HURTS JUST
LIKE LOVE

HURTS JUST LIKE LOVE

M. THOMAS

IMANI PRESS PUBLISHING

CHARLOTTE, NORTH CAROLINA

Library of Congress Control Number: 2017950859
ISBN: 978-0-9641425-3-4

To the Force that has no utterable name.

To my Ancestors.

To Nubian people.

To My Guides, Angels and Cosmic Forces.

To my mom and dad. Molders.

To Monet, Jumaane, and Imani. Love Seeds.

To Josh. Cosmic Child.

To the first man I ever loved, my granddaddy, Jay.

To Tyrone "City" Tripline. Rest in Love.

To Gquan, Deja vu.

To Bert, Asante Sana.

To Believers Who Believe their way to reality.

ACKNOWLEDGMENTS

Chasity, Rosa, Larry, Bill, Trinity, Penny, Audreya and Terri. I am forever indebted to each of you for your consistent encouragement, endless loyalty, and adamant faith in me and this work.

Nita, Val, Elijah, Swami, Dre, Jocelyn, Pat, Mary, Cassandra, Adrena, Claudette, Elder Makheru. No words, just love.

My Oak Fam…Margarette, Adrian.

If I forgot to mention you, please charge it to my head and not my heart!

"If I didn't define myself for myself, I would be crunched into other people's fantasies for me and eaten alive."

Audre Lorde

She's Gone

Myles

I STOOD IN THE doorway paralyzed, and for a split second, if the key had not opened the door I might have thought I had the wrong house. My head swiveled left to right as my eyes quickly darted back and forth across empty rooms that used to hold the contents of my home, but my mind wasn't processing what they saw.

What the fuck! What the hell is going on!

Slamming the door shut behind me, I took off running through the foyer like a madman.

"Mia," I called out, pausing in the middle of the living room. The fact that she didn't answer intensified my fear. I ran in the direction of the library directly across from the living room and stuck my head in the French doors, calling her name and praying for an answer. When she didn't respond this time either, I hurried to the kitchen passing the empty dining and sunroom. I ended up in the family room off the kitchen. As crazy as it sounds, I honestly couldn't remember if a conversation had taken place between Mia and me that would explain why the furniture was gone, and I got upset with myself for not being able to remember. Confusion and fear gripped my chest like a starved pit-bull. I headed downstairs to the basement not sure what to expect. Surprisingly, it was still fully furnished.

Did some motherfuckers rob us?

Even though the rooms were bare, it didn't look like the house had been broken into. Nevertheless, I proceeded back up the stairs with caution. My nine was in the glove compartment out in the car. I considered going to get it and my cell phone, but I was worried my family might be in jeopardy somewhere in the house.

I dashed through the whole downstairs trying to figure out why it looked like we had moved out of our home. What random furniture that did remain made the whole scene appear even stranger. A few family pictures lingered on the living and dining room walls. My worn leather recliner and ottoman sat awkwardly in the middle of the family room floor, and a desk Mia and I used solely for collecting mail and sorting bills had been moved from one side of the family room to the other. It was bare, too.

Why would robbers take the time to steal half the family photos?

I continued to wander through the space in my home that suddenly felt foreign. Wherever our belongings were, the air in the house must have gone with them because I could barely breathe.

Think Myles, think.

I walked in circles pounding my forehead with the heel of my left hand.

Think man, what's today?

I'm not sure what relevance the day had on my empty house, but it was all that came to mind.

Friday, July 22nd, right? Yeah, Friday the 22nd.

"Mia," I called out again.

Did my baby leave me?

I startled myself for having spoken the words I was thinking.

Why would she do that?

Silence.

What the hell is happening?

A haunting quiet that didn't seem to give two shits about me or my questions permeated the air.

No answer.

My thoughts were scattered and I was about to dart out to the car to get my cell phone when the thought of my children hit me like a boulder.

Oh my God!

I sprinted from the dining room toward the spiral staircase and grabbed the handrail. Fueled by the adrenaline that my babies might be in harm's way, I raced up the stairs two by two.

Please God no, please don't let her have taken my children.

At what point I resolved myself to the possibility that Mia might be gone, I can't really say. Logically, it was the only conclusion that made sense given the condition of the house, but I wanted desperately to believe differently.

Tiffany had shut the bright pink bedroom door that had her name painted in black cursive letters diagonally across it before we left this morning, just like she did every morning. I plowed into it shoulder first not quite sure what I'd find, but pleading with a stillness that taunted and overwhelmed me at the same time to give me something I could muster a fragment of hope from. With one hand clutched on the knob, I braced myself against the opened door.

Canopy bed. Dresser. Desk. Computer. Dolls. Curtains.

I took a slow mental inventory of her belongings and it gave me a brief spark of hope to see her things were still intact.

Nevertheless, as I pulled Tiffany's bedroom door halfway closed a sharp pain stabbed at my chest. I tugged on my tie until it fell to the floor. Brandon's room was across the hall from Tiffany's, and after a thorough investigation of his fully furnished room I felt encouraged that there might be some strange explanation about what was going on even though I had no clue what that might be.

I couldn't imagine Mia leaving Tiffany and Brandon unless something was drastically wrong. Her business was growing by leaps and bounds, and as a result, she'd been under a lot of stress over the past few months. Other than that I didn't know what else might be wrong.

Surely she couldn't be far. Where had I been all this time if the feeling in the bottom of my stomach rang true? If this is what she was capable of, if this is where we were? I mean, wouldn't a man have some kind of clue if his wife of nine, almost ten years could just pack up the whole damn house and roll out? Yeah, he would.

My answer was a feeble attempt to console myself.

Not quite sure what to do next, I staggered toward the other end of the hall in the direction of our master bedroom. Nothing could have prepared me for what I saw. Apart from my belongings, the entire room had been emptied. No bed, dresser, night stands, lamps, nothing…just my armoire and personal belongings in the closet.

Indescribable sadness moved inside me. The master bathroom caught my attention and I wandered in. My gaze fixed on two half-burnt cream-colored rectangular candles at the foot of our black Jacuzzi. I walked over and sat on the side of the tub. Confused, I ran my hands over my freshly shaven baldhead several times, propped my elbows on my legs and rested my throbbing head into my cupped hands.

This all must be a motherfucking dream! It can't be happening! I mean, I can't be sitting here wondering whether my wife has left me!

Without warning, I collapsed beside the Jacuzzi.

My baby's gone.

Never in my life had I experienced the type of pain welling up inside of me. It was a strange pain. Not the same kind of pain felt from accidentally cutting yourself or banging your knee into a chair. This was different. Beyond description. There were no words to describe it, but I felt it in my bones, my heart, my chest, my legs and arms, my soul, every part of my being and non-being. Yet despite my emotionally wounded state, somewhere in what was left of my sane mind the inclination to make sure my babies were safe briefly shifted my attention away from the pain. I squinted to focus on my blurry watch; it was five minutes 'til six.

Phone. Gotta get to a phone.

I needed to see my children, needed to believe something in this nightmare was real.

God give me something.

I was mentally and physically drained. Rising from the cold marble floor required assistance. I pulled my lifeless body up by supporting myself on the Jacuzzi, and once on my feet, I needed a moment to regain my balance. Heading back downstairs was more traumatic than going up because it reinforced the fact that I hadn't been dreaming. I made it to the front door and back outside into the record-breaking mid-July heat as fast as I could.

I didn't realize that Kevin, my ain't got no life next-door neighbor was trying to get my attention until I caught a glimpse of his hand waving frantically in the air like he was trying to hail a NY taxi. I had no plans of acknowledging him, but that never made a rat's ass difference to him since he moved into the neighborhood three years ago. Any man who had five cats, a bird, and hamsters, but no woman or children in that formula was suspect as far as I was concerned.

"Hi there, Myles," he shouted loud enough for somebody three blocks away to hear him.

I glanced in his direction and saw he had already wobbled halfway across his lawn a few feet away from me. I parked in the cul-de-sac between our houses and not in my driveway because my plan was to dash in, kiss the children, tell Mia the meeting I had might last about two hours or so, and head back out...so much for that plan.

I wasn't in the mood to be bothered with 'ole dude although his nosey behind probably knew more than I did. Even still, I didn't want to know shit from him about what might be going on in my house. I kept walking.

"You okay, buddy?" Kevin asked falling in stride with me at the bottom of my driveway. He held a hedge trimmer in his pudgy right hand and tried to keep my pace all while gasping for air. I stopped suddenly and he turned to face me. Looking down at his five-foot five, over three-hundred-pound mound of flesh, it took everything in my power to keep from pimp slapping him. Call it paranoia, but I swore I detected a hint of sarcasm in his question.

"I'm good," I managed to say before walking around his ignorant waste of space. I could feel him on my heels as I stepped off the curb.

"You certainly don't look good, buddy. You sure everything's good? If you don't mind my asking, might that troubled look have something to do with that eighteen-wheeler I saw pulling out of your driveway today?"

I stopped so abruptly he almost mowed me down. The smug look on his face confirmed that I had detected cynicism earlier. The urge to snap his bad knee crossed my mind.

He pointed the trimmers at my driveway. "I got back from the doctor's office around three-fifteen. You know my knees still bother me every so often," he wheezed, "but anyway, when I drove up, I saw that moving truck that had come right after you left this morning pull out your driveway, and I thought to myself, my, my, now I know they wouldn't be moving away from here unless they let Kevin know…"

Breathe, man, breathe deeply.

I had to keep telling myself to inhale and exhale because for a brief second it felt like I had stopped breathing. Kevin kept talking, but I didn't hear anything after "moving away." All I saw was his mouth moving.

He had seen a moving truck in my driveway. One that I had no knowledge of and was hearing about for the first time from a neighbor I couldn't stand the sight of.

I wanted to punch him in his face just for being in my business. He'd never get the satisfaction of knowing I had no clue why a moving truck was in my driveway. Instead, I walked away.

I heard him call my name again but I didn't stop. Once I got in the car and shut the door, I couldn't believe the fat bastard had the audacity to be standing at my door looking at me through the window mumbling something.

What an idiot.

I reached for my cell phone laying next to me in the passenger seat and dialed Mia's number.

Fat boy finally got the message to get the fuck away from me and wobbled his big ass back across the lawn.

Come on baby, pick up, please.

My heart dropped when the standard recorded message for a disconnected phone number came on. I tried at least half a dozen more times. Each time the same thing. I called her parents' house and her best friend Daphne three or four times but no one answered. I slammed my hand into the steering wheel numerous times before my head collapsed on it sounding the horn. Crazy motherfucking thoughts raced across my mind at top speeds like a Porsche opened up on the Autobahn.

Did Mia leave me for somebody else? Was she okay? Where the fuck were my children? Is she still in the area?

My cheese felt like it was two inches away from slipping all the way off the cracker. Immediately, I dialed the number to the kid's summer camp.

"The Nzinga Creative Arts Center, how may I help you?" a familiar voice answered.

"Tiffany and Brandon, are they still there?" I gripped the steering wheel with a sweaty palm.

"May I ask who's calling?"

"Sheila?" I questioned impatiently.

"Yes, this is Sheila, who's calling?"

"This is Myles."

"Oh hi Mr. Rollins, I barely recognized your voice. Are you okay?"

"Fine," I snapped, not in the mood for small talk. "The children, are they there?"

My heart thumped in my chest waiting for her reply.

Starting Over

Mia

I MANEUVERED THE CAR in the garage and turned the ignition off. The sound of the garage door closing behind me made my head hurt even worse than it already did. I squeezed my eyes shut and covered my ears until it came to a stop. My eyes burned like someone had thrown sand in them. I pulled the visor down and flipped open the lighted mirror.

Ah Mia, you look like shit.

Hastily closing the visor, I looked down at my phone to check the time…ten-fifteen on the dot.

Faint black streaks of mascara produced by the crying I'd done pretty much the entire drive from Maryland to New Jersey lined both sides of my face. Deep puffy bags were etched under my eyes aging me well past my thirty-five years. I felt weak and worn out.

Mustering the nerve to finally leave Myles once and for all and my children temporarily took everything I had in me. I couldn't play the game anymore. Time had run out.

Between the time Myles left for his office this morning and the movers prompt arrival at fifteen minutes past seven, exactly two minutes after I'd returned from dropping the children off at daycare, I must have hyperventilated ten times. I literally had to walk around inhaling into a brown paper bag. Even though I knew the chances of him popping back up at the house were slim to none, I was still a nervous wreck. It took fifteen movers and a team of three highly competent professional organizers eight hours to pack the house up, load the moving truck and head to New Jersey. I felt guilty for leaving today of all days knowing Myles had finally realized a lifelong dream of being able to buy a building for his dental practice, but if I didn't get out when I did I knew I'd only be prolonging the inevitable.

By the time the truck finally pulled out the driveway and I'd gone by to see my babies before getting on the road, fatigue had already settled in. I thought the drive might give me plenty of time to clear my head, but I ended up thinking about the children and crying most of the trip. When I wasn't crying, I was trying to convince myself not to turn around and go back home.

I gathered my purse from the seat beside me, unhooked my cell phone from the charger and reached in the backseat to get a small bag I'd packed. The car was a mess; packed with odds and ends I'd just thrown in it at the last minute, but I didn't plan on taking any of that stuff out tonight. No way. Before I pulled into the garage, I noticed the moving truck parked around the corner from the house on a side street. Now that I'd gotten in so late, I wished I hadn't made a crack of dawn appointment for the guys to come and unload the damn thing.

The concrete floor of the garage was cold and my bare swollen feet throbbed against it. The drive had taken a toll on me. My whole body ached. All I wanted to do was take a long hot bath and go to bed. I needed to get some sleep.

Meticulously, I had taken time over the past few months to prepare for this day. It made the transition easier knowing I already had everything in the house I needed, even groceries. As far as I knew, Myles didn't suspect that my 'business trips' to NY had more to do with leaving a life I could no longer fake than a business that had grown substantially. On the other hand, maybe he did. Anyway, he'd become so preoccupied with his practice until he didn't notice much anymore, not even me. Maybe now he'd be happy again.

I'd intentionally not scheduled any of my NY clients this week because I figured I'd need at least a week to get all the crying out of my system and to get acclimated to a new environment before meeting with anybody. By next week I might feel differently, but for now, I was glad I had been proactive.

Entering the spacious kitchen from the garage gave me a creepy feeling. The house felt unfamiliar and impersonal, a lot more spacious than I remembered when I decided to buy it. It took four trips and two months before I found my dream house, but once I saw it, I knew immediately that it'd be perfect for the children and me. The backyard was almost the same size, if not a little bigger than the one I'd left behind in Derwood. The major plus was the fact that the schools were the best in the area. Before making a final decision, I took the liberty of talking to a few of my neighbors and found out that most of them had lived in the neighborhood for five years or more. The idea of living in a neighborhood where I didn't know anybody was terrifying; I'm not going to front, but I held onto the thought that the children would be with me soon, and that kept me going. My biggest concern was finding a doctor to treat my migraines, but hopefully after I'd made an appointment to meet with the specialist my doctor back home referred me to, that worry could be put to bed.

I walked over to the phone and picked up the receiver.

Great, dial tone, nothing like being on point, Mia.

I decided to take my things upstairs and put on some music to help ease my anxieties.

Ever since I could remember, I hated long periods of quiet. If there wasn't noise of some kind in the background I got antsy. Something about the demands of silence made me very uncomfortable.

I wished Michelle were around so I could talk to her. Truth be told, my baby sister should have been my older sister because she spent most of her time coaching me through all the madness that made up my life story. I missed having her around, especially now. It had been long overdue for me to learn to stand on my own two feet, but right now her shoulder would have been nice. Michelle didn't need my problems; she had enough to worry about taking care of herself. Dad, momma and I were proud of her for graduating from The FBI Academy with top honors and landing a high-profile assignment. She didn't have time to be babysitting a grown ass woman who needed to take charge of her own life. I hated that I didn't have a chance to say goodbye before she was whisked off on a plane headed for some secret location that was going to keep her away and out of contact with me for at least a year, if not more. If I didn't know any better, I'd swear the gods might be trying to punish me.

I plopped down on the overpriced futon I'd purchased to sleep on, opened my overnight bag and gently removed my favorite picture of Tiff and Brandon that I'd neatly wrapped in tissue paper. It was taken in the lobby of the White House last summer. I'd worked hard on securing a bid to plan a party for a big gala at the White House. When I was awarded the contract, it took two months of busting my butt day and night to pull it off. After all the hard work was done, we were all invited to partake in the festivities. Of course Myles couldn't make it so the children and I went. Watching them explore and play in the White House made it worth all the hard work.

I closed my eyes and kissed their little faces. Determined not to start crying again, I clutched the picture close to my breast fighting back tears.

Mommy loves you Tiff and Brandon, and one day you will understand that I did this for you. One day you will know that sometimes it is better to walk away from a situation that seeps the life out of you than to stay.

My eyes were already swollen, therefore another crying spell was only going to make them worse. Looking into my baby girl's big brown eyes reminded me of the pain I saw in them right before leaving. I knew she didn't buy my 'extended business trip' story for one minute; she knew me too well. Deep in my heart, no matter how I tried to pacify myself, I felt like I was abandoning my children even though I planned to go back and get them.

Suddenly, like an unwelcomed relative, memories of the moment I knew beyond a shadow of a doubt that I had to physically leave crept into my head, triggering a migraine. One day back in February of last year, a day I'll never forget, I woke up and realized I just couldn't do it anymore. Literally. I was bed-ridden. Couldn't move a muscle in my body. It took three full days of laying flat on my back before I could muster the strength to get out of bed and make it to the doctor's office to find out what was wrong.

His words stunned me…

"Well young lady," Dr. Miller said standing over me breaking into a smile that exposed all thirty-two of his teeth. "I've completed a battery of tests on you and I am happy to report that apart from your migraines and an occasional outbreak of hives, you are the epitome of perfect health. We didn't find one thing wrong with you. It looks like your body just shut down for a rest."

Initially I was pissed. I don't know what I expected him to find, but nothing wasn't the answer.

"You mean to tell me I've been on my back for three straight days and all you can tell me is that I need to rest! There has to be something else wrong!" I screamed at him.

There wasn't. Physically, like he said, other than the migraines my body was in tip top shape; it was my mental state that needed a serious overhaul. Mentally, my mind couldn't keep up with all the indecisiveness I'd been feeding it over the past year so it shut my body down. The time had come for me to make some tough decisions in my life or life would make them for me.

My attempts to reach out to Myles were either ignored or minimized, but in all fairness, I'm not sure I even knew what I wanted from him. All my skeletons were trying to escape from the closet at one time and that shit terrified me. I wanted to talk to Myles, come clean, but at the same time I wasn't sure I wanted to stay in the marriage. As selfish as it sounds, I wanted to be free but didn't want to lose him.

Carefully, I placed the picture beside me, grabbed my bag and took out my favorite Will Downing CD, a mango peach candle and a lighter. I went into the bathroom, lit the candle and slipped the CD into the CD player.

Nothing like Will to make it all better.

I got on my knees by the side of the tub to turn on the spigot. I let the soothing hot water shoot through my fingertips before adding a little cold water. When the tub was halfway full I hurried out of my red velour sweatpants, white tank top, matching red underwear and bra, and delicately stepped into the scorching hot liquid, slowly easing my way down until my chin met the water. Closing my eyes, relaxing in the candlelight and listening to Will, I allowed myself to gradually release a fragment of the anxiety I'd traveled to my new home with.

Momma made me promise to call the second I got in. She would have to wait. I had nothing left. She'd worry because first of all her nature required it, but besides that, she had no way of reaching me since I'd cancelled my phone services and intentionally didn't give her the new number before leaving. Sleep deprivation ruled. After my bath, I decided to take a painkiller to ward off the initial symptoms of a migraine. Tomorrow called for a halfway rested body and a somewhat clear head. Everything else would have to wait.

Thank God for Momma

Myles

"YES MR. ROLLINS, they're still here. I tried to call you at your office, but they told me you had already left. I called your house, too, but the phone just kept ringing. I left a message on your cell phone about ten minutes ago. I was beginning to wonder if Mrs. Rollins' remembered to call you and tell you to pick them up," Sheila rambled.

Relief compounded with anger rushed through me.

How the hell did she not have the decency to call and tell me to get the children!

The fog of denial was beginning to dissipate unveiling a probability I wasn't ready to face. Mia obviously didn't give a shit about what was important to me because if she did, she would not have chosen one of the most important days of my life to fuck with my head.

"She must have forgotten. I'm on my way. I should be there in five minutes," I answered while pulling off and trying to hide my frustration.

I wanted to question Sheila about any conversation she may have had with Mia but elected to wait until I got there.

"Okay, see you when you get here and I'll let them know you're on your way."

I disconnected the call and attempted to reach Mia and her parents again but to no avail. Begrudgingly, I conceded that I had no choice but to call Steve to cancel our six-thirty meeting.

Two months of coordinating a lot of folk with busy schedules down the hatch just like that.

The more I pondered what was happening the more pissed off I got. Of all people, Mia knew how much work I'd invested in making this deal go smoothly. She helped me put it together.

My practice had grown beyond the 2,000 square feet it modestly started out in six years ago, and I'd positioned myself to purchase my own building right next door from the one I currently occupied. Double the space for half the price. The meeting tonight would have sealed the deal. Part of me wanted to see if I could still make it happen. I contemplated asking Sheila to babysit, but I knew the children were my priority now. Regardless, it was hard to have to make the phone call to cancel.

"Steve Fisher's Office, this is Marcy, how may I help you?" Steve's assistant answered in her wise and soothing voice.

"Marcy, this is Myles, is Steve available?"

"How are *you,* Mr. Rollins?" She didn't wait for me to answer. "Hold one moment please."

It took Steve a minute to get to the phone, testing my patience.

"Hey buddy sorry about the wait. Kim and I were discussing you on the other line. She'll be a few minutes late, but she's looking forward to finalizing your loan. You on your way?"

"Steve," I paused for a spell. "Something very important has come up, and," I swallowed hard, "I'm not going to be able to make it. I apologize for the short notice, but this requires my undivided attention."

His silence clearly indicated shock. We both knew my hat to purchase the property wasn't the only one in the ring. Not to mention, Steve had busted his ass to make sure I got first dibs on the building when it went on the market.

"Wow man, what's up?" he asked, concern and disappointment in his voice. "You remember there are a lot of variables that could cause you to lose out on this deal, right? Talk to a brother."

"I remember, and I can't go into details now, man. I'm on the way to get my children, but just know this is equally as disappointing to me as it is to you. Look man, I need you to be honest with me. What are my chances of getting this building if we don't finalize today? Can you do anything to hold it? At least through the weekend? What I've got to handle is a crisis. I've pretty much been forced into a situation where my hands are tied. That's all I can say but you've gotta trust me," I pleaded.

Steve and I had been buddies since we met on the tennis court in college. He opened his realty business around the same time I opened my practice. I don't know if he heard the desperation in my voice or if his own determination came into play, but a long pause followed by a sigh preceded his answer.

"Here's what I can do. I'll call Kim and catch her before she gets here and tell her we need to postpone until Monday. I'm not going to make any promises. What I will do is give you my word that I'll do everything I can to hold the sale. Can I reach you on your cell later?"

"No doubt. Hit me up when you know something. Cool?"

"You got it. We'll talk later…and man, keep your head up."

"I'll try."

Steve hung up before I had a chance to say another word. I knew if anybody could create a miracle he was the man. I had total trust in him.

The sudden urge to drive past Mia's office came over me but the children were waiting for me. It would be cruel to make them wait any longer. Even though it was hot as hell, I put the top down on my Saab and braved the heat. Maybe the fresh air might help lessen my frustration before I saw the children.

Driving without the distraction of the radio my thoughts drifted back to last night. I wondered how I could have missed the signs that Mia would wake up and leave us high and dry.

Clue number one should have been the phone call I got from her telling me she was going to pick the children up and start dinner. This summer we both were keeping ridiculous hours. Our schedules were so crazy we'd resorted to relying on the babysitter to pick the children up for us two or three days out of the week, nevertheless I usually beat her home.

Mia had already changed into a pale green tank top and a pair of sexy white spandex shorts that she wore because she knew I liked the way they accentuated the junk in her trunk. She stood over the stove working several pots like a master chef creating aromas from heaven with fresh salmon, red potatoes and stir-fry vegetables. The moment I walked in the door and saw her curves handling them shorts, the only thing on my mind was scoring.

We pecked on the lips lightly. I squeezed her butt on the low and invited her to join me in the Jacuzzi for a nightcap after the children were in bed. She squirmed and giggled trying to avoid knocking over the pans, but accepted the offer with a wink. Since I could count on one hand the number of times we'd made love in the past three months, clue number two should have been her willingness to give me some. Her acceptance put a little pep in a brother's step for the remainder of the night.

I'd become accustomed to trying to make love to her and being denied because of a migraine. Clue number three.

After we ate, I managed bath and story time for Tiff and Brandon before tucking them in bed while Mia cleaned the kitchen. By then, the lust for my wife had escalated to fiend status.

I got in the Jacuzzi with everything we needed to make the night complete right before the phone rang. I heard her laughing hysterically on the phone with her best friend Daphne. They talked while I sat chillin in the Jacuzzi with a glass of XO cognac, smoking one of my favorite cigars and watching the candles I'd lit sketch wild images on the walls. Mia's favorite bottle of white wine was on ice. She loved music and there wasn't a room in our house that didn't allow quick access to it. I clicked the remote that operated the surround system in the bathroom. A mean alto sax blown by some cat that was making love to his horn with the same passion I planned to make love to her flowed through the speaker above my head intensifying the mood. By the time her sexy, fully naked cocoa brown, five foot five frame swayed in the bathroom to the beat of the sax I was ready to dive in.

She barely got one foot in the tub before I grabbed her by the waist and pulled her down in my lap. Straddling me and wrapping her arms around my neck we kissed hungrily like we used to when we first met. The heat between us warmed the water another ten degrees. I cupped a handful of water and watched it cascade down her breast while she reached for my cigar and puffed on it until it produced a thick white smoke over our heads. I took my time sucking, licking, and nibbling each of her supple, wet slippery nipples until her headlights were fully on high beam.

Aroused, her hips began circular motions in my lap. They were slow and gentle at first, but began to pick up speed when I switched to flicking my tongue up and down on her right nipple while gently squeezing the left one. She inhaled deep and slow, followed by a long, low whisper-like moan.

Mia's lovemaking lingo immediately ignited the pulsation that sent my rocket ship into orbit. I poured a glass of wine and engulfed a mouthful. Gently grabbing the back of her head I guided her mouth to mine. Unhurriedly, I emptied the wine from my mouth into hers. She took her time swallowing each gulp until the last drop was gone. Tightening the muscles in her hips she rocked back and forth across my erection teasing and taunting me. The warmth and wetness of her coupled with the cognac and the fact that I hadn't made love to my wife in what seemed like forever created the formula for a deranged man. I didn't waste another ounce of time. I eased inside the warmth of her walls.

Swimming deep inside of her, we both responded to the magic of the moment with passionate inarticulate murmurs. Mia dug her fingernails deep into my back as I steered her erratic movements up, down, deeper, softer, back and forth by holding onto her waist with both hands. I tried to make up for the nights I hadn't gotten any; savoring the ride as long as she gave it to me.

We got in the bed way after one in the morning exhausted from the night of non-stop lovemaking. Somehow, I managed to get up at five a.m. to go for my usual morning run. By six-fifteen, I was in the office ready to see my first patient at seven.

The sight of a big white sign up ahead written in playful purple letters that read, 'Nzinga Creative Arts Center' disrupted my reminiscing. Sheila stood in the door waiting for me to drive up. Instantly my stomach did back flips. Before I had a chance to get to the building, Brandon bolted up the sidewalk heading toward me like a child that hadn't seen his parent in ages.

"Hi daddy," he yelled with every ounce of five-year-old energy he had contained in his body.

"Hi son," I answered lifting him up my arms.

"We're the last ones here daddy and we didn't think you were going to come and get us. Ms. Sheila was going to take us home with her. I like going home with Ms. Sheila, she's a lot of fun! We ate at Red Lobster with mommy today! Tiffany's mad," Brandon exclaimed all in one sentence.

"Whoa little man, slow down! That's a mouthful!" I teased, zeroing in on his statement about their mother. I squeezed my son tight. It did me good to see him.

"Why are you so late?" Tiffany snarled as she walked past us carrying their lunchboxes to the car with Sheila close behind her. She didn't wait for me to answer her question and my heart broke for her. She was biting the nail on her pointing finger, a habit she'd developed out of nowhere about a year ago. I had no idea why she appeared to be snippy, but I'd put everything I owned on it having something to do with Mia. With Brandon clutching my neck I turned to face Sheila.

"I'm sorry I was late Sheila. Mia must have forgotten to call me."

"Where were you daddy? Did you get stuck in a yucky mouth?" Brandon questioned as he played with the small 'M' that hung from my neck on a gold chain they'd given me as a Father's Day gift.

I smiled at Sheila who had reached up to pinch Brandon on the cheek.

"I had some business to take care of son but I apologize to you all for being late. And no I didn't get stuck in a yucky mouth!" I laughed.

"It's okay, Mr. Rollins. I don't have any plans tonight so I had plenty of time to kill. Besides, having these two for company gave me something to do didn't it little giggle bunny," Sheila playfully tickled Brandon who responded by laughing and wiggling in my arms. She was so good with the children and we were fortunate to have her as their provider. They loved her just as much as she loved them.

"Daddy can we go to McDonald's?" Brandon begged.

"Sure we can big boy but do me a favor; go to the car and make sure your sister is okay while I talk to Ms. Sheila."

Brandon bolted from my embrace like a leapfrog.

"Okay daddy! Yeaaaah Tiff, we're going to McDonald's, we're going to McDonald's!" he yelled as he ran to the car.

Once I saw him climb into his booster seat and shut the door, I turned my attention back to Sheila. I didn't know quite where to start.

"Sorry about Brandon. He can ask a million questions but you know that already!" I exclaimed in an effort to gather my thoughts. "Listen Sheila, hopefully Mia told you about the client that's going to require her to be out of town for an indefinite period of time. So, I'm going to need the children to spend the rest of the summer at my parents because as you already know my hours are a little hectic during the summer months. I may even call on you to babysit if that's okay?" I said making the shit up as I went along. My palms were sweating and I hoped she didn't sense my nervousness. Actually, I just wanted her to talk so I could be privy to what Mia may have told her.

"Mrs. Rollins did mention being away for a while and that you'd let me know how much longer they'd be with us for the summer," Sheila divulged. "And I'd love to babysit anytime you need me, Mr. Rollins!"

This shit is getting crazier by the minute. What the hell was Mia up to? Why did everybody seem to know more than I did?

"I don't mean to pry Mr. Rollins, but is everything okay? I've grown attached to Tiff and Brandon and I'd hate to see them go," she said shyly.

"Everything is fine," I lied.

It's time to stop beating around the bush and ask some fucking questions, man. Obviously, I'm the only one in the dark.

"I must have missed her call. What time did Mia stop by?"

"About three forty-five. They went to Red Lobster across the street," she pointed at the shopping center directly across from where we stood, "but they were only gone for about half an hour because Mrs. Rollins had to get on the road to try and avoid the rush hour traffic, you know." Sheila lowered her head and began fidgeting with a small silver Ankh ring on her right pinky finger. "I did want to mention to you that Tiff seemed upset when they returned from the restaurant. She hasn't said much. I asked her if she wanted to talk, but she just shook her head and went outside to sit on the swings. She's been pretty much by herself ever since they got back. Brandon seems fine, but I thought I should mention that to you about Tiff."

"Thanks Sheila. I'll talk to her, and I appreciate everything you've done for them. You have a good evening and I'll be in touch." I squeezed her right arm to signal that I had everything under control. I wanted to ask more questions but didn't want to give off any hints that I was not in the loop of what was happening.

"You're welcome Mr. Rollins, and please let me know if there's anything I can do or if you'd like me to babysit."

"I certainly will."

I gave her a pat on the shoulder and walked away as she waved and blew them kisses. Walking to the car, I was bombarded with my own questions. One part of me wanted to wring Mia's fucking neck and the other part still wanted to believe this wasn't happening. I couldn't fathom the idea that she'd drop a bomb like this on us, not in my wildest dreams. Rubbing the top of my sun-scorched head, I got in the driver's seat unclear where to begin. Tiffany sat limp and distant. Brandon had already strapped himself in and had began coloring in his favorite coloring book. I palmed my throat trying to ease the lumps that felt like they'd gotten lodged in it.

"You alright sweetheart?" I inquired in a calm voice while reaching back to lightly stroke her hand.

An eternity seemed to pass before she barely shook her head to respond with what could have been interpreted as a yes or no.

"Is there something you'd like to talk about?" I prodded further.

"She's upset that mommy has to go away for a while daddy, that's all," Brandon interjected without looking up.

"So mommy told you about the trip?" I proceeded carefully.

"Yeah daddy, she told us at Red Lobster and she said you might let us stay with grandma and grandpa 'til she come back. I wanna go to grandma and grandpa's daddy. Can we go to grammy's?" he asked excitedly.

Thank God for Brandon's innocence. Little did he know how much information he was unknowingly divulging by just being himself.

I'm gathering Mia told them she might be coming back, huh? I wonder if that was before or after she decided to take everything out of the house.

I knew I ought to address Tiffany's sadness, but honestly, I didn't have the mental space to figure out what she needed. This would only be the second time in the seven years of her life she'd been separated from her mother for any length of time and I'm sure it scared the hell out of her. The one time we left her to go to Aruba for our fifth-year anniversary mother said she didn't eat for three days.

The desperation for answers made me anxious to delve deeper into what else they might know but my gut advised me against it.

"I tell you what sweetheart. We'll go to McDonald's and get a bite to eat before heading to grandma and grandpa and when we get there you and I can sit and talk, how's that?"

Staring off into space she did that combination yes, no head shake again. Exhausted, I left it there and drove off.

Tiffany loved her mother. Mia was her idol. She told everybody when she grew up she planned to own an interior designing event planning business just like her mother. One thing was for sure, she'd inherited the genetic coding for shopping and decorating from Mia. Tiffany didn't shop for things girls her age wanted like dolls and clothes. She preferred to buy fabrics, pillows and antique furniture. All the things her mother's fashion etiquette respected.

When we decided to redecorate the house, Tiffany insisted on redoing her own room. She and Mia strategized and planned for weeks non-stop. I'd periodically catch her happily engrossed in a pile of magazines scattered on the floor around her. A big pink poster board held the ideas she'd cut and pasted for the new bedroom concept. Once all her final plans were clipped and attached Mia proudly chauffeured her to estate sales, antique stores, thrift shops, anywhere she thought baby girl could find what she was looking for. They didn't stop until she found each and every item, or a close replica. On occasion, Mia offered her protégé expert advice, but when all was said and done, Tiffany had full reign over her ideas. The completed project made a doting father even prouder.

I couldn't help but wonder how Mia's disappearance was going to affect our daughter.

My emotions were all over the place. One minute anger had me wanting to bust my fist through a wall, worry made me scared, and hurt just left me feeling like a fool.

Man, if you had a spine right about now you'd just face the fact that Mia has left you. I mean what more proof do you need? She played you, man. You got a final goodbye, one for the road, good old fuck.

I didn't like feeling played. My focus should have been on the children but I felt justifiably selfish and resented the fucked up hand I suddenly had been dealt.

When we pulled into the McDonald's parking lot, my neck felt stiff, achy and tense. Brandon barely gave me enough time to park the car before he unbuckled himself and sat perched on the edge of his booster seat ready to bail as soon as I gave the word. My mind was so preoccupied while driving I didn't realize Tiffany had fallen asleep. I hated to wake her largely because I didn't want to feel my baby girl's sadness. Fortunately, though, it gave me a few minutes to make a call.

"Hold on buddy I need to make a quick phone call," I whispered to Brandon.

"K, daddy."

I grabbed my cell phone and dialed the one person who'd have all the answers. After the seventh or eighth ring my mother's winded 'hello' gave me the comfort of a child.

"Hi mother, where were you? You sound out of breath," I noted with worry.

"Oh hi baby," she managed between huffs. "I was down in the basement getting some canned peaches. I thought I heard the phone," she said panting, "but I wasn't sure so I ran up dem steps fast as I could. I'm glad I caught you before you hung up," she gasped.

"I keep telling you and dad to use those cordless phones I got you to carry with you when you go down there! It's too dangerous for you to be running up those steps to the kitchen to grab the phone. You could fall and hurt yourself."

"You right son, but you know how your father is 'bout gadgets, he don't like 'em. That remote control is 'bout as far as he gonna go. He get frustrated when he got to figure all them things out. This one here works fine for us. Whew, let me sit down."

"You all right, mother?" I asked concerned.

"Fine, baby, just fine. Where you at?" she paused, "I thought you was supposed to be at that meeting?"

"As a matter of fact that's why I'm calling. I need to stop by in about an hour to talk to you about something. Will you be home?"

"You know your father and me always at this here house. We ain't going nowhere. Is everything okay, baby?" she questioned in a half knowing tone.

The Past Revisited

Mia

I HAD A SERIES of strange dreams that came to an abrupt halt when the alarm clock jarred me from a deep sleep. In one of them, I was wearing a black wedding dress standing in the middle of a field screaming to the top of my lungs. There was a huge ball of fire moving toward me. I remembered trying to take off and run but my feet wouldn't move. I peeked at the blurry red letters on the clock between half opened eyes. Six-thirty. I'd set the alarm to go off at six-fifteen but must have hit the snooze button to grab a few more minutes of sleep.

No time to shower now. Let's throw on some clothes and fix yourself a cup of coffee before the fun begins, little lady.

Ten minutes before the crew I'd hired to move me in was due to arrive the doorbell rang. It was going to take pretty much the entire morning and mid-afternoon to get things unloaded and arranged in the house.

Here we go.

"Good morning Freddie. How was your drive up?" I questioned the stocky, handsome middle-aged mildly graying Hispanic man standing in the doorway holding a large cup of coffee that smelled a whole lot better than mine by a long shot.

"Good morning, Mrs. Rollins. Without incident, ma'am. And yours?"

"Come on in. Let's see, besides getting caught in traffic right outside Baltimore and once again on the Turnpike which added an hour to my trip, I guess it was okay!" I answered sarcastically while leading Freddie to the living room.

"I'm sorry about that ma'am. Well if you don't mind, I'd like to go ahead and get started. My guys should be here in a few minutes. In the meantime, you wanna show me around the house so I can mark where everything needs to go?" he asked pulling a small worn green notebook and a pencil from his shirt pocket.

"I would love to. Follow me."

It took Freddie and his crew about eight hours to get the entire truck unpacked and all the furniture in place. When they were finished, I was glad to see them go.

In between overseeing the move, I made the dreaded call to momma. She chastised me with all the melodrama and flair she normally carried on in and confessed that she was pissed at me for not calling her last night.

When all was said and done, it made her happy to have contact with me again. Momma mentioned that Myles had called several times but she didn't pick up like I instructed. I could tell by the tone in her voice that she would have preferred not to be in the middle of our affairs. Before hanging up she asked me not to be upset at the fact that she had called my girl Daphne a few times to see if she'd heard from me. Wrong answer. Now I'd have to deal with another drama queen's mouth.

Postponing a call to Daphne would only make matters worse. I sat down on the hardwood floor in the library with my back up against one of the wall to wall built in bookcases waiting for her to pick up.

"Hey girlie what's up?" I asked happy to hear her voice after she answered.

"Ohhh tramp! You finally decided to get up off your backside and call somebody! You know your momma been worried sick about you? And how do I know that you ask? Because she's been calling me all damn night that's how! I'ma tell you what though. If that heifer had called me one more time I would have cussed her and her great-grandmother out! You all settled in baby?" she asked, shifting gears as smooth as a Nascar driver.

"I love you too, Daph, and yes I am."

"You know I had to get that off my chest 'cause Marc was about to put me out the house girl! The damn phone kept ringing and every time

I picked it up it was your momma talking 'bout, "Daaaphneeeee, I ain't heard from my baby yet and I'm so scared something done happened to her," she mimicked in my momma's whiny voice. "She wailed and moaned in my ear like a 'lil baby! As if I was in the mood to be consoling somebody's ass at ungodly hours of the morning! NOT!"

I laughed so hard I could barely breathe. Daphne didn't possess an ounce of sense and I hadn't met anybody that could embellish a story better than her. I know momma must have drove her silly behind crazy with all the phone calls, and if she had kept it up Daphne really would have cursed her out.

"Thanks for covering for me honey. I was too tired to deal with her when I got in."

"I got you, buuut side bar…the next time you sign me up to ride shotgun let a sista know ahead a time! Sooo! You situated? Better yet, you met any fine, delicious chocolate brothas roaming the neighborhood?"

"Daphne! How could you of all people ask me something like that! You know that's not why I'm here. Besides I just got here last night, damn!"

"Yeah, yeah, yeah, I know you trying to find yo'self by running from yo' schizophrenic ass self, but the last time I tried that girl I kept showing up everywhere I went," she laughed hysterically at her own humor. "Sweetie Pie I'm still trying to make sense out of your logic, but that's just me. Listen, if you gonna make a move like you just did, pack up shit and roll the fuck out, you might as well go on and live it to the fullest. Hell, you done did the damn thing now! Be one with that bitch, shit!"

"I didn't call you for a lecture, Daph. Can't you just be my friend for once without judging me or giving me your opinion about everything I do?"

"Okay, is that what we doing? Throwing a pity party for helpless little Mia? You know I ain't never bit my tongue for nobody and I don't plan on starting now."

"Please apologize to Marc for me will you," I asked, trying to redirect the conversation.

"Won't do any good, but I will, and don't think I'm not smart enough to know you're trying to change the subject. So go ahead and tell me 'bout that big fancy house! Is it fly? I looovve the pictures you sent me. You ballin baby!"

Daphne could be tough but I knew she had my back. When we first met six years ago back in the summer of nineteen ninety-five, I'd been hired by one of the Washington Redskins football players to throw a who's who party so he could show off his new multi-million-dollar mansion in Malibu. The evening of the party, a dark chocolate Naomi Campbell looking, five foot eleven very thin sister, rocking a platinum blonde weave that swayed past her hips drove up in a gold tinted out Lamborghini with the music blaring. Daphne stepped out the car in a lime green full-length fur coat, a purple skimpy strapless dress that barely covered her lanky frame and a pair of leopard skin boots that came all the way up to her thighs. Who can say tacky!

All I wanted to know was who invited the escort and how much was she being paid? Imagine my surprise when I found out she topped the VIP list. Daphne Strong, third name on the guest list right below his mother and father's name. Highly disgusted that this guy would invite a groupie and put her on the VIP list with his wife there, I did all I could to steer clear of her. I made sure she knew what I thought about her by shooting an assortment of skanky looks her way whenever our paths crossed.

Mid-way through the night, around the eighth time she'd popped up in my space, grinned at me and walked away laughing, I realized she was entertaining herself at my expense. To make matters worse we represented only a handful of sistas on the expansive twenty-acre property. By no means did I want his guests to think we might be together. Bad enough her appearance made me cringe, but she had a vulgar mouth to boot. Every sentence out her mouth had at least two curse words in it.

It took a minute to pick my face up off the floor when I found out she was Nathan's personal manager. After I apologized for being a snob we struck up a conversation. Daphne confided that she amused herself by purposely trying to get under my skin and thanked me for giving her something to do. She confessed that Nathan's parties usually bored the shit out of her, but my "*class act as a bitch*," as she referred to it, cracked her the fuck up, and she got a kick out of watching me roll my eyes all night.

Daphne schooled me on how hard she had to work to get to the top as a female in a man's game without using her body. Once I came down off my high horse, watching her confidently interact with the snootiest person in the room and turn around and flip it street with a group of fellas was priceless. I always told her she was hiding a set of balls somewhere in her woman parts. Girlfriend could go toe to toe with anybody. God forbid a fool misjudged her and she went in on them!

"Fly ain't the word girl, it's huge! The movers just finished unloading everything and I need to get outta here and go for a walk. A little fresh air might do me some good."

"No see what might do you some good is a real stiff…"

"Spare me Daphne!" I yelled cutting her off. "Get your mind out the gutter girl!"

"See there! Whose mind in the gutter? I was about to say you needed a stiff drink!" she laughed.

"No you weren't and you know it! When you coming to see me?" I nagged.

"As soon as I get a chance, hopefully around the end of the year. I hate that I'm all the way down here in Miami but don't get it twisted, that's just a frog's leap away. If you need me before then you call, okay?"

"I hate it too, Daph. You should just move to Jersey. That way you'll be close."

A sudden rush of loneliness made me want to pour my heart out to anybody who would listen.

"All I want is to be happy, Daph, you know what I mean?"

"No I don't know what you mean. I don't get half the shit you do boo, and I don't think you do either, but that's okay 'cause you still my girl and I got nothing but love for you. Real talk, I don't think you'd know what happiness was if it crawled up in the bed and fucked the shit outta you!"

"Why do I bother to try and explain anything to you, Daphne?" I asked defeated. "You don't understand how tough the last few years have been for me. I've been living a lie. Just caught up in the middle of so much shit. You make me feel like I don't have a reason for feeling the way I do when you of all people know everything I've been through."

"Girl you can work that victim thing like a full-time job!" she laughed. "Get real! We both know your marriage to Myles been over a long time ago, and we also know *why*. Myles is a good brotha, and I don't throw them kind of compliments around easily for no man. I don't give a shit who he is! You haven't trusted him since you made up in your mind he cheated on you, which I don't believe, but that's another story. If shit's been tough for you, it's because you made the bed, laid down, pulled the covers up around your neck, and snuggled the fuck in!"

"You are so far off the mark Daph it's not even funny. I can see you want to make this all my fault as usual. I'm not in the mood this time, so I'm gonna go."

"Go where, Mia?" she continued to dig. "Break out like you always do when the truth gets too close for comfort? Well, you know I was the wrong one to call. I ain't gonna lie to you. Never have, never will. You should 'a called somebody else if you wanted a amen corner. I love you too much to lie to you, baby doll. Don't call me if you want to be stroked. This is too important of a time in your life for you to be playing pretend. You've made a life changing decision. Either accept it and live it like a motherfucker or take your ass back to Derwood and continue to deny the inevitable. Ooops, that's my dime. Gotta go baby! I love you," she said in her 'I'm done with this conversation tone,' and hung up.

I sat listening to the dial tone feeling like I'd been whipped. Daphne had hung up on me.

Something told me I would have been better off calling anybody but her.

I wasn't surprised because that was Daphne. She called it like she saw it. Label me a glutton for punishment but that's what I respected about her. Her words cut deeply given the fact that she was my best friend. However, Daphne was the one person who never sugar coated anything. She always kept it one-hundred.

Determined not to let her throw shade on the rest of my day I got myself ready to go for my walk. I ran upstairs and threw on a pair of shorts, a tee shirt and my sneakers. With keys, water bottle and sunglasses in hand I purposefully avoided the mirror, set the alarm and stepped out into the blistering heat.

By the time I'd walked to the park that was close to my house, I felt some of the tension begin to subside from my body. New Jersey was a far cry from Maryland. The people weren't nearly as friendly and I kept reminding myself it wasn't personal.

The park was crowded. There were families, teens, bikers, joggers, basketball, baseball and soccer players everywhere. I sat down on a bench sheltered from the sun by a mini urban forest of trees and bushes. The view gave me a front row seat to the tennis courts. The courts made me think of how much Myles loved the game. If he hadn't been an orthodontist, he could have easily coached tennis on any level.

The spot supplied me with a picture-perfect intoxicating ambience tucked away from the crowd. I crossed my legs, closed my eyes and leaned my head back to welcome in the feeling of relaxation that promised to subside more of my anxiety. It had been a long time since I allowed myself to let go. It felt wonderful.

"Mia, baby, is that you?" a voice I recognized interrupted my self-induced bliss.

I opened my eyes annoyed at the disturbance. Without warning my paradise instantly turned into hell. The familiar voice belonged to a nightmare.

"Dre, what are you doing here?" I asked sitting up in total shock. Pulling off my sunglasses and shielding my eyes from the sun, I sprang to my feet.

"I might ask you the same question sexy lady! After all, I live closer than you do! Come here and give me a hug!" he demanded, boldly grabbing my hands and pulling me into him.

"Ummmm…you still feel good," he groaned holding my limp body way too familiar and tight.

My mind was racing in twenty different directions. None of them good.

What were the odds of my running into one of Myles frat boys out here? Shit! And Dre of all people!

His sweaty body suggested he was out jogging.

Lucky me.

I freed myself from his aggressive embrace. He stood there biting his bottom lip, gawking at me like I didn't have any clothes on. I felt violated.

"You never answered my question pretty lady," he asked after finally taking his eyes off my breast. "What are you doing here and where are the kids and my frat brotha?" he inquired trying to pretend he cared.

Here goes the interrogation.

"Fuck," I exclaimed right above a whisper.

Out of all the people I could have run into, it would have to be this asshole!

There was no way he could have known I'd left, no way. I doubted very seriously if Myles would have called him. Besides, Dre lived in the city. Unless of course…

Stop it Mia. Stop freaking out. Myles would not have called Dre, for what?

I began filling my lungs with air to keep from hyperventilating.

"I asked first. What are you doing on this side of the bridge?"

"Alright sexy I see what we're doing. We're playing beat around the bush, right? You remembered that I like a little mystery in my woman!" He threw his head back in laughter. "I'll play along but don't tease me too long. I'm here for two reasons: one, to take a run because this park is my usual spot when I'm on this side of town, and two, I'm gathering information for an upcoming case, which by the way if I win might take me all the way to the top, but that's a little side bar, get it, side bar?" He laughed again but I wasn't laughing. "Never mind, I see you left your sense of humor back in Maryland," he said after pinching my arm and purposely grazing my breast. "Okay, okay, your turn," he laughed a third time. Dre flashed that destructive smile at me almost causing me to forgot his arrogance.

Thinking fast I came up with a lie. "I have a client I'm working for the next few days. Myles and the children are at home," I said trying to keep a straight face. Attempting to fabricate a story for someone who made a living pimping deceit was a stretch, but I gave it my best shot.

"That's it! You're not going to tell me the juicy part!" Dre hounded. "Well at least you can tell me where you're staying?"

I could feel my underarms sweating but stood my ground as I looked him dead in his dreamy light brown eyes.

"That's it Dre," I flung my hands up in the air. "I'm sorry to disappoint your curiosity but there is no juicy part," I answered intentionally ignoring his question about where I was staying. I was fully aware of Mr. Westland's charm and had fallen prey to it once. I didn't plan to go there again.

"Who's the client? Is it Whitney and Bobby or some other big celeb you be hanging out with? You can tell me I won't tell anybody," Dre tempted.

"I'm *sure* you won't but that's none of your business. My clients and I share an oath of confidentiality. You know about that don't you Dre?" I answered, suddenly realizing what he meant by *the juicy part*.

"Come on Mia don't be like that. You still upset with me, baby?" he asked, moving closer to me as if he weren't close enough.

I stepped back. Dre thought his charm still carried the same weight it did when I succumbed to it before. I was not in the mood for his bullshit.

"Well now, since you're alone you feel like a little company in your hotel room tonight?" he asked while sliding the tip of his tongue from one corner to the other across his top lip. Mesmerized, I followed it instantly swept into the scary magnetic field that was Dre. I tried to pretend I wasn't admiring his wide chest and well-toned firm arms that were exposed by the rims of his wife beater, or his muscular thighs protruding under the pair of black mid-thigh Jordan shorts he had on. The sun toasted his caramel skin just enough to turn it a shade darker than I'd remembered.

Shit, why did Dre have to be so damn sexy! He know what he doing sliding his tongue across his lips like that! Asshole! Them light brown eyes trying to pull me in again! Looks like he's been working out, too. Mia, you know better! Been there, done that. Get a grip!

Dre was looking at me like I was a slab of ribs straight off the smoker. He intentionally lifted his shirt to wipe the sweat from his forehead, fully exposing his well-defined six-pack. I realized I got busted lingering on his pecks when I looked up at him and our eyes met. He had an overly confident smirk on his face. I put my sunglasses back on to let him know we had nothing further to talk about.

"No Dre, I don't feel like company, but even if I did you'd be my last choice. Besides, Myles is still your frat brother and he might not think too highly of you trying to push up on his wife," I challenged.

The presumptuous bastard moved close enough for me to feel he'd gotten hard. He lifted my chin with his thumb and pointer finger so that our eyes met again. Dre wasn't quite six feet tall but his fit frame loomed over me; temporarily freezing time.

"What he doesn't know won't hurt him, now will it, Mia? Haven't you and I proven we aren't strangers to keeping secrets? We're adults we can handle ourselves. Speaking of handling, I'd love to handle you for another ride," he propositioned.

I stepped back, freeing myself from his grip.

"You and I both know that's not always the case, Dre. Sometimes what you don't know can hurt. A lot. And let's get one thing straight…you and I have no secrets. I made a mistake. One day it's gonna catch up with me, but I don't plan on making that mistake again, got it. Besides, I'm not the only one that has something to lose," I said bluntly.

"I won't take that as a threat because we both know better, but if you change your mind baby doll my digits haven't changed. And I do hope you change your mind," he smirked.

"Do me a favor Dre, hold your breath."

"Sssssss…ummmm…I like it when you give me friction, baby! That shit turns me on like a motherfucker!"

I looked at him in disgust and walked off.

Out of the Mouth of Babes

Myles

"NOT REALLY, BUT we'll talk when I get there."

"Is Mia coming, too?"

"Why'd you ask that?" I questioned, paranoid Mia had already called her.

"Cause she 'yo wife, son?"

How ridiculous of me. She didn't need to answer that question. Nobody could hide anything from her. Mia didn't have to tell her because she felt my pain even when I tried to disguise it. We had a connection beyond words. That became even more evident the time I wrecked my motorcycle at eighteen. My father thought it was macho for me to have a motorcycle and he didn't care if it killed me. If it was manly, it was approved. He made it clear he wasn't going to buy it, but if I earned my own money he didn't have a problem with me having one, which meant mother was out numbered. It was one of the few things my father and I agreed on. I worked three summer jobs and saved every penny to buy my bike. Mother was totally against it, and looking back I wonder if she saw the accident coming long before it happened. Every time I went out the door mother vocalized her disapproval. No matter how late I got home it looked like she was standing in the same spot where she was when I'd left.

Ten months after buying it I crashed her chasing down a car that damn near ran me off the road. I remembered swerving to avoid side swiping the car then going down but nothing after that. Fortunate for me, my boys

Quincy and Stan were riding behind me in Q's brand new Mazda two-seater. When I came out of a coma three days before graduation mother was standing over me smiling. I swore she was an angel.

Q said right after the ambulance went speeding off with me in it, my mother drove up. According to him, she walked over to where my mangled motorcycle lay beside the road, looked at it, walked back to her car without saying a word and drove off in the direction of the hospital. To this day nobody knows how she found out about the accident. She said she just *happened* to be going to the store when she saw it. I know that wasn't true because my parents were creatures of habit. Mother very rarely ventured into Maryland, if at all, and if she did it was with my father. Thirty years of marriage had created some concrete habits between them, most of which I was very familiar.

As time passed I came to accept the fact that my mother simply had a gift. Her instinct didn't fall under the normal definition of women's intuition. Hers was different. Undeniably different, therefore, the fact that she just showed up should not have surprised me at all.

"I see. Well, I'll be there in a bit."

"You just take your time and drive safely. I love you, son," she added.

Those familiar two words. "Drive safely." The two words I'd come accustomed to hearing whenever I was going anywhere.

"I will and I love you, too." I disconnected the call just before Tiffany woke up.

"Daddy are we there yet?" she asked half asleep.

"Yes we are baby girl. Brandon, son, can you climb up here and sit in daddy's seat while I talk to your sister for a minute?"

"Can I pretend drive, daddy?" he asked moving from his booster seat to the passenger seat.

"If you only play with the steering wheel and don't touch anything else, okay?"

"Okay, daddy!"

I got out of the car and walked around to sit beside her while Brandon climbed in the driver's seat.

"Are you hungry sweetheart?" I asked putting my arm around her shoulder to cuddle her.

"No, daddy, I just wanna go home," she said softly.

I hadn't paid attention recently, but it suddenly dawned on me how much she resembled Mia. Big round eyes hidden under long pretty eyelashes, full lips and a round little nose were all Mia's. Her cheeks sat high on her face and a heartwarming smile revealed what I called, 'deep dish dimples.' Although Tiffany was a shade darker than Mia, she still was the spitting image of her mother. Her tall thin frame made her look a lot older than seven.

"I know you do sweetheart. I tell you what, let's go get your brother something to eat and you and I can sit down and talk, how's that?"

"Do I have to go inside, daddy? I really don't feel like it. I just wanna go home," she insisted.

"Your brother has probably been looking forward to playing in those balls in there all day. So why don't we let him have a few minutes to play and eat and after that we'll get out of here, how's that?"

"If we have to I guess it's okay," she conceded.

I kissed her on the cheek and tried to cheer her up by pulling one of her cornrows. She didn't respond. I got out of the car, went around and opened her door like I always did. The three of us went inside. Tiffany clung to my side the entire time I was ordering Brandon's food. She appeared lethargic and tired. We sat at a picnic bench inside the playground area. Brandon had already taken his shoes off and disappeared into one of the big blue tubes. I took his cheeseburger, fries and toy out of the bag and put them on a napkin. He loved ketchup on everything, so I squeezed plenty of it on his fries. I stuck a straw in his chocolate milkshake. The entire time Tiffany sat close to me with her head on my shoulder biting her nail.

"Brandon, here you go son," I called over to him as he chased another little boy up the yellow tube.

He ran over and bit into his sandwich like he hadn't eaten in weeks.

"Sit down young man and eat your food. We have to go in a few minutes," I demanded.

"Where we going daddy?" Brandon asked between a bite of cheeseburger and a sip of his milkshake.

"We're going to see grandma and grandpa."

"Are we going there before we go home, daddy," Tiffany muttered.

For some reason that felt like a trick question. I wasn't quite sure why, but it did. "Yes sweetheart, we need to stop by your grandparents so I can talk to them about something very important."

"I already know you're going to ask them if we can stay there for the summer," she said sarcastically.

"Damn it!"

Obviously, by Tiffany's response Mia had managed to make me look like the bad guy.

How could she leave our daughter so confused and heartbroken? Mia had to know Tiffany would shut down by being away from her. What was she thinking!

In all honesty, I didn't want to deal with trying to figure shit out. As heartless as it might have come across I wanted to get in my car and drive as far away from this shit as I could. I don't know where I would have gone, but vanishing into thin air sounded like a start. It didn't matter if that would have made me equally as guilty as Mia. If she really was gone then understandably the children were gonna need me even more but mentally and physically I was already depleted.

"And what makes you think that, honey?"

"Mommy said you'd do it!" she shot back.

"No she didn't," Brandon retaliated after sucking from the straw in his milkshake. "She said she didn't know what daddy wanted to do. She said he'd tell us."

"Shut up Brandon!"

"Hey, hey, that's not how we talk to one another young lady! Watch your mouth," I scolded. "Apologize to your brother."

"Sorry," she half said.

"It's okay, Tiff. Mommy said we might could go with her but you would be sad if we left, too," Brandon added. "I told her I wanted to stay with you daddy."

Now I understood why Tiffany was so upset with me! She thought I was the reason their mother didn't take them wherever the hell she vanished to! What a coward!

It was bad enough that she'd left, but to leave all this chaos behind for me to deal with made me furious. I was livid, but somehow managed to keep my cool.

"Look you two. Being apart is going to be tough for your mother and me. We both want what's best for you." It took all I had to make the next statement with a straight face. "Since your mother isn't quite sure how long she'll be away, *we* decided it was best for you to stay here, and because of daddy's work I have to ask grandma and grandpa if you can stay with them for a while. Summer is a very busy time for daddy because that's when parents get to schedule appointments for their children without having to take them out of school." I decided to try and lighten things up. "And the best part for me is I get to fix more icky teeth!"

My attempt at humor went over well with Brandon because he laughed and called me silly. Tiffany simply sat listless and uninterested. I hated lying to my children, but given the fact that I had no clue what was going on I did what I had to do.

"It's okay daddy! We don't mind," Brandon mumbled between chews, breaking up a short period of silence. "I like grandpa and grandma's house. Can I go back to play now? I'm finished," he announced sticking a handful of fries in his mouth.

"Five minutes and then we have to go…and chew your food first!"

Brandon took off flying, disappearing into the red tube this time. I put my arm around Tiffany. We were going to have to make it through this together. The last thing I wanted was for us to be enemies. I ached to reassure her that I'd be there when she came around and that I wasn't the bad guy, but I didn't want to make Mia the scapegoat either. She loved her mother too much for me to try and turn her against the woman she idolized.

"Sweetheart, if it's any relief to you I'm going to miss her, too. Let's just pray she comes home real soon and that she won't have to be away long. Can we do that?" I negotiated.

Not a word.

"How about I make you a deal?"

Tiffany looked up at me, not directly, but she took her eyes off the floor and looked past me.

"How about we go and visit her as soon as she lets us know it's okay, would you like that?"

"Could we, daddy!" she exclaimed, her eyes lighting up for the first time since this whole ordeal began.

"As soon as she gives us the word, we're there! I promise!"

My baby girl threw her arms around my waist and squeezed it hard. It took everything in my power to hold it together. I still believed there was a reasonable explanation for all of this. I held fast to the thought that once I had a chance to speak to Mia she'd clear everything up.

"Daddy, can I ask you a question?" she requested out of nowhere.

"Sure sweetheart, you can ask me anything."

She laid her head on my arm.

"Do you still love mommy?"

"Of course I do honey, with all my heart," I answered without hesitation.

It Must Be Fate

Mia

FRAZZLED AND DAZED, I took my time walking home. Fear gripped me every time I thought about what Dre might do. Would he call Myles and tell him he saw me? I hoped his ego would delude him into believing I might call to hook up with his sorry ass so he'd refrain from calling Myles to pry.

I needed something to take my mind off bumping into him. There was no telling what he might do and the idea of being at his mercy made me angry. When I walked back into the house, the temptation to call Daphne for advice vaguely crossed my mind but I'd had enough brow beating by her for the day.

Music, that's what I need.

Proud of myself for coming up with an idea that excited me, I began humming a tune out loud. Michelle's calming voice would have been nice right about now, but since that wasn't an option I decided to take a bath and go shopping.

Mia, you're a genius! A nice long hot shower to soak off Dre's filthy touch, followed by shopping for new music. What a great combination!

Outside of a fabric store and an antique shop, the Wiz was one of my favorite places on earth. It had rows and rows of any and all kinds of music anybody could ever want. Pure heaven.

Rummaging through the closet in my bedroom, I found a denim mini skirt and a red low-cut tank top to throw on after my shower. In one of the boxes I'd marked, *summer shoes,* I pulled out a red pair of wedge sandals and slipped them on. In all, it took me half an hour to shower and get dressed.

Looking in the mirror, I silently thanked my stylist for convincing me to go with a low maintenance short 'fro for the summer. Marcus was no joke when it came to hair.

The fact that there were several malls nearby was another reason I settled on living in Teaneck. I figured I'd go to the Garden State Plaza Mall because it had a Wiz on the outskirts. If time permitted I could go shopping in the mall.

Under half a mile from my destination, bumper-to-bumper cars slowed traffic down to a snail's pace. When I finally got to the mall it took me fifteen minutes to find a park way out in the boonies. I only had a good three hours before the stores closed, so I hopped on the escalator inside the record store and rode it up to paradise where an abundance of music was waiting to greet me.

Let's see, where to start? Jazz, I need more jazz.

My giddiness had to be apparent to anyone in eyesight as I began thumbing through CD after CD. Choices were plentiful. It didn't take long for me to select four and a possible five albums that I wanted.

I laughed to myself imagining what Myles would say if he saw me buying more music. His taste was strictly R&B but he'd become accustomed to listening to whatever I had playing in the house.

"May I suggest Rachelle Ferrell's Live in Montreux?" I heard a deep, sexy baritone voice with a thick New York accent ask over my shoulder. "She does a mean version of "You Don't Know What Love Is," it continued.

For a second I had no desire to move because I wanted him to say something else. The voice sent a tingle from the back of my neck to the bottom of my spine arousing a part of me nobody but Myles had a right to stimulate.

Inquisitive, I rotated my head, glimpsed over my right shoulder, and damn near collapsed! The stranger who'd caused my heart to skip four beats had the letters P-E-R-F-E-C-T flashing in bold neon lights across his frame. I couldn't help but wonder if he knew how drop dead gorgeous he was.

OMG, he is sooooo fiiiiinnnneeee! Compose yourself. Shit, that brotha got it going on! Don't be rude, turn around and say something.

Instantly, I wished I'd worn the pink silk halter top that complimented my bust line more than the one I had on. I turned to face him. His almond-shaped dark brown eyes pierced through me from behind a pair of very expensive gold-rimmed glasses, and he flashed a set of pearly whites from a self-assured smile that lit up the entire room. A broad and powerful nose complimented a set of full luscious lips. Professionally trimmed, every hair in his hint of grey mustache and goatee lay perfectly in place. Brotha man's sexiness made him appear six, six. He had midnight black baby butt smooth skin. His perfectly shaped baldhead was the sexiest thing I'd seen since my husband's. To top it off, his body was chiseled better than any marble statue that could be found on planet earth. Arms, legs, neck, back…muscles were everywhere! Five extremely long thick fingers with nails trimmed to the tee held a CD extended toward me, and I knew if I took the bad boy I'd drop it.

I had to hurriedly step to my right to let a sista parade her big ass between us. She obviously was trying to get his attention because she damned near knocked me to the floor on her way by. When I moved out of the way, I bumped into a rack of CD's, tipping it over.

He and I both fumbled to catch them. The entire time I kept hoping he didn't mistakenly touch me because if he did I might faint. Trying to create some space between him and me, I backed up and struck another rack of CD's!

Damn he smells good! I think that's Clive Christian I'm getting a whiff of! Oh my God how embarrassing is this!

I tried unsuccessfully to keep the damn thing from falling.

Like a mortal god, he sprang into action catching the second rack before it hit the floor.

"Let me get those," he insisted. "And don't you move another muscle, beautiful," he laughed.

Lord have mercy, let this man stop talking before I have an orgasm!

Once he got the second stand stabilized, he gathered the first set of CD's up with one sweep of his large capable hands and placed them on a shelf beside him. The diamonds on his Submariner Rolex glistened like stars under the fluorescent lights in the store. I watched with lust and anticipation. The contour of his muscular thighs bulked under a neatly pressed pair of blue jeans as he knelt to retrieve the CD's from the floor. His Stefano Bemer's were freshly polished and looked as if they'd never been worn before. A black label Ralph Lauren beige sport shirt topped off his style. The brotha reeked of money! Beads of sweat danced boldly on the top of his head and I couldn't help but be envious of them for having the privilege to touch him. When he turned to face me again he had a big grin on his face and I wondered if he were reading my thoughts like a bedtime story.

You're still a married woman Mia, and the shit you're thinking ain't good, not good at all.

"I didn't mean to startle you," he said laughing, "please accept my apology. I saw you thumbing through the CD's and this one happens to be a favorite," he noted holding up the CD again. "I thought I'd offer a suggestion."

Speak Mia.

I pleaded with myself to say something because I must've looked stupid standing there with my mouth wide open.

"No need to apologize. Actually, it was my fault," I blushed.

It was getting hot as hell in the store and I wanted to fan myself but didn't think it would be a good look standing in front of this hunk of black man fanning. I could feel sweat pouring from every pore in my body.

"Let's try this again," he smiled striding confidently into my personal zone. A whiff of his cologne floated pass my nostrils and I felt as if I'd been whisked up and spun around the room like Cinderella.

Stop, damn it! Stop flashing that melting smile at me!

He looked awfully familiar, but undoubtedly, if I knew somebody as fine as this specimen I would not have forgotten him. I smirked at the thought.

"May I suggest Rachelle Ferrell's Live in Montreux?" he asked again, holding the CD out in front of him while checking me out with an up and down.

We simultaneously laughed out loud.

"Yes you may, and thank you," I answered delicately taking the CD.

"Please excuse my manners." He placed his right hand on his left pectoral and slightly bowed.

"My name is Ty. If you don't mind my asking, you are?" he inquired, extending his hand for a shake.

Mia, there is no way you are going to be able to touch this man's hand and keep a straight face and dry panties!

It was bad enough I'd barely contained myself without physical contact. Now he wanted to shake my hand. If I refused, it would be rude and awkward, not to mention totally give me away.

"Thank you. You have good taste," I complimented him shaking his fingers lightly and dropping them like a hot potato. "I happen to love Rachelle's music, but I don't think I have this one," I managed to say without stuttering. "And I'm Mia. It's nice to meet you."

As I predicted, touching his hand set off internal fireworks that caused my nipples to burst through my top.

"Mia. That's an exotic name. I don't think I've ever met anyone by that name before. No wonder you intrigued me. Not only are you extraordinarily beautiful, but you have a name that's equivalent. If I may ask, do you live around here?"

Oh, I can show your fine ass exotic.

"Actually I just moved here from Maryland."

Too much information too soon Mia, don't get beside yourself.

"Oh wow! Aren't *we* lucky. What brings you to Jersey, and let me say, whatever it is allow me to thank it from the bottom of my heart."

Suave, this brotha was suave. He oozed confidence without apology.

I like, I like.

Anybody within ear range could tell he was clearly going for his.

"Work."

"And that would be?"

"I'm an interior designer and event planner."

"Seriously! You gotta be kidding me! You're not going to believe me when I tell you this." He chuckled. "Today must be my lucky day! It just so happens I *need* an interior designer. I bought a condo on Park Avenue and it's a little, mmmmm…how do I say it…bachelor-like. It needs a professional touch, a little softening up." He laughed again.

"Listen to me. I hope I'm not coming across like a male chauvinist or anything like that. I'm a little 'ole school and I think there are some things that women do…okay I'ma quit while I'm ahead!" he noted with his hands in the air.

Ah ha! He wants me to know he's single, huh? Nice. Daphne would approve.

"Great idea," I laughed. But in your defense, I guess there's no tactful way for a man to ask a woman to help him pick out window treatments."

"Exactly! I hope I didn't offend you because I'd never want to insult someone as captivating as you," he remarked, softening his voice and licking his lips. "Might you have a card or some way I can get in touch with you? I'd love to have you come by and see my place?"

Will somebody turn the heat down in this store! All right, that's it.

It was truly time for me to exit stage right. Mad chemistry flowed between us and I had no right to be indulging in the freaky imaginings that were incited by his charisma. Especially given the danger signs that were tugging at my gut like crazy for no apparent reason. Regardless, the stranger intrigued me. I should have cut our conversation short and ran for the door long before now. He'd been straight to the point from the onset and his point was obviously me. I had enough confusion in my life to fill two lifetimes. God knows I didn't need any more.

"No I'm not the least bit offended, it comes with the territory, but my plate is full," I fibbed. I could see the disappointment in his eyes but he wasn't defeated.

"I understand, and I won't pretend that I'm not trying to create an opportunity to see you again, because I am, but business is business." He reached into his back pocket, pulled out his wallet and handed me a business card.

"If you change your mind will you give me a call?" he asked innocently.

I took the card and slipped it into my pocketbook without looking at it. I had no intention of calling him.

"Certainly, now if you'll excuse me, it was nice meeting you and thanks for the recommendation," I said holding up the CD and avoiding his eyes. "I'm sure I'll enjoy it."

Ty stepped in front of me. He loomed over me like God himself, omnipresent and mysterious. My feet were cemented to the floor and my willpower left the room.

"Do you mind my asking if you've had dinner yet?"

"No I haven't, but I can't," I answered without missing a beat.

"You can't or you won't?"

I thought for a moment. No matter which one I chose, my instinct doubted he'd give up.

"I won't," I answered honestly.

"And let me fill in the blanks since you were so forthcoming," he began. "Unquestionably, you're a classy lady. A sexy and intelligent one I might add. You're married and you desire to respect that, but you do acknowledge that there's an energy between us that makes you a little uneasy, maybe even confused. Therefore, you don't trust yourself with me. How'd I do?" he asked with a smile on his face.

Oh this one's got game! Mad game, but I like it!

I admit dinner would have been awesome, but oooh weeee was he on point with my not trusting myself with him! On the other hand, I didn't want to go home because there was nothing to do and I was hungry.

"You're the psychic so I don't need to answer that question, right?"

"Refreshing! A woman who thinks on her feet," he grinned. "I tell you what. Suppose I offered to treat you to dinner in a public place, you can drive yourself there and I promise not to pressure you afterwards. Will you reconsider?"

Ty drove a hard bargain. I wanted to have dinner with him even though there were a hundred reasons why I shouldn't be thinking twice about it. Despite the warning to resist the temptation, I rationalized that his offer to meet in a public place meant no harm could be done. Afterward I'd just drive myself home.

"I don't think that will be possible, but I appreciate the invitation," I heard myself answer before making another attempt to walk away.

"Hold on, hold on, hear me out, one last plea. I'm not asking you to trust *me*. I'm asking you to trust yourself. If you really don't feel comfortable with me and you would rather we not have dinner together, then I'll back off. But if your intuition tells you that I'm a decent guy who will respect your wishes and would just like to treat a beautiful lady to dinner, no strings attached," he motioned with his hand over his heart, "then I beg you to say yes."

My instinct was screaming the opposite but I chose to muffle it.

"What do you have in mind?" I asked, succumbing to his charm.

We both smiled and I felt eager.

"Do you know the city at all?"

"I do. Very well."

"I'd like to recommend Monet's over on 58th and 5th across from Central Park. Are you familiar with it?"

"I am."

You didn't go near Monet's if you had a problem spending money. Hell, you didn't get into Monet's at the last minute because they were always crowded, but I had no plans of mentioning that piece of information either.

Let's see what you're really made of Mr. Ty whatever your last name is.

"Will 8:30 give you enough time to get downtown?"

"Make it 9:00 and you have a deal."

"9:00 it is. I'll meet you there," he smiled. "And don't bother parking, just pull up to valet and they'll take care of you."

"Thank you," I blushed.

"One last question. Do you have a favorite flower?"

I smiled. "Orchids."

"Ahhh, delicate and exotic. Why am I not surprised?"

Silence crept between us offering an opportunity for him to look me over. His head partially cocked to one side, he rubbed his hands together and smiled. I gathered up my stack of CD's, avoiding his stare and strolled toward the register. I felt him watching as I walked off, so I put an extra swing in my hips.

You Can't Hide Love

Myles

B OTH CHILDREN WERE fast asleep when I arrived at my parents' home in the SE section of DC.

Given the day I'd had a round of any kind of dark liquor had my fucking name on it. Once time permitted, I planned to holla at my boy Q to see if he could join me for a few drinks down at the Front Page, one of our 'ole stomping grounds. At least it would give us a chance to catch up since we hadn't hung out in a while.

Like a constant beacon of hope, mother's short but dominating silhouette stood watching and waiting from her favorite spot at the living room window. She'd already partially cracked the front door open for us. I parked the car in the driveway and got out. Opening the back door, I scooped Brandon up in my arms and carried his comatose body inside.

"I'll be right back," I whispered, greeting my mother with a peck on her cheek before proceeding up the stairs to one of the guest bedrooms they kept prepared for the children. Brandon didn't budge when I laid him down, pulled off his sneakers and drew the covers lightly up over him.

"I made a pie earlier today," she informed me with pride from where she now stood on the top step of the porch.

"I smell it. You must have known I'd be coming," I teased going down the steps to get my baby girl.

Despite all the commotion, Tiffany still lay fast asleep and I was glad because that meant my mother and I would have a chance to talk.

"She's getting heavy," I remarked, carrying her limp body in my arms.

"Do they have bags? I can get them out the car for you, suga?"

"No, they don't, but I'll bring them over early tomorrow morning if that's okay," I told her, realizing my mother already had an idea they'd be staying.

I laid Tiffany on the other twin bed and pulled off her sandals. She turned over to readjust her position and fell back off to sleep. I kissed them both on the forehead and closed the door. When I got back downstairs, my mother was hastily searching for something in the refrigerator.

"Did you eat, son?" she asked looking back over her shoulder.

"Not yet. I took the children to McDonald's before coming by but I didn't eat. Tiffany didn't eat either. I imagine she'll probably be hungry in the morning."

"I'll see to it that she gets something to eat if she wakes up tonight."

"Is he downstairs?" I inquired from the bathroom where I had gone to wash my hands.

"You talking 'bout your father?"

"Yes."

"Like you need to ask me that question," she chuckled. "If your daddy ain't out in that yard he in front of that TV sleep. Only two places you gonna find him."

She joined me at the kitchen table carrying an arm full of condiments, a loaf of freshly baked bread, sandwich meat, cheese, a tomato and lettuce she'd probably grown in the garden, the cutting board and a knife. I watched her place each item carefully on the table before going over to the cupboard to get a plate and some napkins.

"It looks good," I said pointing at the apple pie sitting in the windowsill.

"*Something* told me you'd be coming so I started it first thing this morning."

"That's not funny, mother."

"I didn't mean it to be."

"I would offer to make you a sandwich, but I *know* you don't eat processed meat with your high blood pressure," I chided, giving her a disapproving look while cutting the bread.

"Boy don't you come in here telling me how ta eat! My doctor and me taking good care of my blood pressure and I don't need a third party!" she chastised.

"It's only out of love," I laughed. "Would you like me to make you one?"

"I know. No baby I done eat already."

I didn't realize how hungry I was until I saw the bread. Mother continued her busy work, pouring me a tall glass of freshly squeezed lemonade over ice, swiping things off the table when I finished with them and putting them away; all while keeping one eye on me. After I finished making two sandwiches, I pulled my chair up under the table to get comfortable. She sat down across from me with a glass of water in her hand.

"I guess you're wondering what's going on, huh?" I began after taking a big bite out of one of the sandwiches.

"I don't speculate 'bout much son," she said taking a sip of water.

I leaned back in my chair then let out a sigh after swallowing my food.

"I made a quick stop by the house before going to meet Steve." I had to pause prior to speaking the words. "From the looks of things, when I left this morning Mia forgot to tell me that she didn't want to be a mother to our children or married to me anymore. She packed up everything except mine and the children's belongings and disappeared."

I don't quite know how I expected her to respond. She didn't blink an eye or make an expression. All she did was pick up her glass, put it to her lips, take a drink of water and placed it back on the table.

"Have mercy."

"You don't sound surprised."

"No, I'm *not* surprised baby, not at all, but I imagined you were," she stated, our eyes making contact.

"What kind of question is that?" I asked startled. "Why wouldn't I be? Is there something you wanna tell me?" I fired at her, pushing my chair back from the table.

"If you're asking me if I know'ed, the answer's no. If you're asking me if I'm surprised the answers no," she said without apology.

"Well you always have had a way of seeing things most people can't. Forgive me for not having the foresight to know that my wife would pack up our belongings and bounce," I snapped cynically.

"You misunderstood me baby. It musta been horrible for you ta go home and find it that way. I can't imagine," she said tenderly. "Just understand I'm never surprised by nothing people do is all I meant."

Man did I feel like an imbecile! She had been the first person I got a chance to lash out at since this nightmare began but I had no right to take my frustrations out on her. I felt lame for even implying she may have had any knowledge of Mia potentially leaving and not telling me.

"I'm sorry, I was…I was totally outta line. I had no right to come at you like that."

"No need to 'poligize to me. Mercy. I ain't gonna blame you for nothing much you going through right now son. You gotta right to feel whatever comes up."

"I can't even describe it, mother," I replied genuinely. "I wanna understand how my wife walks out on her family without a word. How did she decide to take everything from our children?" I asked rhetorically. "She didn't even leave the living room furniture for us to sit on. Pictures off the wall, plants gone, it's crazy. Why? I mean, was she that pissed off, and if so how long had she been feeling that way? It's got me questioning whether I even knew who she was, you know. We made a promise to each other that we would do everything in our power to keep our family together. If not for us for our children. We didn't want them to be products of a broken home. That was her commitment as well as mine and this is what she does? I don't get it."

"Did you try to call her son?"

"Several times. I even called Mrs. Samuels but of course she didn't pick up. You ready for this? Mia had her phone turned off. It's probably a good thing I can't reach her, especially now that I see how it's affecting Tiffany. I'm sure I'd say some not so nice words," I said shielding what I really wanted to say out of respect for my mother.

"Lord have mercy. I ain't got words for what you must be going through. Them children deserve they mother. What you gonna tell'em?"

"Wait a minute, it gets better. She went by the Center and took them to Red Lobster before sailing off into the sunset. From the bits and pieces I gathered, she told them she'd be away for a while but planned to come back. How convenient, huh? Apparently, she led them to believe that I would be upset if they went with her. Can you believe that? I had to tell them that we both agreed they should stay with me until we figured out how long she'd be away. I know Tiffany saw right through that story even though she's pretending to go along with it for now."

My mother sat at the table shaking her head, an empathetic look on her face. I'm sure her heart went out to all parties involved, even Mia because that's who she was.

Talking about the situation stole my appetite. I shoved the plate with my sandwiches across the table in front of me and rose to my feet.

"Will you excuse me for a minute? I need to make a phone call." I craved a drink to numb the thoughts running rampant in my head.

"Sure baby."

I went out on the front porch and dialed my boy's number.

"Yeah," Q answered.

"Black man! What's going on?" I asked, psyched he'd answered.

"You got me." What up with you?" Quincy hollered over deafening background music.

"Everything's good," I pretended.

"Yo man long time. How the fuck you been? How's the fam?"

"We hanging in," I lied.

"What it look like? Been a minute since I heard from 'yo ass."

"You know how it go with family and shit. What you got going on later, you busy or is that a stupid question?" I laughed lightly.

I could hear the volume of the background music decrease substantially.

"Yeah, that's a dumbass question. Everythang good dawg?" Quincy questioned with suspicion in his voice.

"Yeah, yeah. Everything is everything. Can't a big brother check in?" I asked trying to throw him off.

"Cut the bullshit man. Who the fuck you think you talkin to?"

"That obvious?"

"What you think?"

"You got some time to slide through the Front Page around nine-thirty for a few beers?"

"Sho nuff."

"Cool, I'll see you then."

It was good to know that no matter how much time passed, Q always had my back.

We grew up in the same neighborhood and became friends in third grade despite the fact that we were from opposite sides of the streets. After high school, I went off to Howard. Q never graduated, but instead ended up in the big house on a ten-year bid for voluntary manslaughter.

While on lockdown he literally ran the prison. CO's, sergeants, supervisors and fellow inmates ate out the palm of his hand. Q carried just as much juice locked up as he did when he ran his operation on the streets. Everybody in the hood knew my boy was borderline psycho so his reputation followed him to the pen. After serving five of the ten years, he came home and resumed running his cartel.

I was mad thankful I caught him at home. The odds were high that he already had plans for the evening because my man had a way with the ladies. No doubt a female or two was gonna be blowing up his phone at some point tonight.

Q always said, "love only caught up with motherfuckers who stayed in one place too long." Love almost caught him once in high school.

Imani was smart, fine and she didn't take no shit, however Q was her Achilles heel. The two of them were like night and day. Imani was the class valedictorian and Q was a heartless drug dealer destined to end up dead or locked up and locked up won the roll of the die. Unfortunately, he was one of many sperm donations his drug dealing daddy left fatherless throughout the neighborhood.

Q wanted to keep Imani and his cheating ways but she wasn't playing the game. He pushed the envelope off the fucking table when he slept with her best friend who she'd known since second grade. To add insult to injury, Bev didn't look half as good or have half as much going for herself as Imani did. Everybody but Imani could tell that her so called friend was envious of her and wanted everything she had including my boy. Senior year she went for hers. When Imani walked in and found the two of them getting it in, she came to cry on my shoulder. From that point we became close and looked at each other like play brothers and sisters.

The cold-blooded thing about the whole situation was that when Imani broke it off my boy moved on like she didn't mean shit to him. He even hooked up with Bev for about six months afterward. That's when I first realized the Wizard really forgot to give him a fucking heart. I felt sorry for the parade of women who thought they could tie him down with their good looks, pussy, ass or all the above. What a waste of precious time.

Imani had all the top schools offering her full ride scholarships. She chose the University of Cambridge in England to get away from Q. Last I heard she was living in Paris.

I went back inside and rejoined my mother at the kitchen table.

"I called Q. We're gonna hook-up in a bit. If it's okay with you, depending on how long I'm out, I might hang at his place tonight."

She slowly reached across the table and caressed my hand. "You know you ain't alone in this son, don't you? Your father and I here for you and the chil'ren. I don't know how a mother walks away from her babies," she shook her head, "but it ain't for me to judge. What I do know is that Mia loves them chil'ren and I don't know what she going through to make her leav'em, but I do know that anger won't bring her back, and it sure as heck won't do them babies no good. You got to take care of them now and that's what you focus on. Anger and meanness only makes you bitter," she said with an intense gaze.

"I know what you're saying is right mother, and I appreciate the fact that you're not just taking my side because I'm your son. I'll try to stay focused on Tiff and Brandon through all of this and not let my emotions take over. I might just need a minute to get there. Truthfully, I've thought about walking away a few times already."

"I know, son. You got chil'ren asking you questions you can't answer and on top of that you got questions yo'self, but if you run, who gonna take care of them chil'ren?"

"Yeah but I didn't ask for this," I said defensively.

"Neither did they but it's yours now. You can't just run from life 'cause you don't like the hand you've been dealt. You're stronger than that. Sides, you never done that before so why you gonna start today?" she comforted.

I could feel the tension in my body lighten up a tinge. Her belief in me and encouragement helped to lift my spirits. And she was right, I was not a quitter. It took fortitude to put myself through dental school and work two jobs so that I wouldn't have a bunch of loans to pay off when I finished. I needed to give myself credit for my internal strength and trust I'd be able to get us over this hurdle.

"Why don't you leave the chil'ren with your father and me 'til you figure things out? I'll talk to Phil in the morning but you know he wouldn't like nothing better than to have our grandbabies here."

Here she goes again.

I hadn't even gotten to that conversation yet and already she was on it!

"In case they ask us any questions when they wake up and you not here what you want your father and me to say?"

"Great question. Let's see. I'd say stick to the script and tell them Mia will be back until I find out what's going on. Tiffany is the one who's going to have the most questions. I think she's confused by the sudden change. Keep your eye on her for me, will you?"

"Of course. I tell you. It don't make no sense at all. I'll never understand it," mother said shaking her head.

"I'd like to keep the children away from the house until I can get some new furniture in there. What do you think?"

"Whatever you decide baby."

Mother stood up, walked over to the cupboard and began putting away the few dishes she'd washed.

"I hate her for what she's done. I mean if she really did leave it was pathetic and cowardly," I said out the blue.

"Run on along and go get your mind off things for a while," she said walking over and placing her hand gently on my shoulder. "And don't worry 'bout my babies, they in good hands."

I could see the sadness in her eyes and I felt guilty for burdening her with my problems. "Thanks for everything, mother. It means a lot."

"I'll leave the light on outside…just in case you decide to come back."

"I'll play it by ear. More than likely I'll be coming through in the morning. I'm going to need to pack some clothes for them."

I got up from my chair and stretched. I thought about going downstairs to speak to my 'ole man but I didn't feel like recanting the day's events all over again, especially to him. His whole conversation would have been packed with self-righteous I told you so's, and I really didn't need to have his opinionated ass taking shots at me.

"Why don't you just go ahead? I'll tell your father you'll see him tomorrow," my mother chimed in as if reading my thoughts. "I won't say anything. I think it be better if you tell him, don't you?"

I hugged and squeezed her tight and placed a kiss on her forehead just for being her.

"Thank you. If I don't see you tonight, I'll see you first thing in the morning."

"Drive safely."

We strolled silently to the front door arm in arm. I gave her another kiss, this time on the cheek and walked heavy hearted out the door.

What A Man

Mia

THE CITY'S INTOXICATING energy pulled me in its direction as I drove across the upper level of the George Washington Bridge heading uptown to Monet's. Suspended between the Hudson River below and a crystal-clear sky above, I stole glimpses of the breathtakingly beautiful Manhattan skyline as I crept along stop and go traffic. As far as I was concerned, there was no other sight in the eastern hemisphere more stunning than the view of Manhattan from the George Washington Bridge.

After being charmed by Ty, I left the Wiz and slipped into an upscale boutique at the mall to see if I could find something sexy to wear. I lucked up and found a cute fitted red satin spaghetti strap knee length dress with a classy plunging neckline. It didn't hurt that it complimented my figure without looking too slutty. The sales lady did a fabulous job of accenting the dress with a pair of crystal rhinestone chandelier earrings, a stone and pearl covered black clutch and an overly expensive pair of classic black pumps.

Thank my lucky stars Ty had arranged Valet parking for me. That way I could be cute and didn't have to worry about my feet hurting while trying to break in a new pair of pumps.

I pulled up in valet around five minutes after nine, turned down the volume to my CD player and lowered the driver side window a little. There were three things I knew about Ty for sure: he was drop dead fine, extremely determined and had impeccable taste in music.

"Good evening ma'am, may I ask the reservation name please?" a young handsome valet attendant who'd appeared out of nowhere asked while peeking into the crack in my window.

"My name is Mia, Mia Rollins and I have reservations with Mr. Ty Spencer." Good thing I looked at the card Ty had given me and knew his last name before I got there.

From his reaction you would have thought I said I had reservations with God Himself. In between excitably saying, 'okay, okay' several times, he fumbled nervously with my car door handle trying to get it open, and I smirked wondering if he was going to pull the damn thing off.

"Okay ma'am, I mean, Ms. Rollins, Mr. Spencer is expecting you," he chattered.

He finally got the driver's door open and reached for my hand to escort me out of the car. I grabbed my clutch and followed him into an area of the restaurant I hadn't remembered seeing the few times I'd been to Monet's. The empty private area was off the main dining room, and from the expensively rich décor it obviously was where the VIP's dined. I looked around the large open room in awe trying hard to keep my mouth from flying open.

Say What! This must be where the President and First Lady sit when they eat at Monet's!

The room was elaborately decorated and luxuriously furnished.

The young man excused himself before stepping a few feet away from me. He retrieved a cell phone from his back pocket and began a brief conversation with someone who sounded like they stood right next to us. I listened with one ear open while watching staff members dressed in black tuxedos glide about like ballet dancers through an open door.

"Mr. Kwame, okay, Ms. Rollins has arrived. Okay, yes sir. Okay, thank you, sir."

What a perfect choice for dinner, Mr. Spencer. Two points for you.

The last time I ate at Monet's I remember admiring how someone had pulled off an elegant teal and cream décor in the main dining area. I'd never seen the combination work before then. As if it couldn't get any better, this room boasted a soft sky blue and deep chocolate with a hint of gold thrown in. Perfect.

"Ma'am, Mr. Kwame, our restaurant captain will be here to escort you to the penthouse in a moment. Enjoy your dinner," he sincerely offered before disappearing through the door we'd come in.

The penthouse! Restaurant captain! I never knew Monet's had a penthouse. Impressive. And what the hell was a restaurant captain?

For some reason, I felt the hairs on the back of my neck rise, prompting me to turn around. A gentleman dressed in a black tux, cream shirt and a crooked red bow tie walked nonchalantly in my direction. He had a head full of salt and pepper shoulder length, semi-maintained locs and could have easily been mistaken for a Jamaican. Underneath a pretentious guise I sensed a troubled spirit. His build looked as if it were a lot heavier at one time and he hadn't bothered to buy a more fitting tux. As he got closer, uneasiness settled in the pit of my stomach. His eyes were the coldest, saddest eyes I'd ever met and he didn't look highly excited to see me at all. I avoided more than a momentary glance his way because something about him made me very uncomfortable. I crossed my fingers hoping like hell that he wasn't the one who was going to escort me to Ty.

"Good evening, *Ms.* or *Mrs.* Rollins?" he questioned in a flippant tone.

His inquiry felt cynical but I dismissed it as my own personal guilt.

"*Ms.* Rollins is fine," I answered defensively with a forged smile.

"Please follow me," he demanded before walking off and damn near leaving me in the wind. I trailed hurriedly behind him suddenly feeling stupid for even being there.

This guy must have failed remedial hosting 101.

The minute I saw Ty I planned to let him know how rude this *restaurant captain* had been to me. I wondered if it were safe to be following dude anywhere. When we ended up at an elevator after several twists and turns down long hidden corridors, I had no intention of getting into a closed confined space with him by myself. Bump that!

"Do you mind calling Mr. Spencer to accompany me from this point?" I asked as we stood in front of the elevator. Hell, wasn't no shame in my game! Momma always told me to listen to my instincts and my intuition was telling me to lose this character with a quickness.

"Very well, suit yourself," he said indifferently, and then *poof,* homeboy made a U-turn, banked the corner and vanished. Without another word, he left me standing there in total shock. Dumbfounded, I contemplated whether I should take the elevator, wait, or try to find my way back to the front. I finally concluded that his rudeness was a sign for me to leave, so I turned around and tried to retrace my steps back to valet. We had gone down a long corridor and a few hallways, and halfway back I heard that voice that short-circuited my senses.

"Mia, where are you going?"

It stopped me dead in my tracks. Ty walked up beside me, and my heart rate shifted into overdrive. He was wearing a beige linen shirt and matching slacks that made him look like he just stepped out of 'God Help Me Please Magazine!' Lightly placing a hand on my waist, his pillow soft lips kissed my cheek and I thought I might need to brace myself on something before my knees gave out.

"Who the hell was that Kwame jerk and how did he get a job here?" I blurted out after gaining my composure and remembering I'd just been dissed.

"What happened, Mia?" Ty asked, the bass deepening in his voice.

"Let's see, where do I start…oh yeah, how about he was R-U-D-E! How the hell did he get a job here?" I questioned again. "I have never been treated with such blatant disrespect in all my life! You need to report him to his manager," I insisted.

Ty listened patiently to my temper tantrum. I went off like a wild woman. He probably didn't understand half of what I had said, but he listened attentively until I'd gotten it all out of my system.

"I'll take care of him *trust me*," he reassured me looking keenly into my eyes with an intensity I'd hate to be on the receiving end of. "I have a very special evening planned for you upstairs. Please don't let anything spoil it," he pleaded taking my hand. "I assure you whatever happened will be dealt with, you've got my word," he reiterated. Right now let's enjoy this evening."

As worked up as I'd gotten over that Kwame nobody, Ty managed to bring me right back down on a soft billowy cloud of calm.

"Well, if you promise me that before the evening is over he'll be dealt with, I guess I can let it go temporarily, but don't go easy on him. The next time I come here I don't even want to know he existed."

"I got it covered."

I took that to mean he'd handle his business his way. I didn't care if dude got the axe. He deserved it as far as I was concerned. Restaurant captain my ass.

"Now can we go upstairs?" he gestured with his hand toward the corridor I'd come down.

My smile answered yes as we walked back to the elevator, his hand on the small of my back. He swiped a card through a keypad on the wall and the double-mirrored doors glided open smoothly, awaiting our entrance.

"After you," Ty motioned, directing me into the elevator.

"Thank you," I blushed, the doors flowing softly together behind us.

"I had to bite my tongue downstairs to keep from telling you how beautiful you are. The only reason I held myself back is because I wanted you to know that I took what happened seriously. Mia, my God you are...there are no words," he spoke tenderly and deliberately into my ear as he moved closer to me and placed his hand a little higher on my back. The man generated so much heat he could have easily set off the sprinkler system in the elevator. I tried to pretend I didn't feel the intensity of his attraction or read his erotic thoughts by staring at the wall. My knees were jelly.

"Thank you, you don't look too bad yourself," I murmured, reaching up to run my fingers through my hair, grateful the elevator doors opened when they did.

We walked a few feet down a hallway that had carpet so soft I felt guilty walking on it with my shoes. Both sides of the walls were accentuated with signature artwork from several artists, who ironically, Myles and I owned pieces of their work as well. Karua, a Kenyan painter who had taken the art world by storm in a very short period of time seemed to be the favorite on display. The walls were painted a bright peach that surprisingly created a subtle but powerful backdrop for the artwork. Six beautiful antique marble pedestals each displayed the world-renowned Jiri Pacinek's Ruby Wave Vases. I could tell that whoever had been commissioned to pull things together in the penthouse was on point.

Ty strolled confidently beside me with his hand on my waist smelling and looking sexy. We stopped in front of a mirrored wall and he removed a small remote control from his pocket and pressed one of the buttons.

The wall of mirrors parted in the middle, revealing a room that looked like paradise on earth. Enthralled by an ambiance that rendered me speechless, I was totally unobservant to the fact that he had vanished into a sea of candlelight…the sole illumination in the entire room exposing the extent of his labor. Rachelle's CD played faintly in the background.

Slowly, I tipped-toed into the Penthouse and stopped abruptly because I couldn't believe what was below me. The VIP room on the lower level was visible through tinted glass plates! I couldn't help but wonder if Ty had been watching me the entire time I waited for him.

As if that were not enough to blow my mind, an original carved oak Victorian table was elaborately set for two in front of a jaw dropping view of Central Park.

"OMG," I laughed. "No you didn't!"

There were a ridiculous number of fresh cut exotic Orchids, Casablanca Lillie's, Gardenias and Roses in colors I didn't even know existed, strategically placed in Ruby Wave Vases throughout the room. To say I was flabbergasted would have been an understatement.

Wow, orchids. Where the hell did he find fresh cut exotic orchids in NYC?!

In all the years of owning my business and working with some affluent clients, I'd never seen anything like this before.

Just when I thought the experience couldn't get any better I realized I hadn't noticed a fireplace that spanned an entire wall of one side of the room. It looked like it had been constructed from the finest Black Golden Portoro marble known to man. Limited edition Bibbs, Ringgold and several other famous black artists hung proudly above the mantelpiece. Candles of all different shapes and sizes were everywhere. A fully stocked bar with any liquor you could want was built into the opposite wall and a state of the art home theater system complimented the very back of the room.

Whoever hooked this spot up had flawless taste and a generous checkbook. I couldn't help but wonder why he needed my services if he had access to someone with the skills I was witnessing.

I was impressed. It took a lot for another designer's talents to astound me because I had it going on, however, in this case I had to give props where props were due. Gawking at the room, I wondered how he managed to pull this off with such short notice. Suddenly I remembered our agreement. We were supposed to meet in a public place. Yet despite his transgression, I didn't want to be anywhere else. He'd obviously gone to a lot of trouble to blow me away and man was it working!

My body stiffened when I felt his presence move in close behind me. I turned around to face him and he looked pleased with himself.

"You said we'd…"

"Shhhhhh…Mia, please. Just grant me this moment," he whispered holding a finger up to his lips. His stare penetrated so deeply into my soul I felt him inside of me.

Embarrassed and tickled, not quite sure what to do with myself I shifted my weight from side to side in my pumps. Looking down at the floor I tried to avoid his eyes as he drank me in.

"If you don't mind, ummmm…I hate to interrupt but this is very uncomfortable for me," I confessed.

I inhaled a light trace of his Giorgio Armani cologne to store into my memory bank for later. He effortlessly took my hand and guided me deeper into the room. God knows what little willpower I had left to resist his charisma was fading fast like Stevie Wonder's hairline. Nobody had to tell me that danger lurked in every second that I hung around this man. The linen suit pronouncing every muscle on his body wasn't making my life any easier either. It looked like the damn thing had been tailor made exclusively for him. His eyes were piercing and intense and I could feel myself start to sweat.

"Please forgive me, Mia. The last thing I want to do is make you uncomfortable. It's just that I want to photograph you in my mind. You are complete and beautiful."

"Thank you again, and you're full of compliments tonight aren't you? A girl could get used to all of this you know," I flushed.

He didn't say a word. Instead, he put his hand in mine and led me over to one of the plush leather sofas across from the fireplace where we both sat down. His guide was confident and my mind went straight to the gutter. I put my purse down on the coffee table before crossing my legs revealing just enough thigh to tease but not too much to be obvious. He fixated a gaze on my upper thigh proposing inappropriate subliminal messages, all of which I pretended oblivion.

"Now if I remember correctly you promised a public place," I reprimanded.

"This is a public place. It just happens to have a private setting" he smiled proudly.

"You have a way with words and I haven't quite decided if that's a good thing or a bad thing," I noted, pointing my finger at him.

"Well when you decide pretty lady how do you intend to let me know?" He grinned mischievously.

"You seeee! That's what I mean!" I laughed, shaking my finger at him this time.

"Can I get you something to drink?" he asked as if he didn't have a clue what I meant.

"That would be nice. Might you have cranberry juice by chance?"

"For you, I have any and everything you need. Cranberry juice coming up," he confirmed as he looked over his shoulder at me on the way to the bar.

I wasn't going to touch that statement. Instead, I watched him stride self-assured to the other side of the room. Observing him behind the bar meticulously handling his business was like watching perfection at work. As much as I tried not to, my eyes found themselves glued to his every move.

"By the way I like the Orchids," I smiled.

"I'm glad. Ice?"

"Yes, please. Wow!" I shrieked, suddenly recognizing the box of cigars on the coffee table in front of me. "Are those Aturo Fuente Anejo's?"

"Yeah, as a matter of fact they are. What do you know about cigars?" he queried.

"Not much," I laughed. I have a client who only smokes Anejo's and he told me how rare and expensive they are. Somebody's got classy taste!"

"You wanna try one?"

"Oh no, but thank you."

"So, did you find the restaurant okay? I know you mentioned earlier you'd been here before."

"I had no problem finding it. I never knew Monet's had a penthouse," I commented, looking around the room.

"Most people don't. It's a private space," he admitted strolling back over to where I sat.

"Lucky for me I know the owner. Tell me," he asked, handing me a glass and a napkin, "what did you think of the food when you were last here?"

"Thank you." I took the tall glass of cranberry juice from him making it my business not to touch his hand. We'd done enough of that already. "Honestly, I'd give it five out of five stars."

"Seriously?"

"Seriously. I was very pleased with the food, although I wish I could say that about my experience with the host tonight."

"But we're going to leave him behind us, right," he reminded me.

"Right." A sip of the juice satisfied my thirst. It was nice and cold.

"Do you mind if I show you around the place before we eat dinner?" he asked, reaching for my hand.

"I'd love that."

Ty removed my drink from my hand and set it down on a coaster as I stood up. It felt good to have someone pamper and cater to my every need. He took the time to show me around the penthouse and explained each piece of art and how it ended up at Monet's.

"I'm curious," I stated before taking a seat at the bar, "and only because I'm honored that you'd do this for me, but how did you make all this happen so fast, and how do you know so much about this place? I know from personal experience how hard it is to get reservations at Monet's so I can't imagine what strings you had to pull to get up here," I asked curiously.

"Come here."

He reached for my hand and we walked back over to the couch and sat down. Whatever he was about to say looked serious.

"I'm going to be honest with you Mia because that's the way I want it between us. I don't know if you're married or involved with anyone but I'm feeling you. I would never disrespect you on any level but I'd be upset with myself if I didn't tell you that I'm really attracted to you. I would love to spend more time with you and get to know you if that's an option."

I wasn't sure where this was going but he had my curiosity peaked.

"I own Monet's."

Say what!

You could have blown me over with a feather. It took me a moment but I finally put two and two together. Could it really be? The tycoon, Tyrese Spencer Monroe! I was sitting across from the great Mr. Monroe himself. I'd read about him in Black Entrepreneurs about three years ago.

If my memory served me correctly, his mother died of breast cancer when he was only five. An aunt raised him in the projects of Brownsville in Brooklyn where he joined a gang at twelve. She ended up dying of lung cancer when he was fifteen. He never knew his father or any other relatives. After his aunt passed he continued to live in their apartment for two years by himself while finishing high school. He worked as a busboy in a restaurant at night to feed and clothe himself and pay the two-hundred fifty dollars subsidized rent for the apartment. Before he was twenty-five, he owned his first restaurant. He became a self-made millionaire before his twenty-seventh birthday. There was no mention of him owning Monet's in the article. In fact, he rarely gave interviews and kept a very low profile.

"Oh my God how embarrassing! I feel like I need to apologize for not recognizing you. Wow, I totally had my head in the clouds..."

"Mia please don't trip," he interrupted. "It's refreshing, trust me. I long to be that regular dude nobody recognizes. Don't switch up because you think you know something about me," he stated, reaching for my hands.

I was thinking he looked familiar when I saw him at the Wiz. Now I knew why.

I understood his petition to be treated normal if that were possible. Hell, he was one of the most sought after bachelors in the country, maybe the world because of his fortune. His business ventures had him sitting on a pretty lucrative penny, and with Monet's as a part of his portfolio, there was no telling what his net worth was. I'm sure the invisible shovels came out ready to dig whenever he was in the company of most women. I wasn't going to trip or put on airs because he had fame and money. I dealt with his type all the time on a professional level.

"Alright, let's do this then!" I said in my best ghetto fabulous accent while placing my feet up on the coffee table. I grabbed one of the menus he'd put on the couch next to me and perused it. "Here we go... you can begin by ordering up the appetizers, and I'll have ummmm...two orders of the grilled jumbo stuffed shrimp along with the cob salad and a bowl of Monet's signature Creamy Corn Chowder. Mmmmm…let's see, ahhh, yes. For the main course, you can bring on the baked chicken, marinated with that apricot savory sauce like only Monet's can do, all right. For my sides, I'll have the spinach parmesan rice, grilled asparagus, honey glazed carrots and a basket of Monet's famous sweet honey bread. Ohhhh… unfair, unfair! So many choices for dessert," I laughed. "Let's see, let's see, let's see. Okay, the chocolate cake drizzled with raspberry sauce and a scoop of almond ice cream wins. Lastly, you can go over there and pop a bottle of that Dom Perignon and watch a sista show you how we regular folk get down!"

I thought he was going to burst a blood vessel he was laughing so hard.

"That's what I'm talking about baby girl! I love a woman who knows what she likes! But what I wanna know is, can you handle all that," he teased, before reaching for a phone next to him.

There he goes again with that play on words thing.

"Don't you worry 'bout me, I can handle mines!" I laughed.

"I bet you can," he countered while licking his lips. "Very good selections. Ironically, all of my favorites apart from the baked chicken."

"Hold up, rewind! Is there something you wanna tell a sista about the chicken?" I asked, cutting my eyes at him.

Ty's laughter filled the room once again and I couldn't help but laugh with him. "Only that I've heard it's the best some folks have had, but I'm a semi-vegetarian so I wouldn't know. But don't let me stop you! You go right on ahead and do you baby!" he chuckled.

If you keep calling me baby like that, I might do you.

"I plan to!"

I realized that judging a book by its cover could prove deceiving but Ty made it easy for me to be myself. I was wide open. Realistically, I had no business entertaining a man who made me want to put my underwear on the table and beg him to take me, however lust and curiosity were superseding reality in the moment.

"By the way, from the looks of this place I don't think you'll need my services. The décor in here is meticulous. Actually, outside of my work it's the best I've seen. Who's your designer?" I asked admiringly, canvassing the room for the hundredth time.

"See that's where you're wrong. My home and my business have two different atmospheres. I like my home to feel like a home not an art museum or an establishment." He took a moment and looked around the room before returning to our conversation. "And I do *need* your services because the person that did all of this for me, unfortunately is no longer with us," he said in a solemn tone.

"I'm sorry to hear about your *friend. She* was very talented and I would have loved to have met *her*," I stated intentionally referencing a female. What was her name?"

"Nina."

Nina, huh, mental note.

"Well, let the record stand that Nina knew her stuff!"

One thing I could clearly see is that whoever Nina was she must have been very special. I wondered if they were lovers and itched to ask more questions. Thinking back to what I'd read about him, I didn't recall reading about a wife or fiancé.

I watched him as he ordered our food and I was smitten. I liked the way he took charge of things and I remembered when Myles used to be that way when it came to me. Everything about Ty said he was a man in control of his life. He clearly took care of his body, ate well, and didn't have a problem spending money.

The conversation flowed effortlessly between us as we ate and laughed about everything but nothing in particular. Even though we talked a lot, I still didn't feel like I had learned much about him. After dinner, we kicked back on the sofa like two gluttons. Ty leisurely puffed on one of his cigars and I sat close to him enjoying the rich stimulating aroma it created; sipping from my third glass of Dom Perignon Rose. At some point during dinner, Ty had changed the music to a sensual mix of lovemaking jazz.

"You weren't lying when you said you could put down some food. I thought I was going to have to close the place down for a minute!" he teased.

"You see that's why you gotta watch who you keep it real around, um hummmm! Folk wanna put your business in the streets, but it's all good! Don't matter because anybody that knows me will tell you that I don't mess around in my plate, okay."

"What else would they tell me, Mia," Ty whispered leaning in close to my ear, the smell of the cigar scenting his words.

I looked over at him and guilt set in. Here I was acting as if I were a single woman not even forty-eight hours away from leaving my husband. This is the kind of crap Daphne would use to validate my insanity. My attraction for him was beginning to blur reason.

"They would tell you that I was a woman who loved her children, cherished her parents and thought that her baby sister was her guardian angel," I said, playing it safe and dodging his stare.

"How many children?" he asked attentively.

"Two. Tiffany 7 and my baby Brandon 5."

"I love children. Someday I'd like to have my own or meet somebody special who has her own." He moved closer to me. "What would they say if I asked how you felt about me?"

"They wouldn't because I would never tell a soul."

"Not even me?"

"But as I recall that wasn't the question."

"That's what I like about you Mia, you listen. Do you know how rare that is? Most people are so busy formulating their next thought while you're talking they don't even know what the hell you said. But not you, you really listen," he said amazed.

The sexual energy between us kicked up another notch egged on by the Dom Perignon. The time for me to get the hell up out of Monet's before I did something I'd regret had come.

I shifted my body to face him and when I did, he looked and smelled like a box of Godiva chocolates. What kept us from knocking everything off the table and sexing each other like wild banshees could only be attributed to the gods pulling the reins with everything they had. Surely time was running out.

Gently, Ty put his arm around my shoulder and pulled me closer to him. The part of me that detected I was about to cross the line begged me to leave immediately, but I had no willpower. My mind told me to leave, get up and go, run, but my body said 'girl if you so much as move I'll break both your legs!' I was an internal conflict.

"Ty, I think its best…"

"No, it's not best that you leave," he completed my thought, never once taking his eyes off me, nor his arm from around me. "Mia, you can't imagine how long it's been since I've felt this way about a woman. From the moment I saw you get out your car and walk into the store I knew I had to talk to you."

Is he saying he followed me into the store? That's borderline eerie.

"Ahh…this is way too complicated for me! You have to trust me on that. Besides, we hardly even know each other, and as hard as it is to believe because of my behavior right now, I don't go around picking up guys to sleep with on the first date."

"You wouldn't be here if I thought you were that kind of woman, Mia. Not to sound cocky, but I meet hundreds of women who would give it up just because. I think too highly of myself to fall into that trap. You're a class act, Mia. Any man in his right mind can see that. We're two consenting adults and I'm not about playing games. I honestly don't think your resistance is solely because we barely know each other. I told you from the gate; I'm not going to do anything to disrespect you, but I won't deny what I feel either."

I needed to go, bottom line. Here I was contemplating giving it up to a man I had just met! What the hell was wrong with me! I got up, smoothed down my dress that had crawled way too high up my thighs and walked unsteadily over to the bar where I placed my glass on the countertop. Ty never moved or took his eyes off me.

"You can't go. You're tipsy. I'll send a driver to take you home if you insist on leaving."

"You don't have to do that. I'm fine. Thank you for a wonderful evening. You will never know how on time this was for me," I stated sincerely with a slur.

"I'm going to get some coffee up here for you. After that you can go if you must," he told me, totally ignoring what I'd said. Ty strolled over to the bar and stood directly behind me to use the phone, placing his hand on my shoulder. He vaguely leaned his body against me while he ordered coffee and I didn't move an inch. Instead, I lightly relaxed into him, basking in the way his chest felt against my back and the way the cigar mingled with the smell of his cologne. The two created a titillating elixir. His per-

fect frame towered over me and I prayed his conversation didn't end anytime soon so he'd stay there behind me for an eternity.

After he hung up the phone, he must have read my vibe because he
faintly stroked the back of my head then leaned down and delicately
kissed my neck in different spots. His touch became a powerful aphrodi-
siac awakening the muscles in my vaginal walls. I wanted to slip his hand
down into my black lace underwear so he could feel the floodgate of juices
he'd opened. I felt his masculine left hand slightly grasp the base of my
throat with just enough force to make me quiver. Impulsively, I tilted my
head to the side resting it against his chest so that he could have free reign.
He complied by alternating between sucking the skin on my neck and
making circular motions up and down my neckline with his wet tongue.
He slipped his right hand under my dress, slid it across my naked skin,
and hungrily pulled me into him.

My body surrendered. Grinding against his thick, long, hard penis,
I let myself go. In my mind, I kept thinking I needed to pull away but
things had gone too far. I leaned into him as he moved the hand he'd
slipped under my dress delicately up to my left breast. He cupped and
caressed it several times then with the right intensity clasped my hardened
nipple between his thumb and pointer fingers and rubbed it repeatedly.
My body inadvertently shivered. In chorus we both softly moaned. Ty's
breathing went from a slow deep pace to one that was fast and shallow.
The battle erupting between my flesh and my consciousness triggered a
slight migraine, but I ignored it because I didn't want him to stop.

Time stood still until Myles' face suddenly and unexpectedly flashed
across my mind. Abruptly, I pulled away. An awkward juncture of silence
filled the room as I attempted to regroup by adjusting my dress which had
gathered up around my waist.

"Mia, I'm sorry," he stated while facing me with his hands in the air.
"I got carried away. I didn't mean to overstep my boundaries. I promised
and I'm a man of my word. It's just that you do something to me and…"

"That's not necessary," I told him, trying desperately not to look him
in the eyes. "I'm just as much to blame as you are."

There was a knock at the door and he looked over at me to confirm
that it was okay for them to enter. He allowed me a second to compose

myself and then invited them in. A young woman wheeled over a nicely decorated cart with all different types of coffee and necessities on it. He thanked her and she exited through the opened mirrored doors. Ty fixed a cup of coffee and handed it to me. I took the cup, saucer and napkin from his hands, sipped it lightly then placed it in the saucer.

Just like I like it, not too sweet and not too tart.

He clutched my elbow and guided me back over to the couch where I gratefully sat down. We spent another hour or so sitting close to each other and talking while I drank two cups of coffee.

"Can I see you tomorrow?" he asked shifting from beside me to the coffee table in front of me.

"I don't think that's a good idea," I answered putting my cup in the saucer. The champagne was beginning to wear completely off which gave me the clearance to drive my butt home. It was already way past midnight.

"When can I see you again?"

"Ty, my life is very complex right now. Before I invite anybody else in I've got some house cleaning to do."

"I understand," he offered with no resistance.

His acceptance came too easy. Was this the same man who earlier asked me out three different times and wouldn't take no for an answer? Frankly, I didn't know what his thoughts were but I needed to go.

The coffee hit the spot and before long I felt safe enough to drive. A car would have been nice, but it came with a trip back to Monet's to get my vehicle the next day strategically providing him with another chance to cloud my head. No thank you.

I got up and took my purse off the arm of the sofa. To my surprise, he didn't try to stop me. I was disappointed but happy.

"Let me tell Chris to bring your car around and then we can head down." Ty pulled out his cell phone and sent a text message. Once he got a reply we walked hand in hand to the elevator.

"Did you enjoy yourself, beautiful?" he asked as we waited for the elevator.

"It was magical."

"I'm glad," he responded genuinely.

The elevator doors opened and closed with a soft thump. We rode down to the main floor holding hands in silence. Chris had pulled my car around and graciously opened the door for me. He even had the engine running.

"Thank you, Chris. I'll see my guest off," he said politely.

"You're welcome Mr. Spencer."

The young man vanished into the restaurant.

"I have to see you again Mia, you know that don't you?"

"Maybe," I answered climbing in the car, but leaving the door open.

"Does that mean there'll be a next time?"

"I can't say right now, Ty."

"As long as you don't say no, I'll take that."

I could see this man was not going to give up.

"Can we still do business together?" he insisted.

"I'll give you a ring."

"I'll be waiting no matter how long it takes. Will you give me a quick call just to let me know you made it in okay?"

"I think I might be able to do that."

Ty closed my door and we waved at each other as I drove off.

I toyed with the thought of turning around and going back to the restaurant before I crossed the bridge to Jersey. Reluctantly, I went home.

Grateful for My Homie

Myles

I LINGERED OUTSIDE ON the steps trying to shake the exhaustion and feeling of doom hovering over me. I felt fucked over and stupid, like the walking dead except I was conscious of everything happening in my bad dream. Every time a thought of Mia crossed my mind a sharp pain shot through my chest.

I could feel mother's stare penetrating my back from her infamous spot by the window as I descended the steps, but I didn't turn around to see if she was standing there. I knew she was. When I got in my car, the temptation to drive away from this shit circled back through my mind. Even the thought of bailing sapped what little energy I had left. Besides, the innocent faces of my children were imprinted vividly in my mind and I didn't have the heart to walk out on them.

I ached for Mia. Frankly, I didn't care why she left I just wanted her back. I could smell her, taste her, see her face and hear her voice. I wondered where she was and what she was doing. I even wondered if she was thinking about me.

Yielding onto Seventh Street toward Georgia Ave, I bobbed and weaved my way toward the campus of Howard University. Directly past the campus on the left-hand side, the tacky red and blue neon lights that belonged to the staple hole in the wall joint since I was a child flashed F-R-O-N-T P-A-G-E.

There weren't many cars in the parking lot but that would change just before midnight. I made a left into the parking lot and looked around for Q's pimped out black Escalade. When I didn't see it, I went on inside to secure a table.

The second I walked through the door, Sammy, the brainchild that had birthed the establishment zeroed in on me from where he stood behind the bar way on the other side of the room.

"Well lookie here," he broadcasted in his deep raspy smoker's voice. "Look what the motherfucking cat done drug in here!" All eyes shifted in my direction. Making his way over to me, he greeted me like a long lost son with several pats on the back and a vigorous hug. "Lil' Myles, is that you?" he joked.

Sammy was the neighborhood surrogate 'pop' when I was growing up. He was that guy everybody's momma gave carte blanche to tap that ass if we dared to get out of line. Every year like clockwork he threw a block party for the kids.

"None other than!" I laughed, throwing my hands up.

"You finally decided to drop by the hood, huh boy? It's got to be every bit of what, five years since I done seen you! How's the family and how ya folks?" What brings you down here?" he shouted over the music.

Even though Sammy stood right in front of me, he continued to talk to me like we were on opposite sides of the room. Obviously, listening to loud music over the years had taken its toll on his hearing.

"Everybody's good, man. We have a new addition to the family since I last saw you. A son," I smiled. "As a matter of fact, I just left my parent's a bit ago and mother sends her love. I'm meeting Q for a few rounds, so I thought what better place than here?"

"So what you really saying is the wife let you out the cage for a sec?"

"Something like that!" We both laughed.

"How the rest of them hardhead boys doing?"

"It's been a minute since any of us have gotten together to tell you the truth, Sam. My boy Ron playing football overseas, Cameron been in Afghanistan for over four years now, and Taj is a pilot."

"Nice, nice! Look like you been taking good care of yourself, or has that fine woman of yours been taking care of you if you know what I mean," he joked jabbing at my stomach.

I managed a laugh. "I'm trying," I patted my mid-section. "Still running every day…playing tennis when I can."

"How's the business? Last time I heard you doing pretty good for yourself, Dr. Rollins!"

"It pays the bills."

"Good for you! I always knew you'd be somebody!"

Something behind me had drawn Sammy's attention because I saw him look over my shoulder and smile a big wide grin that flashed two front 'ole school playa gold teeth.

"Now that Quincy! Man, shit that's another story," he bellowed.

I turned around to see my buddy strolling our way with a cigarette hanging from his mouth like usual. Q never moved fast unless he was driving. Half the women in the building stopped what they were doing to watch him walk across the room. A few of them probably didn't even realize they were drooling. Nothing new. Q had that effect on women.

"Why you two low life muthafuckas got my name in 'yo mouth?" he asked serious as a heart attack. Q was the only dude I'd seen talk with a cigarette in his mouth and it not fall out when he spoke.

"Hey man, what's up?" I laughed. We exchanged a handshake; our hands clasped together with thumbs on top then pulled each other's fingers as we drew them apart. He greeted Sammy the same way.

"What's poppin hustler?" Sammy asked Q.

"It ain't nothin." What up with you? You still holdin it down I see."

"No doubt, no doubt, it's what I do, e'ry day, e'ry night!"

Q and I looked at each other. I fell out laughing. Q took a long puff from his cigarette, blew smoke up in the air, dropped it on the floor and put it out with what looked like a fresh new Jordan.

"This muthafucka," Q said.

Sammy's weak attempt at the new school lingo broke the ice. It felt good to laugh and be amongst friends.

"So man what you doing with yo'self?" Sammy asked Q. "Last time I had my ear to the ground they tell me you done got out the joint and went back to 'yo 'ole ways," Sammy cracked.

"Ahhhh, come on Sam give my boy a break," I chimed in on Q's behalf.

"Stay off my dick," was all he said.

That was my cue to end the discord before it went too far.

"Fellas, fellas easy does it. I didn't invite my man out here to be kicked around," I interjected, playfully grabbing Q around the neck.

"Like I said stay off my fuckin dick," Q said again without cracking a smile.

"Alright, alright! I don't mean no harm, son."

"Playtime over boys! Sammy, we gonna grab that spot back there," I notified him pointing at an unoccupied table at the back of the club, my arm still around Q's neck. "Good seeing you man."

"Hey guys first rounds on me! I'll send'em back, and next time don't stay away so long," he warmly reprimanded.

"Make mine a couple a shots of vodka for havin to look at your ugly ass!" Q ordered before he lit another cigarette.

"Grand Mariner for me."

"What up man, how you been?" I asked as we walked to the table.

"Stop frontin son. Who you tryna play? You look like somebody sucka punched you in the gut and you ain't unfolded," he observed off the bat.

Q and I may not have been blood brothers but you never would have known. Mother said he reincarnated as the child she miscarried. She'd tell him whenever he got into trouble, "your mother birthed you but that don't mean I won't put a belt to your butt young man!" She sent him packages, cards and money the entire time he was locked up. Wasn't no secrets between us.

"Oh shit," he blurted out before stopping and removing the cigarette from his mouth.

"Don't tell me you and the 'ole lady in splittsville or nothin like that," Quincy asked looking at me stunned.

I ignored him and sat down at the table. A mixture of stale incense and liquor filled the room. Q dragged out his chair, flipped it around and straddled it with his arms up over the backrest. He took a long deep draw from his cigarette before putting it out in the ashtray on the table.

The place was starting to fill up. Before long it would be standing room only.

So much for a quiet place to spill my guts.

Not quite ready to rehash the story that had suddenly become my fucked-up life, I looked around the room. The Front Page drew a faithful Friday night group of poet heads from all over northern Virginia, Maryland, DC and even as far away as Richmond. To sweeten the pot, it didn't hurt that Sammy somehow managed to find the finest sistas on the planet to host the night's festivities.

"Oh, so now you deaf and shit," Q stated, clearly annoyed.

I inhaled deeply. My palms were sweating and I could feel a knot forming in my throat. Right when I was about to spill the beans my cell phone rang. Without hesitation, I checked to see who was calling. My heart was pounding because deep down inside I hoped it was Mia. It was Steve. Disappointed and relieved, I got up.

"Be right back, I gotta take this," I told Q. "Hello. Hey Steve, how'd it go?" I asked while making my way back outside. "Ahhh man I owe you one brotha! Thanks for working it out for me. Monday at ten a.m. sharp. I got it! I'll be there at nine thirty. Thanks again man."

When I got back inside Q was texting.

"…And you was about to fuckin say?" he said before I had a chance to sit down.

I had no reason to delay the conversation anymore.

"I think Mia rolled out on me," I finally said trying to appear detached. Not that I wanted to be hard or anything, but I didn't plan on breaking down in front of my boy.

"Rolled out? What the fuck that mean?"

I took a quick look around the room just to make sure I didn't recognize anybody within earshot.

"Rolled out, left for good, packed her shit, our shit and moved out," I answered irritated.

Q flipped his chair around and leaned back in it.

"What the fuck happened? You guys throw blows?"

"Your guess is as good as mine and hell no we didn't have a fight! You know Mia and I don't get down like that. I made a quick pit stop by the house earlier today to kiss my wife and kids because I was hyped to be going to a meeting to sign a loan for my own shit only to find my house wiped out. Pretty much everything gone."

"Word?"

"Word!"

"The kids too homie?"

"That's the strange part man. She didn't take them. Don't get me wrong, I'm glad she didn't, but you know Mia when it comes to Tiff and Brandon. She loves our babies, or so I thought." I added.

"They're at my folks right now and will probably stay there until I can sort things out."

"You holla'ed at her?"

"I tried to call her but she disconnected her phones."

"That's some fucked up shit. Somethin ain't right. Why the hell would Mia go out like that? I can't see it. Maybe she went to get her head right for a minute."

I knew Q was trying to keep my spirits up but I didn't want false hope.

"I feel you." I picked a napkin up off the table and began to shred it. "You're the only one I'd admit this shit too, man, but I don't know what to do."

"A brutha can't see walkin in my crib and findin my shit gone 'cause of a trick."

"Dawg, naw you *can't* imagine! Check this out, before she left she stopped by the daycare to pick up Tiff and Brandon and took them to Red Lobster!"

"What the hell for? Did she tell them she was leavin?"

"She gave them some bullshit story about an extended business assignment out of town, that's it. She gassed them up by saying she wanted to take them but I'd be alone so they should stay with me for a while. Can you believe that shit?"

"In a nut shell she threw your ass under the muthafuckin bus."

"Basically."

"Hey guys, how's it going?"

We were interrupted by a soulful voice that belonged to a thick, curvy dark-skinned, fine sister with big eyes and a huge 'fro that I couldn't tell whether or not it was her hair. She was wearing a tight pair of jeans that accentuated her assets, and a low-cut tee shirt that barely held her double d's in. Skillfully positioning herself between Q and me with a tray balanced in her right hand, she locked in on my boy immediately. One by one, she placed two napkins, three Coronas, a glass of Grand Mariner and three shots of vodka on the table in front of us.

"Compliments of Sammy," she smiled, while flashing a set of perfect white teeth at my boy. He raised one of the shot glasses in the air in Sammy's direction and threw it back.

"My man! He remembered the Coronas after all this time," I told Q. "Man, we could put down some Coronas back in the day!"

"If you guys need *anything* else, just give me a holla," she smiled mischievously at Q. "Sammy said your drinks are on him tonight."

"You got a name to go with all that?" Q inquired.

"Lenzie and yours?" she said with confidence.

Q placed his empty glass on a napkin. "Q. That's my man Myles," he said pointing over at me. "Tell Sammy we said good lookin and I'll get at 'ya later," he said after sizing her up.

"I'll be waiting. It was nice to meet you Myles, and enjoy your drinks," Lenzie said walking away with a smile. I'd put my bottom dollar on the fact that she walked off with wet panties.

Poor woman.

By no means did I understand how Q attracted so many unsuspecting women. Most of them ended up like this female more than likely would, a quick pick-up, used and then discarded. We both watched her walk off and disappear in the crowd that had begun to almost triple in size.

"Some things never change," I laughed.

"You muthafuckin right. Have you called her fam?"

I leaned back in my chair. "I called her mom, her sister and her best friend. Nobody answered. It's pretty clear she doesn't want to be found."

"Meanin?" he asked tossing back his second shot.

"You pack up everything in a house while your husband is at work, disconnect your numbers and disappear without a trace, and you ask me what that means? Which one of those isn't clear to you?"

He didn't say anything for a long while and it gave me a chance to drink my Grand Mariner.

"You can crash at the crib."

I was happy he offered because I really didn't want to face my empty house again tonight.

"I don't want to…" I hadn't gotten the words out my mouth before Q's phone rang.

He held up his hand and I knew the case was closed.

"Ain't shit to discuss," he said heading down the same path I'd taken to go outside.

I'd polished off my first beer and was starting on the second one when a beautiful slim, sexy sista a shade darker than Lenzie danced up on the stage to Jill Scott's song, *It's Love.* Her jeans clung to her like a second skin. She had on a simple black tee shirt with the words 'On My Queen Behavior,' written in bold red, black and green letters across the front and back of the tee shirt. Her locs swayed down her back past her hips and they were sexy as hell. Like always, Sammy didn't disappoint. By now the place was standing room only. Turning my attention her way, I suddenly realized it had been a long time since I'd enjoyed a beer and some poetry. Mia hated crowded places, but I didn't mind getting out and mingling once in a while. We had become like two old hermits over the past few years.

"I'ma need you all to get up on your feet and dance!" she told the crowd after grabbing the mic.

Most of the house obeyed her command and the remainder bounced around in their seats.

Prompted by a command from a wave of her hand, the DJ bought the volume of the music halfway down.

"Jambo my fine Kings and beautiful Queens, how ya'll feelin?" she queried with contagious energy. "My name is Lady in Black and I'll be your host tonight. Is that alright?"

The crowd responded with an outburst of claps, snaps and a mixture of whistles as affirmations.

"Asante Sana, Asante Sana! I like the energy in here tonight! You all came to get your word on I see!" She laughed out loud and her laughter filled the room accompanied by more claps and whistles. "Well alright! Hold up, hold up! Because ya'll looking so good to me," she spread her arms and held them out, "I need you to give yourselves a hand! Can you do that for me?" A third round of clapping set the place rocking. It took the crowd a few minutes to settle down. Her energy was electric.

"I ain't *never* been one to waste time no matter what I'm doing," she teased with her hands on her hips.

"So here's what I'd like you to do for me. I want you to sit back, relax and show some love to these poets, 'cause any poet who comes through Sammy's doors," she pointed to the back of the room, "you best believe know how to put it down! We always bring you the most talented, dedicated and conscious brothas and sistas in the game and tonight is no different. They make you think, laugh, cry, introspect, outerspect, love… shiiit, speaking of love, they might make some of ya'll go home and make love, you feel me!" Another loud roar erupted from the audience. The sista knew how to work a crowd. She waited patiently for everybody to settle down.

"Without further-a-do." She paused for a moment. "Umph, umph, umph…all I'ma say is you guys are in for some verbal mental stimulation! All praises to the Ancestors! I can't believe we got this first brotha in the house! He's a personal friend of mine and he a baaad muthafucka!"

"Watch 'yo mouth," the crowd yelled back.

"But I'm talking 'bout Shaka!"

"Well we can dig it!"

She chuckled a deep, high-pitched laugh. "My people, I had to pull a lot of strings to get him here! This King is in high demand but we got him with us tonight," she announced, breaking into dance. "I need some help making him feel sexy…'cause he sho nuff is to me!"

Laughter and a series of amens from the sistas followed her comment.

"Turn the page for my friend… Shaka Zulu X!"

Before she got the brothas name completely out her mouth the crowd erupted into a thunder of applause and whistles.

The house lights went down turning the joint into a partially dark 'ole school blue lights in the basement setting. The audience settled down when a dude who looked like he could have been one of Bob Marley's sons emerged from behind a curtain. He pecked the sista on the cheek before escorting her to a table directly in front of the stage where he pulled out a chair for her to sit in.

Normally I preferred to hear female poets spit for obvious reasons but something about this brotha made me want to hear what he had to say.

I took another swallow of beer and got comfortable in my chair. All the women in the room, even the ones sitting with other dudes were groveling. He took the mic from the stand, lowered his head and paused. Everything about him was heavy…like he had been appointed to carry the weight of the world without his consent. You could hear a pin drop.

"Asante Sana my beautiful Goddess for that Karibu," he mumbled humbly. "I know some of you came out to be inspired or to hear some positive vibes." He hesitated again. "My lady and I just split about a week ago and I've been traveling an inner journey back to myself. I'm cleaning house so to speak, attempting to reintroduce myself to myself as one instead of two, if you with me."

There was a series of aahs, mostly from the females in the room, and immediately I began to feel hot.

"I got this piece I wrote on the way here and I hope you don't mind if I offer it to the Ancestors in front of you 'cause I gotta have her back."

Somebody in the back of the room yelled out, "we don't mind, go 'head brotha, do your thang!"

"I call this piece Unauthorized Despair." The room settled into a quiet hush.

"Kings and Queens it's a pain - it's a pain I can't explain you see I never knew love could hurt like this, so deep…The pain cut so deep when she left me and I never knew how many tears I could cry 'cause a Goddess left me, but I cried, cried like I never cried before but she kept on going walked on out the door. So what do I do now? Somebody's got to tell me how to survive 'cause I don't think I can go on. Get over her? My brotha did you say just get over her? Naaaah see brotha you don't understand you don't understand, trust me you don't understand. See she was no ordinary God. She *was* midnight Black. The kinda black that blended with the night, and her movement was timed with perfection so much so that you could barely tell baby girl was moving. And when she made love to me! Sssssss…ohhhhh…when she made love to me! It took all I had not to give up my soul. Took all I had not to go inside of her and become one. Took all I had not to beg for more. Although I did. I did occasionally beg but see she was no ordinary God. And you don't just get over a Goddess like her. Somehow giving up a Queen like her requires giving up a piece of your soul and we had become one, we had become soul mates… and you don't just get over a Goddess like her."

A silence unlike I'd never experienced settled over the room. All the pain I'd attempted to suppress from missing Mia came roaring up from within me like an eighteen-wheeler out of control. Only this time I couldn't hold it back. No matter how hard I fought, and I gave it a good fight; taking in deep gulps of air and holding them until I almost passed out, squeezing my eyelids tight and clenching them closed were all futile. I could feel tears well up in my eyes. They descended in a mad rush down my face and all I could do was let them go.

Bring on the Drama

Mia

W HEN I WALKED through the garage door and deactivated the alarm around one-thirty in the morning I still wore the smile that hadn't parted from my face since leaving Ty. The smell of his cologne and cigar permeated my hair and dress so deeply that I didn't want to shower or get undressed. I just wanted to bask in the concoction.

God forbid what might have gone down if you hadn't gotten outta there when you did, girl! Screwing on the first date is never a good rule of thumb Mia, and you know that. More importantly, screwing another man when you're still married is even tackier.

The fact that I contemplated knocking boots with Ty made me realize I needed to keep a space equivalent to the Grand Canyon between us.

I forgot to turn the air on before leaving for Monet's so downstairs felt like a furnace and upstairs felt like hell. Reluctantly, I stepped out of my dress and turned the thermostat on to cool off my bedroom. Removing Ty's card from my purse and tossing it on the nightstand I whisked the cordless off the receiver and dove stomach down onto my king-sized bed. Lying there, I imagined making love to him on the Victorian table. If the way his hand took charge of my breast was any indication of his skills, brotha most definitely had it going on!

There were several missed calls on my answering machine that had to be from Daphne or momma because other than a few clients nobody else had the new number.

Whoever it is will have to wait, gotta call Mr. Delicious first.

I dialed Ty's number and attempted to stifle the smile on my face before he picked up.

"Hey, I've been waiting for your call. You got home okay?" he asked after answering on the first ring.

"How'd you know it was me?" I laughed.

"Who else would it be? I was beginning to get worried. You left without giving me your number."

"I didn't mean to make you worry," I noted. "If you don't mind, I have to get something off my chest," I digressed.

"No I don't mind. Go ahead, I'm listening."

"I have mixed emotions about tonight. On one hand, I had an incredible time. It's obvious you went to great lengths to make me feel exceptionally special. On the other, I feel guilty about the way I behaved. Things got way out of hand, and it is by no means representative of the way I conduct myself at all. I don't want you to think I go around allowing random men to fondle my breast."

"For your information I have standards, too. If I judged you, I would have to condemn myself with the same measure. I know you didn't come here with the intent of sleeping with me. Like I said before, I could tell from the onset that you're not that kind of woman. I'm disappointed in myself because I didn't want to do anything to jeopardize seeing you again, but you're a beautiful woman and I let my desires take over. I promise you it will never happen again. I had a wonderful time tonight and I'd be lying if I said I didn't want more. However, I'm willing to go at your pace just as long as you keep me around. If I ever overstep the boundaries, after tonight of course," he conceded; "you can tell me to beat it and I will," he said quietly.

Ty made it hard to resist his allure.

"That sounds fair."

"You got a minute, just a quick minute?" he asked.

"Of course," I answered, happy the conversation didn't have to come to an end yet. I turned over on my back wishing he were kissing my thighs, licking my clit and tasting my juices instead of talking to me on the phone. The thought made me slip my finger into my own wetness.

"Mia, I'm not trying to get in the middle of anything you got going on in your life because I wouldn't handle it well if another man were trying to step into my backyard if you were mine. That being said, I do want you to know that I'm not going anywhere. I'll wait. No pressure, no strings and I'll take whatever you give me in between if it means we can continue to see each other," he stated humbly.

His request felt fair. If I avoided sending mixed messages like I did tonight we might be able to be friends.

"All I can say is that I've got a situation that has to be resolved before I even think about getting involved with anyone else. I'm not gonna lie, I was feeling you tonight but I can't make any promises. We can be friends as long as you don't put any pressure on me, fair?"

"That's all I can ask. You've got my word." He laughed and it made me laugh too, although I didn't know why. "Good night Mia, sweet dreams, baby."

"Good night, Ty."

I sat and held the phone to my chest listening to the dial tone.

What the hell is this man doing to me! He has me sprung like I was sixteen!

I got up and sat on the side of the bed to retrieve my messages. I really wanted to call him back and invite him over.

"Mia, honey, this is your momma. Please call me when you get in sweetheart. I have something to tell you. Bye now."

The second message followed.

"Listen trick, I tell you what, I'm 'bout sick of you and your momma! Call me when you get in! And why is your cell phone off? And where are you this time of night anyway?"

Not again.

I contemplated waiting until after I'd gotten some sleep to call both of them back but as I was mulling over that thought the phone rang.

"Hello," I answered while balancing the receiver between my shoulder and my ear.

"Where the fuck you been at heifer?"

I sighed before answering.

"I guess we gonna plunge right in, huh, Daphne?"

"Spare me, Mia. Not in the mood, okay? Why you ain't been answering your phones?"

"I just got in a bit ago, Daphne."

"We'll come back to that. Have you talked to your momma yet?"

"Not yet, what's up?"

"That's what I wanna know!"

"When were you gonna call me and tell me you ran into Dre?"

What the fuck! That asshole couldn't wait! But how the hell did Daphne know I ran into him?

I sighed. "How did you know I ran into Dre?"

"One guess."

"Momma?"

"By George, she's gotta brain after all!" she shouted.

"Your smart-ass comments get old real fast, Daph."

I got up from the bed and began pacing the floor.

"That doesn't make sense, why would Dre call momma?"

"Alright maybe she doesn't have a brain," she retracted.

"Damn Mia, sometimes I really worry about you. Your momma called to see if I knew where you were. Again. It seems Dre called Myles to have a friendly chat. We both know that's bullshit, but anyway. Dre told Myles he'd ran into you in a park in Teaneck. So then Myles called your momma from a different phone number that she didn't recognize and she picked up. From what I gathered, he told her in that conversation what Dre said. I'm sure your momma can pick it up from there 'cause quite frankly I stopped listening after that."

"Is that all she said?" I asked my heart pounding.

"That's all I remember but I do know this, you need to stop bringing your momma in your business. She's 'bout to lose her fucking mind over petty shit. And as for Dre, you gonna have to stop letting the past hold you hostage and deal with him once and for all. Dre ain't changed and he never gonna change. He'll hold ya'll's little 'tryst' over your head forever and a day if you let him. Time to deal with his ass. He's a con artist. Now, back to where you were and who you were with that you couldn't answer your phone, and don't bullshit me, heifer," she warned.

"I went out to dinner."

"With who? You just got there. Who the hell you going out to dinner with until one in the morning?"

"Why can't I be going out to dinner with myself, Daphne?"

"Bitch please! Who you think you talking to? You ain't going out to dinner by yo'self! You too self-conscious to be seen eating alone! Like I said, don't bullshit me!"

"It's a long story Daph and it's late."

"I got all the time in the world for that story. I want details 'cause I got a feeling you were into something juicy tonight...no pun intended!"

I knew better than to try and avoid Daphne's firing squad. When she wanted something, her ass didn't let go until she got it. Besides, I didn't have the energy to fight her off. She was fucking with my high.

"Do you know Ty Spencer who owns Monet's restaurant in the city?"

"You're asking *me* if I know Tyrese Spencer Monroe, the tycoon? That fine hunk of black man no woman can get close enough to sniff! I know you weren't anywhere in the company of Ty and didn't call me! Oh hell no! I want all the motherfucking details! How did you hook up with him? I know women in the business who flipping cartwheels to try to get next to that man!" she rattled on in octaves higher than my eardrum wanted to be subjected to.

"I heard that brotha got game! He's a smooth talker. Could charm a bottle from a baby. He's supposedly tied to some pretty shady people according to the word on the street. If what I hear is true, you playing with fire momma! Brotha man way out your little naïve ass league!" she professed.

"Daph, spare me the pageantry please. Not in the mood, remember?"

"Don't say I didn't warn your gullible ass," she whined.

"It's not that deep. Why does everything have to be so dramatic with you, damn! Don't you get tired of all the extra some fucking time! Shit," I blew off.

"No, as a matter of fact I don't, and obviously you don't either because that's all you seem to attract."

Daphne yawned, indicating her disinterest. "I done said all I got to say. I'm going back to bed, love ya baby."

Once again, she was gone before I had a chance to say anything else. Our conversation zapped my high and I didn't have the energy to talk to momma, but I was anxious to hear about her conversation with Myles. I took the phone downstairs to get a glass of water and dialed her on the way to the kitchen. She picked up on the first ring.

"Hello."

"Hey momma. Did I wake you?"

"Mia?" she asked half asleep.

"Yes momma, it's me. I'm sorry to wake you but I got your message. Is everything okay?" I asked unsuspecting.

"I dozed off but I ain't asleep yet. I was just about to call you again. I don't mean to keep bothering you, but I got a phone call from Myles yesterday evening and he sounded upset. I had no idea it was him calling 'cause it was a number I didn't recognize so I answered the phone. He told me what you done…that you left and took everything. He asked me if I knew where you were and when was the last time I talked to you. He had a lot of questions. I acted like I didn't know nothing. I'm sure he figured out I wasn't telling the truth. He said somebody ya'll knew named Dre, I think he said, called him and told him he saw you in a park up there. I felt bad about not telling the truth."

"Is that all he said?"

"As far as I can remember."

"Thanks momma. I'm sorry you had to lie. I'm not ready to talk to Myles yet."

Silence filled the gap between her waiting for me to say more and my not sure what more there was to say. My mother didn't want to make waves with Myles and I hated putting her in the middle.

"I understand. What you want me to tell him if he calls back?" she asked with disappointment in your voice.

"Nothing. I promise I'll call him soon."

"Baby I imagine he's confused and my heart goes out to him."

"I know. I'm hurt, too. Momma do me a favor?"

"Yes baby?"

"Please don't call Daphne anymore. She's tired of both of us," I confessed while pouring a glass of water.

"I won't, but somehow she has a way of finding you."

"She's a witch momma," I laughed.

"Tell her I'm sorry and I'll try not to bother her again. You stay in touch with me though."

"I will, good night."

"Good night baby."

It dawned on me when I hung up that she hadn't asked my whereabouts tonight. Maybe she didn't want to know. Maybe Daphne had a point; my mother didn't need to be dealing with the stress of my confusion. I had no right asking her to lie for me knowing she felt uncomfortable with it. From this point forward I planned to keep her out of my affairs.

I sat down at the kitchen table with my glass of water. The urge to call Ty relentlessly hung around in my thoughts, but I fought it off.

I poured another glass of water, gulped it down, turned off the light and went on upstairs to bed. I had no plans to take a shower. I didn't realize how tired my body was until I laid down. With Ty still on the brain it didn't take me long to fall asleep.

When I woke up, the clock on my nightstand read six-thirty. Lying on my back, I thought about all the free time I had on my hands before meeting with my first client in a week. Second thoughts had me entertaining the notion of scheduling one or two clients this week so that I wouldn't die from boredom.

A glowing ball of light peeked into my window, catching my attention. I had a beautiful view of the neighborhood through my windowpane and it promised to be another gorgeous day. Excited to get the day going, I grabbed my robe from the bedpost, slid out of bed and slipped it on. Heaven knows I had enough to do inside the house, but I didn't plan to spend a nice day in the house.

Usually on the Sundays when Myles, the kids and I didn't go to church, we'd lounge around the house all day watching TV, reading or just relaxing in our pajamas. When we did go to church, which wasn't often, I enjoyed the fuss of getting everything and everybody ready. Afterwards, we'd have dinner at Myles' or my parent's house and sometimes both. Tiffany and Brandon looked forward to visiting their grandparents after church. It was the only incentive they needed to sit still through the service.

I ached to call my children, to let them know mommy missed them, but the comfort of knowing they'd be with me soon helped subside my longing a smidgen. Thoughts of the children triggered the onset of a pity party and a migraine. I opted to get out into the fresh air to clean my car before I got sad.

Rummaging through the closet, I found a pair of shorts and a tee shirt to throw on. Once I'd gotten dressed, I went downstairs to fix myself a light breakfast. The food invigorated my energy and charged my spirit.

Maybe I'll finally meet some of my new neighbors outside today.

A picture-perfect day greeted me when I opened the garage door, instantly making me smile. Many of trips I'd made to finalize the details for the house were done in the late winter and early spring so I hadn't gotten a chance to see how charming the neighborhood blossomed in the summer months.

After I backed the car out, I gathered all the necessities to wash it. The brand new water hose I'd purchased on my last visit was already hooked up to the side of the house. I grabbed a few garbage bags from the garage to discard any remaining trash. Next week, I'd have the car fully detailed.

Forgetting my gloves, I went back inside the garage to retrieve them. I heard a car horn, but ignored it because I didn't think anyone would be blowing for me. When I heard it the second time I turned around in the direction of the honking.

What the fuck!

Dre was pulling into my driveway in a black 750 BMW.

No Ladies' Man

Quincy

"YO I'M NOT gonna entertain that fuckin question again," I told this chick one too many times.

"Well I still don't believe you hung out with Myles the whole weekend," Torie continued to bitch.

"I don't give a shit what you believe." I pulled her ova to me and bit her pale white nipple before I mounted her ass for another ride. 'Bout the minute I got ready to stick my dick in her she started bitchin again.

"So I guess you don't feel like you owe me the truth? Just stand me up and tell me another lie like you always do."

It was time for her to get the fuck out. I got out the bed, snatched my pack of Winston's and lighter off the nightstand and put on my boxers.

"Where are you going?" she asked sittin up questionin *me* like she lost her goddamn mind.

"Get the fuck out," I told her stupid ass.

"Are you serious?" she yelled.

"You got five minutes and three of them shits already gone," I told her before going to take a piss.

"You are such a jerk, Q. I don't know why I put up with you!" I heard her bitch on my way downstairs.

She was two seconds from gettin thrown the fuck out my crib butt-ass naked.

I lit a cigarette then hopped up on the kitchen counter and picked up the cordless to holla at my other piece of pussy, Shanise. I heard Torie slam my fuckin bathroom door.

"Yo Nise what's up my sexy lil' freak?" I asked.

"Not you! Where your trifling ass been all weekend? Now you ignoring *my* calls, motherfucker? I better not find out you tryna play me, especially for that white trash."

"You know what I do is my muthafuckin business. What you doing?" I took a deep drag from my cigarette.

"Yeah, okay. Keep feeling yourself with that bullshit. Don't forget who you dealing with over here. I ain't like them other tricks you fucking. And I'm packing."

"Where you going?"

"Seriously! You are so goddamned self-centered! Dammit! You never cease to amaze me. How the hell did you forget you were supposed to take me to the airport today? I can halfway get with your sorry ass failing to recall that we were going to hang out this weekend because that's you, but how the hell you forget that I been complaining about having to take this trip for the past three weeks! Really?!"

"Why you think I'm callin."

"Knock it off, Q! We both know why you didn't return my calls, but that's cool. You're on borrowed time anyway!"

"Chime the fuck down! I already heard enough bitchin for one day. I'll be there in a hour."

"Who the hell said I still want you to take me? I already called for limo service. Ohhh! I see. You need a real woman to break you off. What's the matter? The bitch you had over there this weekend couldn't do the job?" she asked sarcastically.

"Naw and she gettin the fuck out as we speak."

It didn't matter to Shanise if that shit was true or not she didn't care.

"Be here at nine o'clock sharp. That should give me enough time to finish packing and you time to get the lightweight offa your hands. You gonna take me to lunch before my flight, motherfucker. And don't be late."

"I'ma tap that ass when I get there," I told her pullin another drag from my cigarette, "so don't have on shit."

"You're a fucking psycho, Q. You ain't tapping shit ova here!"

"Sho you right. Later, sexy."

I jumped down off the counter and took all the shit from the cabinets I needed to whip up a protein shake. I heard my muthafuckin bedroom door slam. If that bitch slammed another door she was gonna find her face in one. Torie came downstairs with her backpack and parked her ass by my front door like she was waitin for somethin.

Torie didn't have a body like the average white chick. Her ass had curves and shit. Not a sista's ass but a ass for a white chick. The only reason I kept her around was because she had a decent head game.

"I'm leaving, Q."

I ignored her.

"Q, I said I'm leaving!"

I shut the blender down, walked over, and opened the door for her ass to get the fuck out.

"Bounce," I told her blowin smoke in her face.

"I get so upset with myself for allowing you to treat me like this and then I come back and let you do it all over again. I care a lot for you, I mean I really do, but I can't let you keep doing this to me," she whined lookin down at the floor.

"Do what you gotta do."

"That's it?"

"You fuckin right."

The bitch shook her head and walked out the door. I slammed the shit behind her and went back to the blender.

Shanise and Torie was like night and day. Shanise didn't give a fuck how I got down long as she got the dick when she wanted it. She wasn't the type a chick tryna tie a muthafucka down. The only thing Shanise got bent out of shape 'bout was the clock. She hated a muthafucka who didn't know how to be on time. I had to check her ass once for screamin on a brotha for being two minutes late for her birthday party. Shanise went to school on a track scholarship then went and got her masters and doctors in computers. She had one of them big vp titles with a big ass office in one of them high-rise office buildings in Virginia.

I hooked up with Shanise through Myles. She showed up at my man's office ass and titties out 'cause a home wreckin gold diggin hoe she hung around with told her my man was easy on the eyes. Neither one of them gave a fuck he had a wife. Once a month like clockwork she showed up in my man's office actin like somethin was wrong with her perfect set of thirty-two pearly whites. One time she went to his office and Mia was there. Didn't matter to Nise. She stuck her titties in my man's face with Mia right there. A few days later Myles called me to bag her. Muthafucka wasn't foolin me though 'cause I know if he could have hit that he would have.

She owned two cribs. A two-floor condo out in Bethesda and a town-house in Georgetown she rented out for extra change.

Shanise paid big cash to some low life doctor in California on her twenty-first birthday to make sure she neva had kids. A fuckin lifetime present to herself she called it. She had her mom's to thank for that. Nise left the crib at fifteen and neva looked back 'cause all she ever seen was john's and drugs comin and goin. She danced in strip clubs to make enough cash to pay her bills before she went to college.

I rolled up on Torie at a bar in DC one night after I got tired of lis-tenin to some faggot muthafucka tryna get the pussy with weak ass lines. I stepped in to show him how a boss do. I found out the next night when I hit it she was a virgin. Torie made the mistake of thinkin a muthafucka gave a shit just 'cause he fucked a bitch.

Shuttin off the blender, I poured the shake in a glass, tossed it back, took a shower and broke out.

When I got to Nise's house I went in with my key.

"That you Q?"

"Who the fuck else it's gonna be?"

"Close the door and bring your crabby ass upstairs! And put that damn cigarette out! You know I don't allow smoking in my house," she hollered.

I ignored her ass. Nise's crib had muthafuckin candles burnin every-where all the time. Wasn't a place in the joint she didn't have a fuckin candle burnin.

I took the steps two by two up to her bedroom. She was standin in the mirror in a red leather two-piece thong bathin suit checkin out her fat ass.

"Q! Didn't you hear me tell your inconsiderate ass to put that cigarette out! Why do you insist on smoking in my house when I ask you not to?"

"Save it. What time we gotta be at the airport?"

"One o'clock, but I have to drop something off at work first. Sooo, what do you think, you like?"

Shanise flexed her tight ass muscles up and down and squeezed her titties together.

"If I didn't I wouldn't be here."

"Okay, I guess that's a compliment."

I smacked her on the ass and went and took a shower. When I came out the bathroom Shanise was naked and had already put the jimmies on the bed.

"Bring your ass ova here."

"Give me a reason."

"I got your reason," I told her grabbin my shit.

"You motherfucking right and that's a good reason," she said assumin the position on her knees between my legs.

I laid back on the bed when she took both my balls in her mouth, sucked them then let them fall out her mouth. Nise did that until my shit was rock hard. She chocked the bottom of my dick with both hands and licked the tip of my head. Her thick wet lips moved up and down the shaft all the way to the base while she was moanin and groanin in between. She rolled her tongue around the sides of my shit then back up to the top. I reached down and squeezed her titties. Nise got her rhythm and started deep throatin my shit. I gripped the back of her head and kept fuckin her throat as hard as I could. Nise took my balls in her hands and massaged them shits real soft. The thrust that made me come damn near went down her throat.

She didn't waste no time. Her ass straddled me on the bed and thrust her tongue deep down my throat. Nise was grindin and reachin down between my legs hungry for the super dick. I flipped her ova and went down south in the bushes, eatin, lickin, and suckin her clit, walls and g-spot 'til her ass was damn near hangin off the bed. Both my hands were squeezin her titties hard the way she liked it while I was handlin my business in the deep woods. Nise had a fuckin tight grip on the back of my head and was screamin like a damn coyote. Right before she came, I kept one hand workin the left tittie and with the other one I twisted three fingers in and out her wet cave while still gettin at her clit with my tongue.

"Please give it to me now, Q!" her ass begged damned near out of breath.

"Where you want it first?"

"In my ass."

Two hard flicks of my tongue on her spot did the job. Nise's thighs was shakin and her body went into convulsions right before the faucet turned on full throttle.

My shit was ready to handle business so I jimmied up.

Nise turned ova and got on all fours. I pulled up to the bumper and wet the crack of her ass with her juices before working my dick up in her.

"Shit, Q! Damn! That shit feels good! Get it baby!"

Nise started throwin it back when I got it all the way in. I held onto her waist and put it down like a mack.

We went at it fuckin, suckin and eatin until she couldn't take no more.

"Q, don't you want to go to Jamaica with me to keep the Rasta men away?" she moaned while on top of me with her titties in my face.

"You know I don't worry 'bout shit like that."

"Fuck! You so damn sure of yourself, asshole."

Nise sat up all pissed off.

"That's what I hate about you! At least indulge me a little, damn! You so fucked up in the head you can't even tell when a woman is fishing for a compliment. One day your sorry ass gonna get your feelings hurt when somebody else move you out."

"Cool," I laughed slappin her on the ass when she got up off me. She went and put on a robe.

"Get 'yo ass downstairs and fix my breakfast before we jet."

"In your dreams!"

Nise went in the bathroom to take a shower and I followed her.

We fucked again, took a shower and got dressed.

I got everything in the truck before her ass finished blowin out all the damn candles and double checkin to make sure she didn't' miss any.

"Would you do me a favor and check on the house while I'm gone just to make sure everything's okay?"

"Don't I always?"

"And don't bring none of your stray cats to my house either," she bitched climbin in the truck.

"Sho you right."

"I'm serious!" she said, slammin my fuckin door.

"Me too."

Picking up the Pieces

Myles

I LOOKED AROUND MY office wondering how I'd managed to make it through the day. Despite a hectic weekend, Monday offered no mercy. I'd seen fifteen patients and somehow still had time to step out of the office for two hours to finalize the paperwork for my new building. Although the meeting took longer than I anticipated, the fact that Steve succeeded in pulling everything together made the time worthwhile. Admittedly, I needed something in the win column to lift my spirits. Forty-eight hours without hearing from my wife was beginning to take its toll. I'd lost count of the number of times I'd dialed her number hoping she'd pick up.

Most of my thoughts during the day were spent trying to process a phone call I'd gotten late Saturday evening from one of my line brothers who told me he ran into Mia in some park in a place called Teaneck, New Jersey. I didn't know much about Jersey and had never heard of Teaneck. I tried to play it off when he asked why I hadn't come along. He was the last person I expected to hear from with news of my wife's whereabouts. He asked way too many motherfucking questions which let me know she hadn't said much to him. His punk ass acted like his profession as a lawyer gave him a license to pry into other people's affairs.

Regardless, I didn't let on that anything was awry. If he got wind of any turmoil in my affairs no matter how small, his ass would go running off at the mouth to the boys and they'd be blowing up my phone. Before I started entertaining anybody else's questions I wanted my own answered.

Nevertheless, I broke down and called the Samuels from Q's phone because I knew they wouldn't recognize the number. Sure enough, Mrs. Samuels answered. I could tell she was surprised it was me. When she stumbled through a host of obvious lies, my heart sank deeper. It made me wonder if everybody knew something that I didn't.

Dre of all people had no reason to be digging in my backyard. Even though we went to high school together, we were never homies. He held a grudge all the way through our junior and senior year over some female he dug who didn't give him the time of day because she had a thing for me. I didn't get at her because I wasn't interested, but in his small mind he decided that her rejecting him was my fault. Whenever our paths crossed in school he would tell me that one day I'd be sorry for stealing his girl. Delusional motherfucker.

We both ended up accepting offers to attend Howard University. Two years later we were on line pledging the same frat. To this day, I believe the only reason he pledged was to fuck with me. After we crossed over we became brothers but there was no love lost between us.

All the more reason why his supposed sighting of Mia left me confused.

If he was telling the truth I had no idea why Mia would be in New Jersey. It made no sense to me. She didn't have any family up north and none of her close friends lived there either. She did have a lot of affluent clients living in the city and in the northern parts of Jersey but that was it as far as I knew. Periodically, she had hinted about moving the family and our businesses to New York because she thought we might be more successful up there, but I was dead set against it. In my opinion New York was no place to raise children, but equally as significant, I had established my practice in Maryland and it would have made no sense for me to start over.

In an effort to partially refurnish the house I spent the weekend looking for furniture that mimicked what we had. On top of that, I had to run clothes over to the children, stop by the office for an emergency appointment, and tactfully try to answer a million questions thrown at me by the children. By the time it was over, I wanted to crawl in a fucking hole and disappear. The only reprieve was crashing at Q's crib to drown my sorrows in as much alcohol as I could consume.

Mother persuaded me to go to church with her and the children Sunday morning because she thought it would be good for them to have some stability. The only reason I agreed to go was to try and find out if God might have some answers for me. He didn't. After church she suggested that we stick to the usual routine of visiting both grandparents' houses, but given the circumstances there was no way I was gonna sign up for that uncomfortable moment.

Right now, all I wanted to do was hit the tennis courts to work off some of the frustration this whole situation had created. My father picked Tiff and Brandon up from camp to go get ice cream so I had some free time.

Reconnecting with Q had been one of the best things I could have done. We agreed to meet for one of our rivalry tennis matches that we hadn't played in a while. Back in the day we used to refer to ourselves as Ashe and Connors.

My boy had a run to make which gave me a chance to head to the park and warm up a little before he got there.

After locking up the office and changing into my athletic gear, it took me a little under thirty minutes to get to Norwood Park. When I drove up, all twelve courts were occupied with the exception of one at the very far end. Hurriedly, I drove up the block and spotted a park on the opposite side of the street. A quick U-turn made it mine. I grabbed my bag of rackets, water bottle, and towel and darted across the street.

My early morning run had helped relieve a small amount of the anxiety I kept bobbing and weaving in and out of, but the opportunity to beat up on anybody who wanted some would surely knock off a little more. I gave a nod to the fellas next to me before settling in on my court to stretch. The evening's humidity still hung around the high eighties packing a helluva punch. I could hear Mia's voice reminding me to drink plenty of water the way she always did whenever I left the house with my rackets over my shoulder.

I began by hitting a few serves over the net.

Nothing like a good game of tennis to help refocus.

After a rigorous warm up, I thought about hitting Q up to see how much longer he'd be, but opted to give him a few more minutes since it appeared nobody else was waiting for a court.

"Hey young blood you got a partner?" I heard somebody call from behind me. I turned around to face a short, frail, light-skinned, excessively tattooed grey-headed gentleman in his late fifties or early sixties peering through the fence. My man was wearing a bright neon yellow matching short set, yellow headband, some sissy yellow socks that came up to his calf, and a pair of Goodwill faded red, black and green sneakers. He had an arsenal of rackets strapped to his back in a matching neon yellow tennis bag and it took everything in my power to keep from laughing in his face. The other cats on the adjacent court weren't doing as good of a job suppressing their amusement.

"Yes, as a matter of fact I do but he's running a few minutes late," I managed to say without laughing. Dude looked like he was stuck in the 60's.

I intended to hold the court as long as possible with the hopes that Q would get there before somebody with a partner laid claim to it.

Old dude walked around the fence onto my court, lightly laid his rackets on the ground and wiped his forehead with a yellow washcloth he pulled out his back pocket. The guy looked like some kind of whacko, and he'd managed to draw attention to himself from just about everybody in the park.

"Mighty hot out here today ain't it, son?" he noted, looking up toward the sky, shading his eyes from the sun with his hand.

"Yes sir it is," I answered, watching him with dumbfounded puzzlement. I thought about handing him one of my cards because his teeth were horrendous. It looked like the last time he saw a dentist was when he bought that ridiculous looking sweat suit he was wearing.

My serve still needed more practice and I didn't feel like small talk with a nutcase. From the looks of his tennis bag he took his game too seriously. Seemingly a lot more seriously than he took himself. I wasn't impressed. Anybody could walk around with a bunch of rackets and pretend they played the game. What really mattered was the final score.

"Mind if I hit a few with you while you wait for your partner?" he asked. Granddad didn't wait for my response but instead proceeded to open his bag and pull out a bright yellow tightly strung racket. He examined it like it was a woman, holding it up to the sky, staring at it and slowly rotating it round and round, caressing it, and finally testing the strings by tapping them on the palm of his left hand. Pops had a thing for yellow.

In addition to being boarder line rude, he was persistent. He needed to dig in that bag to find his manners. Hell, I wanted to spank him on principle alone. I never backed down from a challenge and I was trying to be respectful, however, this dude rubbed me the wrong way from the moment he opened his mouth. I started to brush him off but the urge to smash some of that super-sized ego corrupted me and I took the bait.

"Let's do it," I told him setting up. "By the way the names Myles," I stated from across the court so he'd stop calling me *son.*

"Big G. Good to meet you son, let's go."

My competitive side kicked in like a motherfucker. I silently hoped Q's delay would give me time to show this cocky bastard how to play the game.

"You can serve young blood," he offered, bending his knees, gripping his racket and setting himself.

"That's mighty kind of you since if I recall you on my court," I answered ironically. "Sure you don't need to warm up, old dawg," I taunted.

"Courts belong to the park. No need, only amateurs warm up, son."

Oh he really wants this ass-whippin. He gonna learn today!

I knew he was trying to get in my head and take me off my game with all the bravado.

My first shot went straight down the line at about ninety miles an hour, and to my surprise he hammered it back over the net to my weak left right passed me.

"You got to do better'n that young blood," he mocked, bending his knees and rocking from side to side.

"You talk a lot of shit, don't you?" I rebutted, tossing the ball up in the air.

"You the one seem to be doing all the talking," he countered. "Love, fifteen," he called out excessively loud.

Unfortunately, I could tell I'd let him get under my skin. My disdain for his cockiness was beginning to impact my game. It pissed me off that he kept ignoring my name and interchanging it with young blood and son. That shit got my blood boiling because it reminded me too much of my father. I couldn't hit a damn thing across the court that he didn't return with precision. I realized too late in the game that I hadn't taken him seriously enough when I found myself running down his shots and not being able to return any of them successfully. Nothing was worse than getting my ass kicked by somebody I had the capacity to beat. Ole dude clearly had skills, I couldn't take that from him, but had I not let my ego get involved at the onset his ass would have gone down.

Big G's strength and stamina deceived me because I expected him to move like an old man. On the contrary, he got down like a man three times his junior. He had me playing his game instead of the other way around. I was all over the court like an amateur. Even when he was killing me 5-1, he continued to hammer the ball as if he forgot the fucking score.

I heard Q laugh right after I fell on my face diving across the court for a shot Big G laid on the baseline. My ego suffered further bruising knowing the ass whopping I was taking provoked the chuckles I heard in the background.

Big G reveled in his audience by mocking my inability to hit anything he sent my way. Through it all he maintained focus and composure, his miniature agile frame bouncing around with little effort.

"Hey Q, we're almost done," I yelled over to him.

"Naw you the one almost done, muthafucka," he laughed with a cigarette dangling from his mouth. "You need some help out there, dawg?" he added, digging the knife in deeper.

"It might give me a little bit of competition if you join your buddy in here. This is a waste of my time," Big G chimed in so that everybody could hear him.

His comment invoked a chorus of ooh's, ahhh's and cackles from the crowd behind us that had now doubled in size. I didn't respond. His psychological mind play had me second guessing myself.

Q didn't rebut Big G's comments out of respect. It was no biggie if we cracked on each other, but as boys it was understood that we didn't join anybody else's diss.

I lost 6-1. To say I was pissed the fuck off would have been a mild description for how I felt. It was no fun to get my ass kicked by somebody's grandfather in front of my boy and a crowd. Even worse, he was openly smug about it. I watched him pack up his flamboyant racket just as confidently as he'd taken it out and my pride and sportsmanship dipped below cordial. He didn't offer to shake hands and I didn't congratulate him either, which anybody who played the game knew was proper protocol win or lose. Instead, I grabbed my water bottle, turned my back to him and tried to wash down some of my shattered ego. To add insult to injury 'ole dude hadn't broken a sweat while I stood there drenched from head to toe.

Q made his way inside the court and began a conversation with Big G like he had just won Wimbledon and shit. In all the years he and I played the game he hadn't beaten me once, so I figured he got a kick out of watching me get my ass kicked.

The crowd was slowly beginning to dissipate and I imagined I must have looked like a sore loser standing there all by myself with my back to everybody. I put my water bottle down on the ground and summoned the heart to walk over to where Big G and Q were running off at the mouth like two homeboys.

"Good game, Big G, I'll give you that one," I said walking over, still not extending my hand. The flashy old bastard looked at me like I slapped his grandma.

"Son ain't nobody ever *gave* me nothing in life. I take whatever I wants. I'ma give you another lesson for free. Don't ever judge a book by its cover," he said, looking me dead in the eyes like we had unsettled beef.

As much as I wanted to come back with something to crush his little yellow ego, I refrained. From my periphery, I could see Q grinning from ear to ear. Clearly he got off watching me sulk over the ass whipping I'd been served.

Big G struck me as a bitter over-confident asshole forever stuck in a moment in his sad little life that he hadn't gotten over. Real talk, I felt that deep down in his frail 'ole bones he knew I could have taken him. It wouldn't have been easy but definitely possible. One thing was for sure, a big part of his strategy relied on him being able to intimidate and bully his opponent until they lost confidence in themselves. From there he set in for the kill. I scoped out his tactic because I'd grown up with an asshole like him. I fell for the okie doke.

"Dawg, Big G say he used to coach them fine ass Watson chicks back in the day."

"Why used to?" I inquired.

"It's a long story," Big G interjected like he didn't want me to know something.

Q let the cat out the bag. "He had beef with da pops."

"Interesting. Why doesn't that surprise me," I smirked.

If looks could kill my time woulda been up. Big G tensed up his body and balled up his fist like he wanted to throw blows. Evidently I'd hit a sore spot. I cracked a smile knowing I'd gotten under his skin this time. His cocky attitude had undoubtedly robbed him of the opportunity to claim the bragging rights for training two of the world's best athletes. Besides, he didn't want any of this. I was already a kettle about to blow with all the shit I was dealing with. All I needed was a reason to put my fist through somebody's yap…even a senior citizen.

He flung the bright yellow bag of rackets across his shoulder so hard he almost took himself down with the force. Dude needed a crash course in anger management. The way his eyes bulged with venom indicated he was in serious danger of blowing a blood vessel. Knowing I'd hit a nerve gave me a small dose of vindication.

"Feel like a winner now young blood?" he asked scarcely containing his anger.

"They say the truth hurts, huh," I laughed, my confidence coming back. "And next time don't you judge this book by the cover."

"Young boy, next times are for people who need a second chance to do what they couldn't do the first time."

Big G nodded his head in Q's direction and huffed his way up a grassy embankment out the park. We both watched him round the corner and disappear out of sight.

"Yo!" Q laughed. "You two muthafuckas was going hard!"

"I didn't go as hard as I should have on his ass! How grandpa gonna come on my court looking like a throwback from the sixties disrespecting me and acting like I need to take tips from his home training manual. I'm a fucking grown ass man! I'll give him his goddamn win this time, but if I get another chance to face off with him, shit gonna go down a whole lot different," I told Q strolling back to the other side of the net. I was furious.

"I feel you bro, but I'm sayin his senior citizen ass did slap you around out there and shit!" Q said after pulling a racket from his bag.

"Let it go, man. It's old news."

"Like the fuck it is! That ass whoppin fresh as a virgin's pussy!" he laughed.

"So what, you gotta ride somebody else's coat tail 'cause you got a goose egg in the win column?"

The unnecessary lost to Big G left me salty as fuck.

"Check yo'self, homie. I ain't the one all up in 'yo head."

I'd left work all hyped and ready to unload the stress I'd accumulated over the weekend and here I was indulging in more.

"You right man, but you and I both know I could have crushed that arrogant Neanderthal. We gonna do this or what?" I asked intentionally changing the subject.

"No doubt."

Regardless of our beef, Q and I never let it cook long. Privately I hungered for the opportunity to get another crack at Big G and I had a strange feeling our paths were going to cross again.

My boy and I got two sets in before the bright lights in the park came on, signaling dusk. I didn't spare an ounce of mercy, beating him 6-2, 6-3.

"Don't stick your chest out muthafucka, I got you next time!" Q said wiping the sweat from his face with his towel.

"Like the last time and the time before that, right? Maybe if you lay off them cancer sticks you'd have some wind and could at least keep up. But you and I both know..." I stopped and looked at Q, attempting not to laugh, "next times for them people need second chances to do what they couldn't do the first time," I quoted Big G, trying to keep a straight face. My impersonation made me laugh.

"For real tho, that dude on the brink. He fresh out the pen. His ass gonna get dressed up in a bag way he poppin off at the mouth. Cats like him always end up fuckin with the wrong person and get they cap pulled back."

"If that mustard sweat suit from the back of his damn closet don't kill him first," I laughed.

I finished packing up my bag, guzzled down the rest of my water and sat down on the court to stretch. An innocent shouting match between a group of young cats in a pickup game on the basketball court adjacent to us caught our attention, but they swiftly resolved matters and got back to the game.

Q sat down and lit a cigarette. "You good man?"

I got what he was asking without directly asking. He had been in the room when Dre called and I hadn't volunteered any information and he didn't ask.

"As well as to be expected," I offered.

"Any word from Mia."

"Not directly." I decided to share what little details I had with him. "I know you heard me talking to Dre Saturday night. Supposedly, he called me to let me know he saw her in some park in NJ."

Q turned to look at me. "And?"

"That's all I got, bruh."

"So you with *that*?" he asked stressing his last word while looking at me like I was from Mars.

"Who knows."

"Yeah okay," he said matter of fact.

"What else I got to go with? I'm tired of the guessing game. I get her point. She was unhappy and I didn't have a clue. I can get to a point where I can handle that, but Tiff and Brandon? They didn't deserve this. It breaks me down every time they ask me when can they talk to her. What the fuck am I supposed to say...I don't know?"

"If that's what it is."

"My man, this ain't about Dre. Mia is the one who hasn't called," I reminded him. "But let's say she's in Jersey, why? Maybe she was creeping all along and I was too far up her ass to see it."

"Maybe this, maybe that, who the fuck know what a trick do on the low. They liars too."

"Yo man, I'd appreciate it if you would refrain from calling my wife a trick," I warned him.

"I call a spade a spade dawg. I don't give a shit who it is. Still I don't see Mia bouncin and leavin her kids for no other dude."

"How the hell you know what she's capable of doing? I was married to her for almost ten years and I didn't think she'd pack up and leave? Did you think she'd do that? You think you know her better than I did…unless you got something to tell me, too?" I asked defensively.

"Back the fuck up. I ain't the one ran out on your ass son," Q cautioned. "All I'm sayin is I don't see Mia leavin for no 'nother dude or droppin her kids off like they orphans."

"Yeah well, I guess neither one of us *knew* her then."

Q flicked a half smoked cigarette to the ground. He didn't know it yet, but I'd made up my mind that the children and I were going to move on.

"I called Kymile this morning," I said.

I realized mentioning a call to my lawyer would set him off because over the weekend when I tossed out the possibility of filing for a divorce and asking for full custody of the children he went ballistic. He thought I should wait and give it more time before I made what he called a 'cross without looking move,' but I strongly disagreed. In my opinion, I didn't need to wait for Mia to do anything else before I went on with my life. As far as I saw it there was no reason to prolong the inevitable.

"I thought you said you was gonna lay low on that move?"

"I know that's what I said but I changed my mind," I snapped.

"Cause?"

"Because a grown ass man has a right to change his fucking mind without asking for permission." Anybody else might have backed off after my outburst. Q saw straight through it.

"Yo punk ass tryin to save face and it's gonna backfire like a bad batch of collard greens."

"You're a psychic and a comedian now, huh?" I barked angrily. "Well take a fucking look in your crystal ball and tell me what it predicts for Mia? Do you see any cloudy days or a fucked up life for her ass in there anywhere, or am I the one destined to catch the short end of the stick!" It pissed me off to think Q was making me out to be the bad guy while letting Mia off the hook.

"I'ma let all that puffin up slide 'cause I know you fucked up in the head," he answered bluntly. "Don't let your pride sit in the muthafuckin driver's seat and take your ass someplace you ain't intend to go, 'sall I'm sayin. But it's your ride bruh."

There weren't many times I could recall, if any when Q gave advice about relationships. That was an area he stayed far away from. In his own way I know he was telling me to slow down, not make rash decisions. And yes I was being reactionary. I wanted to beat Mia to the punch. The thought of receiving divorce papers from her tore me up, so in my mind, the only way to counteract the pain was to try and supersede it. Mia had blindsided me with this one and I didn't know how to handle what I was feeling. We weren't perfect, but nobody could have told me this is how she would have chosen to deal with our problems.

"Look man, I appreciate the advice. I'll weigh my options before I make any final decisions but that doesn't mean I won't go through with it."

"Like I said it's your ride."

My dilemma made me think of something I heard in church yesterday. During the service my prayer request included a punishment for Mia that equaled all the pain she'd caused the children and me. Reverend Gaines insisted that we ask God to forgive us for the things we'd done wrong. I sat there thinking how backwards his "repent, repent, repent," double-talk sounded to me. As a kid I remembered growing up hearing adults say, "boy you better ask God for forgiveness, or if you don't repent you gonna go to hell," on and on. It never made sense to me how God knew everything I was going to do but then when I did it required me to ask Him for forgiveness. Appeared pretty sadistic in my book. If that were the case, I wondered what Mia's punishment was going to be because so far it looked like God had her covered.

"You know," I told Q, "sitting in church yesterday it dawned on me that Mia and I went to church like a lot of families, but look where it got us. It didn't do us a bit of good. We were walking around pretending we didn't have a care in the world, acting as if our shit was tight. Looks like we weren't fooling anybody but ourselves."

"That crap them hypocrites be talkin is a pile of bullshit. Most of them cats ain't practin what they preachin. They just pimps fishin for pussy," Q responded between lighting another cigarette and taking a puff.

"I hear you man, but I mean, we went to church because we followed our parent's examples even though we saw the hypocrisy. I don't know that either of us got anything out of it, at least I didn't. We never talked about God or prayed together as a family. It just seemed like we were going through the motions; it's strange."

"What the fuck is your point?"

"My point is, maybe the writing was on the wall all along and I just kept walking past it pretending I didn't see it."

"Yeah well lookin with the eyes in the back of your head you see all kindsa shit straight."

"I guess you're right."

"What you gettin into later?"

Q's abrupt change of subject should not have caught me off guard. He had zero tolerance for God or church talk. He never did since I'd known him. It's like he came out the womb pissed off at God. Thoughts were running rampant through my head about Mia, my marriage, my future, and I wanted to process them with my boy but he had checked out.

"No plans. I'm going home to take a shower, grab a beer and catch up on the scores. What you got planned, dare I ask?"

"You remember that freak from the FrontPage?"

I laughed. "I remember the *young lady* we met over the weekend. Tell me she's not on deck already?" I asked getting up.

"Straight up," Q answered, getting up and picking up his bag.

We walked out the park and up the street in no particular direction.

"What about Torie, Shanise and all the other females you're juggling? Where do you fit another one in man?"

"Nise in Jamaica for a few weeks and Torie 'bout to get her fuckin walkin papers."

"Why? Did she catch you with another woman *again?*"

"That bitch forgot her position."

"What happened to you, dawg?" I asked half-serious and half-jokingly. "Is there any hope you'll wake up one day with an ounce of decency!"

"When head is a fuckin law!"

"What?!"

"You heard me."

"Okay!" Saying anything more was a waste of time. The women he mistreated deserved better, they just didn't know it.

"Bitches got choices," he added.

"And so do pimps who take advantage of women who don't know better."

"End of story then."

And unfortunately for him that was the end of the story. It blew my mind how he could be so on point when it came to some things and totally out of control when it came to others. He was my boy, but the way he got off disrespecting women didn't sit well with me. The crazy thing about it all was he adored his mother or his Queen as he called her, and if another man *thought* about treating her the way he treated women he'd kill him, no questions asked.

Ms. Scott loved her son despite his faults. She held out hope until she passed that he'd give her grandchildren. Deep down inside, I think Q feared his offspring's might turn out like him and his drug dealing pimp daddy. Maybe there was some rhyme to his reason.

"Later dawg." We bumped fists before turning the corner. "Hey man, holla if you need anything," Q offered.

"No doubt."

I headed across the street to my car. The last thing I wanted to do was go back to the house. A man should never feel the way I felt.

I'm Living in Confusion

Mia

ALTHOUGH I WAS overly excited and giddy that the day had come where I'd get to see Ty again, the anticipation was slightly overshadowed by the tomfoolery Dre pulled Sunday morning. My blood boiled every time I thought about him showing up at my house after he must have followed me home from the park Saturday afternoon. My address wasn't even listed so there was no other way he could have found my house other than stalking me.

The gall of him popping up at my door pretending to coincidentally be in the neighborhood.

Hopefully, after I cussed his ass out and threatened to call the police if he ever pulled up in my driveway again made him think twice about his small minded stunts. Egotistical bastard.

I promptly erased thoughts of Dre from my mind and replaced them with images of Ty. I'd warned myself a thousand times to stay away, but his seductiveness pursued me like a rejected lover. He was consuming my mental space to the point I didn't have the ability to control when he came and went. He didn't make it easy either. After I gave him my cell phone number he started sending me the sweetest 'thinking of you' messages with desperate requests to see me. It had been extremely hard to avoid the longing to return his calls.

To circumvent the temptation of calling him back on Sunday, I stayed busy planting flowers in the yard, running back and forth to the other side of town to buy mulch, and treating myself to dinner at an Italian Bistro I'd found in the neighborhood. Remaining busy helped to ease some of the pain of missing the children, too. Later in the evening I fired up the jets in the Jacuzzi in my master bath and treated myself to a nice hot bubble bath serenaded by music from my new CD's.

Monday morning I got up early and opted for a walk through the neighborhood instead of the park to avoid any chance of running into Dre again. Ty called me just about every hour. I intentionally did not return his calls until I got back home from shopping late at night.

When I did call I kept the conversation short and sweet. He begged me to at least meet with him to discuss his condo because he desperately wanted to get it finished. I agreed. Strictly business was the tone I conveyed. We agreed to meet the following day and I assured him I'd only have a few minutes when we met. He swore to respect my time.

I promised myself that when I saw him there'd be no reminiscing about Saturday night or talk about plans to get together at another time. His voice still sent tingles through my body. Hell, I needed another man in my life like I needed a hole in my head.

To ward off the temptation of accepting any further invitations he might offer or the possibility of staying longer than I ought to, I went ahead and scheduled a few clients in the same vicinity of the restaurant and left a small window of time for me to get to them. He had twenty minutes at the most to discuss his vision for the condo, then good-bye.

Turning around to get one last look in the mirror, I double-checked my business casual outfit one final time. A pair of tight fitting khaki slacks, a simple peach top with a silk belt and a pair of peach pumps met my approval. It had taken me forever and a day to decide what to wear. I wanted something that was perfect for both my clients and Ty. Something not too sexy, but sexy enough. With keys, purse, attaché case and sunglasses in hand, I walked out the door.

Bus 167 stopped at the corner of my block and ended its route at the Port Authority. I settled on public transportation rather than driving. The plan was to hail a taxi to move about once I got to the city.

Standing alone at the bus stop in the scorching mid-morning sun, I peeked under my sunglasses to see if the bus were coming, and just as I did I saw it descending a hill a few blocks away. Once onboard I settled in a window seat in the back, pulled out my MP3 player, and stuck my headphones in my ear.

Ah, Maxwell.

I loved Maxwell's music. It was therapeutic, romantic and relaxing.

Besides myself, there were only three other people on the bus but it would unquestionably get crowded before we got to the city. Leaning my head back on the seat with my eyes closed, I rehearsed the strategy one more time in my head. We'd meet, order coffee, talk for a few minutes, I'd get the specifics about what he wanted in his condo, look at my watch, suck down my coffee, and say I had to run. An air tight plan that didn't leave a minute for him to stall or ask me for another date.

It didn't take the bus long to get to the Port Authority and like I predicted, it was packed like sardines by the time we arrived in the city. As we were rounding 8th Ave heading up the spiral ramp to the depot, I watched people from all walks of life move lightning fast through the streets. Billboards flashed, taxis sped, bikes darted by and businesses advertised food, clothing, jewelry and anything else that attracted tourists and shoppers. There was no place in the world like the energy in New York. Before the bus entered the terminal, I stuck my hand down in the side pocket of my bag and dug out my lipstick case, snapped it open, peered in the mirror and applied a fresh coat of iced chocolate lipstick.

The butterflies in my stomach began flight as soon as the bus came to a stop. They stirred up even worse when I exited the Port Authority and stepped onto Forty-Second Street. With ease, I blended in among all the other souls who drank from the subliminally intoxicating nectar that was Manhattan. I hailed a taxi and made it over to the Upper East Side in thirty minutes. Fifteen minutes ahead of schedule, I had the taxi drop me off a few blocks away from the coffee shop so that I could enjoy the ambiance of the neighborhood.

Strolling along the city streets peering in the window of every fashion boutique and art gallery I passed, reminded me of how much I loved the city, especially the Upper East Side.

I arrived at my destination with five minutes to spare before our one o'clock meeting. The unmerciful ninety-degree temperature had me sweating lightly. The coffee shop had a cute little street side patio with umbrella tables in front of it. As much as I wanted to sit outside so that I could continue enjoying the street scene, it was too hot. I settled on a table inside by the window. Before I had a moment to get comfortable, a young, thin, very pretty chestnut skin-toned sista dressed in a Lapa skirt with vibrant colors and a simple white tank top sashayed over to me.

"Excuse me are you Mia?" she asked with a heavy African accent.

"Who wants to know?" I replied, suspiciously looking around for Ty.

"Mr. Spencer is right this way. Please follow me," she requested, as she turned on the heels of a pair of lime green gladiator sandals. I didn't have time to ask any more questions.

Eagerly, I followed her to the back of the restaurant, up a flight of stairs to a dining area overlooking 5th Ave. Just like before, a table had been extravagantly prepared with all types of coffees, pastries, fruits and finger sandwiches. Rachelle played faintly in the background – a familiar scene.

Everything this man does is sexy!

The cute young lady vanished and I stood there waiting for Ty to make his entrance.

"My God Mia! How is it possible that you are even more beautiful than the last time I saw you?" he remarked from behind me. The sound of his voice made my knees buckle. He walked around in front of me. His attire was modest…a pair of green cargo shorts, an olive green wife-beater and a simple pair of sandals, none of which diminished his sexiness. If there were words to be uttered I wouldn't have been able to speak them.

How the heck could one man be so fine, so sexy and so entrancing all at the same fucking time?

I'm sure the look I gave him read, 'take me now, please!' I was convinced it would only be a matter of time before he broke me down or I gave in. Ty didn't hesitate. He enveloped me in his large ample arms and squeezed me like we had been apart for years. I relaxed comfortably in his embrace. He pecked me lightly on the lips, catching me off guard.

"Who is all of this for?"

"Let's see how good you are at guessing while I wait," he answered taking my attaché case from my hand, wrapping his arm around my lower back, and directing me over to the table. I sat down in the chair he gra-ciously pulled out for me.

"Funny."

"Coffee?" he asked with a childlike grin.

"Tell me Mr. Monroe, are you going to totally ignore the part of our conversation where I informed you that I only had a few minutes because I have clients to see?" I looked at my watch.

"I'm not," he interjected.

"In less than twenty minutes?"

"How much are they paying you Mia?"

"Excuse me?"

He knelt in front of me, took my hands and looked so deeply into my eyes I thought he'd get lost.

"Mia, please hear me out. The last two days have been rough. Since Saturday night I haven't slept, I haven't eaten; I've been a total wreck. It sounds crazy, I know. Maybe creepy, but I have never met anybody like you before. You are like a breath of fresh air in my life. Most of the time when I meet people they want something from me. Not you. You let a brother be himself. The last thing I want to do is scare you off or discredit how you make a living. Come to think of it, I'd be leery of me, too. I don't want to crowd you because I know you're dealing with something right now," he chattered on. "Look, all I'm asking is for you to get to know me, that's all. Just get to know *me*. Not the man you've read about or the one people think they know, but *me*."

The sincerity in his voice and passion in his eyes were enough to melt me like a snowflake in July. I sat there looking down at him wondering where the hell he'd fit into my already complicated life. There wasn't room.

"Maybe we can talk later. Right now let's handle business," I told him.

"Does that mean I can see you later?"

"It might."

Rebuilding Begins

Myles

I T AMAZED ME how sitting at a simple traffic light could conjure up memories. Taking in the rush hour chaos around me, I realized that going straight home after work used to be the highlight of my day. Now it had become the thing I dreaded the most.

Tomorrow would mark a full week without a single word from Mia. My thoughts were consumed with my next move like they were every time I had a free moment to think. Consciously or subconsciously, the denial phase was moving into acceptance.

I wished like hell the stop and go traffic on the Pike could expunge the image of disapproval on my father's face that was etched in my mind when I finally broke the news to him. He immediately went into rationalizing all the reasons why I had to be at fault. He couldn't understand why a woman would uproot herself, especially from her children if a *man* was 'taking care of home.' His inability to ponder the idea that sometimes a man can do everything right and it still not be enough for some women spoke volumes of his rigid nature.

"You know, son," he said, "You should 'a seen this coming. Don't take rocket science. You spend more time at that office then you do at home. You got to know how to balance work and family. I thought I taught you the ropes. You can't spend all your time working or 'fore you know it somebody else be creeping in your back door." My father's holier than thou philosophy was ignorance to me, and I resented him insinuating that I was in anyway responsible for whatever the fuck was going on with Mia.

Besides, what the hell did he know? He must have forgotten the baseball games, tennis matches, track meets and award ceremonies he missed. It was pure comedy to me how his advice didn't measure up to his own example.

Since Mia had been gone, the mere act of turning the corner to our block felt foreign. There were a few times when I'd driven right past our street. Part of me wondered if that were psychological. The house no longer had that welcome home feeling I'd taken for granted and tonight I wished I had somewhere else to go instead of there. Regrettably, I didn't. Everything seemed to be going in slow motion. Like somebody turned down the speed on the clock and every second felt like a thousand eternities.

I parked in the driveway instead of the garage and sat in the car to delay going inside the home that was now just a house. When I finally entered the house, the new black leather sofa set I'd purchased to try and mimic the furniture we had startled me. It felt and looked out of place… like a new suit jacket on an old pair of pants.

I had been anxious all week about the children returning home this weekend for the first time since their mother left, and hoped it wouldn't be too much of a shock for them to see the house the way it was. I'd managed to furnish the whole house with the exception of my bedroom set which was going to be delivered tomorrow evening. Decorating and all that stuff was Mia's forte, not mine, but the situation forced me to do what I had to do. I wanted to try and make things look as normal as possible for them.

Mother didn't think it was a good idea to bring them back so soon. I had run out of excuses as to why they couldn't come home yet. Even though I had no idea how they were going to respond to the changes I felt it was time to deal with their reaction. They couldn't stay in the dark forever.

I went straight upstairs to my bedroom and wandered over to the phone sitting on the floor by the window to check for calls. There weren't any. If time healed all wounds it was sure taking the slowest route to my motherfucking circumstances. In my head, I kept telling myself to get over it, but my heart ached so badly my head couldn't hear shit.

Why baby, why?

I gazed blankly out the window into the backyard.

What was so bad that you couldn't just come and talk to me? I would have done anything to keep it from getting here.

The sad part about my questioning is that I expected an answer.

My thoughts were so heavily preoccupied that I didn't realize the phone had rung. The sound of Tiffany's prerecorded voice echoing from the answering machine snapped me present, and I snatched it off the hook without looking to see who it was.

"Hello," I answered, hoping against all odds that it was Mia.

"My brother, how you doing?"

"Dre?" I questioned, pissed the fuck off and disappointed once again.

This motherfucker!

"Yeah, I was..."

"What you need man?" I asked cutting him off.

"I'm sorry, my bad, you in the middle of something?"

"Nah, but what you want?"

"You know bruh, I thought I'd let you know I saw Mia again and she didn't look too good, but if I'm bothering you I'll catch you later."

Dre was attempting the old lawyer trick...throw the hook and see if they bite tactic. He didn't have me fooled. At this point I had no doubt that he knew we were hiding something. If he did see Mia again, obviously she still hadn't said much because the bastard was fishing in my backyard. I didn't want to shut him down completely, but the fact that he kept running into my wife had my mind going places that wasn't good for him or her.

"Why do you feel obligated to call me and tell me you ran into my wife, dog? Is there something you need to say?" I asked pacing the room.

"Wooo...brother! Slam the brakes on that train! I'm just looking out for you man, that's all. I know you'd do the same thing for me," he lied.

"Nah, man, I wouldn't. I don't go around peeking over another man's fence and I don't appreciate you peeking over mine." Something about dude calling me a second time struck me the wrong way.

How and where did he see her this time? It seemed a bit over the top. Out of all the people in New York and Jersey why did he keep running into my wife?

"I was just looking out for my people."

"Let's clarify something, money. If I wanted you to look after my wife I woulda hollered at you. Now like I said, I'm busy," I told him before slamming the phone down in his ear.

Nothing Dre did was accidental and I couldn't help but feel like he knew exactly where Mia was, but the why enraged me more. Shit wasn't adding up. It had my head spinning. I couldn't allow myself to contemplate the thought that he and Mia might be gaming me.

I picked up my pace and circled the same spot like a lunatic.

What the fuck did Dre mean by "she didn't look good?"

My head was scrambled like the Indianapolis 500 after a fucked up wreck. Thoughts were racing high speed, colliding into each other, smoking and skidding out of control. I needed something to keep me from getting in my ride and driving to Jersey. I went into the rec room across the hall, got the Hennessy X.O. and a shot glass off the top shelf and drank five shots back to back. It didn't take long for the effects of the alcohol to quiet my mind. I settled in my recliner in front of the flat screen and elevated the footrest. That was the last thing I remembered.

In concert with a throbbing headache, my internal clock went off at five o'clock sharp reminding me that it was time for my morning routine.

I sat up trying to get my bearings. Looking around the room I searched for clues that could clarify why my dome felt like it was about to split open. The uncapped bottle of Henney presented the answer. My head was unmercifully waging a war against itself without any regard to the fact that there were no sides. I closed my eyes contemplating whether or not I should still run. The athlete in me decided to go for it. Dragging myself up off the recliner and staggering over to the bar, I screwed the cap back on the liquor before putting it away. I stammered down the hall to my bedroom squinting from the pain of a hangover. Every step I took set off a barrage of thumps across the top of my skull. I found a pair of sweats and a shirt on the floor in a pile of laundry I'd done a few days ago and put them on. Slowly descending the steps, I made my way to the refrigerator and grabbed three bottles of water to dilute the alcohol in my system.

Against my better judgment, I stepped out the door and filled my lungs with the stagnant morning air. It was clear we were in for another hot and humid day. I began my stride with a slow jog to make sure the alcohol stayed down. Once I felt comfortable that it would, I picked up my pace. During the outing, my thoughts scanned a host of reasons that may have contributed to Mia and me being here, wherever here was. I lingered on the notion that the false accusations of infidelity I was constantly reassuring her weren't true was the root. Or perhaps we'd just grown so far apart it was too late to get us back.

All the same, something felt different this morning. I was tired of not knowing. I'd gravitated into accepting what appeared to be the truth... that our marriage was over. The last thing I wanted to do was to give up on my family, but at the same time I didn't want to feel like a fool going all out for somebody who didn't want me.

I pushed the last leg hard and by the time I returned to my block I was starving. On a normal day when I got back home from my run Mia would have breakfast ready. I hadn't quite gotten used to fixing it myself and the interruption of our morning routine still felt unfamiliar. I washed my hands and gathered everything I needed to fix myself some eggs, sausages, and grits.

The alcohol shut down my having to think about shit last night, but now that it had worn off, I needed to deal. Simple as that. A call to Kymile to set up an appointment for her to draw up divorce papers was at the top of my list. It was time to get real. I had no plans of waiting around for Mia to pull another rug out from under me.

By seven-fifteen, I was in the parking lot at work and noticed that the lights were on in the office, which meant Ananda, or Barbara had beaten me in. I didn't see either of their car's in the parking lot, therefore, I had no idea if one or both of them were inside. My first patient wasn't due in until eight-thirty.

"Good morning Barbara. What are you doing here so early?" I asked entering the office and finding her seated behind the receptionist desk.

"Good morning Dr. Rollins! I might ask you the same question!" she answered in her usual upbeat tone.

I placed my briefcase on the counter before sitting down in a chair across from her.

When I opened my practice, Barbara was the first person I hired to manage my employees. It was one of the best business decisions I'd made. She kept everybody and everything running like a well-oiled machine.

"I came in early to finish documenting some of these charts that have been piling up on my desk," I told her. "I didn't expect to find anybody else here. Where's your car?"

She got up and handed me the charts for the day then sat back down at her desk. "Robert took it to the dealer for a tune-up. He dropped me off. Mrs. Rollins stopping by today?" she asked in a manner that was laced with all kinds of innuendos.

I contemplated telling my staff about the situation, but hadn't because I didn't know what the fuck to say. Eventually I'd have to break the news, although I suspected they already had an idea something was up.

"Probably not. She's out of town for a few days. Is Wendell still an eight-thirty?" I asked scrambling to retrieve my briefcase and the charts without making it apparent that I was trying to change the subject.

"Yes sir he is, and it's fine if you don't want to talk about whatever is going on Dr. Rollins, I understand," she said without looking up from her computer. Maybe it was cowardly not to say anything; after all Barbara and Robert were like family. Their son Xavier wanted to be an orthodontist because of me and I had mentored him before he went off to college. Robert and I played golf together. Still, I wasn't ready to share the news with them yet.

It didn't take a mastermind to smell a rat. Mia and my routine had changed drastically over the past week despite my acting like it hadn't. Normally, Mia called the office three or four times a day, and at least twice out the week she'd stop through for no reason other than to say hi. There was no way the sudden change of events wasn't the talk of the office.

When I made up an excuse about why the meeting with Steve had been moved to Monday, Barbara cut me one of those looks that a sista gave you when she wanted to let you know she wasn't stupid. At the end of the day, she was a professional and knew not to ask personal questions unless I opened that door.

"I'm gonna take these in my office and work on them until Ananda gets here," I stated, disregarding her last comment.

"I'll send her in."

"Thanks," I answered before shutting the door to my office. My desk looked like a tornado had ripped through it, which was rarely the case because Mia always kept it organized. I hated missing her the way I did.

"You've got to get it together man. It's time to move on.

I laid the charts and briefcase on my desk before removing my blazer and changing into the neatly dry cleaned lab jacket Barbara had placed on the back of my chair. Eager to get started, I sat in my chair and began absorbing myself in paperwork. The tedious and meticulous process of combing through charts helped to occupy my mind and before I realized it, it was time for the workday to begin. I heard the front door open and detected Ananda's voice out in the reception area. Ananda had mastered punctuality. Very rarely was she late or absent from work.

I hired her two years after one of my other hygienists moved to Atlanta. Although Ananda had gone to school to be a dental hygienist her passion was singing. She'd recently caught the eye of a prominent producer who frequented the same studio she recorded at. Ananda spent every spare moment and dime she had cutting a demo. Lucky for her, perseverance, talent and dedication were about to pay off because the guy had taken her under his wing to produce and shop her sound. There was no doubt she could *sang*. It didn't hurt that she fit the industries standard of acceptable artists; shapely and easy on the eyes. If she stayed focused, learned the business and avoided the field of snakes, I'd be short one hygienist soon.

"Good morning Dr. Rollins! Are you ready for me?" Ananda asked, standing behind the half-opened door with her head peeked in. Ananda was only twenty-two but had the work ethic of a woman twice her age.

"Sure, come on in, I'm just about done."

She sauntered into my office bursting with energy. Her hair was professionally wrapped in Kente cloth and she was overly animated. I could tell she wanted to share something.

"Did you go to the studio last night?" I inquired, already certain of the answer.

"Of course! Guess what?" she asked almost leaping out of the seat she had taken on the other side of my desk.

"I give, what?"

"Dr. Rollins! You didn't even try," she giggled.

"Yes I did, you just didn't read my mind!" I joked.

"I'm serious!" she whined.

"Okay, let me see. You got a contract?" I took a wild guess.

"Yes!" she got up, flew around the desk and threw her arms around my neck. "Do you believe it Dr. Rollins, I'm so excited!"

She hugged me and planted a kiss on my cheek too close to my lips for comfort. Ananda was like a little sister to me so her inadvertent slip-up made me a tad uneasy. I withdrew her hands from around my neck and held onto them.

"Hey, hey no celebrations allowed without me!" Barbara demanded, entering the room.

"Did you hear the good news?" I asked, dropping Ananda's hands like they were on fire.

"Isn't it exciting Dr. Rollins? Sonny Englewood himself wants to sign her! Isn't Trayvon Davis on Signal Records? Xavier loves Trayvon's music!" Barbara noted.

"Sonny Englewood? You got signed by the head honcho himself?" I asked, happy for her. "You didn't tell me that," I chided.

"I was getting ready to," she announced, cocking her head and rolling her eyes at Barbara for having spoiled the surprise.

"Sorry, I was just leaving," Barbara stated before turning on her heels and scurrying back out my office.

Ananda walked around to the other side of my desk and sat back down.

"Okay, now that the cat's out the bag, go ahead and give me all the details."

"Well, Hoffman and I laid down the final track on *It's All About Love* last week right, and he has a homie who works at Signal Records in L.A. So Michael, that's his homie, asked Hoffman to get the demo to him when we finished and he'd make sure Mr. Englewood heard it!" she said in a high-pitched tone. "Soooo! Mr. Englewood heard it and loved it! And are you ready for the best part?" By now Ananda was clapping her hands together like a seal and rocking back and forth in her chair to the point I thought she'd tip it over. "Dr. Rollins, Mr. Englewood called Hoffman and invited us to L.A. this weekend so he could hear me live! All expenses paid! He said there's potentially an opportunity for me to join the Signal family! Do you believe it Dr. Rollins?" She ran back over to me again and wrapped her hands around my neck a second time.

Her neck was close enough to my nose for me to smell the sweet, subtle oil she was wearing. Her full breasts rubbed against my arm, and I felt guilty for being aroused. As fast as I could, I pulled away from her embrace.

"Ananda, I'm so proud of you! This calls for a celebration! Wait a minute, does that mean you're gonna be leaving me?" I asked selfishly.

"No time soon. Hoffman said Mr. Englewood would like to hear a few more tracks, so we have to go back into the studio to lay down two or three more. We already have the music; I just have to add the vocals. It could be anywhere from six months to a year before we get to the contract stage. Oh my God, I can't believe this is happening!" she screamed.

"Sorry to break up the party," Barbara stuck her head in the door and announced, "but Wendell is here."

"Thanks Barbara," I said innocently winking at Ananda. "You and I will talk later young lady."

"Okay Dr. Rollins, I'll go prep Wendell," she snickered as she floated out my office.

Ananda's news helped get me through the day. It was the highlight of every conversation between the staff and the patients. It made the day go by exceptionally fast.

"I can't believe it's almost six o'clock. You and the family doing any-thing special this weekend, Dr. Rollins?" Barbara inquired as she glanced over the top of her glasses across the room at me.

"Not really how about you?"

"Ya'll know what I'm doing!" Ananda chimed in.

"Yeah Nanda we do!" Barbara laughed. "No plans, the usual," she added calmly.

"Ananda, if you need anything just let me know. And good luck with those tracks. Boss lady, whatever you do, try to stay outta trouble," I warned before hurrying out the door to avoid fielding any more questions.

"Have a good weekend, Dr. Rollins; we'll see you bright and early Monday morning."

"Good evening ladies."

I stopped by the grocery store to get flowers for Tiff and my mother, and a bag of M&M's for Brandon before going home to shower.

It was still daylight when I got back in the car to head to my parents. The temptation to drive past the park to see if Big G might be on the prowl tugged at me, but the longing to see my children cancelled that thought. Besides, there was no need to rush fate. He and I would have our day on the courts again.

When I turned down the block, I spotted mother in the yard bent over a bed of flowers, her gloved hands deep in the dirt with Tiffany on her hands and knees beside her. They both had on matching extra wide red brimmed hats to block the sun and it made me smile. Out in the back yard my father was on his riding mower cutting the grass with Brandon in his lap steering the mower. Immediately my smile dissipated.

"Daddy, daddy," Tiff screamed, barreling in the direction of the car. Brandon spotted me and leaped off the mower running full throttle toward me, too. It felt good to see them. I immediately unbuckled my seatbelt and got out of the car.

"Hey there you two!" I said proudly, lifting them up in my arms and squeezing them tight. They both held me firmly.

"I missed you daddy!" Brandon said.

"Me, too, daddy!" Tiffany added.

"I missed you more!" I told them after planting a kiss on their cheeks.

"Hi, mother." I kissed her on the forehead.

"Hi son," she exclaimed.

"Did you bring us something, daddy?" Tiffany asked.

"Why don't you go look in the car and see?" I put them both down. Tiffany skipped to the car with Brandon close behind her.

"Daddy we fixed you spaghetti for dinner and grandma let us do it all by 'ourself, we didn't have no help from grandma. I cooked the noodles and Tiff cooked the sauce!" Brandon broadcasted on the way back from the car with the bag of M&M's in his hand.

"You mean all by *yourself*, and are you sure you didn't have *any* help from grandma?"

Mother listened attentively to our conversation, periodically nodding and smiling.

"It's true daddy," Tiffany confirmed. "And daddy guess what? We used turkey meat instead of hamburger meat 'cause grandma said it's healthier for you, but it tastes the same. We tried it."

She handed mother the bigger arrangement of flowers and stuck her nose close to the pink petals in her assortment. "Can I have this one with the pink flowers in it, grandma," she asked.

"Why of course you can baby! And young man, don't you open that 'til after dinner! Now you both tell your daddy thank you!"

A symphony of thank yous rang in my ear, elevating my spirits higher. "You're welcome."

"Well my mouth is watering and I'm hungry. Can I taste this turkey spaghetti now?" I begged.

"Please, grandma, can we go eat *now*?" Brandon echoed.

"I tell you what, take these with you," mother handed Tiffany her flowers, "you two go run inside, wash your hands and set the table. Then we'll eat. How does that sound?"

"Yeeeaaaah," was all we heard as they both disappeared into the house.

I sat down on the ground and gave my mother another kiss, this time on her cheek. We sat quietly for a moment as I watched her compress dirt in the new multi-colored flowerbed.

"There we go." She leaned back and looked at her work with undeniable satisfaction. "How you doing baby?"

"I'm hanging in," I said, snatching up a hand full of grass from the ground.

"I guess you still ain't heard nothing from Mia, huh?"

"Nope, not yet and I really don't want to talk about her right now. I just want to enjoy those two."

I watched her finish up her work, and then position herself to get up.

I rushed to my feet to offer assistance. We both stood there looking down at the picturesque arrangement of flowers.

"What do you think?" she asked.

"Beautiful, as always."

"Thank you son, you're too kind. Do me a favor," she asked wiping her hands on her apron. "Go tell your father it's time to eat, will you?"

My body language said it all but her request wasn't open for discussion. She lovingly patted me on the back and unhurriedly went in the house through the garage. The last thing I wanted to do was be anywhere alone with my father. Theoretically, I didn't know which one of us despised the other more.

Against my will, I ambled around back and met him coming toward me on the riding mower. I waited for him to get closer, and when he did, he rode by me as if he didn't see me. I felt belittled standing there waiting for him to decide to acknowledge my presence. The moment conjured up unpleasant childhood memories. I used to sometimes wonder if he was really my biological father.

Today was not a good day for him to test my patience.

"We're about to eat dinner," I yelled over his mower when he circled me the second time.

"You heard from your wife yet?" he asked sarcastically after stopping the mower inches away from me.

I didn't say anything. I could feel my blood boiling.

"Did you hear me ask you a question, boy?"

"I heard you," I said, looking him square in the eyes.

"Well why didn't you answer me like you *heard me*?"

"Mother said dinner is ready," I repeated, totally ignoring his bullshit.

He dismounted the riding mower with regimented movement. He steadied himself in front of me wearing a disapproving countenance that felt and looked way too familiar. My father had never managed to separate his role as a Sergeant Major in the Marines from that of a real father. He'd spent forty years in the Marines and was notorious for his ability to send countless enlistee's running back home to their mothers within record breaking time. When he retired from the Marines, he worked as a Police

Advisor for the DC police department for five years. Needless to say, he'd had sufficient training in bullying.

"Don't sass me, boy. I bought you into this world and I can take you out," he threatened more times than I could count.

"Yeah I know, you've been singing that same old song for as long as I can remember," I mocked, fully aware he wanted a fight.

"Are you challenging me boy?" he asked moving closer.

"Call it what you like," I answered, not backing down.

"I suggest you get in line, young'un," he yapped.

"I'm not that little boy who used to…" I felt the sting on the right side of my face, and it took a few seconds for me to realize that he'd just cocked me. I had to dig deep down to restrain myself from knocking him on his ass. As bad as I wanted to finally fuck his shit up, there were several reasons why I had to be the better man just like I did every time he backed me in a corner. More than anything, my children were in the house and they didn't need to see their grandpa leaving the house in a body bag.

"You get that one but I tell you what, if you ever put your hands on me again, you won't walk away, and that's not a threat."

I left his bitter ass standing there and went inside.

Tormented

Mia

TODAY OF ALL *days it has to snow like the bottom fell out of the snow bucket in heaven.*

Lazily propped against the wall, I watched heavy snowflakes from a snowstorm that had begun in the early morning hours accumulate out my bedroom window. Four hours into the blizzard there were already over six inches on the ground. Like soft feathers, they piled on top of each other crafting a thick blanket of white atop everything in their path. I had been standing there for so long admiring Mother Nature weave her artistry, I didn't realize my coffee had grown cold until I took a sip and the bitterness made me cringe. Much to my surprise and dismay, none of the neighborhood children were outside playing in the snow. I desperately craved something to replace the sadness I felt on my husband's birthday.

When I woke up a little after midnight, instinctively I reached over to kiss him and wish him a happy birthday. When reality hit me, I cried myself back to sleep.

Happy 36th birthday, baby.

I felt antsy. Not because of a storm that hadn't been forecasted, or because I was going to have to cancel a shit load of clients next week if it continued, but because as much as I didn't want to face the truth, it hurt like hell knowing today was my husband's birthday and I wasn't with him. Myles always pretended his birthday wasn't a big deal, but the children and I knew better. Everybody's birthday was a big to-do in our home. It was the one event that brought us all closer together as a family. My heart ached knowing this would be the first one we'd miss celebrating together as a family.

I wondered if Q had decided to move forward tonight with the big surprise party he'd been helping me plan since February. A client of mine who spent her winters in Ghana owned a luxurious penthouse out in Virginia. She extended it to me to have a party for Myles. Before I left, more than half the over one hundred people we'd invited had already rsvp'd.

Shifting my attention to a lone car slowly creeping its way up the street, I questioned my sanity for moving to Jersey. I hated cold weather and I especially hated snow. Hell, it was only November second and we'd already had two snowstorms. When I began complaining about the chill in the air back in September, everybody kept reminding me that the real winter months hadn't arrived yet. I didn't own one heavy coat, now I had five, including a full-length mink that I wore every chance I got.

New Jersey winters apparently didn't take any prisoners, and my introduction to city living had more rude awakenings than I bargained for. The gridlock traffic, competition for a cab in Manhattan and obnoxious people made me long for a warmer, less congested and friendlier state.

I abandoned driving my car into the city more than once a week after the first two weeks of arriving in Jersey. No matter what time of day I ventured out onto the roads I got caught in a traffic jam. My new modes of transportation were buses, trains and taxis.

Two nearly exhausted logs in the fireplace directly across from my bed noisily crackled and flickered, beckoning my attention before they threatened to go out. I put my cup down on the nightstand and added a few more logs, stoking them with the poker until they burst into flames of orange and blue. Listlessly, I crawled up onto my bed and sat facing the window to continue watching Mother Nature birth snow.

Business was beginning to pick up unlike anything I had expected. The down side was that it required me to spend the majority of my time in Manhattan and sometimes Connecticut. Ty insisted I let him get me a limo so that I didn't have to worry about transportation. I declined.

The fact that we had been sleeping together for the past two months consumed me with enough guilt as it was. Between the shame that ate at me for sleeping with him, the mess I'd gotten myself into with Dre and missing my husband and children, my nerves were shot. The added pressure from a pending divorce and custody battle for my children was causing me to break out in hives almost weekly.

Call me naïve, but I never expected the consequences of separating from a marriage that had hit a wall to lead my life down the path it had taken. I never intended to get involved with another man or be estranged from my husband and children. I had planned for the children to be with me by the time school started in September. I was devastated because I had already missed Brandon's first day of pre-K and Tiffany's first day of school as a second grader. I didn't plan to lose out on any more milestones in my children's lives.

To add insult to injury, I hadn't heard Tiff and Brandon's voices in almost a month because Myles had resorted to using them as pawns. For a while I was grateful to speak with my babies when my mother-in-law dropped them by my parent's house, but when Myles found out I was talking to them, he forbade Mrs. Rollins from taking them to see my parents. Rightfully so, momma and daddy gave me the cold shoulder every time I called the house. I didn't blame them for being angry with me, I just needed to fix it.

I tried to call Myles at work to reason with him since he wouldn't answer my calls on his cell phone only to find out that he'd instructed Barbara and Ananda not to put my calls through. My patience had grown thin. He didn't leave me much choice but to follow Ty's advice and hire an attorney.

Tommy Cervini was infamous for the Rutherford vs. Rutherford case. He defended Maude Rutherford against her billionaire husband who set out to ruin her reputation and take their four children so he didn't have to part with half his billions in spousal and child support payments. Forty-five years of marriage and the asshole thought he was going to get away with paying her crumbs for sticking by his cheating ass.

According to Ty, Mr. Cervini went into the courtroom day after day for three weeks purposefully presenting amateur facts. Finally, when he got ready to 'slice the fish,' a term Tommy used when he was ready to seal the case, he mentioned a witness who would provide vivid, detailed and substantiated evidence specifying escapades that chronicled a fifteen-year affair Mr. Rutherford was having with a mistress. Particulars that described very personal information about the home Mr. Rutherford shared with his wife, their bank accounts, birthmarks and the DNA of a lovechild Mrs. Rutherford knew nothing of. Ty said Mr. Cervini boasted that the fish began to squirm when Mr. Rutherford's vengeful mistress sat on the row behind Mrs. Rutherford two weeks before closing arguments.

Unbeknownst to Mr. Rutherford, the mistress had found out about other indiscretions and wanted revenge. Needless to say he *willingly* agreed to a more appropriate settlement before the trial was over.

It was imperative for me to have a brutal lawyer because Kymile was no joke. I could see her and Myles trying to paint me as some kind of uncaring mother who just took off and abandoned her husband and two children when it wasn't that black and white. No judge would care about anything that I had to say once Kymile got through with me. It would take somebody like Tommy to go toe to toe with her.

Somehow Dre found out that Myles and I had a court date in mid-January and he had the audacity to send me an email offering to represent me. His ability to slither still flabbergasted me although I don't know why. Dre was a damn good lawyer, probably equally as shrewd as Mr. Cervini, but his intentions were self-serving, and there was nothing he'd like better than to have an opportunity to stick it to Myles. God knows I'd given him enough ammunition to do that already. One day I'd have to cross that bridge, but for now I just wanted my children.

I turned to look out the window and the snow was beginning to fall even harder.

So much for venturing out today.

Tiffany and Brandon would like NJ if but for the snow alone. There were lots of children in the neighborhood for them to play with. Initially, I knew it might prove to be an adjustment for them to live so far away from their grandparents, but I was committed to ensuring that both sets of grands were free to visit whenever they wanted. I even hoped Tiffany and Brandon would be allowed to spend summers with their extended family.

Fortunately for me, not only were many of my client's wealthy they were resourceful. After mentioning the need for a nanny to Sandy, who happened to be the wife of the Chief of Police of Teaneck, she immediately got on the phone with some friends and helped me find Marcia. The moment I interviewed her I knew she was the one. Her calm disposition and genuine smile reminded me of my mother-in-law and her references were impeccable. She had one son who lived in Mexico. He wasn't married and didn't have children so the chances of her commitments being divided weren't going to be an issue. Marcia was willing to move into the house once the children arrived. That was the deciding factor. Sandy also recommended a brilliant child psychologist to help them deal with the separation from the only community they'd ever known. When I met with Dr. Brown to make sure we vibed, she warned me that the initial separation might be the toughest for the children. Her goal was to help ease the transition.

I stared at the divorce papers that were sticking out from under a stack of books on my nightstand knowing full well I didn't need to torture myself by reading them for the hundredth time. Unenthusiastically, I reached for them. Tommy instructed me not to sign anything. I wasn't ready to do that anyway. The only reason Myles petitioned for divorce was either to beat me to the punch or Kymile advised him to be the first one to file. I knew he didn't want a divorce any more than I did. Tommy explained that if I signed the documents it could possibly signal to the court that my move was calculated and premeditated. That felt dishonest because I did calculate my move years before I got the courage to go through with it, however, not for the reasons the judge might think. I did it because my marriage had become a lie and neither one of us was happy anymore. Somewhere in the back of my mind I thought leaving might get his attention and he'd find me and want to work through our problems. So much for that plan.

I read the temporary child custody order of the divorce decree out loud, "custody subject to further order of the Court. Care, custody and control of the two minor children of the parties is hereby granted to the Husband."

Yeah, right. We'll just see about that, Mr. Rollins.

Myles and Kymile must've not really understood what I would do when it came to my children. Mr. Cervini warned me that he planned to leave no rock unturned. At this point I didn't care if the bones from my skeletons fell out the closet. He flat out told me that my relationship with Ty didn't help my case and strongly advised us to call it off until things settled. Ty didn't take that piece of advice too kindly and told him to stay in his lane and focus on getting me what I wanted.

A few times I came close to mentioning my indiscretion with Dre to Mr. Cervini but didn't know how.

"Mia, you're sure we've covered *everything and there is nothing else you care to tell me?*" he'd asked me on several occasions with a raised eyebrow each time. If I didn't know any better, I'd swear he already knew about Dre. Lawyers had a way of finding out whatever they wanted to know. I just hoped and prayed it wouldn't come up.

Honestly, I worried about how both Ty and Myles would react when they found out. Jeopardizing my marriage with the likes of Dre was not the highlight of my life by any stretch of the imagination. Not because Dre and Myles were so called friends but because Myles didn't deserve to be cheated on. I despised Dre for manipulating me at a vulnerable time in my life to settle his own malicious vendetta. Regardless, I should have known better.

Myles and I were married seven years when Dre and I got together. I broke things off after six months and never slept with him or succumbed to his advances after that. Still, every time he saw me, no matter when or where, he acted as if we were still sleeping together or worse yet as if there were some remote chance I'd sleep with his ass ever again. His arrogance was mind blowing. The sad part is; looking back, I can't imagine what the fuck I was thinking or how bad off my head must have been for me to go there. The thought made me nauseous.

Before I met Myles, my confidence suffered a horrible beat down at the expense of my ex-boyfriend's verbal, physical and mental abuse. Jerry and I met at a club the night my girlfriends and I had gone out to celebrate my twenty-first birthday and a new job at Nordstrom's. He and his boys were sitting at the table next to me and my girls. He pretended to be the perfect gentlemen that night. He asked me to dance and we ended up dancing together on and off the entire night. When Jerry found out it was my birthday, he set up a tab for our food and drinks. He and his friends left before we did, so we exchanged numbers on his way out. I really had no intentions of calling him even though he was fine as hell. After he called and texted me every day for a whole week I agreed to meet him for drinks. A woman's intuition never lies, and when I got a strange feeling during our conversation that something didn't jive with the brother, I should have high tailed it out the door.

Foolishly, I gave him a second chance. We went to the movies two weeks later. He relentlessly begged me to be his girl. I detected an abnormal annoyance when I laughed and said we hadn't known each other long enough for him to ask me a question like that. For the second time I made the mistake of dismissing my gut. His pursuit continued, and three months later we were sleeping together. Within six months, I moved into his apartment. Jerry made sure I didn't want for anything. I misread the signs of control as love. In hindsight, all the indicators of an abusive, controlling psychopath were screaming at me from the jump, but my inexperienced ass let good sex, money and low self-esteem blind me.

Once I moved in, the shit hit the fan. The control escalated and I spent two frightening years being brainwashed to believe that nobody cared about me because I was a worthless whore. Jerry reminded me daily that he'd hunt me down like an animal and kill me if I ever tried to leave him. The night he put a loaded gun in my mouth and held me hostage for two days while he raped and tormented me because he said I disrespected him by lusting after some football player on TV, I mustered the courage to leave. By that time my self-worth had a negative zero balance anyway so I wasn't afraid to die. I literally had to uproot a life I'd created in California to move back home.

I moved into my parents' house and got a job at Macy's as a Window Dresser. Every day after work I'd come home and lock myself in my room until it was time for work the next morning. I rarely even ate. Nine months of the same routine, Michelle got tired of seeing me mope around the house isolating myself from the rest of the world. She tricked me into thinking we were going to see a movie one night and took me to a playdate social. That's where I first met Myles. I was immediately attracted to him, but bruised and wounded, I shied away from any man who tried to approach me that night.

The outing made me realize how much I'd missed feeling alive. A few months later I enrolled in a night class at Howard to see if I had what it took to start my own business. Myles and my path crossed again in the library on campus. I was sitting at a table alone, engrossed in rewriting notes from my marketing class when I felt somebody standing over me. I looked up and there he was. He struck up a conversation then asked to share my table.

That day, I learned Myles had just started his sophomore year of dental school. Shamefully, he admitted that the library had become his second home. Our *chance* encounters turned into routine and we began meeting on campus to study. The first few times he asked me out on a date, I turned him down. I wasn't ready. It took a year for me to consider going out with him. Two years and six months after we met, we were married.

In some strange way, I think Dre was the beginning of the end for Myles and me. I had not fully recovered my self-esteem from the hands of Jerry when I started dating Myles. Even though time had passed, my wounds were still fresh and I had no business getting married when I did.

The noise from a plow truck interrupted my daydreaming. The snow was beginning to taper off, but given the accumulation, the Great Mother had decided my fate for the day. A few of my neighbors had already ventured outside with snow blowers and shovels to clear off their driveways. I didn't have to worry about shoveling snow because after the first snowstorm I hired a local guy to clear my driveway and he'd already been by twice this morning.

Ty was out of town on business and not due back until tomorrow morning. We talked for a second late last night and he alerted me that he might not get a chance to call or text today due to back-to-back meetings. Normally that wouldn't have been a problem, but since I was stuck in the house for the rest of the day boredom had me longing to hear his voice.

Ty begged me to go with him to Atlanta. I declined because in all sincerity I didn't want to wake up next to him on my husband's birthday. Besides, our relationship was beginning to get too problematic. He kept dropping subtle hints that he usually got what he wanted and he wanted me. The only issue with that was the fact that over the last month my feelings for Myles were beginning to resurface.

Ty's charm had been irresistible. He was everything and more than

I thought he'd be in bed, but it wasn't enough to shake my feelings for Myles. I still loved my husband. Deeper than that, Ty's overly possessive behavior was starting to look and feel way too familiar.

One night after seeing The Lion King, we were leaving the Minskoff Theatre on Broadway. On the way to Ty's waiting limo, Dre came from out of nowhere and pretended to accidentally bump into me. The fucking bastard had the audacity to grab a chunk of my ass on the sly. I could have castrated him right there on the street but had to play it off.

Ty's limo driver shoved him up against the car so fast, people were scrambling to get out the way. Fortunate for Dre, I don't think either of them saw him touch me. I could tell by the look in his eyes that Haki shook his ass up even though he tried to be cool. He proceeded to apologize directly to me by calling my name, which forced me to make a fucking introduction. Ty gave Haki the signal to let him go and from that moment on Dre proceeded to brown nose with no shame. He went on and on about how much he loved the food at Monet's and how he and his clients only ate there when they were uptown.

The asshole stooped to an even lower low when he seized the opportunity to give Ty his card and suggested the two of them have lunch to talk business. Dre brazenly asked for one of Ty's cards and to my disappointment he obliged. He had the gall to turn to me and hand me a card, too. I stuffed it in my coat pocket to burn later. Just when I thought he couldn't descend any lower than hades, he asked Ty if he'd met Myles. He told him that they were best friends and line brothers. The whole time I wanted the ground to open up so I could disappear. If Ty suspected anything, he was cool as a cucumber. He ignored the question about Myles, graciously apologized for Haki roughing him up, and thanked him for patronizing his establishment. They shook hands, Dre reached over to hug me, and I cooperated despite my trepidation. We got in the limo and drove away.

Ty drilled me all night once we got to his condo and I considered seizing the opportunity to come clean because I so wanted to purge the guilt. However, I felt like my first confession should have been to my husband.

The laughter of two small children making snow angels in the front yard across the street was a welcome distraction from the thoughts swimming around in my head. I had to find something to do before I started feeling sorry for myself. There was one option that kept surfacing to the top of my thoughts. The only thing was it involved Dre. He didn't want to have lunch with Ty for no reason and it was killing me to know what the evil bastard had up his sleeve. I kept imagining the two of them sitting across a table and Dre throwing me under the bus with his fantasies about what happened between us. It was time for me to flush out his motives. Not only did I have to worry about his intentions concerning Ty, but if the birthday party had a green light and he planned to show up uninvited, who knows what he might tell Myles? Dre wouldn't miss a chance to degrade Myles in front of his family and friends. I wouldn't put it pass him to corner Myles and embellish how he'd seen me around town with another man, or God forbid tell him about my moment of insanity with his ass. Dropping that bomb might hurt my case or damage the likelihood of reconciling any type of relationship with my husband.

I wanted to pick through the empty remains of his brain and find out where his thoughts were and how far he'd go to play his little mind games. His unhealthy resentment for my husband was turning into a preoccupation.

Against my better judgment, I decided to see if he were still in town and invite him over under the pretense of being interested in his services instead of Mr. Cervini.

Staring at the phone, I tried to talk myself out of calling but fear made me desperate. Just the thought of being alone with him tied my stomach in knots.

Since I'd made good on my threat to burn his business card, it took me about twenty minutes to retrieve the email I'd deleted with his phone number in it, then I procrastinated for another hour before I sat on the edge of my bed and picked up the phone. With my hands shaking like a leaf and my head pounding like a jackhammer ripping through it, I dialed his number. The phone seemed to ring forever and I prayed the voicemail would kick in so I could leave a message, but lucky me.

"Talk to me."

"Hi Dre," I managed.

"Mia?"

"How'd you guess it was me?"

"I'd know that voice anywhere. So you finally decided to call, huh?"

Stay focused, Mia. Don't let him throw you off! It's early in the game.

"I did. How are you?"

"Better, much better now. I thought you'd never call."

"So that means you've been waiting for my call?" I queried trying to break the ice and give my heartbeat a chance to slow the fuck down.

"You gave me a lot of reasons to hold out hope, baby."

"Did I? Like?"

"Oh I can think of several, but the one that gets my dick hard is remembering how good that tight firm ass felt in my hands."

Come on Mia, you can do this.

Just like Dre to go for the jugular off the top.

"I'm flattered," I lied, "but I have a proposition for you if you're interested?"

"Tell me more."

"Well, it might be better if we spoke in person. Are you available to come by later?" I almost gagged on the words.

"That depends. Will you make it worth my while?"

"Well now you'll just have to come by and see."

"Sweetie, I'm not interested in playing games unless of course we gonna play the ones we used to play between the sheets. You remember, Mia? I especially miss playing that game where you would let me…"

I cut him off to keep from throwing up. My stomach was beginning to turn. "Let's talk more about that in person," I suggested.

"Don't you remember how good it was? I mean, we did it everywhere, on the floor, in the shower, kitchen counter and the table," he laughed. "What took you so long to call me? And don't act like you forgot how I used to give it to you like a motherfucking G! You remember how you used to bite the pillow and scream my name! Ahhh…man I miss that shit, Mia! You cut me off cold, baby."

My confidence was fading and I regretted picking up the phone. He had me on the fence already dodging blows and he knew it. "Look, Dre, I am…"

"Listen baby, unless you giving up some of that good ass you wasting a brother's time."

I jumped up and ran into the bathroom because I literally felt like I was going to throw up! It took all I had not to toss the phone against the wall to try and deafen him in his ear. He was calling my bluff, but I had no idea how to respond to his obscene comments. I remained silent.

"Mia, you still there? Are you undressing so I can come over and stick my…"

"Fucking bastard," I yelled before slamming the phone down as hard as I could. Knowing Dre, he was probably standing there with his hand wrapped around his excuse of a dick jerking off. To say I felt sullied, humiliated and outraged, wouldn't have began to explain how I felt.

My phone rang, and it was him calling back. I started not to answer it, but I did.

"For the record, you're full of shit Mia," he snarled. "It's been almost two years since you dropped me like a bad habit. Out the blue sky you think I'm gonna believe you want something from me? Do you think your shit is that fucking good? You got me all wrong baby, but thanks for the memories; it's been a while since I've *jerked* off on you. Oh yeah, I'll be sure to tell Myles you said happy birthday tonight."

The motherfucker hung up like the bitch that he was.

Fucking bastard was playing me all along! Why did I bother?

What the hell was I thinking? Dre hit it on the head, two, almost three years had gone by, and in that time I had been avoiding him like the plague. Then all of a sudden, I call him and expect him to fall for my weak game. Boy was I a fool. All the air seeped out my deflated ego. Blackmail was still an option, but if I went that route my shit would be entangled in the web, too.

My head pounded so badly I just knew it would explode any minute. Discombobulated, I pulled out the half-empty bottle of sleeping pills from behind the Nyquil in my medicine cabinet. Avoiding the mirror, I poured three of them in my hand, turned on the water in the sink, and filled the glass I'd left on the basin half-full with lukewarm water. Tilting my head back, I tossed all three pills to the back of my throat and took in a mouthful of water, swallowing quick and hard. My reflection and I fastened eyes. Neither of us liked what we saw. Bracing myself on the sink, a rush of questions washed through my mind: How was I going to tell Myles I slept with Dre? Where would I even begin? How was I going to tell Ty that while I was married I'd had an affair with one of Myles' friends? What would my parents and in-laws think of me once they found out?

One thing rang obvious, inevitably I was going to have to face my demons. I gulped down a few more sips of water to try and calm my nerves.

The sleeping pills made me groggy within seconds. I went back into my room to lie down across the bed on my stomach. Before I drifted off to sleep the words from one of Myles favorite songs came to me…"and after the love game has been played, all our illusions are just a parade, and all the reasons start to fade, after all the reasons why, all the reasons were a lie."

Coming up out of a deep sleep, I heard knocking and it felt like someone was banging inside my head. I finally became coherent when I heard the doorbell and realized somebody really was knocking at the door. My thoughts were foggy. The smallest attempt to move my head or sit up made me dizzy. In the middle of trying to get up from the bed and go downstairs, the phone rang. I reached around blindly, searching the bed for the cordless.

"Hello," I grumbled.

"Baby it's me, you up there?"

"Ty, where are you?"

"I'm downstairs. I've been ringing the bell and calling you for about twenty minutes now. You had me worried. Come down and open the door."

"What are you doing back so early? I thought you weren't due back until tomorrow?" I inquired, looking around the room.

"Baby, it's Sunday morning. Come open the door."

"Sunday? What? Wait a minute, what? It can't be," I muttered in shock. I checked my cell phone.

Ten fifteen, November 3rd?

"Mia, come open the door, baby."

"Coming, I'm coming." I shook my head trying to clear the cobwebs but it only got woozier.

The medication must have knocked me out. I crawled slowly off the bed and peeked out the window. Sure enough, Ty stood there waving at me, his limo parked in the driveway. I was surprised to see that most of the snow had melted from an apparent rainfall. Carefully making my way to the closet, I put on my heavy winter robe.

Sluggishly descending the stairs with a firm grip on the handrail, my steps were wobbly and once or twice I almost lost my balance.

It was so good to hear his voice and anticipate seeing his face. I couldn't get the door open fast enough. Ty greeted me with two-dozen beautiful white and yellow roses and a big hungry kiss on the mouth. I wrapped my arms around his neck squeezing him tight, filling my nose with the smell of his cologne. He felt so good, so safe.

"You alright, baby? You had me worried," he admitted, closing the door behind him and removing his scarf, coat and boots without taking his eyes off me. He placed a soft kiss on my forehead.

I took the roses from his hand and stuck my nose deep in them, sucking out the fragrance. We walked into the kitchen holding hands. "Oh honey these are beautiful, thank you!"

"You're welcome, but are you okay?"

"I had an unbearable headache yesterday so I took a few sleeping pills and laid down. I didn't realize they'd knock me into the next day!"

Ty watched me closely as I arranged the flowers in a vase I'd taken from under the sink. He seemed to notice the sadness in my spirit despite the front I tried to put on.

"I thought I'd hear from you before you went to bed," he began delicately. "I called you all through the night. Did you get any of my messages?" he asked, walking up behind me and holding me in his arms. "You've been having a lot of headaches lately. I think it's time to make an appointment with my doctor just to make sure everything is good," he said as a request rather than a statement.

"It's probably stress, that's all," I downplayed.

"How many pills did you take?"

Instantly, I felt myself getting defensive although logically I understood his concerns, especially after he couldn't reach me. I don't know how I hadn't heard the phone, and I began to wonder if I had taken more than three sleeping pills. My head hurt so bad last night I could have easily poured more in my hand than I thought.

"After we talked yesterday morning I spent way too much time preoccupied with a whole lot of shit. By the time the afternoon rolled around my head hurt so bad all I had the strength to do was take a few sleeping pills and lie down," I offered, making one last adjustment to the flowers.

"I understand. Which is exactly why you should have gone with me. We could have slept in separate rooms if that would have made you more comfortable. I don't ever want anything to happen to you baby, you hear me?" he said sincerely, pulling me closer to him.

"I'm sorry I made you worry," I smiled. "Maybe next time I'll take you up on your offer. It did get pretty lonely here without you."

"You don't have a choice. Next time I'm not leaving without you," he responded, holding me tight.

"Is that so? Well, we'll have to see about that now won't we?" It was good to have him back. It didn't dawn on me how attached I had become to him.

"No we won't young lady because I've already decided and that's the end. We did it your way this time, next time I make the decisions."

"I'm not going to fight with you because I'm too happy to see you. You win. For now."

"Good enough. Go get dressed so I can feed you. You need to eat," he demanded, tapping me on the behind.

Ty had no idea how happy it made me to have him cater to me the way he always did. His refusal to accept no for an answer could sometimes be domineering, but in the moment, it was perfect.

I took a shower and got dressed in a simple ankle length denim skirt, red turtleneck and my red snakeskin boots. We were out the house in no time.

Haki weaved his way across the George Washington Bridge into the city. I didn't want to ask because I was curled up in Ty's arms enjoying Kirk Whallum's sax, but I hoped the plan for breakfast didn't include stopping by Monet's.

Kwame still made me nervous the few times our paths crossed. I'd reached the conclusion he didn't like me any more than I liked him. We weren't vying for president of each other's fan club. He gave me the creeps, sort of like a homicidal killer on the loose and nobody knew his real identity. I learned the hard way not to question Ty about Kwame when I jokingly, but seriously one day asked him why he hadn't been dismissed for the treatment I got on our first date. In so many words, Ty told me not to advise him on how to handle his business. He'd promised to limit our encounters and so far so good.

Once or twice through indirect conversation, I tried to find out why he was so loyal to Kwame. Each time he shut me down by simply stating, "Kwame and I go way back. He's like the father I never had." I got the message loud and clear…stay out of it Mia.

Whatever their relationship, the further he stayed away from me the better. I liked the fact that Ty had somebody he trusted to run the business because it gave him more time to spend with me. I just wished it wasn't Kwame.

The ride into the city helped me to relax to the point I felt my appetite come back. We were nearing the piers, approaching the Tribeca section of Manhattan when Ty held up five fingers to indicate he'd be done with a call in five minutes.

No matter where we ate the food was guaranteed to be excellent. The perks of dating a man who owned a restaurant. Since we'd been together, I'd learned never to judge the quality of a restaurant solely by its appearance, especially in NY.

A few of the restaurants he'd introduced me to that had the best food were hole in the wall joints. From the outside, they didn't look inhabitable, let alone places you'd want to eat a meal. Ty taught me how to tell if a restaurant prided itself in what he called CCF. Cleanliness, customers, and food were the ingredients of a five-star restaurant according to Ty. In his opinion, all three were equally as important. If an establishment fell short in one area there was no exception in his mind that it fell short in the other areas. Consequently, it was no wonder that the spots he frequented came with very high standards.

Disconnecting his call and shifting his attention to me, Ty kissed my forehead.

"A quarter for your thoughts," he asked.

"Wait a minute, I thought it was a penny for your thoughts," I chuckled, hastily lifting my head from his chest.

"Normally it is, but you look like you have some pretty expensive thoughts going on up there in that big head of yours," he laughed.

"You're a trip, you know that right?"

"Don't try and change the subject. What's got you so far away from me?"

"I was just admiring the view."

"You wanna share?"

"You got a lifetime."

"If you'll have me."

"Be careful what you ask for, you just might get it."

"I never ask for anything I don't want, or that I can't handle."

"Reserve that."

"Mia, I'm serious."

"So am I," I laughed.

"Mia, look at me."

My intuition sensed a deep conversation brewing that I wasn't in the mood to have. The last few weeks, Ty had been treating me like a fragile china doll. I looked into his big beautiful eyes.

"Mia, when are you going to let me in? I know I said no pressure, but after you got those divorce papers, I've felt shut out. If I'm wrong, paranoid or making too much out of nothing tell me."

He was right. My defenses were up but I had so many balls juggling in the air at one time. How could I tell him about all the thoughts racing through my head like a runaway train without him hating me? How could I tell him I missed my husband, my family? I laid my head back on his chest hoping he'd just let it die.

"I promise, no judgment," he said genuinely.

"I tell you what," I inhaled a deep breath and exhaled. "After we get back to the house, we can talk," I whispered softly in his ear.

Happy Birthday to Me

Myles

WHY Q THOUGHT he was the least bit capable of keeping a secret cracked me up inside. First of all he lacked the patience. It didn't take a lot of planning to have a few drinks with the boys to celebrate my birthday, but the way he acted you'd have thought we were going to LeBron's crib for drinks. The last seven times he called me, I intentionally let it roll to voicemail to fuck with him.

I was already twenty minutes overdue for our arranged six o'clock meet up at my house, but mother and the children had thrown a surprise birthday party for me and they were my priority.

Although both of them tried hard to hide their disappointment because they didn't want to spoil my day, Tiffany and Brandon both seemed sadder than normal. It was the first time either of them had celebrated a birthday without all of us being together. Brandon asked if Mia were coming to surprise me. Tiffany didn't mention her at all. I had no idea what to tell him, but I could have hugged my mother for interceding when she heard him ask.

Maybe it was my imagination, but the closer the time came for a judge to decide our fate the more they acted out. What I may not have been taking into consideration was the fact that my answers about what was *truly* going on no longer appeased them, especially since they hadn't talked to Mia in a while. Tiffany's teachers were calling me almost daily desperately trying to understand how she went from a child that never gave them an ounce of trouble to one who was having sudden outbursts and smart-mouth answers. There was no telling where the fuck I'd be if mother's calm steady hand were not a part of the equation.

All I could do was take one day at a time. Hopefully, after Mia and I got past the custody case we'd be able to do what was best for the children.

Q was sitting in the passenger side of his truck talking on the phone with a cigarette hanging from his mouth when I drove up. He abruptly ended his call when he saw me. I needed a good laugh, and the look on his face did the job.

"I know, I know, save it, money," I said driving up beside his car and laughing.

"See this shit here the reason why your wife might be fuckin another dude," he came at me with.

Nobody else could have made a statement like that without getting their jaw broken.

"That's a low motherfucking blow, son. Remember you ain't the only one carrying a crazy gene," I told him while gathering the gifts and leftovers out the car. I walked up the driveway pass him into the house, leaving the door open behind me.

"I'm scared," he responded.

"What's the rush?" I asked as he followed me to the kitchen. "The fellas won't mind waiting a few minutes for the birthday booooy!" I joked knowing full well we weren't just having drinks with the boys. I put the food away taking note of what Q was wearing. "You dressed mighty fly for a night out with the boys."

"Who you now Sherlock?" Q asked while perched on the arm of the couch. "We need to bounce."

"Hold your horses! I gotta take a quick shower," I called running up the steps. I couldn't help but laugh to myself because Q was bugging. Served his ass right. I told him I wanted to lay low for my birthday. Drinks, maybe a strip club and then call it a night. Now I knew he was trying to hide something.

"That's that bullshit, muthafucka!"

Thirty minutes later we were driving up the highway in Q's Escalade bumping a hyped mixed CD on our way to who knows where. Mia was thick on the brain. My ego was taking a hell of a beating because she hadn't called yet to wish me a happy birthday. Something about that fact signaled the end for real. I missed the big fuss that would have been made over my birthday. Tiffany and Brandon had done their best to try and keep the tradition alive, bless their little hearts, but, Mia's absence made a huge difference.

"Park that shit running through your head homie," Q advised.

"Easier said than done."

"You ain't bringin no bitch shit up in here. Drop it off dawg. You feel me?"

"You the one acting like the bitch. When did you become my mother, motherfucker?"

"I got 'yo moma," he said grabbing his shit.

"Like I said, easier said than done, bruh. Until you've stepped foot in a brother's size thirteen's, back off."

"A trick'll trick you every time."

"You didn't hear me the first time when I told you to nix the disrespectful names for my wife, man?"

"Like it meant shit to me then."

Q popped opened the glove compartment and pulled out a bottle of Cognac, twisted the cap off and handed the bottle and cap to me. "Hit that."

"Are you serious?"

"What you a bitch now son? Hit that muthafucka!"

I looked around to make sure the coast was clear before taking a swig. Q lifted the armrest, pulled out a blunt and sparked it up. Part of me wanted to cop out for real because the last thing I needed to do was get caught drinking and smoking weed, but the don't give a fuck, it's my fucking birthday motherfucker was on deck tonight. I hit the Cognac two more times, screwed the top back on then stuck it back in the glove compartment. Two pulls from the blunt and I was blazing!

"That's the muthafuckin dawg I know!" Q boasted. "You ready for some titties and ass?" he asked before taking a toke.

"Hell yeah!" I slurred.

For a minute, I thought I had an idea where we might be going until he headed toward Arlington throwing me off. I sat back to enjoy my high.

"You good over there partna," Q asked after ending a call on his cell phone.

"Yeah, I'm good. I was just admiring that moon."

My boy took a quick peek out the window. "That shit full. You know what they say about a full moon…the freaks come out at night!" he sang off key.

"The freaks out day and night in your world, homie," I chuckled.

"You muthafuckin right! A chick that ain't a freak is useless." Q took a few more tokes, passed the blunt to me and I finished it off.

He turned off the highway and onto another freeway unfamiliar to me. "Where the hell we going man?"

Instead of answering my question he cranked up the music.

We'd been riding for over an hour when Q drove through a tall metal gate that fully enclosed two high-rise buildings.

"When you gonna tell me what's going on?" It had been a long time since I'd gotten high. The combination of alcohol and weed had my head right. I put the window down to get some fresh air.

"When a fuckin monkey fly!"

"What's this?"

"Stop whinin," Q retorted, parking the truck at a valet stand in front of one of the high rise buildings. "Let's go," he told me hopping out and tossing the keys to valet.

"Fuck with my shit and I'll slit 'yo muthafuckin throat," he warned the young kid.

"So you couldn't find something closer to home, my man?"

I stumbled out and collected my balance before catching up with him. Q walked through the double doors held open by a doorman and I followed close behind. He swaggered over to a desk with me on his heels. The inside of the building had the look of a hotel but not the feel. Although the lobby was impressive, I still wondered why we had to go so far away from home to celebrate my birthday. A young preppy white kid exchanged a few words with Q before picking up a phone and conversing with someone on the other end. After he hung up, he handed Q a card and pointed to an elevator isolated from two others.

"Enjoy yourselves," he said with a big Kool–Aid smile. Q led the way and once again I followed. My ass was so high; I didn't really give a crap where we were going. He could have been leading me up to the roof to jump off and I would have been down. I felt good as shit! Whatever his big secret entailed, it obviously had nothing to do with a few buddies simply having drinks. Q swiped the card on a keypad on the wall and both of us watched the red numbers above our heads descend from thirty to one.

"Bet you ain't neva balled like this before muthafucka!" Q mocked much louder than he should have.

I felt like a kid on Christmas day. Anytime Q was the head Negro in charge there was no telling what to expect, but one thing was for sure, the blunt and cognac combination had my adrenaline off the Richter.

I stared up at the bright red one above the top of the elevator door. Smooth and soft, the doors parted like butter. When they opened fully, I stumbled backwards.

"Get the hell outta here!"

I looked over at Q and gave him some dap. The fucking elevator was laid out like a living room. It had a red loveseat and armchair, a chandelier, and a white coffee table! The ceiling was mirrored and the floor had a bed of thick ass rich looking red carpet!

"That's what the fuck I'm talking about!" I laughed before strutting in with my coolest rendition of a pimp walk. I wasn't sure whether to stand up or sit down. I opted to sit down on the loveseat.

"Which one of your street pharmacist ballin like this?" I laughed.

"Don't worry 'bout the logistics bruh."

"Hell fucking yeah!" I yelled out for no reason.

"Your monkey ass need to get out more," Q said shaking his head.

My dawg pushed a red button marked P. The doors quietly met in the middle and the elevator took off slow and effortlessly. I enjoyed every moment of the ascend despite the fact that the furniture on the elevator confused the hell out of me.

"Who the muthafuckin man!" Q demanded from nobody in particu-

lar. "It's your birthday and you gonna party like its 2016 you feel me?" Q
sang snapping his fingers and dancing around the elevator.

"The fucking song say 1999, man! Party like it's 1999!"

"That's that purple faggots shit! Mines say 2016 muthafucka!"

For the first time since we'd left the house, I wondered if I were underdressed in my jeans, collared shirt and favorite black suede sports jacket.
Even though I gave my boy a hard time for being mum about our plans,
I was suddenly grateful that he'd gotten me out the house. More than
anybody, he knew how the past few months had almost tipped a brother
over the edge.

I faintly heard music as we approached the top of the building and
I couldn't wait to get off the elevator. Q was texting the entire time we
were ascending. My high kicked into second gear, co-signing a room jam-
packed full of fine ass sistas with skin tones from light to midnight black
waiting to party with me.

When we came to a stop and the doors glided open, Q took the lead
exiting. He walked up to the only door on the floor where the loud music
was coming from and flung it open. Somebody pulled the plug on the
music and flipped the lights on in the pitch-black penthouse. The sight of
a room full of people caught me off guard.

Voices erupted into a melody of surprise, happy birthday screams, followed by Stevie's version of happy birthday. Kazoos, cowbells, whistles
and horns were all mixed in with the celebration. I was floored.

The penthouse was by far one of the dopiest cribs I'd laid eyes on! It
had four levels of wall to floor glass windows all the way around the entire
circumference of the building that accentuated views of the Virginia, DC
and the Maryland skyline. The shit had bedrooms, bathrooms, dining and
living rooms, a movie theatre, a kitchen, and a bar on every floor. Every
bedroom had a sliding glass door that led to a private balcony. All of the
furniture was white. The floors had the tightest, smoothest marble surfaces
my shoes had ever walked across. The bottom level had a pool outside and
a fully equipped dancehall right next to a game room.

The joint was packed! Faces I hadn't seen in years bum rushed me. I
hugged, kissed, shook hands, high fived, fist bumped and greeted family
members, friends, frat brothers, teachers, professors and former co-work-

ers for almost an hour and a half. I was speechless. Q and his cahoots had even gone so far as to have the penthouse decked out in royal purple and old gold…true Omega Psi Phi style. Food and alcohol was plentiful and the eating and drinking began the minute I walked through the door.

Every time I moved, somebody put a drink in my hand even though I hadn't finished the one I already had. Needless to say, the alcohol and weed I'd already consumed on top of what I was being given had a brother lifted.

Q finally revealed that Mia contacted him early in the year to help plan the party. When I told him that she had taken off, he kept the ball rolling. My dawg. They'd managed to find people I hadn't seen or heard from since elementary school.

Out of everybody in the spot, Sammy's presence choked a brother up the most. As far as I could remember, he never left the Front Page for anything or anybody, especially on a Saturday night. It was his pride and joy and he didn't trust anybody to run it like he did.

The only person missing other than Mia was Kymile. Q said she had a case on Monday morning that required her undivided attention. She did give him a gift for me. Just like her to always be looking out for a brother.

Mid-way through the night, Sammy, me and a group of brothers were standing around talking major shit in the game room. One of my totally wasted line brothers was getting his ass handed to him because he was trying to convince the rest of us that Kobe was the best baller of all times. I was about to go ham on him when someone crept up behind me and covered my eyes with a pair of soft, sweet smelling hands. I could tell they belonged to a fairly short person because she was straining to keep her balance.

"Guess who?" she asked attempting to disguise her voice with a baritone influence. She snickered like a little girl.

I ran my hands over her ring finger to see if a wedding band might be the starting point for a clue, but she wasn't wearing one. I ruled out Mia. I would have recognized her smell anywhere.

"Let's see, I can't identify the voice so there goes half my guesses. Can you give me a hint?" I asked incoherently. "Guys, you wanna help a brother out?" I petitioned from my boys.

"We can't help you with this one," Sammy said.

She was having a hard time balancing herself, so I kept my eyes closed, held onto her hands while removing them from my eyes and turned around.

"Don't peek!" she giggled louder.

Honoring her request, I reached down to touch her hair. The close-cropped haircut didn't give me any hints either. "If I had a kiss might that help me remember?" I asked flirtatiously.

"Nope, that won't do you any good," she laughed.

"Okay, shit I give up! It ain't no more fun then!"

She broke out into a hefty laugh, pulled her hands away and slapped me on the shoulder. "You're still the same old Myles!"

I opened my eyes. "Imani," I yelled, the shock of seeing her reflected in my exclaim. She looked goooood! Baby girl's assets had filled out since high school and her body was banging! The light blue sexy short mini dress she had on flattered every curve. I stared down at ten freshly pedicured toes in a pair of white stilettos and internally reprimanded myself for the thoughts running through my head. Whatever the hell she had been doing was working like a champ!

"Happy Birthday, Myles!" She flung her arms around my neck as I picked her up off the floor and squeezed her tight. It was good to see my old friend.

"Imani, is that really you?" I asked stepping back just to make sure my eyes weren't playing tricks on me. She struck a pose with her hands on her curvaceous hips and flashed that same old school girl smile I remembered from back in the day. She turned around slowly so that I could get a view from front to back.

"In the flesh, big brother!"

"You cut your hair! Not fair. I never would have guessed it was you. Come here, woman!" We hugged again.

"You like it?" she asked hesitantly, running her fingers through her hair.

"Baby you could be bald with an eye in the back of your head and you'd still be fine!"

"Ewwww...that's a scary visual," she laughed.

"When did you get here?"

"I just arrived."

I turned to Sammy. "Is this your doing?"

"Not this time! Come here and give a 'ole man a hug girl!" They embraced.

"Hi Mr. Sammy! I don't think I've ever seen you outside of the Front Page!" she noted.

"And you won't again!"

One of my frat brothers cleared his throat to request an introduction. I gave him the overly protective big brother eye, and he got the drift immediately.

"Everybody, this is a very *good* friend of mine from high school," I said with an emphasis on good to make sure Scooby clearly understood that Imani was off limits to playas. Especially married ones. "Imani, meet everybody. Now if you'll excuse us, we have some catching up to do," I told the group after grabbing Imani's hand and walking off.

"Now was that necessary Myles," she laughed, poking me in the side.

"Yes, very much so."

To escape the crowd, Imani and I went upstairs to the master bedroom that had been designated for me with a 'do not enter' handwritten sign on the door by Q. I still wasn't sure why I needed an exclusive room, but knowing my boy, a stripper or an escort was on the agenda at some point in the night. I embraced her a third time. Seeing how good she looked made me feel sorry for Q.

"Do you know Q's here?" I asked concerned.

"No, I didn't. Thanks for the heads up," she answered, looking around nervously. "I'm not going to stay. I just wanted to stop through and wish you a happy birthday."

"Stop through? Are you back in the states? Last I heard you were still in Paris."

"Yes and no. I own two boutiques, one in Atlanta and the other one in Paris, so I'm back and forth."

"That's boss, baby. I always knew you were going places, Imani."

"Thanks Myles. You've always had faith in me," she said looking at the floor.

"Hotlanta? How long you been there?"

"Three years."

"How'd you find out about the party?"

"One guess?" Imani grinned.

"My mother?"

"Your mother! You know our parents still play bid whist once a month," she laughed.

"So she was in on this, too, huh? And to think, she never said a word, but are we surprised?"

We both got a kick out of the inside joke about mother. My mother and her ability to know everything had made her somewhat of a local celebrity. She had quite a reputation in DC and the surrounding areas for predicting everything from births to deaths and everything in between.

"Myles, I really didn't plan to stay. I have an…"

"Oh hell no! There is no way I'm gonna let you get away that fast! It's been too long!" I interrupted. "At least catch me up pretty lady! Husband, man, lover, children, what's going on in your life?" I asked after a tap on the door brought in a fresh round of drinks from one of the waiters. I gave him a thumbs up.

Imani simulated a time out signal with her hands while trying not to spill her drink.

"Slow your roll, doc!" she laughed. "We're here to celebrate a birthday party not write my autobiography!" She vaguely took a sip from her drink. "How about I give you the condensed version and we can catch up on the rest later. Fair?"

"If that's my only option, I guess I'll have to go with it," I told her taking a seat on one of the three sofas in the bedroom. It was getting harder for me to keep my balance with all the alcohol I'd consumed. Imani sat beside me.

"No husband, man, boyfriend or lover, but I do have a Yorkie named Bear. My life's too busy right now for anything that requires more than a bowl of food and water once a day."

I could tell she was getting uneasy and wanted to go. She put the barely touched drink on a coaster on the table behind her and reached for my hands.

"I'm sorry about you and your wife, Myles. You don't have to feel the need to go into details. I just wanted to let you know I was sorry and I'm here for you."

I wondered when the elephant in the room was going to be called out by somebody. Up to this point nobody had said anything about Mia all night. On one hand, it was a relief to finally have someone mention her and on the other it was painful. Thankfully, the first person to address it was somebody I didn't have to front with.

"I appreciate that, sis, I really do. It's been a tough road I ain't gonna lie. Equally for our children too, you know?"

"I can't imagine what you must be going through."

"What the fuck you doing in here, homie."

The moment I'm one hundred percent sure Imani wanted to avoid had come. Q entered the room without knocking and stopped just shy of the threshold. Imani gazed at him as if she were trying to fill in the blanks from missing chapters of her life that hadn't included my boy. His face was expressionless. My allegiance was split, just like old times. I scrabbled to stand up.

"What up Imani?" he asked, turning his attention to me. I read the number one question on his face, but wanted to ask him how I could have known that Imani would be at my *surprise* party!

"I'm good, and you, Quincy?" Her barely audible voice cracked when she spoke. Imani got up and stood beside me. Neither of them made a move in the direction of the other.

When it looked like Imani was about to pass out from holding her breath, I grabbed her hand, pulled her close and put my arm around her. She shifted her weight back and forth in her heels.

"Hangin."

Q had always been a hard motherfucker to read and it was no different now. I would have thought that encountering the one woman who could have had a remote chance of setting his ass straight might faze him. If it did he didn't show it at all. The only thing I caught was him checking out her curves but that was it. I wished that I could have left them alone so they might be able to talk, but I knew that was the last thing Imani wanted. Besides, I couldn't move anyway because she was leaning on me and I was supporting her full weight.

"You cut your hair," Q noted indifferently.

"Yeah, I thought a change might do me good," she ran her hand through her hair like before.

"You wanted downstairs," he said shifting his eyes from her for an instant.

"Cool."

The whole scene was heavy. I was about to excuse Imani and me from the room when Shanise walked her tipsy ass in.

Fuck.

"Hey baby, where you been? I been looking for you! They playing my song downstairs and I wanna dance!" Shanise was making a spectacle of herself dancing unsteadily with her drink in the air to a beat only her ass was hearing.

"Did you read the sign on the fuckin door?"

She stumbled, tried to get her balance and ended up falling on Q. He grabbed her arm and shoved her away from him. Shanise somehow managed to regain her equilibrium.

"No I didn't, but anyways." Shanise turned her attention to me. "Ohhhh Myles! Who's that? She's cute," she said incoherently. Shanise stared at me, stuck her finger in her drink and swirled it around. She pulled her finger out, stuck it in her mouth and began to suck it. Nothing about Shanise turned me on.

"Imani this is Shanise, Shanise, Imani. I was just about to walk her out."

Shanise floundered over to shake Imani's hand.

"Nice to meet you cutie." She leaned in close to Imani, swaying back and forth. With her free hand cupped on the right side of her mouth she supported herself on Imani's shoulder.

"Myles is a good catch. I tried to catch him but his wife kept getting in the way," she whispered then chuckled. "But don't fret, *you* won't have to worry 'cause she's no longer in the picture." Shanise attempted a wink, but it ended up contorting her face. "Keep that between me and you, or would that be you and me, never mind."

Q snatched her by the arm so hard I thought he tore it from the socket. He hauled her out the room like a ragdoll and slammed the door. He didn't say anything to Imani before he walked off and I felt bad for her.

"Imani, I'm sorry."

I attempted to apologize to her but she stopped me with a wave of her hand.

"You don't have to apologize for anything, Myles," she said sincerely.

I could tell she was relieved they were gone, but it was short lived. There was a tap on the door. Before I could tell them to come in, it opened.

"Imani?" Dre inquired after stepping into the room, totally ignoring the sign on the door. "Is that really you? Sammy told me you were here!"

I had been purposely avoiding Dre the entire night. How Mia thought it was cool to invite him to my shit was the million dollar question.

"Dre, what's up?" Imani screamed. She ran over to him and they hugged.

"Damn! Look at you girl! Mercy! You looking good enough to eat! And I mean that literally!" his disrespectful dumbass said slobbering over her like she was naked.

"Same ole Dre!" Imani scolded.

"You got that right! And that haircut sexy as hell, baby! I knew you had it going on in high school, but DAMN! You done let the freak out I see!"

"Dre! Stop it! You're embarrassing me!"

"Listen my man, I'ma need you to have some respect. I know you have a hard time telling the difference between a lady and a ho, but you know Imani, so chill with that," I warned, eager to kick his ass for a number of reasons.

"Come on, Myles! You know *every* woman got a little freak in'em! You should know that. Ain't that right, Imani?"

All the fucking alcohol I'd devoured felt like it evaporated from my system after his comment. His remarks resonated like a low blow on the sly. It took everything in my power to keep from punching him in his face. He and Imani continued to talk but I kept replaying his last comment in my head.

What the fuck did he mean every woman got a little freak in'em? And why did he say I should know that? Was he indirectly trying to make a reference to Mia?

The time had come for the two of us to have a man to man.

"Well I'm going to put it this way, the only person who should know a woman is a freak, is her man." Imani tastefully stated.

"Exactly my point!" Dre laughed looking at me.

"Imani, would you excuse us?"

"Huh? Okay."

"I wanna holla at Dre for a minute."

"As long as you make it quick Myles, I really have to head out." She looked around apprehensively and I knew she was looking for Q. She didn't want to be caught alone with him.

"I tell you what, why don't you find Sammy and wait with him so I can walk you out."

"Sure, but promise me you'll be quick?"

"I promise." I kissed her on the cheek.

"Imani, if I don't see you again tonight, keep doing whatever the hell you doing 'cause it's working, baby!"

"Whatever! Goodbye Dre," Imani said rolling her eyes and throwing up her hand before turning to walk out the room.

We both watched her walk away. I was convinced Q had no brain cells after seeing the woman Imani had evolved into.

"Let's take a ride downstairs," I told him already walking off.

"This sounds serious, should I bring backup, man?"

I didn't answer.

Who Is She and What Is She to You?

Mia

AN EMERGENCY CALL from Kwame unexpectedly ended our brunch. We hadn't long settled into a secluded booth at one of Ty's favorite places to eat when he answered his private cell. The moment he ended the call he said we had to leave. In the four months that I'd known him, Ty had never been required to handle an urgent situation at Monet's so it had to be serious. Ty didn't want me to go home and I had no desire to see Kwame. Against my better judgment, I gave in and agreed to let Haki drop me off at his condo instead of at home. Honestly, I wanted to go back home, but Ty wasn't having it. Besides, I know he still wanted to have 'the talk.'

Boredom and anxiety set in the moment I stepped foot in his apartment. Unenthusiastically, I slipped out of my coat and boots, flopped down on the sofa in the living room and flung my purse beside me. I placed my feet on the coffee table and reached for the remote that controlled everything electronic in the room. With the push of a button, I watched the motorized window treatments descend simultaneously. The entire room went from bright to dark in a matter of seconds. I hit another button. The home theatre screen silently came down from its concealed nook in the ceiling until it reached its final destination and stopped. I flipped through a hundred channels before settling on highlights of the NY Marathon because it reminded me of how much Myles loved watching marathons. Numerous times he talked about running in one, but thus far had not attempted to fulfill that dream.

Two hours into the television watching me instead of the other way around rendered me even more bored than I was when I walked through the door. I decided to call Daphne. Things were strained between us after she cautioned me about getting serious with Ty, and I told her to mind her business. I reached for the remote, opened the blinds and retrieved my cell phone from my purse. Standing and stretching, I made my way over to one of the huge windows that overlooked bustling Park Avenue.

Ty referred to his luxurious five-bedroom apartment as a refuge in the center of chaos and I could see his rationale. Down below, traffic and people bustled about endlessly, moving like little statues. The more I watched, the more I wished I'd gone home.

Just as I was about to dial Daphne, Ty's cordless phone rang. I stood watching it ring, biting the nail on my pinky finger contemplating what to do.

Okay, should I pick it up?

Answering each other's phones was a bridge we hadn't crossed partly because the situation never presented itself. By the time I opted to just let it ring, the recorded message on his machine came on. I turned to call Daphne when I heard a woman's voice leaving a message.

"Heeey Spence, guess who?" she asked. "What ya doing tonight? I'm in a layover at JFK for a few days. I'm gonna call your cell phone. If I don't reach you maybe I'll stop by the restaurant later for some *dessert*. Call me! You have the digits!"

A long beep preceded a flashing red number one on the display. I walked over, circled the phone a few times, and stared at it as if it were going to ring again.

"Spence? Love to see you? I'll stop by for some *dessert!*" I repeated aloud at the phone, my hands on my hips mocking the caller. "You have the digits, huh?" I blurted out.

My first inclination was to call Ty and request an explanation, but I wanted to see his face when I demanded to know who this chick was.

The fact that little missy was throwing out pet names and felt comfortable enough to leave messages on his home phone indicated that their relationship was more than platonic.

So whoever this chick is, she *isn't worried about another woman hearing her message. Why I wonder? She's a little too comfortable for me, especially since I don't know anything about her ass.*

My emotions vacillated between anger and jealously. Ty never once mentioned another woman or gave me any reason to believe one was close enough to be calling him intimate names. On the other hand, if he were seeing somebody else of course I'd be the last to know. I began to wonder if I'd been delusional.

Come on Mia, three months of good sex doesn't mean squat! Get a grip! As fine and rich as Ty is, I can't believe you thought you were the only one? And besides, NEWS FLASH! Did you forget you are a married woman with two children?

Regardless, I had been monogamous and in my mind I deserved the same.

Exclusive and forthcoming are two different things, Mia.

Spots interchanged with wavy lines in my vision signaled the onset of a migraine. I sat back down, closed my eyes and began to massage my temples to ward it off. Within ten minutes I felt the migraine tentatively back off. Jealousy gnawed at me. I didn't like what I'd just heard but I wanted to wait before I passed judgment.

The longing to subtly pick Daphne's brain about Ty's untold story was even more enticing now. I dialed her number.

"Come on Daphne, where are you?" I pleaded after getting her voicemail twice. I called her house but got no answer there either. I left her a message to call me as soon as she got a chance.

I made my way over to the bar. After finishing a glass of wine and a shot of cognac, I heard Ty's key opening the door. I jumped up from the barstool and tried to act normal even though I wanted to hit him with a shit load of questions the moment he walked through the door.

Who the fuck is this woman that called here like she knows you and what is she to you?

"Hi there sexy, come here." Ty danced across the large room toward me, arms open wide, eyes hungry. "I'm sorry for having to run off like that. I missed you so much you'd think it was days instead of hours." We embraced and kissed…mine with a hint of hesitancy, his with passion.

"Everything okay at the restaurant?" I asked, my body rigid.

"Yeah, just some scheduling conflicts for a couple of big events happening tonight that needed to be hashed out. I promised a buddy the VIP room not knowing Kwame already had a party booked. So a little switch-a-roo settled everything. I put my buddy in the private banquet hall. It's more space than he needs but now everybody's happy."

Ty must have picked up on my energy because he leaned back and looked at me strange. "You aren't mad at me are you? You know I wouldn't have gone if it weren't important, right?"

"Sure."

He tried to embrace me again. My body tensed up.

"Okay, out with it baby. I can tell something's wrong."

"You got a phone call. I think you should listen to it," I said stepping back.

His expression said everything. He knew exactly who had called. I saw it in his eyes.

"Let's sit down baby. I think we both have a lot to get out in the open."

He reached for my hand and we walked over to the sofa. Ty sat on the coffee table in front of me and I sat on the edge of the seat with my knees between his.

"If you'd like, I'll go first," he offered gently.

"Aren't you going to listen to the message?"

Ty took my hands and rubbed them. He stared in my eyes. "That's not necessary. She left a message on my cell phone. But let's back up a little bit. I have to tell you the whole story before we talk about India."

"Do you remember our first night at Monet's?"

"How could I not?"

He smiled and kissed me softly on the cheek.

"You were admiring the décor in the penthouse and I mentioned the person responsible for it was a very special friend, but unfortunately no longer with us, remember?"

A knot formed in my stomach and tightened because I had no idea where he was going with this conversation. I got anxious waiting for him to get to the point.

"Nina was my fiancée. We were engaged and planned to get married two years ago, but she was…" his voice trailed off…"killed… in a…a car accident." He took several deep breaths.

"Before I met you Mia, I didn't think another woman could make me feel anything close to what Nina did."

So this was the story that Daphne had referred to. When she told me about it, I went to every website that brought up his name. None of them mentioned a fiancée or an accident. As a matter of fact, there was very little information about him at all on the web. It was like he didn't exist.

"How did you two meet?"

"We met in Hawaii at Pono's."

"Your friend the wine and art coinsurer?"

"Exactly. You remembered!" he smiled.

Ty talked to Pono at least once a week and I'd overheard a few of their conversations. They were always conversing about acquiring new artwork from up and coming artists before they became famous. We were going to his estate for New Year's Eve. Ty said people literally came from all over the world to get their hands on the paintings of Pono's newly found artists before they attained fame. He was proud of the fact that his friend played a huge role in making quite a few artist and collectors millionaires.

"You recall me telling you about Pono's annual New Year's Eve parties, right? The ones where he's been showcasing an up-and-coming painter for the past ten years?"

I gave him the 'keep going' look.

"Well, four years ago Nina showed up with Matu."

His eyes lit up as if she'd walked in the room.

"*The* Matu Karua from Kenya?" I exclaimed in shock.

"Yes. *The* Matu Karua."

"Was Nina from east Africa?" I asked curious.

"No. She was born in Jamaica. Her mother was Jamaican. She didn't know her father."

Ty cleared his throat. I could tell by looking in his eyes that discussing

Nina was not easy for him. His hands were getting clammy and his voice was nearly a whisper.

"You probably are already aware of this Mia because you know your stuff, but prior to his fame, Matu was an unknown struggling artist. To make a long story short, Pono featured him the year Nina and I met. They were good friends. She was his guest at the showcase. I remember the moment she walked into the room on Matu's arm."

Ty paused dead in the middle of his thoughts and gave me an odd look. If I read him right, he probably was wondering if hearing him pine over another woman made me uncomfortable, and it did, but I wanted to hear it anyway. Even though she posed no threat in the flesh, any fool could see her memory still had his heart.

"You sure it's cool for me to talk about Nina with you? I mean, I've wanted to tell you about her for a while. She was such a big part of my life and it didn't feel right leaving her out. At the same time, I didn't want to jeopardize us. It's been a tug-of-war, baby."

"I understand. Trust me I can relate. Listen to me, and I mean this Ty, I want you to be open, share things with me, no judgment, and I want the same from you."

Once again, his eyes said everything. Whether I liked it or not, no other woman would ever replace Nina's piece of his heart, not even me. I wondered if I'd eventually find myself trying to compete with a memory that would never die. "Are you okay to finish?" I asked.

He nodded. "Nina and I made eye contact several times throughout the night. I thought she and Matu were a couple so I didn't approach her."

"Sort of like you did with me," I said sarcastically.

"I'm not sure what you mean by that, Mia. My attraction for you is different. I don't compare you to Nina or her to you."

"I'm sorry. I didn't mean it the way it came out."

"Look baby, if this conversation is going to cause problems between us I'd rather we have it at another time. You're what matters to me at the present moment. I don't want to mess up what we're growing."

"No, no baby you won't, you won't," I reassured him. "I ain't gonna lie, it's tough seeing the love you still have for another woman in your eyes, but I'm a big girl, I can handle it. I need us to be able to talk to one another without feeling like we have to hold back because we're afraid of losing each other."

"I feel the same way."

"Please, go on."

He searched my eyes as he often did to see if my words were in alignment with his instinctual ability to read me.

"Call it fate, but out of over a hundred people at dinner that night on Pono's lawn, Nina and I ended up at the same table right next to each other. The attraction between us was evident from the beginning. She made it a point to let me know she was single once we had a chance to talk. Fast forward, I proposed to her two months after we met but she turned me down. A year later on New Year's Eve, I proposed again. This time she agreed to marry me." He drifted off once more.

"My Nina was killed six months before our wedding day. The rest, as they say, is history. We were getting married on her birthday. September first...," his voice went to that distant inaudible place.

His hand gently slid out from mine. He leaned back on the table, took a deep breath and held it for a while before releasing it through his nose. Gazing about the room with an empty stare, he got up, walked over to the window in his dining room, and steadied himself with his shoulder against the glass. I wanted to console him, but didn't know if I should interfere, or if he wanted me to. Quietly, I got up from the couch and went into the kitchen to pour him a glass of water. I walked over and handed it to him, then sat back down on the sofa to give him space.

"Mia," he whispered. "Can you come here?"

I got up and stood in front of him. "Yes?"

"Promise me you won't ever leave me."

My stomach felt queasy. I was in no position to make such a promise. I began to wonder if part of the reason he was with me was because he was trying to fill Nina's void. I felt silly resenting a dead woman, but she had a part of his heart I'd never have and it made me envious.

Ty slipped his arms around me and tucked his head in the cradle of my neck. The warmth of his breath aroused me. He held me tight, almost too tight, but I didn't resist. When he finally lifted his head, I saw conflict disguised with pain in his gaze. He missed her deeply and probably hadn't allowed himself to mourn in a while.

"Mia, before I met you I didn't know my heart had the capacity to let anyone else in."

"You miss her don't you?" I asked softly caressing his face. I intentionally did not answer his question about leaving him.

He didn't hesitate to answer.

"Yeah, I do. I try not to let it get this bad too often," he sniffled, "because when I do I feel like I'm gonna, I'm gonna lose it," he stuttered.

"I think I understand. Do you mind talking about what happened?"

He squeezed his eyes shut tight and took another deep breath.

"Kwame called me and told me she had been in an accident. I was in California on business at the time, and I swear to you Mia my jet couldn't fly home fast enough. When I landed at the hanger, Kwame was waiting with Haki to drive me to the hospital. He and Nina were very close. She loved him like a father." Ty's body tightened as if he were reliving that moment. "I hardly recognized her, tubes were everywhere, her face was completely bandaged hiding those big beautiful eyes that had gotten me through so much. Machines were pumping. Doctors and nurses were in and out. Whispers. And without a warning she was gone. She held on long enough for me to get there. Six months before our wedding day…I was alone."

My eyes welled up. I finally understood why he had been single for so long. Daphne was right when she said he couldn't be caught, but this explained why.

"I'm sorry for spending so much time talking about Nina, baby. I guess it's been a much needed release," he said almost embarrassingly.

"Stop it," I chided. "If we can't cry on each other's shoulder, what's the point? You suffered a terrible loss. You didn't have a chance to say good-bye. I'm so sorry," I said sincerely. My heart went out to him. If there was a way I could make his pain disappear I would have done it.

"Mia, I care for you and I hope you don't think I'm in this because I'm using you to get over Nina 'cause it's not like that. When I saw you, my heart skipped a beat. I guess what I'm trying to say is, I meet a lot of women, baby you know that, and very rarely does one stand out for me.

I've lost too many of the women in my life that I love. That's made it hard for a brother to put his feelings on the line. I'm very guarded. Nina gave me the gift of love. You came along and breathed new life into me."

The concept was beautiful, but the idea of being in the shadow of another woman tarnished it. Now I wanted to know how this India chick fit in the picture because she obviously was more than a friend.

"Do you know how the accident happened?"

Ty sat down on the exorbitantly plush virgin white carpet facing the window. I sat next to him clutching my knees. "I've been tormented in so many ways since Nina died. Her death was ruled a homicide because the brakes on her car appeared to have been tampered with." Ty inhaled deeply.

"Nina didn't have an enemy in the world but it seems somebody must've wished her harm. She was killed shortly after leaving her house, less than a mile away. Her car hit a tree. The car she was...driving...was a gift from me so it was registered in my name. I was the first person they tried to contact. They traced me to Monet's and Kwame got the call."

"No!" I gasped. "That's horrible!" Now I understood the bond between him and Kwame. He continued almost as if I weren't there.

"Whoever tampered with the brakes didn't leave much for the police to go on. As far as I was concerned they weren't doing enough to find her killer. I hired the best Private Investigator money could buy the day after we buried her. He didn't find any leads either. Nothing. I still don't know what happened, and I won't rest until whoever is responsible pays."

"You mean to tell me you don't have any clues? No leads whatsoever?" I asked confused.

"None. The police just filed it away as an unsolved murder. The closest lead we got was from a neighbor who thought she saw a man hanging around Nina's house while she was walking her dog a few days prior to her car hitting the tree. When he went back to talk to her, she couldn't remember anything. When my PI went back the third time the neighbor was gone. House packed up, for sale sign in the yard. No signs of her anywhere. We think somebody got to her."

"You gotta be kidding me!"

"I wish I were, Mia. God I wish I were. Theodore even looked into the possibility of somebody going after Nina to get to me, but he didn't find anything there either."

"Wow, that's crazy. It's bad enough when you lose someone you love, but to have them cast aside as an unsolved murder has got to be heart wrenching. What about her family? How have they dealt with all of this?"

Another level of sadness came over his spirit.

"Nina's mother died when she was sixteen. Like I said before, she never knew her father. We had so much in common. Neither of us had siblings and we both were on our own at a very young age. She never spoke of any other family members. Matu was pretty much all she had in terms of family."

"Do you and he stay in touch?"

"Certainly."

"Did they interrogate you? I've always heard that they suspect the person closest to the victim."

"In a case like Nina's, you're right it's protocol. The husband, boyfriend or lover is usually the first one to be deemed guilty. They came for me relentlessly because everything pointed to me. My car, my house. I was out of town and they didn't have any other leads. I was questioned and followed for over a month. When I passed two lie detector tests with ease they finally left me alone. Precious time wasted where they could have gone after the real culprit."

"God that breaks my heart."

My neck felt tense and I gave it a rub, rolling my shoulders in backward circular motions to release some of the stress. My curiosity about India still hadn't been satisfied. I couldn't tell if he was intentionally avoiding the subject or not. He looked worn out and I felt guilty for wanting to push the issue.

"Would you like something to eat?" I asked trying to lighten the air.

"No, the water's fine, you? I'll get whatever you like."

Ty attempted to get up but I encouraged him to stay seated.

"I'm good. Is India a friend of Nina's," I asked nonchalantly. One way or another I was determined to get the details.

"No. I met India at a very low point in my life. Dealing with Nina's death left me open for any and everything. I was so fucked up in the head.

All I wanted to do was die. Before the accident, everything in my life was going right for once. I was in love, the restaurant was growing, my investments and joint ventures were moving me toward the billionaire status, you name it, I supposedly had it all. Then with the blink of an eye, my reason for living was snatched away. Just like that," he snapped his fingers. "One day I'm on a high, planning a wedding with the woman I love more than life itself and the next I'm preparing her funeral."

He closed his eyes.

"Have you ever pretended you had it all together until you couldn't fake it anymore?" he asked rhetorically. "For me that moment came on the anniversary of Nina's death. Nina's birthday, our wedding day. The front I was trying to maintain fell completely apart. I thought if I just stayed busy and drowned myself in work I'd be able to sleepwalk from exhaustion through the pain. The joke was on me. My life was unraveling slowly. Monet's was taking a hard hit because I just wasn't present. Kwame took the helm and kept things afloat. He's not perfect, Mia, but he's been very faithful and loyal to me."

I'm not quite sure why he thought he needed to interject a sidebar on behalf of Kwame's character, but whatever. As bad as I wanted to drop a smartass come back I refrained. It only further explained why he hadn't gotten the boot like I thought he should have.

"Prior to Nina's death my board and I were considering opening a line of vegan restaurants in California. We foresaw it being the next hot trend in the restaurant business. A friend of Pono's wanted to fund the venture. To take my mind off things, the president of my board suggested we honor Nina's memory by arranging the meeting around what would have been our anniversary. To say I was a complete mess would have only scratched the surface of my predicament. I was in no shape to be presenting a million-dollar investment opportunity, you know? Nevertheless, we took the trip. The pain of missing Nina grew more and more unbearable the closer it got to her birthday."

He paused for what seemed like forever.

"India and I officially met on that flight."

"Wait a minute. Why did you say you two officially met on that flight?"

"Because she'd been an attendant on the aircraft of a business acquaintance. We all used the same agency to staff our planes."

"Did you two ever converse on any of those flights?"

"No, not at all. They're very professional, Mia. They're not escorts if that's what you're suggesting. They don't go around picking up clients on the job."

I bet they don't.

"Okay, continue."

"During the flight to Cali, India and Tracey, the other attendant aboard my jet were lifesavers. They did an exceptional job of entertaining my board because I was useless. I spent ninety-nine percent of the flight caged up in my suite trying to drown my sorrows in alcohol. India immediately peeped my condition and took charge. She made sure the other guests on the flight were comfortable. When we landed that night she invited me to her room for drinks. I accepted. One thing led to another and we ended up in bed together. It was a one-night stand, Mia."

"So why is she calling you now?" I asked with a trace of distrust.

"Being the gentleman that I am, I felt really bad afterward. When I agreed to go to her room, I knew it was not a good move because of my state of mind. At that time, if I can keep it real, I needed to lie between the legs of a woman and pretend they were Nina's. We both knew what we were there for. It was just sex. More importantly, she let me pour my heart out by talking about Nina. She didn't judge me or try to give me advice, she just listened."

I don't care what he thinks, that trick had an agenda.

"I respected her for getting me through a rough patch. After that, India called periodically to check in on me. Truthfully Mia, had it not been for her, I don't know what I would have done that night once I was alone. Could she be lying in the cut waiting for more? Sure. I've picked up on her innuendoes, the subtle flirting, but that's not what I want. I've made it very clear I have nothing else to offer her."

"Why not?" I asked, intrigued.

"Because I never would have slept with her had it not been for the circumstances. I used sex for one night to try and fill a void. India is a good person, but I don't have those kinds of feelings for her."

"*If you don't have those kinds of feelings for her,* why is she at liberty to call your home and leave intimate messages? Seems to me you're leading her on."

Ty looked at me as if he never contemplated that theory before. "I didn't intend to lead her on but I can see your logic. If I'm authentic, I'll admit to a bit of guilt about what happened between India and me. And yes, there is a sense of obligation because she came to my aid, however, I can't control what goes on in her head, Mia. If India thinks flirting with me is going to buy her a relationship she's delusional. I haven't talked to her in over six months. She doesn't know about you, but she will."

For the first time I was beginning to question Ty's integrity. Something about his story didn't sit well in my gut. Any woman could smell India's plan a mile away. She wanted more than a friendship and she was the type of woman who didn't mind playing the game until her real chance to pounce introduced itself. I wouldn't put it pass her to have arranged to be on his jet once she found out it had been scheduled for flight. The question was, had Ty given her any indication he might eventually hook-up with her. I decided to prod further. "How often do you two get to see each other?"

"Maybe once or twice out of the year when a flight brings her to NY. And in case you're wondering Mia, she doesn't service my flights anymore. She's working international now."

I bet she is.

"Baby you don't have to worry about India. I don't have anything to hide. If you answered my phone, which you have a right to do anytime, you'd see India poses no threat to you."

Even though I should have been satisfied, I couldn't let it go.

"What do you two talk about?" I asked.

"Okay, I want to entertain your questions but I'm beginning to feel like I'm on trial. I've told you everything. I'm not going to defend myself against something that doesn't exist," he said depleted.

The gall of me! I had the audacity to be pushing an issue that was clearly from his past with the shit I had dangling out my closet! Most of what he'd said about 'ole girl I could half way believe except the part where he slept with her one time. She was a little too comfortable for them to have only slept together once.

"I'm not asking you to defend yourself. I don't want to be played. If we are going to shed everything that has to be the whole shebang. We can't pick and choose what we are going to share hoping it won't come out later. Personally, I don't understand why you would maintain a friendship with someone you had a one night stand with. Looks like she got what she wanted and so did you. Move the fuck on!"

Ty scooted up behind me and I sat between his legs, my head on his chest. "Mia, you're absolutely right. I have maintained a friendship with India because I felt guilty about sleeping with her. The fact that she hasn't put any pressure on me made it easy for me to justify continuing a friendship with her. Our conversations aren't deep, we talk about the restaurant, her travels, general stuff, but I'm not willing to let her or any other person potentially risk what I'm trying to build with you. You're my number one priority. You've got to believe that."

The sincerity in his voice softened my heart and diminished some of the mistrust. It didn't take a gold digger to see that Ty was a catch. India was just playing her game slow and sweet but she had a plan, you best believe she did. She had gotten the inside scoop straight from the horse's mouth. She understood that the chances of another woman getting close to his heart as long as he mourned Nina was slim to none so she had time, or so she thought.

We were rounding the corner on Ty's confessionals and my turn was fast approaching. In my mind I had run through several different deliveries, one starting with Myles, the other with Dre, all in an effort to try to figure out which one was less crazier, if that were possible. God knows if he stuck around after I finished with my testimonial he'd be a definite keeper! Hell, I don't even know if I'd stick around after hearing my story!

"You still want to keep me?" he asked playfully.

"Let's hold off on that question until I'm finished," I joked seriously.

As soon as I cuddled into his arms to begin diving into the chaos that was my life, his cell phone rang.

Reading Between the Lines

Myles

I DIDN'T SAY ANYTHING to Dre while we were waiting for the elevator or on the ride down. His cell phone kept him preoccupied. Thoughts of beating his head against the pavement consumed me. He followed me out into the parking lot where I intentionally scoped out an area far enough away from the lobby where nobody had time to stop me from handling my business. He leaned smugly up against the hood of somebody's candy apple red chromed out seven series BMW with his foot on the grill.

"What's so top secret that we couldn't discuss upstairs, bro," he asked still engaged with his phone. "It's cold as shit out here!"

I positioned myself a few feet in front of him eyeball to eyeball. I wanted to be able to read his fucking face and body language when I asked him about Mia. I waited for a couple that had run past us huddled up together to get to their car before I spoke.

"Who invited you here?"

Dre looked up from his phone for a second with a smirk on his face and proceeded to finish a text. He laughed.

"Wow! So that's how you treat a frat brother who flies in from out of town to help celebrate your big day?"

I moved in closer. "I asked you a question?"

"Are you serious, brother?"

I didn't crack a smile.

"He looked up from his phone. "Oh you are serious," he laughed again. "Mia invited me."

"You got something you want to tell me?"

"I'm not following. Is this some kind of joke? You're the one who obviously has something on his mind bruh…hence why we're here playing 99 questions!" he chuckled.

"You got something you want to tell me?"

"I seriously don't follow, man. What is this, like April Fools," he laughed once more.

"You got something you want to tell me?" I repeated for a third time to allow him the opportunity to man up before I broke his nose.

"Yo man, you're beginning to sound like a fucking broken record. If I had something to tell you I would," he boasted. "I'm a man. I ain't never been afraid to say what's on my mind to *no* fucking body."

"So why aren't you man enough to tell me you fucked my wife?"

Call a punk ass motherfuckers bluff and if he's guilty, he'll flinch. Dre flinched. The look on his face said it all despite his attempt to maintain the lie. I could tell he was wondering what I knew. Call it a man thing, instinct, intuition, what the fuck ever you wanted, but the cat was out the bag. Everything in his body language read defense.

The times I'd caught the two of them looking foul but shook that shit off as an overactive imagination replayed in my mind like the scene in a scary movie you couldn't shake from your memory. My pride had willingly allowed me to dismiss the idea that Mia would cheat on me even though the signs were right in front of my face.

I saw red. Truth be told, I was hurt but anger dominated.

Dre of all people, Mia! Damn!

He made the mistake of trying to flex. "I fucked your wife! Yeah right! And where did that bullshit piece of information come from? Check it my man, if 'yo wife out there ho'ing around don't look at me," he answered between text messages. "You're the only one that didn't see her for the lying, conniving, deceitful…"

A left hook caught Dre on the left side of his face dead in the muzzle. The cell phone went flying out his hand and bounced across the windshield of the BMW. He tried to counter but I blocked it and caught him with another left to the ribs. He buckled like a bitch. I landed a few more rounds to his face before he crumpled to the ground like a deck of cards. His bitch ass wasn't giving me a fight and it intensified my fury. He grabbed my ankles and tried to bring me down, but I caught myself on the door handle of the car and recovered my footing. Between the alcohol, weed and pent-up rage, my objective was to kill him. Dre scrambled to his feet and tried to run away. I caught him by the shoulder, body slammed him to the ground, then leaned over his semi-conscious body and grabbed him around the throat. I tried to crack the back of his head open by pounding it against the sidewalk. I don't recall how many times I slammed his head against the pavement, but when somebody yanked me off of him he was unconscious.

I blindly attempted to spa with whoever was trying to pull me off Dre, but ended up with my arm locked behind my back and my feet swept out from under me in one move. I hit the pavement lightly, face down, shielded by a firm grip on my arm. A knee lodged itself in my back and as enraged as I was, nothing I tried freed me from the brute strength that suddenly held me hostage.

"What the fuck you doing, 'yo!" Q asked right up in my ear.

"What I should have done a long time ago!" I wrestled to try and free myself, but he had a tight hold. My chest was on fire from the pressure of his knee pressing it into the sidewalk.

"You wanna get your fucking knee out my back!"

"Not 'til you cool 'yo ass down," he said calmly.

I took a few deep breaths. "I'm cool."

"Solid?"

"Yeah."

I heard a siren in the distance and I prayed it was on the way to get Dre's dead body. Q raised his knee off my back and heaved me to my feet. He didn't let go of my arm until he led me over to the entrance of the building where I sat down on the ground with my back up against one of the pillars. The moment I was seated all the shit I'd eaten, drank and smoked threatened to come up.

"Look dawg 'yo ass in a seat that's 'bout to get real hot, ya heard. Focus up," he instructed from a kneeling position in front of me.

I closed my eyes and shook my head a few times to try and clear it. When I opened them, Taj, and five or six of my frat boys had formed a circle around me shielding me from the crowd of partygoers and residents that had spilled out of the building. I couldn't see where Dre lie on the ground. I did see another large group of people over behind the BMW. The scene was mayhem, and the number of people surrounding him kept growing. My knuckles and hands were full of blood. I didn't feel any physical pain, just emotional.

Not long after I saw an ambulance drive up, four or five police cars followed. The reality of going to jail didn't faze me one bit. I was more interested in confirming that Dre was dead.

"You down a notch?" Q asked, his hand on my shoulder.

I didn't say anything just nodded affirmative.

"You flyin solo now?"

"What?"

"This shit here. This my muthafuckin lane. What that punk bitch do to make you flip?"

"Like you can't guess."

Q took a pack of cigarettes and a lighter from his pocket before squatting beside me. He removed one, stuck the pack back in his pocket and cupped his hands to light it. "Fuck a guessin game, man. What he do?"

"Slept with my fucking wife! I never thought Mia would do that shit to me, man!" I screamed pounding the sidewalk with my fist. It took a few seconds for the pain from my knuckles hitting the concrete to register with my brain. When it did, the sting reverberated through my entire body without mercy.

"That muthafucka fessed up?" he asked, inhaling deep on his cigarette.

"It's what he didn't say."

In the background I heard a barrage of commotion. "Look Q, I need you to call Kymile and let her know what happened. I'm sure they're gonna take me down. I left my phone upstairs in my jacket pocket. Her number's programmed in there."

"Taj let me holla at you!" Q got up and shouted to my frat brother. "Breakout upstairs and get my man's jacket from the room with the sign on the door."

Taj took off toward the entrance of the lobby like a bat out of hell.

"Camel!" Camel ran over. "Get a update."

Q delegated a few more orders to the party of brothers who had not left my side. When one took off another one replaced the circle to ensure nobody got close to me. The inside of my head throbbed like a stampede of elephants were trying to escape from it.

"Q," Smokey hollered from the second semi-circle encasing me.

"There's a female named Imani wanna talk to Myles. Is it okay if I let her in?" he asked.

"Yeah but keep them other muthafuckas back."

Smokey gave instructions to let Imani through and demanded that everybody else move back. A few other partygoers were asking permission to see me too, but Smokey rejected their requests. Imani walked over quietly, her eyes sad. She looked at Q who was pacing back and forth deep in thought. Imani sat down on the ground next to me despite the fact that her dress barely covered her thighs. She stuck her arm through mine and put her head on my shoulder. Her soft warm body comforted me and as ridiculous as it sounds I couldn't help but wish she was Mia. Q came over, tossed somebody's jacket over her legs, and handed her another one for her shoulders. She thanked him with her eyes.

"I'm sorry. I didn't mean to cause problems at your birthday party, Myles."

"Don't you dare. It's not your fault. This has been brewing for a long time. You know that."

She reached up and gently touched a knot on my forehead. I grimaced from the pain.

"That looks like it hurts. You're gonna catch a cold out here without your jacket," she scolded, huddling closer to me.

"I'll be fine."

"You sure?"

I nodded, answering her core concern.

"I'm certain he deserved whatever he got," Imani said nodding toward Dre.

"If he's still alive he didn't."

"I know a good lawyer if you need one."

"I have one, but thank you."

She took a business card from her pocketbook. The smell of her perfume lingered on it. The fragrance was familiar. "Here, put this in your pocket," she demanded, handing it to me.

"I'll be in town another week. If you need anything, and I mean anything, call me, okay? That card has all my contact information so you have zero excuses not to stay in touch. Nada one!" She attempted to smile.

I stuck the card in my back pants pocket. She leaned over and hugged me tightly around the neck then lightly kissed me on the lips.

"Looks like we've got company," she informed me before rising to her feet with a hand from Q.

He took a stance by my left side.

Three police officers were walking in our direction. "Sir, would you please stand up," the taller, slimmer of the three asked in a deep southern drawl. He had his hand on the handle of his gun.

"Sir, ma'am, can I get you two to go stand over there," the lone female officer requested firmly by pointing off to the left of the building. Q gave me a hand to my feet before backing off, but not where he had been instructed to move. Imani stood directly behind him with the jacket over her shoulders. My footing hadn't stabilized and it took me a few seconds to steady myself.

"Do you have any weapons on you?" the female officer asked.

"No."

"Do you have an ID on you?"

Taj held up my wallet which he'd taken from inside my jacket pocket. "Here it is."

"Do you give him permission to retrieve your ID from your wallet?" the third officer inquired.

"Yes."

Taj removed my license and handed it to the officer.

"Are you Myles Rollins?," he asked after looking at my license.

"I am."

"Have you been drinking tonight?"

"I have. It's my birthday."

"You want to tell me what happened?"

The formality and all the fucking questions was getting on my nerves.

"Basically, I found out Mr. Westland was fucking my wife and I tried to kill him," I said cutting to the chase.

"Watch your language," the female police officer warned, looking annoyed. "Mr. Westland is in a coma for your information."

I didn't say anything.

"Sir, we're going to have to place you under arrest for aggravated assault," the third officer announced.

He proceeded to read me my rights. When he finished, he patted me down and then put his handcuffs on my wrist. I understood the severity of what I'd done but I didn't give a fuck. All I wanted to do was finish the job. A coma wasn't good enough. I wanted him to hurt ten times worse than I did right now. My mind kept conjuring up images of him touching my wife and it made me sick to my stomach. Instigated by an overactive imagination, my stomach began to churn and bubble on the walk to the police cruiser. I felt the liquor and food settle in my throat.

"I gotta earl."

Southern drawl took one look at my face before hurriedly escorting me over to a patch of grass. He quickly unfastened the handcuffs and backed up a few feet. Immediately, everything came rushing up out my stomach with a vengeance. The officers congregated together and began discussing my predicament unconcerned that I could hear them. An ambulance screamed off down the road, and for no particular reason I wondered what Mia was doing.

They waited patiently while earl and I finished our conversation so that I didn't throw up in their car.

Before the cruisers left for the police station, Q let me know he was going to follow us. He loudly proclaimed without giving a fuck who heard him, that it wasn't safe for a black man to be in the back of a police car in this neck of the woods. He wasn't taking any chances and I appreciated the precaution.

When we parked in front of the station I couldn't help but think it looked like something straight out of a movie. The building was a small, one story, dimly lit red brick structure with a phone booth, mailbox and bench out front. There was nothing else surrounding it as far as the eye could see. Scary. Right after we parked, Q's truck rolled up alongside the patrol car and I was shocked to see Imani sitting in the passenger seat looking down at me. She gave me a quick wave and blew me a kiss. My head still throbbed like hell but I managed a smile. I tapped my wrist several times with my pointing finger to ask her the time. She held up two fingers a zero and a five.

Two of the officers escorted me into the station and released me to a fourth one who began the booking process. By the time they finished questioning, photographing, fingerprinting, collecting my belongings and patting me down again, I felt humiliated. I'd never personally been subjected to the penal system before, and after what I experienced, I wondered how people allowed themselves to be exposed to that bullshit at all.

Once they finish with your ass that's about all you had left was your ass.

I certainly didn't need this type of publicity for my practice. After 'processing' as he called it, the same officer led me down a corridor to an unoccupied cell that had the nastiest looking cot, toilet and sink imaginable. The jail cell was dim, damp and cold and smelled like piss, shit and vomit. The only thing that gave it an ounce of character was all the initials and names carved sporadically on the walls. My stomach still hadn't fully recovered but I fought hard to keep anything left on it down. Luckily, I didn't have to share the cell with anyone else.

"You sure you don't want that phone call, buddy?"

"I'm sure," I confirmed before he locked the bars behind him.

"Your choice."

I listened to the sound of clanking keys disappear into an eerie silence.

One phone call to Kymile at this time of morning would be plenty.

I already knew what was in store for me when she showed up at the police station. I'd rather hear it once she got there instead of on the phone. Looking down at the nasty ass cot I contemplated standing up until Kymile came but my legs were mush. Besides, standing up made me feel like I was going to earl again so I sat down lightly on the edge of the cot trying not to think about its condition.

In my mind, I could hear Kymile ranting and raving about the potential damage my actions might cost me in the custody case. She had already reminded me that we were fighting an uphill battle based on her knowledge of Mia's lawyer. She referred to him as ruthless and warned me not to take anything for granted. No doubt, she was going to chew my ass out for tonight.

I dozed off and on until the faint sound of voices jarred me fully awake. I jumped to my feet and shuddered when I realized I'd succumbed to stretching out on the cot. In a flash, I was at the bars pressing my ear to the cold metal hoping like hell one of the voices belonged to Kymile.

I heard the footsteps belonging to two shadows that moved along the floor heading in my direction. I felt like a kid whose mother had come to rescue him from the principal's office. My heart pounded in my chest. The figures turned the corner. I wanted to slob Kymile down tongue and all when I saw her face. Her expression said everything her words couldn't in the presence of a cop. She wore a navy blue pinstriped pantsuit that hugged her five nine slender body perfectly. She was carrying her infamous cup of coffee in her left hand. Her midnight black dark skin and naturally curly hair complimented her effortless beauty. I never figured out how she managed to be flawless all the time, even at damn near four in the morning.

Kymile was not only fine and smart as all get out, but she was intuitively gifted when it came to her craft. Nevertheless, despite her intellect and good looks she couldn't keep a dude. Kymile dug in the bottom of the barrel for boyfriends. She dragged in a low life off the streets and married him six months after they met. The jive turkey damn near bankrupted her because she was too ashamed to admit he was a gold digging pimp. She ignored the smell of bullshit masked behind a leased Bentley and a four-hundred-thousand-dollar house he was paying rent in all because she gave in to the pressure of the maternal ticking clock.

He masqueraded as an investment banker but forgot to mention his personal bank accounts were in the red. Kymile refused to listen to anybody who tried to warn her about the riff-raff. By the time she did get a clue they'd been married for two years. Brother man had to have been putting it down in the bedroom because he didn't have shit else going for himself. Kymile got caught without a prenup and needless to say the cost of divorcing him and alimony payments left her soured on the idea of happily ever after. No prenup made her have to pay up.

Keys clanging against the cell lock sounded like sweet freedom to my ears. Kymile waited behind the officer clutching the Kenneth Cole briefcase I'd given her for her birthday. She stared me down like a madwoman. Heeding the officer's command to exit the cell, I stepped out.

"Mr. Rollins, after you sign some paperwork you're free to go... *for now.*"

"Thanks, Kymile," I said humbly. "I owe you one." I went to place a kiss on her cheek. Her stiff posture demanded that I think again.

The officer led the procession back down the hall in silence with me by his side and Kymile directly behind us.

You could have blown me over with a feather when I spotted Q and Imani waiting in the tiny lobby with Styrofoam cups in their hands. She had my jacket over her arms. My first reaction was to gauge her comfortability level with Q. She must have detected my concern because she winked and gave me a thumbs up. Seeing them together made me wonder if some good may potentially come out of a fucked-up situation. I sat down in the same chair by the officer's desk.

Kymile hovered over me policing the entire release process, reviewing every detail on all the documents before giving me permission to sign them. They went back and forth over one particular issue until she requested a supervisor. He reluctantly made a change, initialed it and shoved the paper across the desk in front of me. I had no clue what I was signing. I trusted her to hold me down since I had never had a run in with the law before. The depth of how much trouble I was in unexpectedly sank in as I sat there signing my life away.

Finally, he handed her an envelope that contained the few items I had on me at booking. Kymile requested that I verify all my belongings were inside. I poured the contents on the desk and confirmed that they were. When all was said and done, she cordially reminded him that she was doing her job, too.

"You're going to take a ride with me. I'll be right back," she instructed before going outside to use her cell phone.

I joined Q and Imani. She grabbed my hand and gave me a big hug and squeeze.

"You good?" Q asked.

"I've been better."

"I thought you might want this back," Q said handing me my cell phone. "It was blowin up so I turned it off."

"Thanks man."

"What's up with her?" Q asked.

"Your guess is as good as mine. I'm sure she's not happy about getting outta bed at two in the morning to get some knuckle head outta jail. I'm not sure where we're going but you best believe my ass is gonna get the book thrown at me," I joked halfheartedly.

"Are your children okay?" Imani inquired.

"Yeah, yeah, yeah, they're fine, my mother has them. I appreciate the concern. Why don't you two get out of here and go get some rest. I know you're exhausted."

"When you leave we leave," Q said.

"I like her," Imani remarked, presumably referring to Kymile. We watched her through a small window pace back and forth in the cold morning air with her cell phone glued to her right ear, her briefcase hanging from the strap on her shoulder and the cup of coffee still in her left hand.

"She's good people. I'm in good hands."

"I hate to break up this little gathering but Myles and I have to get going," Kymile interrupted, sticking her head in the door with a look of impatience on her face.

"Loosen up your balls," Q laughed.

"Come on, man, was that necessary?" I wanted to laugh, but refrained.

"I will when you grow some," Kymile delivered perfectly.

Shockingly, Q didn't offer a comeback. She closed the door and walked off.

"I'ma take Imani to her car. Hit me up when you get in."

I assessed Imani's response and once again she winked at me.

"No doubt, and thanks for everything, man. I really appreciate it."

"Next time you decide to rock-a-bye a muthafucka, holla, ya heard."

Imani side-eyed Q like she used to do back in the day.

"Right," I laughed.

"Now that makes a lot of sense. If both of you imbeciles get in trouble," she pointed at us, "who's gonna look out for the other one?"

"She's got a point there," I contemplated.

"Good lookin ma," Q chimed in.

The fact that he'd slipped up and referenced the pet name he used to call her back in high school created an awkward moment. I saw Imani blush and I hoped she wasn't being sucked back into Q's charismatic web of emptiness.

We walked outside in silence. Imani handed me my jacket and hugged me one last time before climbing in Q's truck through the door he held open for her. The last time I saw my boy open the door for a woman it was his moms. I could tell Imani had unrealistic illusions dancing in her head about who she thought Q had morphed into, but nothing was further from the truth.

I had my own problems to deal with and didn't have time to address anybody else's. Besides, the look on Kymile's face as she sat waiting for me to get in her car said enough.

Fruits of Deception

Mia

"DO YOU WANT me to take this call or not?" Ty asked.

"Please do."

"What's up, India?"

I figured she'd call again. Especially if Ty hadn't returned her call before he came home. Anybody could see that sista girl had an agenda. Ty's innocent act didn't fool me. I smelled a rat. Home girl was a little too persistent for them to have just had a one-night stand. For her to leave the type of message she left on his voicemail meant she felt confident about her position despite what he was telling me.

"Yeah I got your messages. How you been? Cool. How long you gonna be in town?"

Since I was lying on his chest, I heard every word they both said.

"Today won't work, but listen, I do have somebody special I want you to meet if you're not busy tomorrow for lunch?" Ty looked at me for approval and I responded with a half-smile, not sure I wanted to commit to lunch yet, but I continued to keep my ears open.

"Baby, what's your schedule like tomorrow?" he asked kissing me on the forehead.

So he called me baby in front of her, huh? Okay, that restores a few points of credibility.

I heard her ask him if he were positive he was not available today.

"No India, like I said, I'm not available today. Why don't you meet us at Monet's for lunch tomorrow, say noon?" he confirmed without consulting with me.

The chick said something else that I couldn't make out.

"Perfect! See you at noon."

My ego didn't mind the stroke Ty had given it by letting Ms. Thang know she wasn't the only kitty on the block. She had to be wondering who the woman was that had thrown a monkey wrench in her potential goldmine. What I would have given to see the look on her face! I did notice, however, that he never responded to the comment I missed.

"I hope you didn't mind me putting you on the spot like that, baby? I figured the sooner you two met the better."

Ty obviously wanted to let me know that I had nothing to worry about by arranging lunch with missy, and while the gesture gave him a few brownie points, I wasn't ready to openly claim him given my situation.

"Tomorrow might be a problem for me. I have to drive to Connecticut in the morning. I'll probably be there most of the day, but you know I would have told you that had you asked before confirming with her."

"Mia, do you want to meet India or not?" he asked seemingly annoyed.

It never failed. Ty had a way of getting straight to the point. "Truthfully baby, in a way I do and in a way I don't. She's somebody you slept with. I mean, it makes me feel better that you don't have a problem with me meeting her. I just don't know what meeting her will really prove," I lied.

"Sounds a bit dishonest to me, but if you change your mind, let me know."

What exactly does that mean?

"So does that mean you two are going to have lunch anyway?" I asked.

"Why not? I'm confused, Mia. Are you asking me not to be friends with India anymore?"

Duuhhhh! That's exactly what I'm asking you! What about that don't you get? Confused my ass!

I thought I had done a pretty good job of explaining to him why he needed to cut her loose. Now my suspicions crept back in. So much so that my head got that tight feeling signaling the migraine I'd been able to curb earlier might come back with a vengeance. I didn't have my painkillers with me, which meant trouble. The thought made me anxious and I jumped when his private cell phone rang again.

Ty removed it from his pocket and looked at the number.

"Hey Kwame, this better be good," he answered coldly. "I thought we already took care of those details!" He got up, excused himself and began pacing on the other side of the room.

"No, that's not correct! Were you listening to anything I said? Those guys can't use the banquet hall because my guests have it. I understand that. If they don't like the arrangement they're more than welcome to find another establishment to accommodate them! They requested the VIP room, so now it's my problem they overestimated? I don't give a fuck how much business they bring me! I'm not going to let anybody intimidate me with my own shit! I own the motherfucking restaurant, remember! Tell them to take it or leave it!" he yelled.

When Ty got pissed off he paced in circles. If he was agitated, he'd tug on the top of his right earlobe like he was doing now.

"I'll only be another minute, I promise baby," he said muffling the phone.

"Take your time. I'll be upstairs." With the onset of a migraine, the last thing I wanted to hear was an argument. I had never heard Ty raise his voice at Kwame. I walked into his enormous master bedroom full of African artifacts from different parts of the continent, turned the TV on and muted the volume before I lay across his Grand King bed. A throbbing pain began its journey through my right temple and my stomach got queasy. I needed a miracle to happen so that I could get home or I was going to have to create one myself.

Out my peripheral, I saw Ty standing silently in the doorway. He walked over to where I was lying down, sat at the foot of the bed and began massaging both my feet.

"What happened," I asked, my body succumbing to the pleasure.

"I still don't know, but I've got some bad news," he announced digging his thumbs gently in the balls of my feet.

"What now?"

"I have to go back to the restaurant," he treaded lightly. "A pretty significant client is playing bully. I'm not confident Kwame's going to honor my directives for tonight. Do you mind if we go check things out?"

There is a God.

Now I could go home and take my meds.

"Of course I don't mind," I said trying to contain my gratefulness to the gods for interceding. "That's a first. Kwame can run Monet's with his eyes closed. You sure he's okay?" I queried.

"I wish I could say that he was. I am a little concerned, but like I said, I'd feel more comfortable going over there to see for myself. You want to stay here until I get back? I shouldn't be long," he asked. "Haki is on his way with the car. He can zip me there and..."

"No, I need to get home," I interrupted. "I have some work to finish up for my client tomorrow. You're welcome to come by after you've finished," I answered sitting up on the bed.

"You sure? Haki can take you home to get what you need," he appealed.

"Are you serious? All my supplies are at home! I'm not dragging that stuff around like a bag lady! No! You're welcome to come by when you're done. Maybe we can watch a movie, take a bubble bath and relax without all the interruptions. How does that sound?" I teased.

"Mmmmm...that sounds good, baby. Listen, I know you don't want me to continue a friendship with India, and I get your rationale. When I get back we'll talk about it, along with whatever it is that keeps that pretty little head of yours so preoccupied," he said before alternating wet kisses on the inside of my thighs heading north toward the space where men have ventured never to be the same again.

Truthfully, I wanted to make love and forget all the petty shit we were dealing with. I basked in his seductive foreplay anticipating the moment he'd reach my island. I was dripping wet between my legs, but the headache warned me not to prolong its antidote.

Besides, if I was reading between the lines correctly, Ty was telling me he had no plans of cutting India loose. We'd cross that bridge when we got to it. Right now I needed to get home.

"Later, baby. I don't want any more interruptions for that." I kissed his lips.

"Okay."

I grabbed his outstretched hand as he escorted me to my feet. We descended the steps hand in hand without talking, preoccupied with our own thoughts.

Instinctively, I felt like something had changed since he received the second phone call from Kwame. I didn't have the energy to engage him so I ignored the obvious. He guided me to one of the chairs by the door and I sat down. Ty helped me slip into my boots and zipped them up.

"Positive you want to go home, baby? We can finish what we started when I get back."

"We can finish at my house, too."

Ty rarely stayed overnight at my house and I got it. He didn't know if Myles or any other man might show up.

"Here we go!" he laughed. "Why does it always have to be tit for tat with you, little lady!"

The doorman buzzed in to tell him Haki had arrived with the car right before I could respond.

"You ready?" He went over to the intercom and had a brief conversation with Paul. When he was finished, he got my coat and scarf, wrapped my neck with the scarf, helped me slip into my coat and buttoned it for me. Ty picked up his attaché case and cashmere coat.

"After you pretty lady."

Riding down Fifth Avenue I was amazed at how the frigid temperatures didn't seem to deter New Yorkers from shopping. They wrapped up like Eskimos and kept it moving. Being a country girl I would never understand city folk as long as I lived. Here it was Sunday afternoon and the traffic was just as congested as it was during the week.

Neither of us said much during the ride. Ty periodically caressed my leg and smiled at me as I sat curled up close to him gazing out the window at everything and nothing. Consumed by random thoughts, I tried to remain calm so that my head wouldn't get any worse while Haki skillfully maneuvered his way through traffic as if we were invisible.

About twenty-five minutes after leaving Ty's condo we pulled up in front of Monet's. Chris was right there to open the door the minute the limo came to a stop. Ty rolled down the window.

"Hey there Chris, what's up my man?"

"Nothing much, sir! How are you and Ms. Mia?"

"Good my brotha, good. Do me a favor. Take this and give it to Kwame," he said sticking the briefcase out the window. "Ask him to put it on my desk. And tell him I'll be there in a few minutes."

"Yes sir, Mr. Spencer."

I watched Chris delicately take Ty's briefcase from his hands like it was a newborn baby. He took off running but cuddled the briefcase close to his chest.

As we were saying our goodbyes, I thought I saw a woman peek out the main entrance of the restaurant. My head hurt so badly I chalked it up to hallucinations until she stuck her head out a second, then a third time. Immediately, pieces started to fall into place. I surmised that India and Kwame were plotting to get Ty back to Monet's.

"Do you mind if I come in for a minute?"

If Ty had any idea as to what might be transpiring, his reaction to my sudden request to go inside didn't give him away.

"Of course, you okay? I thought you wanted to go home?"

"Yeah, I'm fine, and I do. I should have gone to the bathroom before we left. I don't want to take a chance and get caught in traffic and pee on myself," I joked as a distraction.

Even though the thought of having to see Kwame made my head hurt worse, I was not about to be played. We got out the limo and went in the restaurant through Ty's private entrance. I discreetly scanned the spaces we moved through looking for anything suspicious. When he moved toward the elevators to his penthouse, I grabbed his arm.

"I'm going to go to the one down here. I really gotta go! I'll meet you upstairs." I scurried to the front of the restaurant with Ty on my heels.

"What! Wait a minute," he chuckled. "I'll wait for you out here."

I saw her strutting our way from the front lobby. Without a doubt, I knew it was India. She wore a pair of red tight fitting slacks that accentuated her long legs and shapely body with a white ribbed turtleneck that emphasized her exceptionally large firm breasts. The red Hermes Birkin handbag she boasted on her arm was top of the line. She looked Ethiopian or Somalian, but whatever her nationality, she was very attractive. Her shoulder length brunette hair swayed back and forth in sync with the sway of her curvy hips as she moved in our direction with a big smile on her excessively red lips. Kwame followed closely behind her, sweat pouring from his face; his stunned gaze fixed on Ty.

"Hi Spence, what a surprise! I see my *suggestion* to Kwame worked!" she said proudly.

India tried to hug Ty, but he deflected her advance by placing his hand in front of him. There were two options that explained what was happening…the heifer blackmailed Kwame with something to get Ty back to the restaurant or the two of them were partners in crime.

Soooo, this is India. I had this chick pegged spot on for the gold-digging slut that she was. Either he knew this trick was going to be here and he was playing me or he just got played.

"Come on, Spence! Don't be mad at Kwame! He didn't have a choice. He had to play along, didn't you Kwame?" she asked looking at me.

The plot was thickening. I wanted to grab her by the neck and choke her ass until she couldn't breathe. The bitch had gotten her feelings hurt earlier now she wanted to retaliate.

Ty was cool as a cucumber. "I'm trusting that the two of you realize you're standing in the middle of *my* establishment with *my* patrons. Since you both know a little something about me, you understand the ramifications of any disharmony in my business. That being said…let's go," he stated before leading the way.

Ty did not bother to look back to confirm that we were all following him to wherever he was going. I trailed closely behind him with Kwame following India. I could feel the smirk on her face from behind me but I was ready to show her a thing or two about deception. Ty removed a chair from under a table in the VIP room and I sat down crossing my legs. He stood behind me. India grabbed her a chair and sat right in front of me. Kwame positioned himself in front of the door after closing it behind himself.

"Who wants to go first?" Ty asked bracing himself on the back of my chair.

"I was at my desk," Kwame jumped in, "when India walked in and told me that she was on her way to your house and that she had the keys to let herself in. She told me I either persuade you to come down here or she would…" he took a deep breath, "show up at your apartment and tell you that I've fallen off the wagon."

India turned around to face Kwame and laughed. She clapped her hands vigorously in Kwame's direction. "Ohh! Poor, Kwame! That was very good! If I didn't know any better, I'd almost feel sorry for you."

"India!" Ty roared as he walked toward her. "Are you *sure* you want to play this game?"

Her whole demeanor changed with that one question. All the confidence and self-assuredness her ass walked in with went out the window real quick. She almost looked like a little girl being chastised by her father. Whatever deflated her balloon had to be some heavy shit. I wanted her to bluff so that Ty would divulge it. Cocky ass bitch. A flood of questions ran through my mind. How did she know Kwame had a drinking problem? Did she really have keys to Ty's apartment? Why did she back down with Ty's question?

"I didn't think so. It's unfortunate that you would try to bribe Kwame with something I was already privy to," Ty looked at Kwame to show his disapproval. "I'm very disappointed in you, India. You need to leave the premises. Kwame, see her out and meet me in my office when she's gone."

India's expression could have been the precursor for Ty's funeral. Obviously, there were a whole lot of secrets and innuendos floating around in the room. Unfortunately, I was not going to have the pleasure of finding out what they were. Without another word, home girl uncrossed her legs and got up from her chair. When Ty reached out his hand to escort me up, I made sure to let her know who held the number one position by standing in front of him and wrapping his arms around my waist.

No one could have told me in a million years that Kwame would have played Ty for any reason. The trap proved my gut instinct about him had been right all along. He was a snake whose days were numbered. If any of what had just happened impacted Ty at all, his 'business as usual' attitude didn't give him away.

As much as I would have loved to have stuck around for the Kwame ass kicking party, the circus was taking its toll on my head. If I didn't get home to some medication soon, I'd be on my way to the nearest emergency room.

"How's your head? You don't look too well," Ty noted after guiding me around to face him.

"It's at a nine. I'm not feeling good at all," I said grabbing my head.

"Migraine?"

"Yeah, and it's pretty intense. I gotta get home to take my medication. I forgot to bring it with me."

"I'm sorry you had to be subjected to this bullshit. I promise you that I plan to get to the bottom of things. There are going to be some serious repercussions if I find out Kwame betrayed me," he said sternly.

Ty put his arm around me and speed dialed the limo while we walked back outside. "Mia and I are headed that way. I need you to take her straight home."

"You sure you're going to be okay at home alone?"

"Yes. I'm sure. I hate to say I told you so, but I told you so." I couldn't resist the opportunity to remind him of how I felt about Kwame. "I hope you take this seriously. He's got too much clout not to be one-hundred percent trustworthy," I reminded Ty.

He kissed me on the cheek. "I always listen to what you have to say and your input about Kwame is no different. Call me when you get home, baby," he instructed, kissing me before I got in the car.

"Yes sir."

I settled comfortably in the back of the warm limo waiting for Ty to finish a conversation with Haki. I felt no empathy for Kwame and the wrath of anger he was about to experience.

The nerve of him to set us up like that.

Homeboy had stooped a little lower than I gave him credit. I wondered how much of his part in India's plot was an attempt to try and get me out the picture.

Well if that's the case, Kwame, looks like you might be the one packing. Low down dirty bastard.

India struck me as the type of woman that had the potential to get ugly over a man. Her ass needed to know she'd met her match. I wasn't going to lower my standards and get into a catfight with her, but I wasn't going to take any shit either.

I was about to doze off when I felt my cell phone vibrate in my coat pocket. There were two text messages, one from Daphne, and the other one from a number I didn't recognize.

My heart raced and my hands trembled as I read the message…should I call U MRS ROLLINS? Chick your stupid ass type come/go. BTW Spence is GOOD right? Did he tell U I was a 1 night stand. She interjected a mad face emoji. What I would give to C yo face right now. lol"

India? How the fuck did she get my cell phone number? Unless of course…

The idea that India may have gotten my number from Ty's phone and that she had turned the tables on me intensified my migraine to the point of implosion. I was dumbfounded she'd referred to me as Mrs. Rollins.

Who told her I was married and how much did she know about me?

I got light-headed trying to sort through what had just happened. I felt humiliated, deceived, and foolish. Was Ty playing me like she said? Hadn't Daphne warned me about Ty's lifestyle? Part of me wanted to dismiss India's tirade and chalk her up as a jealous rejected whore, but she had too much personal information. Her text made me wonder what I'd gotten myself into.

The Deeper the Darker

Myles

HALFWAY THROUGH WHAT felt like the ride to hell and being subjected to every sad ass song Teddy P. ever sang made me want to punch a fucking wall. Kymile and I hadn't exchanged one word since leaving the police station. There weren't too many things I hated more than the silent treatment from a woman. I understood her reasons for being angry, but hell, they were all water under the bridge at this point.

I entertained myself by counting the few cars that were whizzing along on the interstate with us in the wee hours of the morning. The entire time we'd been driving her cell phone was ringing like crazy. I asked her if she wanted me to answer it only to be ignored.

I got as comfortable as possible in her two-seater Jaguar that clearly wasn't made for a brother my height. She exercised driver privilege by rolling my window back up when I cracked it to take in some fresh air. I longed for a nice big breakfast with a steak, some eggs, grits and mother's homemade biscuits to replenish my energy.

Kymile didn't give me any indication where we were going. Given her mood I decided not to ask. I reached over beside me to try and push the seat back a little more and she swiftly cocked her head in my direction like I was annoying her.

"I'm wondering when you're going to tell me exactly what happened, Myles?"

I looked at her to make sure she was serious. "Oh we talking now? If I remember correctly, I tried to talk to you several times despite the cold shoulder. I don't know, maybe it's me, but you seem to be awfully pissed off when it's my ass that's on the line."

"Grow the fuck up Myles! You don't think I have a right to be upset?" She rolled her neck and pointed her finger at me…another pet peeve. "You're the one that woke me up at two in the morning to drive an hour and some change to bail your ass out of jail, not the other way around, might I remind you," she blasted at me, taking her eyes off the road way longer than I felt comfortable with.

"On top of that, I'm the one who's trying to fight a damn near impossible battle for you and your children, and this is what you give me to work with? A fight? How old are you? You know better! This is going to risk everything we've worked for over the past few months. All I asked you to do was lay low and you go get into a fight and almost kill a man? Drinking and smoking weed like you're in college again. Do you even want your children, Myles? My God! Because if you don't I have better things to do with my time."

As usual she was right. I didn't even think about how this incident would look in front of a judge. Bad enough I was a man fighting a woman for custody of two children. In my current situation all I could do was eat a big slice of humble pie. "I got a lot going on in my head. The last thing I wanna do is fight with you. I appreciate you bailing me out," I told her sincerely.

"Look Myles, I need you to act like you understand what's at stake. Since this whole ordeal went down with you and Mia I don't recognize you anymore. You're doing some crazy shit, making some fucked up choices. And I get it, but when is enough, enough?" she said with cynicism. "You and Mia are forgetting that you have two children that didn't ask for any of this. They're in the middle watching everything both of you do. What would have happened if you had killed Dre? And mind you let's hope that's not the case. You know what would happen? They would be with their mother right now and you'd be in a jail cell. You would have thrown everything you say you wanted down the drain. The way both of you are acting, I'm questioning if either of you deserve those children. You two have regressed way past some kindergarten bullshit."

Lucky for me I didn't get to see this side of Kymile often. I'm sure the pending custody case and all the hard work she'd put into it had her stressed. This was the worst time for me to be getting in trouble.

"I concede. I'm not too big to admit that I let my temper get the best of me. Even still I'd whoop that motherfucker's ass if I had it to do over again," I said unapologetically.

"I'm not interested in your inability to act like a grown ass man, Myles!" she yelled, hitting the steering wheel and causing the car to swerve a little over into the left lane. "What I am concerned about is your decision to jeopardize your chance of keeping your children." She looked at me again.

"Big deal I'm upset, and yeah I have an attitude, but I'm the one who has to represent you. You can't make my job any harder than it already is."

She had a point.

"You're right," I agreed. "I'm sorry for getting you up at two in the morning, and…"

"How could you have been so stupid? What possessed you to try and kill your own frat brother?" she jumped in before I finished.

"Dre and Mia had an affair," I told her flatly.

"What?"

"You heard me."

"How do you know that?" she asked, her question directed at me with distaste. "I mean, Mia doesn't strike me as the type of person that would cheat," she said, trying to soften the blow.

"Does it matter how I know?" I asked looking at her in disbelief.

"You damn skippy it does! When you have a man in a hospital fighting for his life and you are the one that put him there! You better have a damn good reason *that matters*."

Her reaction wasn't the one I expected given I'd just told her my wife and line brother had fucked. Kymile and I were more than lawyer and client; we were friends. She knew me better than most people I'd known for years.

"Wow, okay. So much for my track record, huh?"

"Fuck the empathy route, Myles! I deal with facts not hypothesis. I repeat…h-o-w d-o y-o-u k-n-o-w t-h-a-t?" she said slowly. "Where did you get the idea that Dre and Mia would even have an affair? Did Dre tell you he had an affair with Mia?"

I didn't have any concrete verification but I didn't have any doubts either. Her line of questioning made me feel like I was the one guilty of something.

"Not directly. The motherfucker didn't come out and admit it when I asked him, but that still doesn't change the fact that he had an affair with my wife."

"That's it! What the fuck! You aren't making any sense at all! Did he say something, anything? What? Did Mia confess? Give me something so that I don't think your ass has gone off the deep end!"

"A man knows when another man has crossed the line on his beach. Whether Dre confessed or not is irrelevant to me. I know the truth."

Kymile vacillated between staring at me and the road. I felt like she was being a little over-the-top about the whole thing. I figured as a lawyer she understood instinct better than anybody. Her livelihood depended on it.

Kymile merged back over to the right lane. "Please tell me you have substantial evidence that Mia was having an affair with Dre other than a gut feeling?"

"That's enough for me. You know I'm not the type of dude that runs around starting fights," I told her exhausted from trying to explain the same 'ole shit over and over.

She sped off the exit ramp, made a quick left and drove down Pennsylvania Avenue toward what I assumed was her office downtown. I didn't understand why she was being so hostile toward me, even though her point about the children was well taken.

"You almost kill a man based on what you're telling me is pure speculation. You can't fathom why that seems a bit far-fetched to me?"

I saw clearly how it could appear ludicrous to someone who might not know me, but Kymile should have known this was out of character for me, and the fact that she didn't pissed me off. Something about her whole disposition didn't sit well with me. "Let me ask you a question. When have you ever known me to act on a whim?" I asked her directly.

"I'll admit that's not your style," she confessed after a long pause.

"Well, if I tell you Dre admitted in so many words that he and Mia violated our marriage why don't you believe me? If you really know me, you know I have a damn good reason to feel the way I do even if I don't have concrete evidence. Check it. Wasn't he the first person to call me and tell me where she was when she left, then turned around and called back to say he saw her a second time?"

"Fucking bastard," I thought I heard Kymile whisper under her breath. She parked the car in front of the large high-rise glass building with blue panes where her office was on the tenth floor.

"Let's go up here and see what we're dealing with," she said after sending a text.

I scrambled out of the car, grateful for the opportunity to stretch my cramped legs. My body was beginning to feel the effects of the hangover and sleep deprivation.

What a way to celebrate a birthday.

"How long do you think this is going to take?" I asked before following her into the building.

"As long as it needs to take. You do remember that Dre is a lawyer, right? And a damn good one I might add. We need to make sure we cover all our bases," she answered, as she swiped her badge and continued to text while walking inside the elevator. Kymile didn't talk to me on the ride up the ten stories to her office. Instead, she maintained her nonstop texting. The high-speed elevator reminded my stomach that it had not fully recovered from the night's abuse.

Entering her huge office overlooking downtown, Kymile flipped on the lights and immediately did a beeline over to her coffee maker to turn it on.

"Make yourself comfortable."

She walked away from the machine only after finishing half of the first cup she'd made. I looked around the familiar dark oak furnished room and zeroed in on four neatly stacked bookshelves. Everything in her office was obsessively in place.

"You want some coffee?"

"No, I'm good." I settled in one of the two leather arm chairs directly in front of her oversized OCD desk. She glided her expensive looking dark brown leather chair out and plopped down in it. Placing her refilled cup of coffee on the edge of her desk, Kymile grabbed a notebook and pen from a top drawer. I noticed it had my name across the top.

"Here's how this is going to go. I want you to give me all the details of what happened early this morning. Everything. Don't leave out a word even if you think it's not important. When I say we're done, I'll call Gary to take you home. Hopefully you'll get some rest when you get there. Alright?"

"Let's do it."

Kymile proceeded to drill me for over an hour. She didn't hold anything back, and at one point I felt like she was getting a little too invasive. I didn't think it was any of her business whether Mia and I were having sex before she left. Her questioning and constant texting was getting on my fucking nerves near the end, and I think she picked up on it. My misery finally ended after five full pages of notes, three cups of black coffee, and two mysterious phone calls that Kymile stepped out of the office to take.

"There. I think that covers everything." She let out a deep sigh. "How you feeling?"

"Like I got a pimp named Tyrone and I need to count the cash on the dresser," I said sarcastically.

Kymile thought that shit was funny for some reason. "I've never known you to be so dramatic, Myles," she said before going back over to the coffee machine.

"I've never known you to play hardball with a friend, so we even."

"Shit, if you think that's hardball you just wait until Tommy gets a piece of your ass! You're going to feel more like you're working for three Tyrone's," she said laughing.

I really didn't know what to say to that, and was glad I didn't have to respond because Kymile's office phone rang.

"That's gotta be Gary," she said walking back to her desk to get it. "Hello? Okay, give him five minutes."

I got up before she had a chance to tell me the driver was downstairs.

"You heading out, too?" I asked concerned about her being in the building by herself.

"No, I have a few phone calls to make. I need to find out if my client is going to be charged with manslaughter."

I remained silent. I'd had enough.

Kymile came out from behind the desk and reached for my hand. "Sorry for earlier. It wasn't personal. I'm just highly disappointed in your actions. Regardless, I'm going to do everything I can to protect your best interests no matter what. Some of your fate depends on Dre's condition. If he recovers and we're looking at emotional damage, not too bad, but if God forbid he has some type of brain damage or something along those lines then we could be dealing with a whole different set of circumstances," she demonstrated by making a circle with her right hand. "Go home, turn off your phones, rest and get up tomorrow morning and go see your babies. I think that'll do you a wealth of good," she smiled.

We embraced. "No need to apologize. If anybody should be eating crow, it's me." I wanted to say more but fatigue had shut down my thought system. "I appreciate you," I told her before kissing her on the cheek and walking out the door to the elevators. I rode the elevator back down to the main lobby.

When I exited the double doors of the building, a mid-height overweight, balding white guy who looked to be in his late sixties jumped out the black Lincoln and opened the back door. I don't know what I expected, but he wasn't it.

"Greetings, Mr. Rollins," he said in a raspy voice. He stretched his hand toward me.

"Myles will do. Nice to meet you," I said shaking his hand.

"Pleased to meet you, brother! The name's Gary," he smiled enthusiastically.

I got in the backseat through the door Gary held open for me and laid my head on the headrest. He gently closed the door before walking back around to the driver's side to get in.

"I take it you know where to?"

"Yes sir. I know exactly where we're going! Relax and leave the driving to me," he stated proudly while looking at me through the rearview mirror.

I fell asleep the second he exited the parking lot and miraculously woke up right when he turned the corner to my block. With the exception of two early morning joggers, one by himself and the other running stride for stride with her 'I dare you to fuck with me' Boerboel, the neighborhood was lifeless. I could feel my body reminding me that it had past the time for my morning run. There was no way that was gonna happen. All I had left was the strength to lift a spoon to my face to eat a bowl of cereal, take a shower and crash.

I thanked Gary with a generous tip before getting out the backseat and all but crawled up my walkway to the front door. The moment I walked in the house sadness greeted me. Since Mia's departure, a cold silence had moved in. One that didn't care if I were comfortable with it or not.

Tossing my keys and cell phone on the island in the kitchen, I could hear Tiffany ask me if I'd washed my hands before gathering what I needed for my cereal. It made me chuckle before going to do it. The children and I were slowly finding an awkward routine. No matter, I knew they missed Mia more than they let on. To create as much normalcy as possible, I let them hangout with my parents on the weekends. Ironically, the conditions that allowed my mother the extra time to spend with them came with bittersweet circumstances.

Sitting at the table eating, I fought hard to keep myself from conjuring up images of Mia and Dre together. His comments weren't by mistake. Man to man we both understood what he was implying. I was the fool. Mia might as well have put a knife through my fucking heart. I had gotten enough confirmation to finally accept that we were over.

Once I'd finished my third bowl of cereal and placed the spoon and bowl in the sink, I sat down on the sofa in front of the TV with the intent of calling Q.

The sound of my neighbor's car alarm going off awakened me an hour later. I got up, grabbed my cell phone, turned it back on and went upstairs to my bedroom. There were five missed calls and two text messages from Q. The text messages demanded that I call him back immediately. Likewise, there were four messages on my answering machine from him along with tons more that I suspected were from people at the party who were calling to check on me.

Before I had a chance to dial Q, my cell rang.

"What's up?"

"Where the fuck you been?"

"I came in and knocked out."

"Got some crazy shit for 'yo ass."

"Please tell me Imani is not there with you," I asked, suddenly remembering they'd left together.

"Yeah and she's suckin my dick."

I didn't know whether to believe him or not.

"Check it," Q preceded without missing a beat. "Imani couldn't sleep 'cause she was worried your punk ass was goin down for fuckin Dre over. She got on the horn and called a homie with connections. She finds out what hospital the bitch at, jumps in her whip and ride out there. When she get there they only lettin the muthafucka's family in. The nurse tells her to chill 'cause his ass got a visitor in the room and maybe she could get a word when they came out, right? Take one muthafuckin guess who comes out?"

"Who?" I asked, thinking he was going to say Mia. I backed into the wall.

"Kymile."

"Kymile?" I repeated.

Kymile? Kymile never told me she was going to the hospital. She said she was going to call around, but she never said she was going to the hospital. Unless of course he got worse...

"Yo trick ass lawyer."

"That shit don't add up. Why would Kymile go see Dre in the hospital?"

Q hurled out a string of obscenities. "Homie Dre been bangin your lawyer," he said bluntly.

"What? They don't know each other," I informed him.

"You gettin soft dawg! Kymile *ain't* family and she ain't his lawyer. Why the fuck would they let the lawyer of the guy who beat down the muthafuckin in his room, son?"

Q was making a valid point. One I didn't want to believe because I couldn't bear any more betrayal.

"According to the chick Imani got the 411 from, Kymile and Dre been kickin it on the low low for the last four or five months. They hooked up at some lawyer's conference in NY and he been hittin it ever since."

Q's words took the air out of me like I'd been hit in the chest by a Tyson punch. Shit was becoming crystal clear real fast: Kymile's response to my suspicion about Mia and Dre, the fact that she didn't initially have shit to say in the car, her wanting to know if they fucked, the back to back phone calls she didn't answer, the comment I thought I heard her say. It all added up. I felt sick to my stomach. As much as I wanted to try and deny what Imani had discovered it explained a whole lot of shit. Q hadn't stopped talking in the background but I unconsciously tuned him out.

"Wait a minute. How did she find all that out?"

"Didn't I tell you she had connections?"

"You trying to tell me that the woman who is going to defend me in a life or death situation is fucking the motherfucker she has to defend me against?" I laughed; an attempt to hide everything I was feeling.

"Jackpot. Seems that faggot been layin pipe all ova 'yo backyard."

"Not the time, dawg."

"He ain't dead. The docs got the bleedin stopped, but I can arrange that for you."

"Nah, man. I need him alive. I'll hit you up later, and tell Imani I said thanks if you talk to her before I do."

"No doubt. Holla if you change your mind."

I disconnected the call and froze with the phone in my hand. The nightmare was getting worse. How the hell was I going to trust Kymile to defend me if she and Dre were fucking? Her allegiance would be compromised. I felt like my world was full of lies and deceit. I was beginning to question my judgment and my ability to read people. Somebody was going to give me some fucking answers once and for all. I dialed Kymile's cell phone on my way downstairs to get my keys.

"Myles?" she inquired.

"You home?"

"Yes, what's up?"

"I'm on my way," I told her and hung up.

Surprise, Surprise

Q

"BLOW WHEN YOU get here," I told Lenzie.

Five freaks a limo all the fuckin liquor a pimp could drank and a Charlie Wilson and Fateema concert. If there was a muth-afucka that had it betta than me he was frontin. Fateema and Lenzie grew up in the same buildin back in Philly. They was homies since second grade. Fateema blew up when she got picked up by Signal Records after hustlin her own joint on the street. Whenever she came through DC her fine sexy ass gave Lenzie tickets to catch her show and hangout backstage. On the real it wasn't a brother's style to roll with a bunch of bitches but Uncle Charlie was my man. I dug his style when he was with the Gap band and Unc still had a tight pimp game.

The limo driver hit the horn right before I snatched my trench out the closet. Back in November the muthafuckin hawk swooped down and landed like we owed her ass somethin. Two months later the bitch still had a grip on our asses.

"What up?" I asked the young cat who stood by the back of the Hummer with the door open.

"It's all good my brother."

"Who you be?"

"Marquis."

"Where you from my man?"

"Chi town," he answered with a nod of his head. "Just moved here a few months ago with the wifey and kids."

"Word."

Any muthafucka rollin my ass around town had to be cleared first. I was familiar with cats who moonlighted as limo drivers 'til they got they weight up and fucked around and crossed ova to another muthafuckas terf. Cool with the setup I got in and sat next to Lenzie. He shut the door and rolled out.

The fuckin Hummer was boss level. The bitch had flat screens and TVs in the headrests, runnin lights in the ceilin, surround sound, a bar and two stripper poles in the middle of the floor. My man Luda was pumpin from the speakers. I caught a whiff of some powerful shit they'd already been smokin.

Lenzie gave up a hug and a peck on the face 'cause she knew a brother didn't put on no show. The other four chicks sat across from us. Stacey was the only one I seen before.

"Q, you know Stacey," she said pointin at home girl on the end. Baby girl held her drink up toward me licked her lips and smiled. She had on a little ass sexy black dress.

"Hi, Q."

"What up, baby."

Me, Stacey and Lenzie had hooked up for a threesome a few weeks after me and Lenzie fucked. Stacey was a red bone with a fat ass a decent rack and a fuckin weave that looked like she let her dogs play with that shit before she put it on her head. She could take a dick and throw her shit back like a pro but her head game was way off.

I was checkin the dangerous curves on the double D chocolate chip chick sittin with her legs crossed next to Stacey with a champagne glass in her hand. She had squeezed a whole lot of junk in a red skintight cat suit. The bitch had curves a blind muthafucka could see. She bit her bottom lip and winked at a brother.

"That's Monika."

"What's up Q?" she purred.

"What's up, baby?" I asked. "I'm feelin dat sexy ass outfit," I told Monika lickin my lips.

"Thank you."

I was pissed at Lenzie for not hookin a brother up with Monika instead of red bone.

"Down, trick!" Lenzie told Monika.

"Anyway, that's my cousin, Queenie, and bestie, Rasheeda." Lenzie pointed at the two chicks next to Monika.

"Hi, Q!" both of them said at the same time.

"What up." The two of them wasn't nothin to write home about. The cousin was a fat chick and the other one looked blank like a piece of bread.

"Damn, Len, you didn't' lie! He fine as shit!" the chubby one said. Her fat ass was squirmin and twistin like she was 'bout to have a orgasm. They all was high as a muthafuckin kite.

"Preciate that baby."

"You 'mo than welcome, d-e-l-i-c-i-o-u-s!"

"Queenie, stay in your lane bitch!" Lenzie told her. "Ya'll some thirsty bitches, okay, but I ain't mad at ya 'cause he is FINE! You do look good, baby," Lenzie moaned after she sat in my lap to get her grind on. She took a sniff on a brothas neck. "Shit! You smell good, too!" The bitch neva wore panties and could come at the drop of a dime so I had to slow her ass down before she came all ova my shit.

Lenzie had a fat ass but it didn't hold a candle to Monika's.

"You might have to share him, girl," chocolate chip told Lenzie. She plucked a fat blunt out her bag and fired it up.

"That's not up to her," I told chocolate chip.

"Ahhhh, hello! Really? How you gonna disrespect me with mines? Stay in 'yo lane heifer!" Lenzie said waving her hands in the air.

I moved her ass off my lap then sat between Stacey and chocolate chip. I took the blunt from her and hit it a few times.

Lenzie jumped up and went to the other end of the Hummer. Like I gave a shit. The bitch musta forgot who she was fuckin with.

"Get this shotgun."

Monika turned and put her thick thighs between mine. The bitch smelled like pussy. She took the blunt turned it backwards and clenched it with her teeth. I gripped her thick thighs then put my mouth on her wet lips and sucked hard while she blew on the blunt. I could tell the bitch wanted to come out her clothes the way her legs was tremblin.

My high set in with two shotguns.

"You good ma?"

"Not quite," she answered lookin down at my shit.

The other chicks laughed.

"You don't wanna fuck with that."

"I can handle mines."

"Ohhhhhhh…"all they asses sang like background singers.

"Monika, enough already," Stacey laughed before taking the joint from chocolate chip and sticking it in her mouth. I did the shotgun between her and Monika a few more times. Lenzie finally bought her sulkin ass out the corner and joined the party. Dranks and blunts was flowin nonstop.

Driver boy put on Jodeci's Freek' n You. The lights on the poles flashed and the limo went dark.

"Ahhhhhhh, shit, that's my song!" red bone hollered. They bum rushed the poles like a bunch of thirsty strippers. Monika worked her shit like a pro starin at a brother the whole time.

By the time we rolled up in front of Union Station all they asses was drunk, high and horny. Young blood opened the door and I let the tricks hop out.

Lenzie peeped Chocolate Chips' game tryna fall back to get out the Hummer in front of me and damn near pushed her ass face first out the fuckin joint.

A cat I used to run with back in the day was runnin thangs at the joint we was gonna grub at. His punk ass fucked around and slapped a dude's sister. Dude and his boys came to handle family business with they uzis and gats. My queen was seein his pops so I did what I do. He asked how high whenever I told his bitch ass to jump.

I followed the chicks through the Station to Catherine's. The fuckin place was crawlin with zombies. We had a VIP table with a personal waiter in front of the house band. My ass had the munchies like a muthafucka. Clarence dropped by the table after the waiter got our orders.

"Q! What up man?"

"Everythang," I said standin to give him some dap.

"You and the lovely ladies straight?"

"We good. Monika, Lenzie, Stacey, Queenie, Rasheeda, this Clarence." They all got a hello in.

"You still got it playa!" Clarence said after kissing the back of all they hands. "Let me know if you need anything, my brother. My staff will take good care of you. Ladies, enjoy!"

"Solid."

My goddamn phone kept vibratin all while we was waitin for appetizers.

"I'll be right back."

"Okay, but hurry back, baby," Lenzie slurred in the middle of taking a sip from her glass of cognac.

I stopped by the coat check and copped my trench to go outside and take a smoke. When I got outside I lit a cigarette took a hit and checked my phone. I had calls from a number with a 201 area code but no messages. I didn't know nobody with a 201 area code. I hit redial to see who the fuck was blowin me up.

"Hello."

"Who dis," I asked.

"Q, is that you?"

"Who dis?"

"Q, it's Mia."

Mia was the last person I expected to be blowin me up.

"What's up?"

"I'm hanging in Q, how about you?"

"I'm straight." I paced to keep warm.

"Are you busy? Do you have a moment to talk?"

"Naw."

"Can you call me back when you get a chance?"

"For?"

"I need to talk to you about Myles."

"About?" I asked takin another drag from my cigarette.

"I miss him, Q. He still won't talk to me and I didn't do this to hurt him. Really I didn't." She started cryin.

Mia and me neva had beef but after findin out she fucked Dre wasn't shit her ho ass could say to me.

"I don't give a shit."

"Please Q, I'm begging you, I need you to hear me out. I don't have anybody else to talk to and I'm asking you to just hear me out, that's all I ask, just hear me out," she begged in between snorts.

"For the record I don't give a fuck 'bout you. I'll hit you back sometime tomorrow."

I hung up from the whinin bitch's call finished my cigarette and dialed Myles.

"Hello."

"I just got a call from your trick."

"Okay? I'm assuming you're referring to Mia? Why is she calling you?"

"Not sure. Don't give a fuck. She was whinin some shit but I wasn't listenin. You interested?"

"Ahhhh, yeah, I guess. I'd be curious to know what she wants."

"I'll hit 'ya back tomorrow."

"Cool, man, and thanks."

I hung up and stuck my phone back in my pocket. I pulled on my cigarette one last time tossed it on the ground and put it out with my shoe. When I got back to the table they was bringin out the food.

"What took you so long, we missed you," Monika asked.

Chocolate Chip wasn't no joke. I liked how she got down. "If you was so worried 'bout a brotha why didn't you come check'em?"

"Cause she know I woulda broke her fucking neck if she had," Lenzie said pointing her knife at Monika. "I'm gonna tell you this for the last time, heifer," Lenzie raised up, "back the fuck off."

Monika smiled and winked at me. "Won't be the first time you shared him," she whispered under her breath.

I laughed.

Everything was on the money. We ate and drank damn near everything on the menu. Lenzie sent limo boy a text when we finished. He had 'bout an hour to jet us across town to the concert. On the way out the chicks went to the bathroom and I shot the breeze with Clarence 'til they got back.

We were headin out the station when I spotted a chick who looked like Torie eye ballin the train schedule.

"Go ahead, I'll catch up," I said walkin away. I strolled closer to be sure the weed and alcohol wasn't playin tricks. They wasn't. I rolled up close on her.

"Waitin for somebody?" I asked over her shoulder.

Her ass damn near jumped across the room. When she turned around she was white as Casper.

"Q! What the hell are you doing here?" she had the fuckin nerve to ask me.

Torie was did up with makeup. She neva put that shit on. I couldn't tell what fit she had on 'cause she was wearin a coat. Her ass was shakin and she kept peepin around all nervous and shit like a ho lookin for her pimp.

"I'm askin the fuckin questions. You waitin for somebody?"

"I am," her bitch ass said with too much fuckin 'tude. She tried to walk off. I snatched her arm. I looked up at the board her ass was studyin and the only train I saw comin in anytime soon was from NY.

"Who you waitin for?"

"Ahhh…if you have to know *my* business, umm…I have a friend coming in on the train and, ahhh…I came to pick *her* up," she said, still lookin around like a fuckin schizoid on crack.

"You're hurting my arm, Q." She tried to free it.

The bitch was singin too many ahhhs and ummms. "Anybody I know?"

"Huh, oh no you don't know *her*. Look Q, I was on my way downstairs to meet my friend, so if you'll excuse me."

She tried to walk off. Soon as I was 'bout to tell her I'd walk with her downstairs I heard a dude call T's name and my dick got hard.

"Torie! Over here!"

I turned around. Dre had a overnight bag on his shoulder. I was decidin if I was gonna twist her neck or cap her ass when I felt a hand tappin me on my shoulder and somebody talkin in my fuckin ear.

Bitch ass Dre turned around and went back down the stairs he'd come up when he saw me.

"Q, we waiting for you. Who the hell is she?" Lenzie asked barely able to stand.

"Go back to the fuckin limo and wait for me." Lenzie cut her eyes at Torie before backin away. Torie didn't try to move again. I smelled her fear and rightfully so.

"You fuckin that muthafucka?" I yelled spit flyin in her face.

"Q, you're hurting my arm! You know better than that! I would never do that to you! I know how you feel about Dre. He called me and asked me to pick him up. I swear!"

"How he get 'yo number bitch?"

"What?"

The trick was gamin.

"Yeah I got 'yo what. You fuckin that dude?" I yelled in her face. Muthafuckas was starin.

"No Q, you know me better than that, I wouldn't do that!"

"Why that muthafucka got a bag and why you tell me you was waitin for a chick?"

Torie tried to get her arm loose and I snapped that shit out the socket. The bitch knew better than to make a scene. I looked around to see if Dre had come back but his punk ass was nowhere in sight. "Move trick." I yanked her ass down the steps he'd gone. The bottom floor of the station was filled with restaurants and I walked up and down both sides pullin the bitch with me. Dre had fuckin bailed. I bought her ass back up the stairs.

"Q, my arm," she whispered.

"Shut the fuck up!"

"Nothing happened I promise. Dre called me and asked me to pick him up from the train station, that's all."

I stopped quick and jerked her ass around snappin her arm back in the socket. She cringed.

"Why he call you?" The ho's body language fessed up. The bitch was lyin and even if she wasn't it didn't matter. She had bought that mutha-fucka too close.

"Move." Torie tried to resist me by standin her ground.

"We can handle this now or later," I told her lettin go of her arm. She caught my drift. Even if she went home and packed all her shit and left tonight I'd find her ass. The trick started cryin. I pushed her in the direction of the limo. When we got outside she hung back. I tapped on the glass and Lenzie got out.

"I got some business to handle."

Lenzie looked at Torie all crazy but the bitch knew betta than to get in my business.

"Okay. I'll leave your name at will call so you'll know where to find us," she said lookin confused. Lenzie took a second look at Torie sucked her teeth and got back in the Hummer.

I shoved Torie back inside. She followed me over to Catherine's. In a muthafucka's head I was going back and forth 'bout snappin her neck crackin her windpipe or blowin her brains out. Neither one of them satisfied me.

"Stay here," I told her.

I walked into Catherine's past the chick at the door through the kitchen into Clarence's office. He was sittin at his desk with his back to me.

"Hand ova 'yo keys," I said slammin the door behind me.

"Say what?" he asked spinning around in his chair.

The look on my face shut all the muthafuckin questions down.

Clarence had a storage room that doubled as a place for him to crash on days he had to pull OT. It was where his punk ass hid out 'til his situation was handled.

"Did I fuckin stutter muthafucka."

"Calm the fuck down, shit!" Clarence jumped up outta his chair and went to a box got the keys and tossed them to me.

"What you gonna do, man?" he asked followin me out the restaurant.

"Q!"

"I'll leave them in there when I'm done."

I snatched Torie's arm and slung her round back of the restaurant with Clarence right behind me.

"Don't your crazy muthafuckin ass kill that white bitch and leave her body on me!"

"Fuck you."

"Yo, Q, I'm for real!"

I didn't answer.

I pushed Torie in the dark ass room and locked the door. I slapped her with the back of my hand and heard her ass knock over some boxes before she hit the floor. Torie had a ninety-nine percent chance of being a homicide. Her fear made me horny.

"Get up and take 'yo shit off."

I flipped on the lights and took off my shirt.

"Get the fuck up!"

"Q, please don't do this, I'm begging you, please don't."

Her pale ass got up and did what she was told then balled up like a baby in one of the corners of the futon. She wasn't dressed to meet no chick.

"Did you fuck him?"

"No Q, I swear! I swear I didn't!" she cried.

I leaned over her. "Did he ever touch you? And before you answer you better think hard."

She was mute for too fuckin long.

"What do you mean? That's not fair, Q, and you know it!"

"You think you a big dawg bitch. You think you a big dawg right?"

"Q, please, don't do this, please!" she begged grabbin hold of my arms.

The more she begged the more that shit turned me on. I slapped her hands away.

"You a big dawg right bitch?" I screamed in her face.

"He never touched me the way you're trying to make it seem Q."

I wasn't interested in hearin her ass talk no more. It didn't matter 'cause she didn't matter. I picked her naked ass up by the throat and dragged her offa the futon. She was gaspin and scramblin for air so I choked her harder. She didn't have the strength to fight back. I pushed her down on the floor in front of my dick. I took a jimmie out my pocket and bit the wrapper open unbuckled my pants and dropped them and my boxers to my ankles.

"Suck my dick bitch."

"Q, please don't…"

I grabbed her by the throat and raised her ass up off the floor like I was wringin a chickens neck. She gurgled and tried to get at my hand. I considered finishin her off.

"Shut the fuck up and do what I said!" I shoved her pale ass back on the floor.

She took my shit in her mouth and I grabbed the back of her fuckin head and rammed it down her throat to where I could feel the back. I kept rammin my shit down her throat until she passed out. I sat on the back of the futon lit a cigarette and waited for her to come to.

"Do it again," I told her.

Torie got back on her knees and took my shit in her mouth like I told her. I grabbed the back of her head and pumped my shit down her throat until I came.

"You a bad bitch huh? A muthafuckin big dog bitch!" I taunted her. "You big enuf to gun for me huh?"

I slung her ass on the futon by her hair and bent her ova the arm. I pressed my forearm in her back then strapped up and shoved my shit up in her dry ass. I put my other hand over her mouth. The whole time I was breakin her back open she was tryna get away. Torie was a fuckin poodle in a starvin Rottweiler's jaws. I busted a nut up her ass twice and when I was done I shoved her useless ass down on the floor. If that muthafucka had fucked her ass I wasn't goin up behind his punk ass.

"Get dressed," I ordered standin by the door. I lit a cigarette. I could tell her ass was burnin by how slow she was movin.

"Check it," I said, puttin my shit back on. "Since you think you got game, you got next bitch and you betta come hard." Under the roar of the trains I could hear her whinin. The bitch had crossed the line into my world. There was no rules in that shit.

"Hurry the fuck up!" I yelled at her stupid ass.

I grabbed her face and squeezed 'til her jaws was meetin.

"I'm comin through later so keep the chain off the door, ya heard."

"Yes."

She looked like shit.

"Where's yo fuckin ride."

"In the garage."

I opened the door and the trick followed me. "Go ahead." We walked to where she parked her car. When we got there I waited for her to open the door and get in. I held the door open and bent down.

"Stay woke," I said slammin her door. I watched her back up and pull off down the ramp her tires screamin round the curve. If she was smart the bitch would go home and slit her wrists.

I lit a cigarette and went upstairs to the street. A line of taxis was parked outside the station so I hopped in one and headed to the concert.

I figured the show had started by now. The taxi got me there in 'bout twenty minutes. I gave my name to the slim momie behind the booth. She walked to the front where Lenzie and the other females was shakin her ass for a brotha. Before I sat down she slipped me her digits.

I got there while Fateema was doin her thang. The chick could blow. Unc followed her and shut it down. He ran through all the classic 'ole jams.

After the show we bounced backstage behind Fateemas swole body-guard. Groupies and everybody who thought they ass was somebody was crowdin the fuckin hallway tryna get a peep at Unc or Fateema. Big boy knocked on a door and somebody yelled for us to come in.

"Len!" Fateema screamed runnin over to hug her. They kissed in the mouth.

"Hey Momma, you put it down out there! You still got it just like back in the day, baby girl!"

"Stop it! You know I'm only doing what I love! You guys were the best audience ever!" They hugged again and then showed us some love. "Okay, I know Queenie and Sheeda, but you gonna have to introduce me to the fine brotha and those two beautiful sisters!" she said huggin the two chicks she knew.

"Well," she said standin by me. "The fine brotha is mine." She looked at Monika. "Q, Fateema, Teema, Q."

"Ummm…so this is Q." Teema sized me up. "Girl, you didn't lie, brotha is fine!"

Baby girl was thicker than she looked on TV. "You did your thang out there. That fuckin chair gone need a shower." We hugged.

"Ohhhh Len, I like this one, he's smooth!"

"I know. He might be a keeper if he act right. That's Monika and Stacey," she said flippin her hands at them. They hugged. Chocolate chip slipped me the digits on the low while we sat around shootin the shit. People was comin in and out the room brown nosin. Fateema had to jet so we didn't hang out long.

Lenzie hit up Marquis to tell him we was comin down. She and Fateema said they goodbyes before we left. The limo was waitin when we got outside. Monika didn't waste no time pickin up where she left off. She got in the limo in front of me makin sure I got a good view of her fat ass. Lenzie instructed the driver to take the long way home and we all got wasted again. The tricks was fiendin to get freaky.

I told boss man to drop me off first. Lenzie tried to talk me into lettin her come in but I told her ass to go home. I gave each of the ladies a peck on the cheek. Monika whispered for me to call her.

It was two-thirty when I got to T's house. She had left a light on like she usually do when I came through. I opened the door went inside plopped down on the couch and pulled my shoes off. I headed up the stairs to her bedroom and went in.

I took a shower and got in the bed. She was naked. After tonight I never wanted to see the bitch again. I hadn't decided if one of my boys was gonna make that happen.

Emotionally Drained

Myles

HAPPY NEW YEAR to me.
What a way to start things off, man! Four weeks after ringing in a New Year, you're sitting in a courtroom waiting to see if your heart is about to be ripped out through your throat.

The judge's deliberation lasted one week. Kymile wouldn't tell me if that meant good news or bad news. As much as I was trying to stay optimistic, my gut felt the latter. Waiting for the judge to exit her chambers was what I imagined it felt like waiting to be strapped in the electric chair.

Mia's henchman had managed to get the judge to approve a temporary visitation order for her to see the children over the Christmas holiday. Now, we were back in the courtroom for the verdict sooner than Kymile predicted. Something told me I was about to be dealt a devastating blow.

Shit was getting crazy. Anybody who thought for a minute that divorce didn't bring out the worse in people could not have gone through one. When Mia showed up at my parent's house on Christmas Day, I couldn't bring myself to be in the same room with her. Not even for my babies. Tiff and Brandon's only wish for Christmas was to see their mother. I was happy it came true, but I didn't have shit to say to her that would have been suitable for my children to hear. To avoid a spectacle, the kids and I opened our gifts early that morning and I broke out before she got there. I spent the rest of the day drunk as a fucking skunk. Mother didn't say a word about my decision to skip out. The asshole who referred to himself as my father took the opportunity to tell me how childish he thought I was being. Like I suddenly gave a shit what he thought.

The constant on again off again tap, tap tapping of Kymile's pen on the long wood desk where we sat side by side in the courtroom with rows of papers neatly stacked in perfect order was getting on my nerves and making me jumpy. Bad enough I hadn't slept the past four days. Every time I thought she'd quit, it would begin again - tap, tap, tap, tap, tap, tap.

My relationship with Kymile shifted to an awkward space after I confronted her about Dre. She still hadn't admitted to sleeping with him. Her way out of disclosing anything was to insist that her professional and personal lives were separate. Normally I might agree, but this shit right here represented extenuating circumstances. She could spit that mumbo jumbo protocol bullshit all she wanted, but from my perspective, her personal and professional lives had collided in my lane. I had too much at stake for secrets.

When I approached her about visiting Dre at the hospital things got heated. She kept wanting to know how I was privy to so much info. The lawyer in her felt outsmarted. I didn't give up my source and for a while we both held our positions. Kymile went all intellectual on me, but I assured her that she was my lawyer because of her track record not because of the degrees she had on her wall. When her soapbox speech was done, she reluctantly admitted to understanding how I *might* feel like both my cases could be compromised. However, her ego had to get a jab in by reminding me that Dre's near death experience was entirely on me.

At the end of the conversation, Kymile advised me that I had to either trust her or not. The decision was mine. She suggested that I take a few days to think it over.

Bottom line, I had to trust that she wouldn't take the opportunity to seek revenge on Dre and Mia at my expense. After a lot of thought and little sleep, I went with what I knew about Kymile. She was a hell of an attorney that knew me better than anybody outside of my family and Q. Kymile was a beast in the courtroom. More importantly, her professional etiquette gave her the edge in and out the courtroom. Equally as important, I didn't have time to secure a new lawyer in the middle of all the shit I had going on even if I wanted to. We eventually reached an amicable agreement but the damage was done.

Now that it looked like the cards were stacking against me, I was beginning to second-guess my decision to stay with her.

Out my peripheral I could feel Mia staring in my direction from where she sat on the opposite side of the courtroom. What she had to say to me at this point or whatever she was feeling had no relevance to me at all. The only thing left to settle was the matter of our children. The same children she walked out on and now was trying to convince everybody she wanted back.

Besides, she'd clearly moved on. Kymile briefed me on all the sordid details that were going to come out months before I had to sit through hearing them. I don't know how she thought traipsing around with another dude a month after she left me and the kids wouldn't come to light. I wondered what kind of man would be okay with funding a married woman's attempt to take her children from their father. The motherfucker must not have any kids of his own.

During the hearings, Kymile instructed me that under no circumstances was I to talk to Mia. I pretended that suited me just fine, but secretly I wanted to understand why she walked away from us. Why she didn't feel like she could talk to me. In my quiet moments, I questioned who the hell I had been married to for nine years. All the shit I'd endured over the past six months was slowly breaking a brother down. I didn't know if I could take anymore. The thought of her sleeping with Dre and a new dude cut deep.

We both kept our families and friends away from the courtroom for different reasons. I'm sure Mia didn't want the people she had worn a mask for all these years to see that her innocent girl character was all a facade. I talked Q and mother into staying away because Q was a loose cannon and I didn't want mother to feel like she had to take sides.

Without warning Kymile's pencil stopped tapping. She sat straight up in her seat like a dog sensing his master coming down the road miles off. She looked toward the judge's chambers and then rapidly over at me.

"Here we go," she whispered.

I leaned closer to her. "What?" I asked perplexed.

"The judge, she's on her way out," she said trance-like, staring in the direction of the chambers.

Of all the things I'd learned about Kymile, her instinct and intuition in a courtroom were weapons of mass destruction. They were unequivocally keen. It was the edge that set her apart from other lawyers. Regardless of what I thought about her personal choices, home girls ability to handle herself in the courtroom commanded respect.

I trusted her when she pleaded with me not to have any contact with Dre after he got out of the hospital even though the brazen bastard was calling me. Kymile convinced me to stay calm and promised she would get him to drop the charges against me but I couldn't do anything to blow it.

I listened because to tell the truth I didn't have a choice. Eventually, the fucking punk agreed to a deal. Kymile and his dirt bag lawyer settled on a payoff that included medical expenses and lost wages. In exchange, he agreed to drop the charges. After that my faith in her was fifty percent restored. With that in mind, when Kymile said the judge was on her way out, I believed her.

My heart began an unnerving overdrive pace. I broke out in a cold sweat and my mouth dried up like I'd eaten cotton balls. Kymile began sweeping up the stacks of papers on the desk. I wanted to grab her hands and hold them still.

Sure enough, less than forty-five seconds after her prophecy, the bailiff ordered us to stand. The judge's chamber door swung open and the full-sized dark-skinned woman with excessively red lips and a mini afro dressed in a black robe emerged. The judge acknowledged us with a quick glance and a half smile before taking the bench. Mia gave one last desperate attempt to get my attention. I ignored her.

With the bailiff's orders everybody sat down. I had no clue what was about to happen, but if the energy Kymile gave off was any indication it didn't feel good. I thought about mother's plea for me to stay open to the possibility that Mia could be given custody and take the children to New Jersey and my heart dropped.

"All parties in the matter of Rollins vs. Rollins, please stand," the tall, buffed bailiff ordered.

I comprehended his words but my legs weren't cooperating. The two times I tried to stand on my own left me fastened to my seat. Kymile didn't even look at me; she just reached down, lugged me up and held onto my arm until I got my balance.

The sound of my heartbeat thumping in my ears grew louder and louder to the point it began to muffle out the judge's words. Between thumps, I'd make out a word or phrase… "I order…the children… Tiffany… their mother… the two of you… for the sake of the children…"

The more I tried to focus on what she was saying the more my brain zoned out and my heart raced. Everything began to get blurry and my head pounded so hard it felt like somebody had taken a sledgehammer to it. I bent down to lean on the table hoping it'd keep me from passing out.

Deep breaths, bruh, deep breaths.

I don't know when she had leaned into me, but I suddenly realized Kymile's body was supporting mine to keep me from hitting the floor.

Through a haze, I saw the judge raise her arm and bring down the gavel creating a sound so loud it shook the courtroom.

"You alright, Myles?" Kymile questioned. "Sit down and drink this." She guided me to my chair and shoved a glass of water to my mouth. I took a few sips, cupping her hands as she held onto the glass.

"My head feels like it's going to explode."

"Take a few deep breaths and relax," she instructed.

It took a moment, but eventually the room stopped spinning and the sprinter's pace of my heart slowed down with each breath I inhaled. The look in Kymile's eyes caught my attention.

"What's going on?" I asked, trying to decipher the bewildered and dazed look on her face.

I glanced over and saw Mia and her lawyer embracing and smiling; I got nauseous. I turned back around to face Kymile, looking for answers.

"Do you want to go out in the hall and talk," she asked as if reading my mind.

"No, dammit! I want to know what's going on!"

"Did you hear any of what the judge said?" she asked as if she were talking to a five-year old.

"Kymile, what the fuck happened!"

"Myles, you need to remember that you are still in a courtroom so I suggest you keep your voice down and watch your language," she demanded in a stern hushed tone.

Based on her reaction and the elation coming from Mia's camp it didn't take a rocket scientist to figure out that things hadn't gone in my favor.

Kymile stared me directly in the eye, her trademark for cutting to the chase. "To tell you the truth Myles, I don't know what just happened. I'm flabbergasted. Judge Freeman is known for being one of the fairest judges in cases like this, especially when it comes to children, that's one of the reasons why I felt confident going with her. She's never compromised her standards, which is why this is even more confusing."

"Oh my God, What!"

"I'm sorry Myles, this is bullshit," Kymile concluded, slamming the table with her hand. She let out a deep slow sigh. "In layman's terms, despite all the evidence we presented, the judge seems to believe that it's in the best interest of the children to be with their mother in NJ. She's ordered that you retain custody of Tiffany and Brandon until the first week in July. Mia gets weekend visitation until then. You get the children during the summer months of July and August starting next year. Basically, Mia was given full custody. Myles I'm so sorry."

Her words weren't registering with me at all. My mind had no way of accepting the idea of being without my children. Somebody made a mistake. I wanted to talk to the judge but she had already left the bench.

"Exactly what does that mean, Kymile?"

"That means Tiffany and Brandon finish out the school year here in Maryland with you and the first week in July you take them to New Jersey, or Mia picks them up, whichever. For some strange reason the judge stipulated that the case be re-evaluated by the court in one year," she added, almost talking to herself. "Very rarely does a judge do that in these kinds of cases. There must have been something that she thinks is going to change."

"You've got to be bullshitting me! How do I stop this! There has to be something I can do! I can't just let her take my children like that! She walked out on them. Doesn't that count for something?" I shouted, jumping up from my chair, knocking it over and pointing at Mia.

"What about an appeal, can't I appeal? What do we have to do to appeal this, Kymile?"

"Calm down Myles, you don't want to make matters worse for yourself. We can't appeal, remember? We mediated that option out at the onset of the hearing."

"Yeah, well maybe now's the time to tell everybody she's a whore!" I announced. "Maybe it wasn't a good idea to leave that out after all!"

"Myles! I'm going to need you to calm down before you're held in contempt!"

No sooner had she gotten those words out of her mouth, I barreled across the floor heading for Mia. I could hear Kymile's chair hit the floor.

"It'll be over my dead body before I let you take my babies from me you slut! You walked out and took everything! You did that shit not me! I hope you don't think this is finished!" I shouted up in her face; saliva flying out my mouth in every direction. I was livid.

Her lawyer attempted to intervene playing right into my hands because I desperately wanted a piece of his lowlife ass. Before I could swing on him, the bailiff caught my hand with a strong hold, shoved my arm up behind my back and forced me out the room. I didn't struggle because my beef wasn't with him.

"Not in my courtroom, brotha. You gotta take that outta here," he growled after letting go of my arm.

Kymile wedged herself between us and with her eyes spoke to the deranged man that I'd become.

"We're leaving. I apologize sir. Let's go. Right now!" she yelled while pointing at me like a mother whose last nerve had been plucked.

I didn't appreciate her raising her voice at me. She dragged me back down the dimly lit corridor we'd come up, her heels clicking on the cement floor and out a revolving door into the street. With her hands on her waist, she began walking in circles on the sidewalk. I was numb. I wanted somebody to tell me this wasn't happening. Kymile's body was trembling from either being cold or pissed the fuck off.

"So now you think it was a good idea not to bring up an affair!" I screamed at the top of my lungs. "I lost my reason for living in there just now, Kymile! Maybe that one piece of information would have made all the difference!"

"And where's the proof, Myles? How were you going to substantiate it? We just can't drop circumstantial evidence without something to stand on. You know that! Despite your conviction, we don't have an admission from either of them that they slept together. Have you ever accused Mia of cheating before? Have you ever had a reason to suspect she was cheating? We based our case on abandonment. That's the concrete foundation we had. I don't just go dragging cats, dogs and flying monkeys into my case without a reason for them being there and I'm not going to start now!"

"Circumstantial! Fucking for real, Kymile? You're gonna keep acting like we both don't know the truth?"

"Listen Myles, I don't come to your practice and tell you how to do your job, do I? No, I don't! How about you give me the same fucking respect!" We both paced around each other and she began again. "When did you start settling shit with fights, Myles?" she asked rhetorically. "Granted, I know this situation is all fucked up no matter how you slice it, but damn! Why are you trying to make it worse for yourself? Mia's lawyer built his whole case around you and your temper and the danger it might *eventually* pose to your children, which the judge obviously bought, and you decide to prove her right! Don't you see, Myles? At some point you've got to stop blaming other people and accept where you are. *You* almost killed a man by banging his head into the pavement. Now you go after a total stranger because you're full of jealously, rage and anger. Where does it stop? Hell yeah, you have a right to be angry! Hell yeah, you've been deceived, played, whatever you want to call it, but at some point you've got to decide to move on, let it go. Not for Mia, your children or anybody else, but for you Myles, for you."

Kymile sounded physically worn out. I could relate. Her slumped over posture said it all as she walked up the steps and back into the building. I stood there for a moment hoping I'd wake up from this nightmare. Nobody had a clue what I had just gone through. Easy for her to tell me what I needed to do. She could kiss my ass. My children were my world. They were just beginning to try and move past the chaos Mia had caused them when she left, now she wanted to turn their lives upside down again. For what? To prove a point? How was she gonna explain another man to them? If Kymile didn't understand that, then fuck her, too.

We drove to my parent's house in silence; something we'd come accustomed to amidst all the secrets and lies that were separating us. How was I gonna break the news to the children? How was I gonna tell them that they were moving to some foreign state far away from me and their extended family?

"Weekend custody and summer months," I repeated audibly. "What the hell was that supposed to mean and why didn't she get weekend custody? What am I supposed to do, drive up to NJ every weekend and keep my children in a hotel room to visit with them? What kind of sense does that make?" I questioned aloud. Kymile glanced at me but turned and looked away.

Perplexed, I stared out the window wondering what the hell I was going to do without my children. I had never been without them and couldn't fathom not having them with me. The very thought had me contemplating some crazy shit.

After what seemed like an eternity, Kymile pulled up in front of my parent's home. She didn't look at me but continued to look straight ahead. She didn't cut the engine.

"Do you want to come in?" I asked, hoping she'd say no.

"I think you'd better go in alone. If I come in it might look suspect, you know. Tell your parents I send my love though."

"Sure."

I felt like we both wanted to say more but the words weren't readily available to either of us. Instead, I turned to look out the window and noticed mom and dad had new neighbors across the street. Somebody had moved into the Finch's house. Mr. and Mrs. Finch lived across the street from my parents for over forty years. After Mrs. Finch passed away five years ago, Mr. Finch was never the same. They didn't have any children and both of them outlived their siblings. Mother and the ladies in her church had taken up looking after him. They did his grocery shopping, got his prescriptions filled, took him to church, to the doctor or wherever he needed to go. Two years ago he passed away leaving the house to a distant cousin who put it on the market for sale. It looked strange to see somebody else's touch on the house. I wondered how long it'd been occupied.

"Kymile, I appreciate…"

"That's not necessary Myles. I'm just sorry things went the way they did. I hope you know I did everything I could for you to be victorious. As much as I hate to admit it, unfortunately, even in the judicial system things aren't always cut and dry."

"Tell me about it."

"I apologize for yelling at you back there. I know the decision was difficult to swallow. Believe it or not it was for me as well."

"No need to apologize."

We both turned our heads and looked at each other at the same time and the mutual respect hadn't gone anywhere. I had no right to judge Kymile. How she chose to live her personal life was her choice.

"Myles, there's something I've been wanting to say to you," she said, cutting the engine and turning her body toward me. "I lost a many a night's sleep pondering whether I should move forward as your counsel in this custody battle. Part of me wanted to bail out mainly because it was important to me that you got the best representation possible, but I knew that could only be me. I don't mean to sound cocky, I simply mean it to say nobody could have done a better job in there for you but me. I hope you trust that."

I could tell Kymile's words were heartfelt. I didn't need the tears she was fighting hard to hold back to prove it. I trusted she did everything in her power to fight for us.

"I appreciate your saying that Kymile, I really do. Why this all went down the way it did I don't know, but I have to believe that in the end it'll all work out one way or another, that's all I've got to hold onto. I just know I can't give up on my children."

"Have you ever considered the idea that sharing Tiffany and Brandon with their mother doesn't mean you're giving up on them? Quite the contrary in my book. It makes you the better man. Look, I'm not here to defend Mia, but she left your children with you. She didn't abandon them with a stranger, she left them with their father. What better place could they be? She could have taken them with her. Maybe she planned to talk to you about a fair and equitable arrangement…remember we filed for full custody, not her. Maybe we forced her hand?"

Her observation was the first time I saw it from that viewpoint. There was never an excuse for Mia to have left our children in the first place, but if she did have to leave them with someone what better person than me. Maybe her plan was to figure out a way we could work together.

"Thanks for that perspective, Kymile. It takes the sting down a notch," I admitted with a slight smile.

"You're welcome, my friend." We gave each other a hug. "Don't hesitate to call me if you need anything, my door is always open. And Myles, listen," she grinned. "Try and have faith in the process. Don't let other people turn you into somebody you're not. Sometimes life just isn't fair, but that don't make it stop. It goes on. We gotta find a way to keep it moving or we get stuck."

"I'll try to remember that." Her advice was all over the place, and I couldn't help but wonder if she were talking to herself. We hugged one last time before I stepped out the Jaguar onto the curb. She fired up the engine and drove off down the street as I waved goodbye.

I felt mother's presence standing in her favorite spot in the window where she had more than likely been watching Kymile and me the entire time. I sat down on the bottom step to gather myself before going inside to answer the bombardment of spoken and unspoken questions both mother and my sperm donor would have. I was grateful the children were in school. I didn't doubt for a second that mother intuitively predicted the outcome, and I found myself wondering what else she knew about the way this entire mess would end up.

My life was falling apart at the seams. A cloud of funk settled over me.

In the middle of my pity party, I spotted a timid looking, chunky, light-skinned boy of about eleven or twelve bounce out of Mr. Finch's house. He went running down the street with a football in his hand and I wondered why he wasn't in school. He didn't have on a jacket and was underdressed for the weather in a pair of jeans and a thin red short-sleeved shirt. My preoccupation with Mia and this case had been an obsession for way too long. It worried me that all the times I'd come by my parents' home I didn't notice that someone had moved into a house directly across the street.

I heard the door open behind me and looked up to see mother coming out the house bundled up from head to toe. I jumped to my feet to escort her down the steps. We both sat on the cold concrete steps. She nuzzled next to me, placed her arm around my shoulder and planted a kiss on my cheek. We sat in silence watching cars pass by.

"When did somebody move into Mr. Finch's house," I asked, purposefully starting the conversation with something other than the details of the hearing.

"A woman and that 'lil boy just went running up the street a minute ago moved in been 'bout two months I'd say. They pretty much keep to they selves most of the time. I don't think she got a husband, at least I ain't seen none," mother interjected. "Tillie said she a nurse. Said she was a divorcee but I don't believe much of what Tillie say," mother laughed.

"Yeah, well you know Ms. Tillie. She knows everybody's business but her own."

Mother nodded her head at my last comment. "I'm surprised she let him out 'cause most of the time he cooped up in that house under her. I don't even think she got him in school yet."

"Have you been over there to introduce yourself?"

"You knows I did. When they first moved in…and baby I hope you don't mind me saying this, but she remind me of April."

The mention of April's name gave me that bottomless pit feeling.

April and I dated on and off throughout my four years of college. When I was ready to take it to the next level, she wasn't and vice versa. We hooked back up while I was in grad school and I proposed to her, but she was already involved with someone else.

"Are you serious?" I asked looking over at her.

"As I can be. I went over there with one of my peach cobblers and knocked on that door for about ten minutes. I knew she was in there 'cause I seen her go in. When she finally opened the door she stood in it peeking through a tiny little crack talking to me," mother demonstrated the size of the crack with two of her fingers. Her names Veronica and that lil' boy of hers named Brooklyn. Anyway, she took the cobbler, mumbled thank you and darn near closed the door in my face."

"Huh, interesting," I noted. I was grateful for the few moments my mind was preoccupied with something other than what I'd just experienced. Mother gently rubbed my back as we watched Mr. Finch's house.

Sitting there with her, I begged the gods to never birth the day when

I'd have to find out what it would be like to be without my mother. Being in her presence always held an air of calm no matter how dark a situation appeared. She had a way of trusting something beyond herself that I didn't understand.

Right as I was getting ready to go into the day's events, the front door of Mr. Finch's old house swung open and a frantic looking woman stood clinging to the doorknob. She pivoted her head left and right several times before running out onto the sidewalk in front of the house. Mother wasn't kidding; she looked like she could have been April's twin! Although she was a tad bit thicker than April and had locs, their facial features and complexions were the same. They were even the same height.

"She must be looking for that boy a her's," mother whispered as if she might hear her.

Driven by my fatherly impulse, I leaped from the steps, ran blindly across the street and barely missed getting hit by an oncoming car whose driver frantically blew the horn as it skidded around me. Before I got to her side of the street she had already taken off in the direction of the park. I caught up with her just as she was about to cross an adjacent street.

"Excuse me, are you looking for a young man about eleven or twelve so high?" I asked while attempting to approximate his height from the ground with my hand slightly below my waist. Only another parent could sense the fear that emanated from her spirit. Despite an effort to hide her panic she was shaking.

"And you are?" she asked looking at me with suspicion.

"I'm sorry, my name is Myles. Myles Rollins. My mother and father are Mr. & Mrs. Rollins and they live across the street." I pointed to my parents house.

"Oh yes, I've met your mother," she said trying to conceal her anxiety. "My son, he's gone from the house and I don't know where he is." Her voice quivered with each word she spoke.

"I saw a young man come out of your house about five minutes ago with a football. He headed down the street toward the park over there," I told her pointing up the street. "I'll be happy to go with you to look for him."

Other than Tiffany and Brandon asking me about their mother, I can't remember anyone piercing my soul so deeply with a stare. I suspected that for whatever reason she didn't trust easily. Her spirit reeked fear, distrust and worry.

"Thank you, that won't be necessary. I think I can find it." She lowered her eyes and walked off.

What just happened I wasn't sure, but as I watched her turn the corner toward the park, I had no question about what had awakened in me. It was something I hadn't experienced in a minute and it made me nervous and excited at the same time. I wanted to follow her but decided that might be a little creepy. Instead, I walked back to my parent's house realizing she'd suspended thoughts of Mia in my head for those few seconds.

Will the Real Truth Please Step Forward

Mia

MIA, YOU CAN'T *do this, you just can't,* I told myself for the third time in five minutes, tapping the steering wheel with my thumb. I knew I shouldn't be doing it, but driving with my nose damn near up against the windshield down the lonely pitch black, two-lane road to the hotel, I had already made up my mind to follow through because I didn't have much of a choice.

I had no business letting Dre talk me into meeting him at two o'clock in the morning at some out the way hotel for reasons he refused to divulge. Twice, I'd pulled over on the side of the road to turn around trying to convince myself that I wasn't going to be bullied by Dre, but the fear of him threatening to ruin my life with the sordid details of our affair and God knows what else drove me forward.

I held my breath throughout the entire hearing waiting for the shoe to drop, but it never did. The only conclusion I could come to as to why Kymile didn't bring up the affair is because she didn't have anything tangible the way she did about Ty and me. Now Dre was threatening to give Myles the dirt he needed that could allow him to take my children away.

Not gonna happen, buddy. I've only got two more months before I have my babies with me, and I'm not going to let you or anybody else blow that for me.

Sleeping with Dre had cost me enough. I wanted the memory and him to go away. For my own sanity the time had come to be honest with

Myles. The longer I tried to act like I hadn't betrayed my husband the longer I set myself up to be Dre's puppet.

Up ahead I could see the sign for the sleazy hotel, "Town House Hotel." The knot in my stomach tightened. I pulled off the road into the half-empty gravel lot and found a parking space between Dre's BMW and a grey Toyota Corolla. My life was unraveling like a cat playing with a ball of yarn and I felt out of control.

Thankful I'd tossed my purse in the trunk before I left home; I read the room number from the piece of paper lying in the passenger's seat.

Room 215. May 21st.

I wondered if that room number were some kind of omen because it was the same date as Ty's birthday which was two weeks away on the 21st of May.

Straight ahead up a flight of concrete steps on a green door in desperate need of a paint job, I spotted the number 215. The room was dimly lit and the curtains were fully drawn. It looked dirty and creepy. My face began to itch and I knew if I didn't calm down I'd break out in hives. Ignoring the urge to scratch my face, I exited my car and looked around cautiously then ran up the stairs as fast as I could. I wore a sweat suit and my sneakers just in case I had to make a quick exit.

Why did I let Dre talk me into this shit!

I stood in front of the door and just as I held my hand up to knock it squeaked open.

"Come in and close the door," I heard Dre command from somewhere in the room. I didn't see him but I could smell his cologne. Looking around one last time, I reluctantly stepped inside. The pit of my stomach churned and my instinct instructed me to get the fuck out of there, but I couldn't move. My feet felt cemented to the floor.

"Mia, close the damn door!" he demanded again.

"Now is it necessary for you to yell at a lady like that," a voice I recognized chastised from behind me.

What the...

I looked back and felt my knees crumple when I saw Ty. He walked in the room, flipped on the lights, and shut the door behind him. He was dressed in a long black duster, a black baseball cap and a pair of black

Nikes. He looked like he was ready to shoot the joint up. He stood beside me. The fully illuminated room revealed Dre sitting smugly in an armchair next to the queen-size bed. I wanted to run. One of my worst fears had come alive.

What was Ty doing here? Had Dre set me up?

"We all meet again! How lovely!" Dre said cynically.

I was trying to figure out how Dre opened the door, and got back to the chair in such a short span of time. Nervously, I eyeballed the room to see if someone else were there.

"You got a whole lotta shit twisted my man, but for the fun of it, entertain me," Ty said walking past me and making his way a few feet away from Dre.

Dre stood up and stuck his hands in the pockets of his grey sweatpants. He wore a matching jacket that was zipped all the way up to his neck. There they stood, two men who were as unpredictable as a baby's bowels, positioned face to face fueled by 'ole man ego. I pictured the two of them drawing guns from their waists and Ty being the quicker of the two, beating Dre to the punch, firing off two shots to his chest...killing him instantly.

"I'm figuring you didn't tell her I'd been invited to the party, is that true, Mia?" Ty turned around to ask me.

I couldn't speak.

"I'm going to take that as a no."

I squeezed my eyes shut hopeful that when they opened both of them would have disappeared. They didn't.

"So how does it feel to stand between two of your fuck buddies, Mia?" Dre taunted.

Ty stepped closer to Dre. "You don't get to insult a lady with me in the room. Put your cards on the table and you better pray for a royal flush," Ty advised.

"What the hell is this?!" I snapped at Dre.

Ty turned around again and looked at me. This time his countenance reminded me of the day he checked India and Kwame at Monet's. Everything about his expression told me to shut the fuck up. I didn't like seeing that side of him. It frightened the shit out of me. Dre had sunk lower than

I ever thought he could go. The audacity of him to set me up! The fury I felt made my body tremble. Ty reached in his coat pocket and I snapped my eyes shut and held them closed. When I didn't hear any shots, I peeked out my right eye. Ty had pulled a piece of paper out of his pocket.

"I'll deal the first hand. Let's see what we have here. Andrew Kenneth Westland. That would be you. Parents John Sr. and Vicki Westland, married thirty-two years. Middle child…between Donald and Brian. That would be you again. Donald, the eldest sibling, a graduate of West Point. Brian, the youngest, a homeless junkie somewhere in a street gutter in California. John carried on a five-year relationship with his secretary until he got caught, but not before a bastard child was spawned. That secretary would be Cindy, a white chick by the way, and that child would be Harold. Harold is currently shacked up with a Chinese female by the name of Jun in Hawaii. They have three kids…all girls: Lee 7, Nao 5 and Qing 3. Should I go on?" he asked.

How the hell did he get all of that information on Dre? What a stupid question given who he is! But wait a minute, Mia! That means if he has a rap sheet on Dre, he more than likely has one on you, too! Shit! Could Ty have known about me and Dre's affair all along! If he did, it would explain why Mr. Cervini repeatedly kept asking me if there was anything else I wanted to share during our briefings!

The room was spinning fast and I was getting dizzy as shit.

"I'll take your silence as a no, too. Your faggot ass lure me here with the intent of telling me a *secret*?"

Ty walked back over to me and put his arm around my stiff waist.

"A secret you didn't think I already knew?"

What the fuck was he talking about? Was he trying to throw Dre off? If he really didn't know about me and Dre maybe he was bluffing to save face. I'd filled him in on every aspect of my life except my affair with Dre.

Never in my wildest dream could I have conjured up the nightmare I'd found myself smack dab in the middle of. From what I gathered, this entire fiasco was Dre's elaborate scheme to avenge rejection. He wanted to ruin my life by throwing me under the bus. The reality that he didn't stand a chance in hell finally sunk in now that Ty was in the picture.

I felt disregarded. A pawn in the middle of their pissing contest.

Whether I wanted to accept it or not Daphne's warnings were beginning to ring true.

"I see you did your homework!" Dre retorted, clapping his hands. "The real questions is, did you do the same for missy over there," he added glancing at me. "And oh, by the way, you forgot to mention that Cindy and my father had two children together. One was a stillborn," Dre added in his smug manner. He stepped to the left of Ty. "It's good to see Missy is no longer keeping secrets. I didn't think she wanted anybody to know the freaky shit we did, but she's full of surprises!" he said totally ignoring Ty's demand to address him.

"You're a fucking low down dirty bitch!" I yelled, trying to go after Dre, but Ty held me back.

"Let him go on."

"Did either of you stop to think that this isn't amusing to me! You're acting like I'm not in the fucking room! How dare you, Dre!" I struggled to free myself but Ty impeded my efforts.

"He wants me to go on, Mia. Are all your men gluttons for punishment? You sure know how to pick'em!" Dre laughed. "Or maybe it's that goddamn good ass pussy you throwing around."

"Dre! Stop it!" I yelled.

"I said let him go on!" Ty yelled.

"I'll spare you the details, besides, I'm sure you already know you've got a freak on your hands unless of course you don't have what it takes to unleash the freak in her! I do wanna caution you brother, she's got a thing for her man's best friends. Don't underestimate that pretty lil' face."

"Dre you're going to regret this, I promise you!" I spewed while trying to get at him. I was hysterical.

"Watch this. I'll prove my point. I'll bet my bottom dollar she didn't tell you she hit a brother up for 'ole time's sake on her husband's birthday? If my source is correct, you were out of town on a business trip. Damn! That look says she's still keeping secrets!"

Before Dre could say another word, Ty transformed into a lightning bolt and sprang across the room, grabbing him by the neck. His grip had been so tight on me that when he let go I fell to the floor. He fastened Dre up in a brutal headlock that immediately cut off his windpipe rendering him limp in Ty's arms. I attempted to scramble to my feet, but the room began to spin once more and I had to grab the bed to find a shred of balance. Things were happening so fast. I could hear Dre gagging for air and it scared the shit out of me. The last thing I wanted was to be an accessory to a murder, even Dre's.

"Ty, please! Let him go, he's not worth it," I begged inching my way along the bed with my hands to steady myself. My request fell on deaf ears. Dre hit the floor with a thud, his body lifeless. My heart dropped, too.

Everything I thought I knew about Ty went out the window in that moment. His eyes weren't the same eyes I had affectionately gazed into for the past ten months. Something about them looked cold, heartless and vindictive.

He came toward me and shoved me down on the bed. I saw my life flash before my eyes, but at the same time, I wondered if Dre were dead or alive.

"You trying to run game? You been fucking that dude when I was out of town? You gonna question me about my moves and yet you hoeing behind my back? Is that what I am, a fucking game to you, huh? You and dude was gaming me that night at the Minskoff?" he asked too calm for comfort. He kept asking me question after question but didn't wait for an answer to any of them.

"You got me thinking we're going to build together, bring your kids here and become a family," he went on.

I honed in on his last statement. I don't know where he got the idea that he was going to play any part in raising Tiff and Brandon. They had a father. I never gave him any indication he'd play a role in their lives. The last thing I planned to do was jump out of one marriage into another. In fact, this whole situation was beginning to shed light on how deep of a hole I'd dug for myself. Besides that, he had some nerve! I never mentioned India's text message to him or anyone else for that matter. The only place she could have gotten my number was from him. I had just as much right to wonder if I had been played, too.

All that aside, right now I needed an exit strategy. The immediate objective was to get out of this nightmare alive. That one goal overruled a fear that threatened to paralyze me. I thought about what I could say to try and pacify him, at least so he would calm down. I wanted to ask him if Dre was okay, but didn't want him to read anything into my concern for the asshole. I just decided to start explaining.

"I tried to tell you about Dre more than once, but the right moment never presented itself and I didn't know where to start. On top of that, I felt guilty and ashamed. I made a terrible mistake. I'm not proud of what I did. God knows if I could take it back I would. Dre took advantage of me at a very vulnerable and low period in my life. He's been holding this over my head for so long, and as crazy as it sounds, I'm glad it's out. He can't use it to manipulate me anymore. It happened once and that was it. I don't know what Dre told you to get you to come here, but that's the truth."

I exhaled. Releasing the guilt and shame attached to the betrayal I'd carried for so long equated to someone taking a boulder off my chest. Provided, I'd rather it was Myles who heard it from me first, but given the circumstances I had no choice.

"You still haven't answered my question."

Which one I wondered. I took a stab that he was referencing my calling Dre on Myles' birthday.

"Yes I did call him, but it was nothing like he made it out to be. I was desperate. I figured he'd planned to crash Myles' birthday party, and I was afraid he'd take that opportunity to tell him what I'd done. I thought he might interfere with me getting my children back. I had no plans of sleeping with him. Dre was the one who took it there. I just wanted to get in his head. See where he was. It's been damn near forever and a day since that happened. I despise him!"

"Why did you cheat on your husband?" he asked standing over me.

I was getting worried Dre might be dead. He wasn't moving.

"Is he alive?" I took a chance and asked.

"Why would you give a shit about a motherfucker that set you up?"

I felt cornered. Ty had shifted gears on me. I didn't know how to deal with this new temperament. My ability to schmooze him over wasn't working in my favor like it had in the past.

"Are you angry with me for cheating on my husband or because you think I'm not telling you the truth?" I asked, wanting to get a feel for which of the two made him the angriest.

"You're not smart enough to play mind games, Mia. I suggest you answer my question," he said coldly.

My heart began to race and my face itched like crazy. I didn't know what he wanted and I certainly couldn't match his savvy. Exhaustion and a fuck it attitude opened the confessional floodgate.

"I suspected Myles was cheating on me with a woman he dealt with in college," I began.

"April," I heard myself say. I'd never once said April's name audibly.

"One night over dinner, his dad sarcastically revealed that Myles had asked her to marry him around the same time we met. Myles never mentioned her. During that same conversation, I found out that at some point she got engaged. Apparently, Myles begged her to marry him instead. She chose the other guy. I tried to question him about her, but all he'd say was that she was his past. We got married, however, as you can imagine, I felt like second pickings." I tried to gauge his reaction to what I'd said thus far, but he maintained a mean poker face.

"About six years into our marriage, Dre revealed that April's marriage was on the rocks. He told me that she was secretly reaching out to Myles for solace. I believed him, one because they were line brothers and two because Myles wouldn't talk to me about her. At first I tried to brush his comments off, but my insecurities surfaced and I began believing the lies Dre fed me. I tried to talk to Myles several times. He wanted to know where the random questions were coming from. What was I supposed to say…Dre told me? I thought I'd eventually be able to shake my doubts and just trust my husband. Dre didn't make it easy because he and Myles were frat brothers and they hung out sometimes. He pretended to know my husband's whereabouts when he wasn't with me. Needless to say, most of them included details about rendezvous with April."

Ty didn't give me any indication whether I should stop talking or keep going. I kept going.

"The final straw came when Myles went to a dental conference in Seattle for a week. The moment he left, Dre revealed to me that April had gone on a business trip that *happened* to be in Seattle, too. He gave me her name and the name of the hotel she was staying at which coincidently was the same hotel where Myles was staying. Of course I checked, and sure enough, she was a guest there. The night after he arrived, I called him several times in his room and on his cell phone but couldn't reach him. When I finally got a hold of him he was always too busy to talk long. My imagination began to work overtime. The combination of Dre's selfish motives and my paranoia created a fertile ground for me to fall prey. I didn't intend to sleep with Dre, Ty.

It started out with him consoling me under the pretense that my husband was having an affair behind my back, and from there turned into my sick interpretation of getting back at him for hurting me. The entire time Dre and I were deceiving my husband he kept feeding me more and more lies. It took me six months to finally put the pieces together and discover the truth, but by that time, I didn't have the nerve to tell Myles what I had done. The damage had been rendered to my marriage, and yes I stayed, but the guilt, shame and disgrace I'd accumulated carried a price. They kept me from giving my all. Every day I lived with the fear of being found out. When I ended the affair, Dre constantly reminded me that he could destroy my marriage anytime he chose. I lived with the fear that what I had done would cause Myles to walk out on me. In a way, I guess I walked out on him first. In my heart I don't believe Myles ever cheated on me and I don't think he ever would. Deep down inside I never felt worthy of him after I slept with Dre. I never forgave myself."

Excavating those buried fears felt freeing, but trying to read Ty's reaction was like trying to read a foreign language. He displayed no emotion.

"Why didn't you tell me the truth when you had the chance?"

"Because I've been a coward. Because my first line of defense is to slip into denial when life gets tough. Because running is all I've known how to do. I was trying to avoid this very moment. I thought I could quiet the devil by making a pact with him. I rationalized that Myles had a right to hear it from me first. I was waiting for the chance to tell him and afterward I planned to come clean with you. In the meantime, I agreed to meet with Dre to let him know he could do whatever the hell he wanted to do, I wasn't going to be held prisoner by him anymore."

"Want to know what I think, Mia?"

"Yes, of course I do."

"You're full of shit. You already knew that scum couldn't be trusted. You didn't have to come here to tell him anything. You could have told him everything you had to say on the phone and been done with it. Let the chips fall where they may. So you want to try telling the truth for once. Why did you *really* come here?"

How the fuck did I tell him I was through running scared in a way he could hear me! Here I was pouring my heart out with the truth and all he wanted to do was chastise me. I was getting angry.

"Forgive me if I don't handle the affairs of my life according to your standards."

"You're sadly mistaken if you think playing the innocent victim is going to work with me."

"Innocent victim?" I stated mimicking quotation marks with my fingers. "You should know something about that!" I shouted. "You're the one who's pretending to be oblivious to the fact that your heart belongs to a dead woman! Me, India or any other woman you're stringing along are fools to think we could have your heart! There's no room because Nina has every room filled up!" I screamed. "We're gullible little women wishing on a star!"

Ty grimaced. I'd struck a nerve.

In the background I heard Dre gagging for air as he came to and I felt a tinge of relief. The world would have been a much better place without the likes of his ass, but I didn't want to be the one to have anything to do with that option. His time would come without my intervention. Ty continued to stare down at me with that unexpressive look on his face ignoring Dre.

Dre slowly sat on his butt, backed himself against the wall and stared wide-eyed at Ty while he clenched his neck with both hands.

I'd often heard or read about people who described a moment when time stood still for them. Some of those moments were dramatic and others were simple. Until now the experience wasn't one I could relate to. Everything in my body felt like it had shut down. When I tuned back to reality, Ty was gone.

The last place I wanted to be was in a hotel room with Dre. I got up to leave.

"Mia, can I talk to you for a minute?" He asked faintly.

"No," was what I thought, but I stopped right at the door.

"Despite what you think I care a lot about you."

I didn't move or respond.

"Look, that dude is shady. He's tied to some dangerous people. Not everything about him is all that meets the eye. I just want you to be careful."

Mia, this is your second warning! Dre's words echoed Daphne's.

"I'm a big girl. I can take care of myself," I told him and left.

The mid-morning theatricals consumed my thoughts on the drive back home. My head hurt past pain. It was somewhere in the explosion zone.

For my own sanity, it was time I came clean with my husband. Seeing him in court rekindled old feelings, and the fact that he wouldn't even acknowledge me stung deep. Too much damage had already been done. There was probably nothing to salvage, nevertheless, I owed him the truth.

At this point I had no idea where things stood with Ty. After tonight, I could care less. The timing was perfect because my babies would be home in two months. I had no intention of inviting them into another round of chaos. I had been trying to figure out how I was going to tell him that we needed to take a break once they were with me. Thankfully, I might not have to worry about having that discussion.

"Shit!" I exclaimed after slamming my brakes to avoid running a red light. I cracked my window slightly to let in some fresh air while waiting for the light to change. I had to adjust my rearview mirror because the headlights from a SUV behind me were damn near blinding. My thoughts were a hodge-podge of the last ten months of my life.

I noticed the same headlights that had blinded me at the red light back on Cedar Lane seemed like the same ones at the light before I turned down my block.

That's strange. Don't get paranoid, Mia. They're probably going the same way you are.

As a precaution, I made a right turn on Teaneck Avenue instead of going straight and the SUV turned right, too. I paused at the stop sign on the corner of Irvington Road only to have the beams distort my vision again. I squinted my eyes to see if I could make out what type of SUV it was but the lights were too bright. I decided to make another right but signaled left to throw them off and when I made the right, the SUV followed me. There was no doubt I was being tailed! The first person I thought to call was Ty. I dialed his personal cell.

"Come on, Ty answer! Please answer!" I pleaded with each ring. Fearful, I kept turning down random streets and the vehicle copied my every move. I dialed him again but this time it went straight to voicemail. Ty never allowed my calls to go to voicemail.

"Crap!" I whispered. I checked the rearview mirror. The SUV pulled up close to my bumper as I traveled down Voorhees Street at twenty-five miles an hour.

Why is somebody following me?

I dialed Ty for a third time and got his voicemail. I decided to leave a message this time.

"Ty, I know you're upset with me right now, and I get it, but I'm headed home and it looks like somebody is following me! I don't know what to do. Please call me back as soon as you get this message."

My hands were trembling as I made a left onto Teaneck Road to jump onto Route 4 and head to the GW Bridge, but the SUV made a right and disappeared. I pulled over in the parking lot of a Laundromat to compose myself. My hands were trembling uncontrollably and my heartbeat was racing out of control.

Mia, you live too far on the edge for me, heifer!

I traveled up and down random blocks for about twenty minutes to make sure I wasn't being followed. Once I was satisfied that the coast was clear, I cruised past my house and circled the neighborhood to ensure there were no strange cars hanging around. When I didn't see anything out of the ordinary, I pulled in the garage as quickly as I could and let the garage door down, watching it descend in the rearview mirror. I turned off the ignition, dropped my head on the steering wheel and closed my eyes. I was exhausted.

I didn't need another problem on my plate. Seriously. I popped the trunk, got out, snatched my purse out and slammed it and the car door shut. I had come accustomed to leaving the door from the garage to the house unlocked but that was going to change pronto. The moment I walked in the house my landline rang. Thinking it was Ty calling me back, I hurried to turn the alarm off and get to the kitchen to answer it.

"Hello," I answered. "Hello?"

Whoever was on the other end didn't respond. I heard a click. I dropped the phone and backed into the island. I felt defenseless. Somebody wanted me to know they were watching me. I ran over to the alarm and activated it, then picked the phone up off the floor to check the caller ID. Private. I waited for a dial tone. My hands were shaking even worse, but I managed to dial Ty's cell phone again. It went straight to voicemail. I called his condo, and when he didn't answer after two attempts, I dialed Monet's thinking he may have gone there for the remainder of the morning. While I listened to the phone ring, I grabbed my purse, tiptoed upstairs to my bathroom, opened the medicine cabinet, took out two painkillers, and swallowed them down without water. No answer there either. I drew all of the curtains in my bedroom closed before peeling off my jeans. I slumped down on the cold hardwood floor in front of my bed.

At this point it was obvious Ty was avoiding me on purpose. I sat there wondering what to do. A stalker was not a cool look right before my children were due to arrive in Jersey. I didn't want to let my imagination run wild, so I elected to call Daphne.

She and I had rang in the New Year together in Miami. One of my declarations was to call her before I made any more blunders in my life. Even though she was in Norway for a photo shoot with an up and coming model she'd recently signed to her agency, I decided to cash in one of my promises.

"Hey baby," Daph, answered wide awake.

It was comforting to hear a familiar voice and I almost broke down and cried. I tried hard to articulate a cheerful disposition. "Hey momma, what ya doing?"

"Sitting out here in the sunshine sipping on a Motorcycle watching Lexi kill it with her skinny ass! This little anorexic bitch know she can work a camera!"

"A Motorcycle! It's not even afternoon! What a life! I wish I was there."

"No you don't heifer! Who you trying to fool! You hate cold places!"

"Is it cold there?"

"No, but it ain't hot either!"

"Maybe you're right."

I was barely holding it together.

"Mia, you alright baby?"

"I'm fine, why you ask me that?"

"Because it's almost five o'clock in the morning back home and despite your effort to put on the valley girl persona you're failing miserably."

Her words opened the portals for my tears to escape. I began to cry like a baby. Trying to hold all the shit in that I had been going through over the past few months poured out of me.

"No Daph, I'm not alright," I confessed.

"What's going on, baby? Talk to me."

"Daph, I feel like I'm going to lose it," I sobbed.

"I understand," she said compassionately. "Talk to me."

I blew my nose on the bottom of my shirt, inhaled and emptied a deep sigh from my mouth. The pills were starting to ease a small portion of the headache I'd amassed since the day began. Lethargically, I picked myself up off the floor, crawled to the middle of the bed and laid down on my left side. I shifted the phone to my right ear.

"Well my secret is out. Dre told Ty everything."

"Noooo, Mia! Are you serious? Wait a minute! What do you mean by *everything*? How? When? What the hell! Girl details!" Daphne demanded.

"Unfortunately, I am serious, and no, not *everything*." I blew my nose again. "You're the only one I told about the miscarriage, Daph."

"Okay, I'm glad to hear that. That is one piece of information you want to take to the grave, baby girl! I hope you know that. Trust me, you don't *ever* want Myles to find out that he stopped his sperm from meeting his semen after Brandon was born for you to get pregnant by another man. Excuse me a minute, sugar," she interjected.

"Rico, you've got two more hours of our time, not a second more. After that the fat lady is gonna sing! Do we understand each other? Good. I'm sorry, Mia. This motherfucker acting like he got all day for this shoot! He better make it happen...we on the clock! Go on."

"I'll give you the long and short of it. You remember when Dre pretended to bump into Ty and me on Broadway and I told you they exchanged cards?"

"Yeah, I remember go head."

"Well Dre called me and told me he was going to give Myles the sordid details of our affair if I didn't meet him. I agreed and not even a minute after I got there Ty shows up."

"Get the fuck outta here! Where did this go down?"

"At some seedy hotel in Patterson."

"Huh?"

"Right, go figure. He set me up by inviting Ty, but Ty turned the tables on him!"

"How?"

"He pulls this sheet of paper out of his pocket with Dre's life story on it. He mentioned some things I didn't even know."

"Say word! Like what?"

"For one, his dad had an affair and a child with his secretary! Actually, he had two children with her but one was stillborn. On top of that, Dre's got a homeless brother, girl! There was some more shit, too but I forgot."

"Damn!"

"You're not gonna believe this, but interestingly enough it seems Ty already knew about me and Dre. Either that or he was saving face by pretending to know when Dre told him. Ty almost choked the shit out of him. I thought his ass was dead!"

"And you would care if he was?"

"Not the least bit, but I don't plan on going to jail as an accessory to anybody's bullshit."

"So what happened?"

"He's fine. While Dre was knocked out, I told him about what I'd done."

"What did he say?"

"He accused me of lying and walked out."

"What? Wow, Mia. That's some crazy shit! Dre is filth. So does that mean you and rich boy are over?"

"As far as I'm concerned we are. The timing is perfect with the kids coming soon. I wasn't quite sure how to tell him I had to move on when they got here anyway. My main goal is to focus on them and work on getting Myles to trust me again."

"Woooo…backup Sally, rewind! Trust you again? That sounds like reunionville?"

"I've been telling you all along that I still love my husband, Daphne. I've never stopped loving him."

"I heard you but that's not how you been acting. If that's the case, why leave and immediately start fucking another man if you had a clue you wanted to work things out with Myles?"

"It wasn't immediately, Daph. Anyways, hindsight is always fifty-fifty," I reminded her before yawning. The painkillers were beginning to make me groggy.

"You sounding real crazy right now I'ma hafta tell you. Too much, too much! You doing way too much, momma! My head hurt fooling with you. I'm trying to be compassionate, but you making it hard, baby girl. So now you want Myles back? I swear, Mia, I can't! It ain't even been a year and you got two penises to tell him about on top of explaining why you packed up everything and left. Myles is a good dude, but I don't think he's that good."

I wasn't the least bit upset that Daphne thought I was a raving lunatic. Hell, I thought I was going crazy, too. I didn't dare tell her someone had followed me home. That would have sent her over the edge.

Moving Forward Toward the Past

Myles

THE BLUE SIGN with red lettering read, *Welcome To Teaneck. Welcome my ass.*

I didn't feel welcomed. If anything, I was numb. I captured glances of the town while waiting at a traffic light behind a red Volkswagen with its top down. It looked like an okay place from what I could tell. Flags lined the light poles up and down the street in preparation for what I assumed was going to be a Fourth of July parade. I checked my rearview mirror to see if Tiff and Brandon were still asleep given the pace of the car had slowed down since we got off the turnpike, and they were. I was pleased to see that my plan to leave Maryland in the early morning hours so they would sleep all the way to their new home worked.

Time seemed to have taken wings after the court date back in January. Nothing in the world could have prepared me for this moment. Mia initiated the first contact that began the process of uprooting our children. I was detached when I heard her voice. The first few exchanges were anything but pleasant. We argued, cussed and fussed before one of us ended up hanging up. It took a minute for us to be able to talk without arguing or hanging up on each other. Our conversations were brief and painful. Eventually, with my mother's subtle intervention we agreed that the best way to handle the inevitable was to tell them that they'd be visiting her for the summer. As soon as they were settled into their new environment, we'd find a way to break the news.

I had mixed emotions about seeing Mia again. Although she'd made several trips down to see Tiff and Brandon when the logistics of her visitations were ironed out, I avoided her each time. The down side to that was the unhealthy emotional rollercoaster I rode between hating her and trying to ignore the feelings I still had for her. As much as I tried to deny it, a part of me still loved my wife.

My GPS beeped to communicate the next turn and I instinctively obeyed. My nerves were on edge from replaying what I'd say once we came face to face. The children hadn't seen us together in almost a year. They had to be looking for honest answers even though we both tried in our own way to explain the unexplainable.

Mother overheard Tiffany telling Brandon that 'mommy and daddy were getting a divorce' one night when they were supposed to be asleep. From my perspective, nothing prepares a man for any kind of pain or harm directed toward his children, no matter where it came from. It set off shit that could bring an end to humanity if he was any kind of man. Sadly though, in this case I was that man. Having to watch Tiffany and Brandon mask their feelings was fucking me up inside. The rulebook to my life didn't have a chapter on how to deal with helping my children cope with separation because I never anticipated it happening.

Before the GPS confirmed that we had arrived, I spotted Mia's house sitting up on a hill on the right-hand side of the street. Everything about it said it was hers. It looked like a model home. As a matter of fact, it almost looked out of place from the rest of the houses on the block.

"Are we there yet?" Tiffany asked, waking up. She yawned, stretched and looked around to take in her surroundings.

"We are. Perfect timing. How did you sleep?" I asked pulling in the driveway and coming to a stop. I turned off the ignition.

"Okay," she answered while surveying the house. She unbuckled her seatbelt and shook Brandon gently.

"Brandon, we're here."

"Huh, we're here?" he asked half asleep.

Brandon yawned then shot straight up with a smile on his face. "Where's mommy?" he asked while unbuckling himself. "Can we get out now, daddy?" Brandon inquired.

"Put your shoes on," Tiffany advised. They both clambered to put on their sneakers.

Preoccupied with my own feelings, I checked out for a moment. My sweaty palms gripping the steering wheel was the only sensation I processed.

I wasn't quite prepared for the flood of emotions that swept over me when she rounded the corner from the back of the house. Her appearance transported me back to reality. All the macho I'd used to remain indifferent ran off like black folk with the first sign of trouble in a scary movie. Watching her walk over to my car in a pair of tight jean shorts and a simple white tank top was like old times. Tiffany and Brandon fought to get their doors open and bolted from the car before Mia had a chance to get to them.

"Mommy, mommy," they screamed, grabbing her around the neck almost knocking her over. Both of them wrapped their arms around her, hugged, and kissed her with tears in their eyes. She dropped to her knees and squeezed them tight, then planted kisses on their faces one after the other. They tucked their little faces in her neck and squeezed it so hard I don't know how Mia could breathe. I watched them peek out from under her neck and look at her like they wanted to make sure they weren't dreaming.

I sat in the car taking it all in. Mia was facing me, and our eyes met intermittently. I saw her lips mimic thank you.

"Daddy, daddy!" I heard Tiffany call. "Come say hi to mommy!"

Watching the three of them together made it easier for me to comprehend why she fought so hard to get them back. I would have been disappointed if she hadn't. Although I still didn't understand how she could have ever walked away from our children, the love was not in question. Awkwardly, I got out of the car.

"Daddy aren't you gonna come and give mommy a kiss?" Brandon asked innocently.

Hard Core

Q

"HEY Q, HOW are you? This is Imani. Listen, when you get a second I'd like to talk to you about something. Give me a call, I'm in town visiting my parents. You can reach me on my cell at 555-555-1212. Okay, thanks."

Fresh out the shower, I sat on the edge of my bed listenin to Imani's voicemail. I checked to see what time she called. Eight thirty-five.

I was no more interested in what the fuck she wanted than I was to know why mutherfuckin sidewalks cracked. Bitches was being reshuffled.

Nise was on the top of the fuckin list to get the boot 'cause she was runnin game. Last time I seen her she acted like she was borrowin the keys she gave a brother but the bitch neva gave'em back. Game.

Her ass was 'bout to get a surprise visit.

By nine-fifteen I was rollin to her crib.

When I pulled up her whip was in the driveway. The only time the trick parked her ride in the driveway was when she had company. I finished my smoke and parked on the other side of the street and got out. I walked up the driveway and peeked in her car. Her windows was tinted out so really wasn't shit to see.

I banged on the door. Her ass didn't answer.

"You betta open this shit or I'll blow the fuckin lock off!"

"Who the fuck is it!" she asked without openin the door.

"Yo fuckin momma! Open the gotdamn door."

"How the hell you gonna come to my house unannounced, Q!" she asked peekin through a crack in the door.

"When I ever tell 'yo ass I was comin, trick?" I asked pushin my way in the crib. Some thug wanna be lookin muthafuckin was standin behind her with no fuckin shirt on. He had his arms folded lookin like Popeye. Shanise had on a robe.

"You never told me you was gonna bring 'yo hoes to my house either lowlife."

"Who dat homo?"

"Who you?" the bitch asked with way too much bass in his voice.

I chuckled and put my arm round Nise's neck. Dude made the mistake of steppin out his lane. Before his pussy ass could blink he had a barrel at his throat.

"Your move."

He raised his hands up and fell back.

"I'ma holla at this trick for a minute and you can have her back when I'm done." I stuck my piece back in my waist.

"I'll be right back, Tariq."

I followed Shanise up the stairs to her bedroom and shut the fuckin door behind me. She sat on the edge of her unmade bed with her feet up on the footboard. I stood in front of her.

"What right do you have coming over here busting up in my place like you pay the goddamn mortgage and putting a gun to my friend's neck! You and me ain't never got down like that! You know what time it is! What, you forgot? I swear to God your screws is loose! Urghhh! What the hell do you want anyway?" she screamed outta fuckin control.

I reached to grab one of her titties that had popped outta her robe. She slapped my hand and jumped up to go stand across the room with her arms folded like a fuckin kid.

"I want you out my house, Q!"

I sat down on the bed and laid back on my elbows.

"When was you gonna tell me you was fuckin faggots?"

"The same time you were gonna tell me you were fucking hoes and sluts."

"I ain't flip."

"Right! Thanks for the reminder. No, you haven't changed but I have. Are we done now, Q?"

I looked at the bed. "Looks like you the same 'ole ho I took off Myles hands."

She frowned and cocked her head side to side like she was tryin to read somethin.

"Really, Q? You know what, you need to go, okay? I'm not going to stand here and let you disrespect me in my own house."

Shanise walked to the door and opened it.

I got up and walked ova to her trick ass.

"I really don't give a shit what you do bitch. I never have and I never will. I always told you if another pimp could do you betta get yours."

"Bitch! Oh now you gonna call me a bitch to my face? You know what Q, I'm done! Is that what you wanted? To come over here and see for yourself? Well now you got your fucking answer! Now get the fuck outta my house and stay the fuck out my life!"

"Cool."

I turned to bounce but Shansie got froggy and jumped in my face.

"See Q, that's exactly what I'm talking about! I was the ride or die chick who took everything you dished out and this is how you treat me? You and I both knew the deal. I ain't ashamed of mine! But you ain't no different from me motherfucker! Crazy ass Nise! I was the one outta all them hoes you drug in from the street who really cared for your selfish ass! I had no problem with you doing your thing. But you know what I'm realizing, Q? You're incapable of caring. You don't have a caring bone in your fucking body and I'm so disgusted with myself for wasting so much of my precious time with 'yo bitch ass!"

Her ass was borin the shit outta me. "What you thought? Your ass ain't no different. I don't give a shit 'bout no trick. You made that shit up in 'yo head and if your trick ass don't wanna be gettin up off the floor you betta get the fuck outta my face."

"Or what? What you gone do? I ain't Torie. Your punk ass don't scare…"

I snatched her by the throat shoved her ass against the wall and pinned her there. She fought to get my hand loose like that was gonna happen. The bitch was barely breathin but still tryna fight.

"If you know so much 'bout what I did to Torie your ass wouldn't be runnin your mouth 'cause you'd have my dick in it."

I let her ass go and she fell to the floor chokin for air. I lit a cigarette and went down stairs. She came down behind me still runnin her mouth.

"You raped that girl because you think she fucking around on you! *You* of all people? So you can do it, but when it comes back around you gonna resort to rape? You are one sick bastard, Q!"

"Go fuck yourself bitch."

I wanted to put a cap in the pussy she had in the house for not mannin up, but his ass was ghost.

I slammed the door and went back to my ride. My phone rang. It was Imani.

"What's up?"

"Hey Q, did you get my message?"

"Yeah. What's up?"

"I just wanted to know how Myles was doing. I gave him my number but I haven't heard from him, so I wanted to follow up."

"He's good."

"Next time you talk to him, would you tell him I said he's in my prayers and if he needs anything to call?"

"Yeah, later."

"Wait a minute, Q, there's one more thing. You doing anything later?" she stuttered.

"Yeah."

"Oh, okay. Sorry to bother you."

Imani didn't call me to check up on Myles. She didn't understand nothing had changed.

Me and Monika was gonna catch a movie later. I didn't have shit else to do 'til then so I banked back to the crib to catch the Yankees. I parked my ride in the driveway and walked back to check my fuckin mailbox. I hadn't checked that shit all week. The bitch was overflowin.

I lit a blunt and sat in front of the TV and tossed the mail on the table in front of me. A big yellow envelope caught my eye. I picked the shit up to see what the fuck it was. There was no return address but the postage stamp was from Hackensack, NJ. I put my joint in the ashtray. When I opened the envelope and turned it upside down a small cardboard box and a yellow piece of paper fell out. Two discs was inside the box.

I unfolded the paper and read a note that was typed.

"Q, I KNOW YOU'RE WONDERING WHAT THIS IS AND WHO IT'S FROM. WELL, ONCE YOU WATCH THE CD'S YOU WILL UNDERSTAND. I FIGURED ONE DAY MYLES MIGHT NEED TO REMIND DRE THAT HE HAS SKELETONS, TOO. AFTER YOU'VE WATCHED THEM, GOOGLE JUDGE ROYAL IN NYC. I WISH I COULD SEE YOUR FACE WHEN THE PIECES FALL IN PLACE. EITHER WAY, DO WHATEVER YOU'D LIKE WITH THEM, BUT I HAVE A FEELING *YOU* WILL ENJOY MAKING SURE THEY GET IN THE RIGHT HANDS.

I picked up the discs.

In The Early Morning Hours

Myles

I UNPACKED THE NEW tennis racket I'd gotten in Jersey and put it in the closet in the guest bedroom that had pretty much become a room for my tennis equipment. My favorite racket, Lady in Red lay across the bed by herself like she owned the place. She was my number one lady because I found out that Serena Williams had one just like it. I could have damn near paid a month's mortgage with what I paid for the thing.

The drive back from up north was emotionally and physically exhausting. Despite getting back home after two in the morning, I didn't feel like going to sleep. Descending the steps to the kitchen, I couldn't help but notice the house carried a different kind of sadness now that Tiff and Brandon were gone. I'd become accustomed to stepping over toys, books and Tiffany's creations after Mia left because I didn't make them clean up the way she did. Not having them around was going to be hell for all of us, especially mother. She'd spent the majority of time with them since this fiasco began and she was sure to feel the void in the next coming weeks.

All kinds of thoughts were running through my mind as I stood in the refrigerator looking for something to eat. I missed Tiff and Brandon to the point that I ached in places I didn't know I could feel pain. If there were a silver lining in the cloud of having to drop them off to Mia, it was the distraction provided by the Fourth of July activities. Between the parade, fireworks and food, there weren't as many uncomfortable moments as there could have been.

The first greeting was the most challenging, especially after Brandon suggested that I give Mia a kiss. It surprised me how easily we both were able to play the role for the children, pretending to be on good terms, faking the funk while they were in our presence.

I tried to leave Mia alone with them as much as possible so they could recapture some of the time they'd lost with her and they clung to her side every minute. I had to admit, she did a good job of making sure the house, neighborhood and atmosphere was conducive and welcoming. I especially liked Marcia, the caregiver she'd found for the children and was glad she'd be moving in next month. At one point I took a walk around the neighborhood and noticed swing sets in several backyards, a park across the street from Mia's house, and one around the corner, which hopefully signaled the neighborhood had plenty of children.

The hardest part of the entire weekend came after Tiff and Brandon went to bed Saturday night. They hung around until I finally bribed them to bed with a bedtime story. I had booked a hotel room not far from her house, but Mia insisted I stay there...for the children, of course.

After they went to bed she gave me another tour of the house. Seeing all of our furniture almost broke a brother down.

. We sat up in her family room and carried on a semi-cordial conversation in front of the TV until about three in the morning. Not once did either of us mention the trial, Dre or the new dude. I retired to my room about three-fifteen. The attraction I had for my wife hadn't gone away; despite everything, however, I had no desire to sleep with her...too much fresh water under the bridge. I spent most of the night trying to figure out how we'd come to this bizarre place.

Leaving my children behind was a tough and strange experience. It made me wonder how Mia could have done it. The mental preparation it required to psych myself up to leave on Sunday left me drained before I even got on the road later that night. Walking away from them fucked my head up, I ain't gonna lie.

They cried when I left and I held it together until I reached the Turnpike.

Do You Still Care For Me

Mia

DOUBLE-CHECKING THE LOCK on the screen door after Myles pulled out the driveway, I wondered if he had detected the Fort Knox feel my home had taken with the security system, dead bolt doors, and motion detectors throughout the house. If he did, he didn't say anything. The last thing I wanted to do was confess that the children might be in danger and I didn't have a clue why. After the first time I'd been followed back in May, I became paranoid. I paid extra attention to cars, license plates and faces just in case I saw any strangers hanging around the house. The hang-ups continued so I changed the number. Knock on wood, that stopped them for now. Nevertheless, I got my permit and bought a gun. Thanks to my dad, Michelle and I were comfortable handling weapons. Consequently, I wouldn't hesitate to shoot to kill if I had to.

Satisfied that the house was secure, I went upstairs to the bedroom where Myles had slept and sprawled out across the bed on my stomach. I closed my eyes and stuck my nose deep in the covers hoping to extract any cologne or natural body aromas that still clung to the sheets. Although I was super excited to see the children, spending time with him was the highlight of the weekend. It was like old times again.

After we were able to break the ice with a laugh when Brandon asked if he were going to give me a kiss, the rest of the visit went better than I expected given what we'd been through. Myles seemed to relax even more when he met Marcia.

I noticed that he stayed absent fairly regularly. I was hoping it was because he wanted to give me and the children time to get reacquainted. At one point, he took a walk around the neighborhood for over an hour by himself, returning with a new tennis racket he got at a specialty sports store down in Englewood.

Saturday night we packed a picnic and drove to the cliff-tops on the Palisades Interstate Parkway to watch the fireworks. I think Myles enjoyed himself just as much, if not more than the children did. Once we got back to the house, they bathe themselves, he read them a bedtime story and tucked them in bed like old times.

I gave him a tour of the house. Afterward we sat up talking until three in the morning. Our conversation was very generic and safe. There were so many things I wanted to say, apologies I wanted to offer but I didn't feel like the time was right.

I had to give it to him, he did a good job pretending that he was with the whole family thing, but I could tell his mind was somewhere else. I didn't have the heart to imagine that another woman might be in the picture. I was disappointed that he didn't try to make a move. It made me feel some kind of way to think that I was no longer attractive or irresistible to my husband. When he indicated that it was time for him to go to bed because he had a long drive back, I attempted to give him a hug good-night, but he resisted my advance. I went to bed and cried myself to sleep.

Another Woman Will

Myles

MY BOY Q took it upon himself to parade a flock of women in front of me. His way of overtly saying it was time to get back in the game. One or two of them wanted to give up the ass the first time we met. Granted, I'd reached a point where I was horny as hell, but I didn't want a side dish of crabs, herpes, or gonorrhea to go along with the cookie.

Sitting out on my back deck killing a few minutes before heading out, I couldn't help but laugh at my boy. His answer to solving any and everything in life was fucking. If you had a damn toothache, in my man's playbook fucking would take the pain away.

I hadn't told Q that I was seeing Veronica. Part of me felt guilty for feeling another woman.

Right after Veronica and my paths initially crossed fate arranged subsequent encounters. In the beginning, I thought the attraction had more to do with trying to recapture what I'd lost with April, but she genuinely intrigued me. I started out by trying to engage her in small talk. She would rarely look me in the eye and kept her words to a minimum.

The opening came back in March when mother asked me to take a cookbook she'd promised to deliver over to her. I was determined to make her talk and had made up my mind I wasn't leaving until she opened up. I kept the conversation light; mostly about me and the kids which seemed to lessen her apprehension. We ended up talking for a few minutes. The following week I invited her out to dinner. She declined because she said she didn't have a sitter. Two weeks later, I pulled up to my parent's house and she was taking groceries out the trunk of her car so I went over to give her a hand. As we were carrying the bags into the house she casually mentioned that Brooklyn was going to Virginia to visit her sister for spring break. I took that as my cue and asked for her number. The day he left, I called to ask her out a second time but she declined. I finally got her to agree to join me for dinner the Saturday night before he came back home.

Surprisingly, I enjoyed her company even though she was a bit uptight the whole night. When I dropped her back off and walked her to the door, I detected that she didn't want to go in alone, so I asked if I could come in to use the bathroom. That's when I realized there was a strong sexual energy between us. I didn't make a move out of respect.

By the time June rolled around, she'd let her guard down about sixty percent and we'd been on a few dates. There were several times when we both almost lost the bet to passion. I hadn't put any pressure on her for sex despite going home with blue balls a many a nights. The fact that we had good chemistry, not just physically, kept me interested.

I could tell mother suspected Veronica and I were close to taking things to the next level because one day she walked by me and casually said, "make sure you get all the fish out the creek before you go sticking your pole in the lake." I think I understood where she was going.

With Tiff and Brandon in NJ and Brooklyn spending the summer with Veronica's younger sister it afforded us more time to hang out.

From where I stood, Veronica took first place for being the most overprotective mother I'd ever known. There was something extra about her fears when it came to her son. Whenever I tried to broach the subject of allowing him more space to be a boy, she pretty much told me to mind my own business. Her response got even more curt when I asked about his father one night. Her manner shifted from pleasant to standoffish and she didn't have much to say for the rest of the evening. I refrained from asking any more questions about him. I would have given my Nike shoe collection to find out how Veronica's sister got her to let Brooklyn spend the summer with them.

I polished off the fourth bottled water and checked my watch. Tonight would be the first time Veronica agreed to come to my house since we'd been hanging out. I hoped like hell that meant she was ready to break a brother off.

The only thing I had to do was stop by to give mother an update on my trip to Jersey. After that it was on.

I dialed my parent's landline.

"Hello."

"Good afternoon my favorite lady, how are you?"

"Hey baby, I'm just fine! You still in that NJ?"

"No. I got back early this morning, and yes I took a nap when I got in," I blurted out before she could ask.

"Well you ackin like you know me, huh?" she laughed. "I see Veronica didn't go to work today either. Does that mean you two might be up to something?"

"Now who "ackin" like they know who?" I joked.

"Did you say ackin? Who you mockin boy?" she laughed vibrantly.

"Nobody!"

"That's what I thought. You on your way here?"

"Yes, I should be there in about an hour."

"Well you be safe and I'll see you when you get here. I made the two of you some hot biscuits. They be waiting for you."

"You're the best."

"I love you, son."

"I love you, too, mother."

Sweeping the empty water bottles off the table, I dumped them in the trash and went back inside the house to shower. Within the hour I was pulling out the garage.

Q called while I was getting dressed and I hit him back with a text message to let him know I'd call him when I got on the road. Word was circulating amongst the fellas that he had raped Torie. No woman deserved to be raped under any circumstances. If it were true, Torie would never press charges because she was terrified of my man. Sad. I liked Torie and never understood why she gave Q any of her time, but then again I never understood why any woman gave Q time. Last I heard, she'd moved to Richmond and was staying with a friend.

I hit my man back on his cell.

"What up, dawg," I asked.

"I think we got that muthafucka on the ropes. I'll hit you back."

"What motherfucker?"

"The only muthafucka I know. Later."

Motherfucker was the term Q used for just about everybody on his shit list. I had no idea who he could have been referring to or what he meant.

I saw Veronica's blinds open when I drove up on the block, something she never did, so I decided to stop by for a hug and tell her I'd see her in a few.

My parent's neighborhood was one of the few hoods where people still felt comfortable leaving their front doors unlocked, but not Veronica. She kept her shit bolted tight twenty-four seven. I skipped up the wooden steps two by two and rang the bell, anxious for her to open the door. After what seemed like an eternity, I watched her peep through the tightly drawn curtains like she did every time. Her smile aroused me and I could tell she was equally happy to see a brother.

The second she opened the door I pulled her into me and wrapped my arms around her. She felt good, real good. I held her tight without saying anything, enjoying the sensation of her braless voluptuous breast against my chest. There was nothing sexier to me than a simple sundress on a woman. I slid my hands down over the smooth silk navy blue dress and stopped when I reached her pantiles hips.

"Damn Ronica, I missed you," I said brushing a loc from her face and leaning down to kiss her lightly on the lips. Veronica wasn't comfortable with PDA's and I tried to respect that.

"I missed you, too."

I backed her into the house just in case mother was watching, kicked the door closed behind me with my foot and kissed her like I really wanted to. I guided her over to the couch with my hand on her hips and gingerly maneuvered myself down on top of her. She flowed with me, wrapping her soft thick thighs around my back stroking the top of my head with both hands. I caressed each leg slowly, enjoying every inch of them. My hands moved up her quivering stomach, underneath her dress. I caressed each breast equally with undivided attention. We were breathing like two asthmatics.

She softly kissed my neck. The intensity between Veronica and me was way past the cosmos. It was different then what I remembered with Mia, or maybe it had been so long since I'd had some horny had clouded my mind. Whatever the case, the anticipation to cross the threshold had reached its peak. Just as I was about to lift her dress up higher so that I could work her breasts like a newborn baby, she stopped me.

"Later," she whispered in my ear.

Her proposal made my Johnson jump and stiffen to brick status.

You 'bout to get some tonight!

We kissed one last time and I pulled her dress down, but not before stealing another feel of her breast. I assisted her up from the couch.

"I'm gonna go over and talk to mother for a little bit," I mentioned as we walked hand in hand to the door. "I should be back in a jiffy."

"Take as long as you need. I think I can wait."

Veronica was teasing me but she didn't understand how dangerous that could be. No doubt she might find out later. I hung around for a few minutes to let my hard-on subside.

"I can text you when I'm done or you can leave the door unlocked," I told her reassuringly.

She looked embarrassed. "Do you mind texting me?" she asked looking pass me.

My intention was not to dismiss her concerns whatever they were. I wanted desperately to understand what she was afraid of. I lifted her chin so that we were looking each other in the eye.

"Ronica, I'm not sure what's going on and I won't press the matter, but as long as I'm around nobody is going to hurt you or Brooklyn, I promise you that," I said sincerely.

Her shoulders eased. She smiled and reached up to kiss me on the cheek.

"I trust that," she said. "You need to get going. I want to spend as much time with you as possible, so scoot! Text me when you're on your way," she demanded, slapping me on the ass.

She didn't have to tell me twice. I was out the house across the street at my parent's door before she had a chance to lock up her fortress. Mother saw me approaching and stood in the door with it wide open waiting for me to come up the steps.

"Hi there you beautiful Queen," I said, planting a kiss on her forehead.

"I bet you say that to all the women," she laughed, patting my cheek.

"Only if it's true!"

"We're in a good mood, aren't we?" she teased. "I made ice tea and warmed you both some biscuits. They out back," she said, leading the way to the screened porch on the back of the house. I caught up with her and put my arm around her neck. She clasped her fingers into mine as we walked side by side. I sat in my favorite pale blue rocking chair with my back to the sweltering sun. Mother immediately got busy pouring two glasses of tea, spreading homemade blackberry jam on my biscuit like she always did and proudly placing everything on a tray in front of me. When she finished, she sat down in the swing across from me and sipped her tea.

"How she doing?"

"She's fine," I unintentionally blushed.

"You like her don't you?"

"Yeah, I do. I mean of course I still love Mia, I'll be honest, but my marriage is over and at some point I have to move on."

"I know son. Just make sure you not hoppin from the pot to the pan," she cautioned without a blink.

Mothers one liners were as wise and ancient as time.

"What is that supposed to mean?" I asked, looking at her.

She began a slow steady swing. "Son, you don't want to find yo'self going from a woman you love with all your heart to another woman that lights 'yo fire 'til you sure you can give her everything you got. What you think happens to all that love, all that pain, all that anger, all that disappointment and God only knows what else you got inside you somewhere? You can't just tuck it away like it never was. It got life. Somewhere, somehow it's gonna come up for fixin."

"What do you suggest I do, mother? Lock myself away in a closet and stop living until I get the answers to why all this crap was dumped in my lap?" I asked, honestly looking for a resolution.

"Is what you saying you ain't had *nothing* to do with none of this going on 'tween Mia and you?"

"No, that's not what I'm saying, and by the way, you're beginning to sound a lot like somebody else I know," I said defensively, referring to my father. "I'll admit I may have played a part in our marriage falling apart, but I was willing to work it out, not walk away. What does that solve? Most adults talk things through no matter how difficult they are and if they have to walk away after that, so be it."

"Baby, that's life. Everything ain't a tree or a bush, flat or straight. Listen to me. Ain't nobody perfect. Sometimes we don't know when the road gonna curve or the hill gonna drop."

"Yeah, well my road seemed to turn into an endless curve and my hill doesn't appear to have a bottom, but let you tell it, it's all my fault," I said sarcastically.

"I ain't said or 'plied nothing 'bout fault. You the one used that word. There's a difference 'tween 'countability and fault, you know?" she said, raising her eyebrow at me. "Countability takes courage, fault points fingers. People who 'fraid to face theyself blame. The others look inside. They stand in the truth even if it hurts. You and Mia's troubles didn't show up when she left. I know that, and you know it too if you honest with yo'self. Question is, did you really want to *know* it? Was you ready to face the truth? Was you listening or was you turning a deaf ear and blind eye so you didn't have to face what you already know'ed 'cause you had to do something 'bout it?"

I watched mother close her eyes and go to that place only sages got an invitation to enter. A peaceful look came over her face, and she smiled that wide grin that spanned the entire width of the universe. Her head tilted slightly back, she inhaled a slow deep breath of the thick humid air that could be cut like a piece of chocolate cake. It was as if she were physically there on the porch but her spirit was somewhere else. I always thought my mother was beautiful, but it seemed the older she got, the more stunning she became. I closed my eyes to take in the peaceful aura she had invited into our space and it wasn't long before she began again.

"Problems come. Problems go. Most of what life throws at us we can handle and keep on moving. Every so often we get blindsided…knocked to our knees and can't move for a period of time. Sometimes we think we 'vancing when we really not. We just moving forward back to the past."

She opened her eyes and looked at me as if discerning the fact that I hadn't comprehended much of what she said.

"You've said a lot that I don't understand. This thing hurts. It hurts real bad. I don't know what to do with the pain. I don't have a place to put it. It won't go away. And how do you move forward back to the past? I never heard that before."

"I knows it do baby. I see the pain all ova you. It hurts just like love. The good and bad of it. Some days love is a beautiful thing. Other days it hurt like hell. One day a child is born another day somebody dies. One person cry tears of joy the other one cry tears from hurt. When love hurts you gotta go back and look at what caused the pain 'fore you can move forward. Sit still with yo'self 'stead of jumping 'tween the legs of another woman or hoping on the penis of some other man."

"I hear you, and no disrespect, but I don't plan on sitting around sulking like an old man. I deserve to be happy."

"Sitting still ain't 'bout doing *nothing*, baby. More moving happening when you sitting still then when you moving case you didn't know it. See this world wants you to believe that when you busy doing something you making strides. You somebody. Quiet got no value in today's time. You ever *hear* a tree, the grass or a plant grow? Ever hear the wind when it's not blowing? You won't if you always moving. But if you learn to sit quiet and listen, you learn yo'self and when you learn yo'self, you learn nature. See how it work, baby? Nature open the door when you sit still long enough. You learn things 'bout yo'self and the world you neva gonna learn runnin round in circles."

"I don't know mother that's a little over my head. I'm not above admitting that Mia and I had problems that didn't happen overnight. And yes, I denied that we weren't happy far longer than I should have, but I never would have guessed that she'd just up and leave," I admitted, taking a bite out of one of my biscuits.

"Always remember son, life has a funny way of showing us ova and ova everything we need to learn until we get it. Sometimes we gotta go backward to get the lesson before we can move forward. Everything we need to learn will keep showing up one way the other until we learn it. That way, we don't keep hoppin from the pot to the pan. Now tell me, how happy was my grandbabies to see they mother?" she asked, changing the subject with the precision and tact that only she could pull off.

Although I wanted to continue our conversation because I felt like some of what she was saying was clicking, I was ready to go hang out with Veronica.

"There aren't words that could get close to explaining their reaction. They were asleep when we got up to her house, but the moment they saw her they came alive. It was truly amazing to witness. Mia looks great and the house she bought is beautiful. I met the nanny and I like her a lot. She reminds me of you in a strange way. I mean, I have to give it to Mia, she handled every little detail for Tiff and Brandon."

"Sooo…," she said looking at me with a mischievous grin on her face.

"So what?" I asked, fully aware of what she wanted to know.

"You gone call my bluff!" she laughed.

"Okay, okay! No we weren't intimate! Not a conversation I want to have with my mother!" I laughed. "Things were way too awkward. I don't know that we'll ever go there again. After she crossed the line with Dre and now a new guy…nah. I'll pass."

"You know what I'ma say to that."

"Never say never, right?"

"You said it not me," she smirked.

It was good to sit and talk to my mother. I missed the time she and I used to spend together. Back when my father was gone, most of the time it was just her and I. We talked for another twenty minutes or so while I ate. I didn't want to go but I didn't want to leave Veronica hanging too much longer either. Intuitively mother detected my restlessness and got up. She began putting things away. While she did that, I sent Veronica a text letting her know I was on my way.

"Thanks for the words of wisdom. Despite what you might think, I heard you," I assured her after popping the final piece of buttery bread in my mouth. Mother put the container with the biscuits for Veronica in my hands.

She smiled. "I know you did, son. Get on! Tell her I said hello and enjoy them biscuits."

"Will do!"

We walked back to the front of the house hand in hand in silence. I kissed her on the forehead.

"I love you."

"I love you, too, son."

I hurried back to Veronica's house like a dope fiend with ten dollars heading to the crack house. She came out the door as I was ascending the steps. Veronica was breathtaking and her curvaceous highway made a brotha pause in his footsteps. The song Brick House had to have been written with her in mind. She had changed into a pair of denim short shorts and a sexy low cut camouflage tank top with no bra. Her locs were wrapped up and off her shoulders in a green bandana. I wanted to skip lunch and have her instead. I noticed a red overnight bag on her shoulder instead of her pocketbook.

"Damn girl! Where you been hiding all that at!"

"You like," she asked turning around so I could get a full view.

"Oh yeah!"

I met her at the top of the stairs and put my arms around her waist. We pecked on the lips. "You look and smell like dinner and dessert," I whispered in her ear.

"Do I now?"

"Let me get that for you." I locked the two deadbolts for her. She checked them behind me on the low. "You mind if we go to my place first and grab dinner later," I asked, cutting to the chase.

"That would be a yes I mind! You're going to feed me and take me to a movie before we go to your house, mister."

"Can't blame a brother for trying," I laughed. "These are for you." I gave her the container with the biscuits. "She sends her love."

"How sweet! Your mom is the best. I'll have to thank her later."

"You can thank me for her if you'd like?" I suggested.

"Side eye, whatever!" she countered giving me the side eye.

"Is that a maybe?"

"You don't give up, do you!?"

We both laughed. I took her bag and threw it over my shoulder as we walked to my car. I wanted to hold her hand but knew it would make her uncomfortable if mother happened to be watching us. Veronica didn't say it, but I knew she didn't want mother to know we'd been intimate in any way, shape or form since I was technically still a married man.

She go into the car through the door I held opened for her and I slammed it shut once she got in. Her thick, toned thighs planted perfectly on the passenger seat of my car and a glimpse of her firm breasts made me feel like a teenager again. Veronica was not the typical sized six super model female. She was thicker and fuller. A little different from the women I was usually attracted to, but man had I been missing out.

By the time we'd seen the movie, had dinner and made a run to the drugstore in case I got lucky, it was way past nine when we pulled into my garage. I gave her a grand tour of the place after dropping the mysterious red bag off in my bedroom. Afterwards, we settled in the kitchen with a glass of red wine for her and a beer for me.

"Your home is warm. It feels good," she said genuinely.

"I appreciate that. Its' been a long road getting it back here. You're actually the first person outside of family and a few of my buddies who's been inside since I refurnished it," I told her.

"Well I'm honored," she said smiling.

Her sexy ass body had been testing my gentlemen status all day. My throbbing solider was giving me hints that it was time to move things along. "You mind if we go upstairs?" I asked hopeful.

"Not at all."

I held her hand going up the stairs. Both of my heads were full of anticipation. Veronica and I were both in the medical field, so we'd talked about the benefits of having to be tested for STD's once a year subtly revealing our clean statuses on the low. As far as I was concerned, it was going down tonight.

Veronica paused by my bedroom door to read a plaque on the wall that I'd received from the national chapter of the NAACP for an outstanding Black business. I put my arms around her waist pressing my body lightly up against her ass. She reached for my hand when she finished reading the plaque and led me over to the bed. The hunger in her eyes gave me the green light to proceed.

It had been almost thirteen years since I'd been with anybody other than Mia. Straight up, I was a little nervous. Veronica was a lot of woman. I wanted to take my time and enjoy all of her, not just rush in and bust a nut.

"Ronica," I whispered in her ear after backing her against the bed. "You sure you want to do this?"

"I'm sure, Myles," she said, breathing heavily.

Her consent was all I needed. I picked her up and laid her down lightly on the black satin comforter admiring the architecture of her body from head to toe. There was so much to her, I didn't know where to start. I felt like a kid in a candy store. My third leg was erect, pulsating and throbbing, damn near making threats to jump in the lake if I didn't get on with it. I obeyed. She spread her legs open and beckoned me to come aboard with a sultry fixed stare into my eyes. Veronica wrapped her soft, firm thighs around me and caressed the back of my head while guiding my lips toward hers. Our kisses were intermingled with long stimulating moans and heavy breathing. Her hips were rhythmically rocking the boat left and right, up and down while her hands were under my tee shirt exploring my naked back. I could feel the heat coming from her good, good. Everything in my body was tingling. I slipped my hand up under her top and lightly circled each nipple with my finger. Her body responded with erratic mini jerks.

"Ummm…that feels good, Myles."

I didn't respond verbally but instead tenderly kissed her on the shoulder, inching my tongue up her neck, across the left side of her face and into her mouth. This time our kisses were hard and deep. I took hold of her right hand, guided it up under my tee shirt directly over my racing heart and held it there. I wanted her to be fully aware of what she was doing to me.

She freed her hand from my grip and glided it down into my boxers, gently caressing my Johnson. Her touch made my body jerk involuntarily. Her gaze remained fixated into the depths of my soul as she placed her warm slender fingers confidently around the middle of my shaft. A deep sigh escaped my mouth. Veronica began to eagerly but tenderly explore the head, width and girth of my rock-hard dick like it was a work of priceless art. Even though she wasn't stroking me, I felt like I was going to come all over her hand. It took all I had not to rip her clothes off and lose myself deep inside her.

Ascending to the next level, she maneuvered her other hand down into my boxers and stroked my balls with just the right force. I braced myself above her licking and sucking her breasts to the music of her moans and groans. We both were breathing off chorus while pleasuring each other, finding moments to kiss in between. I was teetering on the boarder of exploding in her hands, so I slowly removed them and placed them around my waist. Unintentionally, I'd left the lights on in my room and was privately grateful for the opportunity to witness just how beautiful Veronica was. I lifted her tee shirt up over her head and tossed it on the floor beside the bed. Her naked, chocolate covered breasts stood firm with the headlights on high beam. They looked like two chocolate covered bon bons.

"Baby let's slow down. I want to enjoy all of you," I whispered.

"Do you have candles?" she purred.

"No," I lied. "You want music?" I asked picking up the remote to my surround sound.

Candles were Mia and my thing. I didn't want to spoil the mood with her surfacing into my thoughts.

"Naw, I like our music."

"Me, too."

I pulled her up to a sitting position and unknotted the bandana that secured her locs. I watched in awe as each one settled around the nape of her neck, stimulating me equally as much as the rest of her beauty. Unfastening one button at a time on her waist high shorts, my fingers brushed up against her pubic hairs revealing the fact that she didn't have on panties and she hadn't shaven. That discovery made me anvil hard. I drank in every inch, hill, mountain, arch, birthmark, mole, scar, stretch mark and crevice of her banging body. From a kneeling position, I pulled my tee shirt off baring a six-pack I was proud to expose. She reached up and helped me pull off my shorts and boxers. We were both in the raw.

"Ohhh…Myles you got it going on! How many packs you got there?" she asked with a lust that made my manhood jump. She traced each ab light as a feather with her long slender manicured pointer finger while counting in her head. "I could get used to this," she sang between planting small wet kisses all over my chest and stomach.

She steered me onto my back and straddled me with precision. With her on top of me, the gates of heaven opened revealing multiple universes. As if she hadn't gifted me enough, Veronica leaned down alternating each breast in my mouth for suckling. Grateful for the offering, I licked and sucked each one while my hands were squeezing, rubbing and spreading her mountainous ass. With her eyes closed and her hips dancing in my hands, she continued to serenade me with musical moans and groans from native Africa. My second head had gotten so hard it throbbed. I know I was only imagining it, but I tasted peaches, strawberries and melons dripping from her nipples as I hungrily circled and sucked for more to flow.

We'd both reached the zone. There was no turning back. Ronica came up for another kiss, her eyes rolling with pleasure in their sockets. I wanted to be inside her so bad a brother almost begged for permission to enter.

Veronica pinned my hands to the bed, then began erratically kissing and licking my face, my neck, my chest, my stomach, my groin area. That's when the stars and planets aligned.

She didn't give me a chance to prepare for what happened next. In a way I'm glad she didn't because my heart might have given out.

When her moist lips met the head of my pulsating muscle, my brain didn't connect with what was going down. It wasn't until she took me in deeper that it registered and I let out a bitch cry all my neighbors probably heard. The room was spinning so fast I felt like I was gonna be thrown from the bed! I wanted to stop her before I came in her mouth, but the suction of her jaws, the wetness, the sounds, the heat, the perfect timing of her stroke on my shaft synchronized with the up and down movement of her head rendered me helpless. All I could do was drop my head back, release the tension in my body and go with the slaughtering. Her skills were impeccably masterful. I lay there, a prisoner between the bars of ecstasy and heaven. Veronica took complete control of me. Her locs flapped like eagle wings…up and down, wide and majestic. I never had a woman go down on me the way she was handling her business. As much as I hated to, I had to stop her. I didn't want to punk out by coming in her mouth, but if she kept it up, it was undeniably going to be a wrap.

"Shit baby, what the fuck are you doing to me!" I asked in between trying to catch my breath. The fireworks in my body were in the finale stage with no end in sight. "Ronica, baby, I'm about to come," I stammered, slowing her next deep descent. She had almost worked her way up to taking all of me in.

"That's the objective," she whispered still circling the head like a fresh kill. "You don't know how long I've fantasized about doing this for you, Myles."

"I love it but I don't want to bust a nut in your mouth. At least not yet."

"Look who's playing by the rules now."

She got up from the bed and strutted across the floor like a Goddess. Her body mimicked a tree dancing in the wind, her locs the branches. I watched her mesmerized, restraining the urge to bow at her feet. I was experiencing the same feeling I got the first time I rode a rollercoaster: anticipation, excitement and a tinge of butterflies. She dug in her red overnight bag and came back to the bed with two boxes of condoms and a small tube of massage oil. "I got these just for you," she announced holding them up.

"Red or black?"

Veronica had gotten the exact size and brand of condoms I'd purchased earlier at the drugstore.

"Black!"

She tossed the red box across the room, climbed back on the bed and kneeled by my waist. I rubbed the baby smooth soft skin of her back and ass.

"You ready?"

"I think so," I laughed. "You promise not to take all my pride?"

"That depends on how far you're willing to go."

"Sounds like I'm in trouble."

Veronica put the oil by the pillow, ripped into the box of black condoms, and retrieved three from the box. Between her eagerness and my anticipation of satisfying her with long, slow strokes, I was giddy as a teenage boy about to dip into his first taste of paradise. She reached for the tube and squeezed a quarter sized quantity of the liquid into her left hand. I watched her every move like the climax scene in a good movie.

In all the time we'd spent together, I never peeped an inkling of this seductive side of Veronica. For the most part, she was usually conservative and shy in my presence. Nevertheless, I had no motherfucking complaints about meeting her alter ego!

Veronica rubbed her hands together then encased my erection. I closed my eyes and rolled my head side to side while moaning shamelessly. Skillfully, she began a circular up and down rhythmic stroke, not too fast and not too slow until I'd reached a rock stiff hard on again.

"Ahh...oh shit, Ronica, that's it, ahh...baby, yes, that's it baby," I affirmed.

Satisfied with the results of her efforts, she ripped into one of the packaging with her teeth. I leaned forward to watch her masterfully dress my erection with a condom she'd placed in her mouth. Taking the reins, Veronica mounted me. Slowly and skillfully as if riding a mechanical bull, she rocked back and forth, inching me inside of her bliss. Her tunnel was tight as a baby's grip on a fresh bottle.

"Ahhh...babe...that's it! Shit, you feel so...AH!"

"It's so good...sssss, Myles, ahhhh, yes! Deeper...I can't...shit...I'm gonna...DEEPER!"

Concurrently, we both were testifying. I didn't have to do anything but enjoy the ride. Veronica dominated, and I consented. I was her prey. I was a moaning, groaning fool. Baby girl worked her gift like a pro, rolling back and forth, round and round, fast and slow, deep and rough. I watched her breasts bounce up and down like the balls in the lottery cage. I counted four screaming orgasms, but she may have had more.

Once I was sure she had been satisfied, I flipped her over on her hands and knees and went to work. Driving up close to her bumper, I eased my hand in between her legs and stroked her clit from the back until the plug came out of the damn and overflowed. She let out soft screams and moans every time I hit her spot.

"Shit...slap my ass, Myles," she requested.

"Is that what you want," I asked still stroking her cat and licking her lower back.

"Yes...yes...ahhh, yes, please!"

I licked the palm of my hand then paddled her right cheek firmly while still stroking her clit. Her whole body quaked.

"Mmmm...ahhhhh...its'...I'm...yes...please, Myles, harder!"

I landed a few more whacks, each one harder than the last. I was about to land another one when the floodgates opened and she squirmed and slithered as she came. She tried to get away from me, but I strapped up again, held onto her waist and slipped in.

"Ahhhh...Ahhhh...Ahhhh...Get it, Myles...Get it, baby...Yes...Oh my God...Get it...Yes!"

Veronica was out of control. She reached around; fumbled for my ass and pulled me into her while she threw everything she had back at me. I was happy to comply, but I made sure not to lose control or hurt her while getting mine in. She begged me to stop, to keep going, to go deeper, to slow down, to take it. Her instructions had no rhyme or reason.

"Myles, you feel so fucking good, damn," she said looking back at me. Veronica was breathing so hard I thought she was going to hyperventilate. Her locs were hanging over her face and she looked beautiful from that angle. When our volcano's finally erupted together, we collapsed in each other's arms relishing in the aftermath.

Four condoms and three hours later we were both weak and happy. We lay intermingled and content, listening to Miles Davis. I played in her locs while she closed her eyes and smiled.

"You're amazing, Myles."

Just as I was about to kiss her the phone rang. I could tell the interruption made her uncomfortable by the way her body tensed up in my arms.

"The machine will get it baby," I tried to reassure her. I attempted to kiss her a second time, and it rang again.

"Baby you might need to get that. It could be important," Veronica said trying to hide her disappointment.

"They can leave a message. Let's not spoil our time together," I said, trying to recapture the moment by kissing her. No sooner had I said that, my cell phone rang. At that point, I wondered if something were wrong with the children.

"Myles, I insist that you answer it. Really, it's okay," Veronica said in her comforting voice.

"You don't mind? I'm afraid it could be about the children and they're so far away."

"You don't have to explain. I'm not going anywhere," she cooed.

My cell phone stopped ringing and the house phone rang a third time. She stretched out on the bed. I laid close behind her with the cordless in my hand. I glanced at the display and it was Mia. I gave myself an internal pep talk before answering.

"Hello."

"Hi Myles, I'm sorry to bother you, but Tiffany wanted to talk to you. I think she misses home. I hope I'm not disturbing you?" she said apologetically.

"No Mia, it's no problem, where is she?"

"Hold on."

"Daddy, when are you coming back to get us? I miss grandma," Tiffany whined.

"Baby, we agreed you'd spend a few months with your mother, do you remember?" I reminded her, trying to slow the pace of my breathing.

"Yes, daddy, I know and I remember, but I don't like it here. I want to come back home."

Veronica moved as if she were about to get up. I held her close to me with my free hand so she couldn't leave.

"Sweetheart, daddy will be there next weekend to see you. We can talk about what you're feeling then, okay?"

"I guess."

"Where's your brother?"

"He's right here."

"Does he want to talk to me?"

"No daddy, he's fine. He likes it here."

"Well, I love you both and I'll see you the weekend, okay?"

"I love you too, daddy. Mommy wants to talk to you."

"Myles, I'm sorry for calling you back to back like that, but she really wanted to talk to you."

"Don't apologize, it's no problem. I want them to have access to me anytime. Don't hesitate to call me if you need me or if they want to talk."

"Myles, can I ask you a question?"

Fuck, why was she doing this shit to me!

"Right now isn't a good time."

"Oh, okay. I'm sorry. We'll talk later?"

"Yeah," I said, hanging up the phone.

All that good sex went down the drain. Talking to Mia made me feel guilty as shit, like I had done something wrong. I didn't want her to know I had another woman in my bed. At the same time, I didn't want to disrespect Veronica by pretending she wasn't there. I felt torn for feeling the way I did.

"You still love her don't you," Veronica asked out the blue.

What was I supposed to say to that? Of course I did.

I Want You Back

Mia

I WAS TAKING TWO painkillers every other day. The realization that my headaches might be more psychological than physical was one I could no longer deny. They were coming on more intensely, too. Back in May, I'd toyed with the idea of seeing a shrink but never followed up. Now I was seriously pondering it. I scooted my vanity chair closer to the mirror in my bathroom and applied another layer of foundation to try and conceal the dark circles under my eyes. Insomnia was running havoc on my body internally and externally. Not only was I losing sleep, but I'd lost a few pounds as well. Fortunately, I still managed to maintain the curves Myles always found irresistible.

Standing up and turning around to check out my figure-flattering red sundress one last time, I winked at my image in the mirror. If there was anything Myles couldn't resist it was me in a sundress, and a red one at that. I spritz a few more sprays of his favorite perfume under my dress and headed downstairs to wait for him to arrive.

Marcia had packed a lunch and taken the children to the Bronx Zoo early this morning. A plan I concocted to give Myles and me a chance to spend some time together once he arrived for the weekend.

Intuitively, I suspected he was with another woman when Tiffany called to speak to him Monday night, but whatever. All I can say is the bitch better be ready for a fight. He was still my husband.

I missed Myles and wanted desperately to give our marriage another chance even if that required moving back home. The time apart made me realize that I was running from myself and not our problems. It was me that needed to be fixed. Oddly enough, my involvement with Ty made me realize that a large percentage of the problems Myles and I had were mostly my fault because the same issues showed up in my relationship with him. At the end of the day, I was the common denominator.

Facing the fear of coming clean about my affair with Dre revealed how guilt, shame and humiliation was causing me to self-sabotage my own happiness. I was projecting my guilt off on Myles. His faithfulness never should have come into question based on an outsider's input, especially Dre's.

In the middle of self-reflecting, I saw Myles pull up in the driveway in a rental stirring up the butterflies in my stomach. I gushed at his fine ass from behind the sheer curtains in my living room as he got out the car. He was casually dressed in khaki shorts, a Nike sleeveless tee shirt, sandals and sunglasses that hid his eyes, and I noticed he didn't have an overnight bag with him. My heart doubled its pace. I wondered what the hell was on my mind that I let a gorgeous specimen of a man like him get away.

Mia your ass seriously need some counseling!

I bit my bottom lip as I watched him and all of his sexiness walk up the driveway. Perspiration began breaking out everywhere there was a pore on my body as I gawked at him and fantasized about the last time we made love. That moment was exactly what I wanted now.

Surely no other woman could have erased how good we were together from his mind in this short period of time.

The doorbell rang, snapping me out of my daydream. I took a few seconds to gather myself, tugging on my sundress to make sure it was in place. I eagerly unlocked the door and swung it open.

Okay, girl! Here's your chance to go for it! Don't blow it!

"Hey there," I said, giving him a friendly embrace and sniffing him on the low. His hug was light and superficial. "How was your flight?"

"It was good, thanks for asking," he said sticking his hands in his pocket and walking inside.

"You look great," I confessed.

"So do you."

Myles appeared uncomfortable, almost shamefaced, but I didn't plan on letting that deter me. If all went the way I planned, we were going to get in a quickie before Marcia and the children returned.

"Did you bring a bag?"

"Ah, yeah, I did, but it's, it's in the car. I thought it might be best if I got a room this time," he said, without looking me in the eyes. "I don't want to confuse the children. Speaking of, where are they?" he asked looking over my shoulder attempting to evade anymore conversation about the topic.

"Marcia took them to the zoo, and I won't have any such thing! What's going to confuse them is your staying at some hotel and not here with us. Now go get that bag!" I demanded turning him around back out the door.

"It should be fine."

I held my hands up for him to stop. "Are we going to do this again? End of conversation. Moreover, you're outnumbered," I laughed. "The children have a full night planned for you," I fibbed. "Popcorn and a whole stack of movies lined up. Now if this is about you not trusting yourself around me, we'll just have to talk about that," I hinted to test the waters.

"Naw, it's not that. I just don't want to make this anymore confusing for the children, that's all."

So he didn't take the bait.

"Then skedaddle!" I asserted, sweeping him out the door with a gesture of my hands.

"No, honestly, Mia, I..."

"Myles, do you hear yourself?"

"You're not thinking about Tiff and Brandon. You know it'll break their hearts if you don't stay here," I told him applying the guilt trip.

He inhaled a deep sigh. "I guess you're right. "I'll be right back."

My suspicions were correct. Myles was involved with another woman. I felt it. I smelled it in the air. I knew him too well. He was trying extremely hard to avoid eye contact, and his sudden concern about sleeping arrangements didn't fool me one bit. Fine. We'd see how much self-control he really had when it came to resisting me.

No worries, Mia. Time to pull out all the stops.

When he returned with his bag, an ominous mood hovered over him.

He had not planned on staying in the house for reasons other than being tempted by me. I suspected he'd told his new woman he would be sleeping at a hotel to make her comfortable.

"Follow me silly."

I made sure to put a little extra something, something in the sway of my hips as I led him up the stairway to the bedroom next to mine. The sundress was hurting him. I could feel his eyes on my ass. I walked into the bedroom and sat on the bed. He dropped the bag on the floor by the dresser and turned as if he were going to leave the room.

"Sit down for a second," I invited him tapping the space beside me on the bed.

"I'm good," he stuttered.

I got up, grasped his sweaty hand and escorted him over to the bed where he reluctantly sat down. The connection between my husband and I hadn't gone anywhere. It still had a pulse. My pride silently demanded that I not attempt to kiss him, but I didn't listen. I reached for his moist hands and leaned in toward him. He didn't resist my advance until our lips met.

"Mia, I can't," he whispered unconvinced. He tried to remove his hands from mine, but I wouldn't let go.

"Why not, Myles?" I didn't retreat.

"Because it's not right. There's been too much pain," he said exhaling.

"So how do we make it right?"

He paused for what felt like forever before saying anything. "I don't know that we can," he answered looking me in the eyes.

"We can if we take it one step at a time," I suggested. "Do you still love me, Myles?"

He inhaled another deep sigh. "I'd be lying if I said I didn't, Mia. I love the hell outta you and I hate myself for it. But I'm still fucked up. Really fucked up. I'm a broken man acting like I'm whole. My heart is still in pieces. There are places in my mind I can't go because if I do…God only knows. You were my wife. That shit meant everything to me. How do I ever touch you again knowing you cheated on me?"

It felt like Myles had hit me in the stomach with everything he had. Now the cat was out the bag. That was exactly what we needed, to put all the shit that had happened out on the table once and for all. I wasn't the least bit discouraged. Actually, the fact that he was talking to me gave me hope.

"Look at me, Myles," I pleaded. "I messed up. I did the worse thing a wife could do to her husband in the worse way. You didn't deserve that and there's nothing I can do or say to try and make it right. No apology is going to make it go away overnight. The only thing I can do is show you who I am now, fuck ups and all and ask you to give me another chance. Ask you to forgive me. Tell me what I have to do to help you trust me again and I'll do it. I'm willing to do whatever it takes to show you that I made a mistake and there's no excuse for it. I love you, Myles that never changed. I've been waiting for the opportunity to apologize to you for all the pain I've caused this family. We're here because of me. Not you, but me. I can't make excuses for what I've done but I can tell you I'm so sorry Myles. I'm so sorry."

I'd seen Myles cry three times; once when we got married and when the children were born. His father had taught him how to suppress his emotions well, so seeing tears well up in his eyes before streaming down his face like a quiet waterfall made me feel like shit. I reached to pull him close to me but he got up and went back downstairs.

I felt numb. Stupid. Defeated. Like he'd slapped me in my face without a single blow. I didn't know what to do. All I'd dreamt about since I saw him back in January was having my husband back. The way things were playing out, it looked like that wasn't going to happen. I couldn't give up that easily. I followed him downstairs and found him in the living room on the sofa with his face cupped in his hands. I placed my hand gently on his back. He didn't ward it off.

"Myles, what can I do to try and make this up to you?" I begged.

"Why did you leave the way you did?"

This time I sighed. "Guilt. Not having the courage to face my own fears, my own mistakes. Hoping it would make me forget how bad I felt about myself. Thinking I could just start all over and leave the past behind and somehow things would get better. I was selfish, Myles. There's just no other way to put it."

"Did you leave me for Dre?"

"No! Dre is the scum of the earth and every day I have to live with myself knowing what I did to you."

"Do you love him?" he asked still holding his head.

I assumed he was talking about Ty.

"No, Myles, I don't. I love you."

"Can you help me to understand how you could say you love me but run right into the arms of another man?"

I began to cry. "I didn't leave you with the intention of running to another man. I know that's how it looks but that's not how it happened. Shit! I mean that wasn't my plan. When I left home, I thought I was doing the best thing for you and our children because I was so confused. I was a mess, Myles. I chose to believe that you were miserable and I was to blame. I was making all kinds of shit up in my irrational mind. Now I understand that I didn't love myself because of the betrayal I'd been carrying around. Baby, I took you for granted and because of my own insecurities I chose to run instead of taking ownership of my mistakes. My heart has been yours since I first saw you, Myles. You're the only man I love. I need you to believe me."

He didn't respond. Sitting there with him in the silence, it hit me for the first time that I may have lost my husband for good.

"I don't know that I could ever trust you again, Mia. You hurt me to the core. I never want to feel that kind of pain ever. It almost took me out."

The phone rang and it startled me. "That's probably Marcia and the children." I assumed it was Marcia and without checking I answered the cordless phone next to me.

"Hello."

"Hey, Mia," Ty said.

My body froze. I could tell Myles read the look on my face like a book because he hastily got up and exited from the room.

"Ahh, hey," I said turning around to see where he was going, while trying to remain calm and not arouse his suspicions.

"You don't seem happy to hear from me."

I had no idea why Ty had to pick this moment out of all the time in the world to call me. I hadn't heard from him since the incident at the hotel back in May. I'd called him and left several messages. He never returned any of my calls. It was clear I'd been played. I suspected that many of his out of town 'business' trips were India related rather than business related. They could have each other.

"What do you want?" I whispered trying to contain my anger.

"Now is that anyway to talk to a long-lost lover," he had the audacity to ask.

"Cut the bullshit, Ty. Clearly, we have nothing to talk about and my husband is here," I purposely revealed. "I gotta go."

"Oh, it's like that?"

"Yeah. It is. Goodbye."

I hung up and went looking for Myles with the phone in my hand. I found him standing outside on the patio staring into space.

"Which one was that, Mia?" he asked with his back to me.

"That was Ty, and for the record I haven't spoken to him in over two months."

"Why?"

"It's a long story," I confessed exhausted.

"Gotcha. If you'll excuse me I have a phone call to make before Tiff and Brandon get back."

"I'm sorry, Myles," I said, trying to talk to him.

He continued past me.

"Look, if you want to hear it we can talk."

"It really won't make a difference one way or another, Mia," he shot back over his shoulder before disappearing in the house and up the stairs.

The phone rang again. This time I checked the caller ID. It was Marcia.

"Hey Marcia, where are you guys? That close? Okay, we'll see you in about ten minutes."

I wanted to go upstairs to let Myles know that the children were on their way home, but didn't want to invade his space any more than I already had. I decided to fix a light dinner instead. I longed to touch him, get back to where we were before things fell apart. I wasn't quite sure what to say to bridge the universe that had formed between us.

Opening the freezer I removed the salmon, turkey burgers, a few steaks and a pack of chicken. Hopefully, cooking out on the grill would subside some of the tension in the air and renew a family atmosphere so that Myles could remember how good we used to be.

"You need help with anything?" he asked sneaking up on me. I almost dropped the salad bowl.

"Of course. I figured we'd cook out on the grill unless you wanted to go out to eat?"

"Either one is fine with me. How long before Tiff and Brandon get back?"

"Is my company that bad?" I asked trying to make a light joke.

"Mia, damn! Let it fucking go!" he blurted out.

I put the bowl on the counter. "No Myles, I won't let it go. Don't you see that's what got us here? Letting shit go! Talk to me. Hell, curse me out if you need to! I can handle it. Say what's on your mind. Ask questions, but don't shut me out. Please."

"I got all the information I need to know at this point, Mia."

I walked over to him and stood in front of him.

"Do you know what I *need*, Myles? I need you to love me again. I don't want to hurt you and I don't want you to hurt me. I need you to tell me you love me and kiss me like you used to before our lives became one big lie. I need you to tell me we can be a family again. I need you to be able to forgive me and yourself so that you can be free from the pain I caused you. I need you to trust me again. I need you, Myles," I said softly and sincerely.

This time he looked me in my eyes instead of through me. His hard exterior cracked the door for a brief second allowing me to catch a glimpse of the love we used to share in his eyes. I was careful not to expose it by saying anything although it made me hopeful. We didn't need to spoil the moment with any further dialogue. Instead, like old times we moved in unison around each other getting things ready to cookout in the backyard. I felt like the luckiest woman in the world.

Marcia and the children walked through the door shortly after Myles and I silently proposed a truce.

"Daddy, daddy!" they both charged at him shouting.

"How are you, Mr. Rollins?"

"I'm better now, and you, Marcia?" Myles exclaimed while scooping the children up in his arms.

"Hot and sticky!" she laughed.

"Mrs. Rollins, would you like for me to put the car in the garage?"

"No, Marcia, its fine in the driveway. You two, off to the bathroom to wash your hands before you contaminate your daddy with monkey dirt!"

"Monkey dirt?" Brandon repeated with laughter. "There's no such thing as monkey dirt, mommy!"

"Oh yeah? Hold up those hands and you'll see it. Go wash it off!" I told him whacking his little bottom.

"Well if everyone will excuse me, I'm going upstairs to my room to wash the monkey, giraffe and lion dirt off of me!"

"Thanks for everything Marcia, we'll see you in a bit."

The children came back from the bathroom and spent the next hour or so filling Myles in on the details of each animal they'd seen in the zoo, where and what they ate, how long it took them to get there, on and on. He sat and listened attentively to their every word, asking questions, laughing hysterically at Brandon's interpretation of how the animals moved and the sounds they made. He patiently examined every single souvenir with care and uninterrupted attention.

My family together. What a miracle.

God and I weren't the best of friends for several reasons. Sometimes I felt as if I were part of a mold he intended to throw away but somehow ended up using. However, observing our children interact with their father from the sidelines secretly made me want to thank him for this moment.

Marcia rejoined us in the family room carrying a tray of fresh cut fruit, crackers, cups, paper plates and lemonade. Tiffany and Brandon both needed baths before dinner, but I wasn't about to disturb the peace.

For no reason that I could put my finger on my stomach felt jittery. Seconds later the phone rang. I tried to move but couldn't. Marcia swiftly answered it and went into the kitchen. When she came back into the room she gave me a look that let me know it was another hang up call. I didn't like what was going on and for the first time I felt scared.

Cut And Dry

Q

I LAID IN THE cut across the street from Monika's apartment buildin finishin my smoke before goin up.

I was gettin up with my man Myles in about an hour for a round of tennis since he wasn't gonna go to Jersey to sniff up Mia's ass the weekend.

I made copies of them joints I got in the mail to hand off when I seen him. They was sex tapes of bitch ass Dre bonin some crooked judge trick ass wife he was pimpin. I had no idea who sent the shit to me.

I googled the 'ole fart like the note said and seen them all over the fuckin internet like the three fuckin Stooges. On one site the wrinkly ole geezer was being interviewed and his ho and Dre was standin right next to his clueless ass.

Flickin the cigarette butt on the street I cut across the grass and went to the buzzer on the side of the buildin. Monika lived in a buildin with a bunch of nosey ass white muthafuckas. They acted like they neva saw a fuckin god before. One time some stuffy ass white dude did a triple take when he looked up and saw me comin down the hall. I lifted my shirt and gave him a real reason to be spooked. He doubled back to his crib and dropped his keys twice tryna get in his spot. His hands was shakin like he had Parkinson's and shit. A few minutes later the pigs was roamin. Muthafuckas.

I pushed the button on the intercom.

"Is that you, Q?"

"Buzz me up."

I rode the elevator up to the seventh floor and got off. Monika was waitin inside her door with nothin on. My kind of bitch.

I grabbed the back of her head and tongued her down.

Monika was a freak that knew how to keep her fuckin mouth shut and handle her business.

When I was done layin it down and showerin I got ready to bounce.

"What you doing later?"

"Chillin."

"You gonna come back by to finish what you started?" she asked brushin her naked ass against my shit.

"Depends," I told her going out the door.

My cell phone rang on the way to my ride.

"What's up Imani?" I answered lightin a smoke.

"How are you, Q?"

"Hangin." I took the smoke deep in my lungs and held it.

"I'm going to cut to the chase. There's something we need to talk about."

We didn't have shit we *needed* to talk about.

"Like," I asked after releasin the smoke from my lungs.

"I have to do it in person not over the phone. Are you busy now?" she asked.

"Yeah."

"Do you think you can squeeze me in any today?"

"Naw."

"When then, Q?"

"Friday."

"I'll take it. Where and what time?"

"Randolph's."

"On the Wharf?"

"Yeah. Eight o'clock."

"PM or AM."

"PM."

"That's perfect. I'll be there. This coming Friday, eight o'clock at Randolph's," she repeated. I appreciate it, Q, see you then."

"Yeah."

I got in my ride and bogarted out into traffic to make my way over to Norwood. I had no interest in what Imani wanted to talk to me about. I dialed Myles.

"Yo man, I was just about to call you!"

"What up?"

"I'm running behind. Give me another fifteen-twenty minutes."

"Cool."

"In a minute, bruh!"

I figured Myles musta got caught up tappin Veronica's ass. He was fuckin mute when it came to the broad. Like sayin nothin wasn't sayin somethin.

Every fuckin body and they momma was at the park. I dropped the ride off two blocks away walked back to the park dumped my shit on a bench and lit a cigarette. It wasn't as hot as it had been the last few weekends 'cause it rained Thursday and Friday but the suns dial was still set on bake. I had a bird's eye view of two thick'ems workin they game like they thought they was Venus and Serena. One of'em had ass for lifetimes.

The court to the left of them had two Spanish dudes who was ridin each other 'bout the ball being in or out every time they hit that shit. They asses was gonna be on the court all fuckin day just tryna get they game started.

Ova on one of the far courts down at the end I couldn't believe what I saw.

"Yo my man," I called to the two dudes on the court I was waitin for. "I got next."

"No problem, man," the taller cat yelled back, "we got you."

When I got down there and saw the little scrawny ass dude in a bright yellow fuckin sweat suit I knew it was Big G. I chuckled to myself. This shit was too good to be true. Whoever the dude he was spankin had a mean game but Big G was bitch slappin his ass around the court like he fucked his momma.

'Ole pimp had no clue today was his unlucky muthafuckin day. Myles was gonna finally get his chance to get at'em.

Right when I was about to hit my man up the kid holla'ed to let me know they was done. Headin back that way I saw my boy comin down the street.

"What up!" his way too chipper ass said with his hands in the air.

"You one happy grinnin skinnin sambo. Yo ass nothing but a fuckin wall of teeth."

We dapped. He sat down on the ground and unloaded the bag off his shoulder so he could stretch.

"It's a beautiful day, why wouldn't I be!"

"You got Lady in there?"

"Say what! You want to get a beat down like that, dawg!" his corny ass laughed.

"You got fuckin jokes. She might wanna spank Big G. Take a look down there," I told him pointin at the far end of the courts.

You woulda thought I said Janet was callin his name the way he jumped up picked up his shit and jetted off.

"Yo, you done with that court, my man?" some young wanna be thug walked up on me and questioned.

"Who wanna know?"

His punk ass figured it out quick. I went down to check out the ass whoppin Big G was 'bout to get. My man didn't waste no time. He went right in for the kill.

"Well, well, well, if it ain't the little old tennis court bully in the yellow sweat suit trying to find a prey so he can have his pint sized ego stroked," my dawg said, strollin big willy on the court and circlin Big G. Myles was actin like he was havin flashbacks from that ass whippin he got earlier. The other dude looked fuckin confused as shit.

"Looks like you still ain't learned no manners, son. Now if you'll excuse us, we were in the middle of a match."

Shit was gonna get heated real fast. Myles dropped his bag on the ground like he forgot Lady was in it. He took her out and tossed the bag behind the court. My man pointed Lady in the direction of the dude who was clueless.

"I'll take over from here. What's the score my man?"

"Ahh...I was serving and down thirty, love," he stuttered.

"Perfect!"

"Yo, my man!" I called ova to dude. "Step off the court."

Myles was already on the other side set. Big G knew he couldn't bitch out. Besides that his ego wasn't turnin down no challenge. Stupid muthafucka didn't even see the beat down comin. Myles was neva gonna let him whip his ass twice.

"Kenny, if you'll excuse this very bad-mannered boy, I'll make this quick," Big G told the cat.

"Yup." His punk ass walked off and sat down on the bench behind the court.

"Usually I don't entertain losers, but you know, son," Big G told Myles walkin to his side of the court, "I got this strange feeling your old man forgot to teach you a valuable lesson about respect, or maybe you were too busy being hard-headed to listen. Now your boy back there he seems to be a levelheaded young man, and I can't believe he's never told you that it ain't good for a young blood like yourself to walk around so cocky. It's a very dangerous thing."

For Big G to bring Myles' pop up was the wrong answer. Ole pimp was sealin his coffin with his big ass mouth. This shit was gonna be better than I thought.

"You running your mouth too much granddaddy. Giving out a lot of parental advice. Let's me know that fortunately that opportunity musta passed ya by. Well in case nobody told you, it's a little too late for you in that arena so keep your weak ass parenting skills to yo'self, granddad. And that psychology bullshit may have worked last time. You gonna have to come with a new hustle this go round, pops. Let's do this."

That bitch Lady in Red set Myles back close to a grand and was strung tight as a virgin's pussy. Her ass was flippin round and round in his hands. She was 'bout to have Big G callin his 'ole ass momma from the grave.

Homie sent his first shot barrelin down the line pass granddaddy. From there my man was all up dat ass. 'Ole dude didn't stand a chance. He couldn't hit shit my man slammed across the net. The ancient dinosaur was gettin that ass tore up so bad the muthafucka punked out and walked off. Dude didn't wanna give my man his braggin rights. He snatched up his shit like a little fuckin boy and bounced. The shit wasn't even a competition. I had seen dawg play his top game before but he took it to another level on Big G.

"Damn man! Did you have to strip the muthafucka down like that?" I laughed watchin him walk out the park and cross the street almost gettin hit. "You better watch 'yo back. That muthafucka might be goin ta get some heat out the trunk the way he stomped off."

"I got his heat. Man that shit felt good! One thing I hate is a coward," My boy said chuggin down a Gatorade he pulled out his bag. "I knew I could beat him if I got another chance. He took me off my game last time, but I wasn't going to fall for that shit again."

"That dude is a time bomb. He the type you just gotta cap," I told Myles who was checkin his phone.

"Yeah, well he ain't the only crazy grape in the bunch."

"Man where do you come up with the lame ass shit you say sometimes?"

"That's one of mother's."

"Now why you gonna go lie like that!" I asked him after sittin on the ground next to my bag. I pulled out the envelope with the note and copies of the discs I made.

"What's that?" He took his eyes off the phone for a split second and went back to textin.

"Your insurance policy."

Myles copped a squat. "Is that what the secrecy's all about?"

"You got it." I handed ova the envelope.

Myles pulled out the note and read it. "Where'd you get this?"

"It was in my mailbox in that envelope."

"What's on them? Did you google the guy?" he asked readin the note again.

"You'll see. We gone do this?"

"Yeah, yeah for sure. I think I got a little whoop ass left."

"Fuck you."

"Check it, I need to ask you a question first and I'ma just go straight, no chaser. Word is you raped Torie. Is that true?"

"That's some bitch shit."

"People talk, man."

"And I gives a fuck."

"That's your problem, you *don't* give a fuck, homie."

I laughed. "Yo B you crackin me the fuck up right now."

"Listen man, I ain't here to try and change you because we both know that's a waste of time. I got a daughter man, and if my baby came to me and told me some motherfucker raped her I automatically got a case. You with me?"

"What's that got to do with me?"

"If you did it just own your shit. Don't play word games or justify it, man."

"Justify? You a funny muthafucka. Im'a school you on some real shit 'cause you my man. You wanna do somethin for a trick? Tell her ass dudes like me is real. We don't gives a fuck. About shit. As much as you muthafuckas like to think we do we don't. Cats like me don't live by them empty bullshit moral codes the thugs who made dem shits up don't even respect. They pullin 'yo strings got 'yo ass dancin to a lie while they laughin all the way to the muthafuckin bank. Me. I'm 'bout as real as you muthafuckin get. I'm the thug without a fuckin mask. You see me comin you know what you get. Justifyin shit don't cross my muthafuckin mind homie. Shit simply is or it ain't. Straight up."

"So there's no line, man? You just do whatever the fuck you want to whoever?"

"Yeah, my man there's a line. The same fuckin line you drew when you tried to knock that bitch ass Dre off."

"So you comparing what you did to Torie with Dre?"

"I just told 'yo ass I don't compare. Shit simply is or it ain't. E'rebody makin the shit up as they go along includin you. You handle your beefs your way and I handle mine's mine."

Wasn't like Myles to preach to me about no chick. I packed my shit and got the fuck up to roll out.

"It's not that cut and dry, Q."

"In who's muthafuckin world homie?"

It All Makes Sense

Myles

VERONICA WAS BLOWING up my cell phone while Q was talking. His logic, or lack thereof never ceased to amaze me. As a matter of fact it had gotten crazier. I wondered how much the absence of a father played a part in creating the heartless gangsta he'd become, but then again if that was the case I should have been in the same boat with him. Even though I had a father it was like I really didn't. As close as my man and I were, I felt like there was a part of him that I didn't know. Granted, there were no secrets between us, but there was a gap. Something that kept us on opposites sides of reality. One day he was going to make a choice that he was truly sorry for.

I tried to call Veronica back several times after Q left, but each time her phone went directly to voicemail.

I gathered up my things and decided to go home, take a shower, and head over to her house. I'd be early but I didn't think she'd mind. The eagerness to see Veronica had me showered and out the house in under forty-five minutes. It had me speeding down the Parkway and turning the corner to my destination in twenty minutes instead of the usual thirty, but when I turned into the neighborhood, I saw two ambulances, police officers and yellow tape obstructing the entrance. Immediately, the air got thinner making it hard to breath. I came to a screeching stop in the middle of the street, threw my car in park, got out and ran toward my parents' house. Although most of the commotion was in front of Veronica's house, my first priority was to make sure my parents were okay. I attempted to go under the yellow tape but was instantly stopped by a female officer.

"Excuse me sir, this is a restricted area, you can't go in there," she said standing firmly in front of me.

"That's my parents' house!" I said, pointing to the big brick house.

"Sir, I'm going to need you to back up. No one is allowed on this street."

"Officer I need to go and check on my parents!"

"Boy, step down," I heard my father's voice demand. "Let him in Clarisse. That's my son."

"Yes sir." She respectfully stepped aside.

I didn't say anything to him. The only thing I wanted to know was that my mother was okay. I ran up the steps two by two and bust in the front door. I saw her standing in the usual spot by the window. Despite the troubled look on her face, I felt relieved. I walked over and hugged her.

"You okay?" I inquired holding her in my arms.

"We fine baby."

"What's going on?" I asked looking out the window across the street at Veronica's house.

Before she could say a word, a police cruiser drove off and I spotted a white sheet on the ground near the sidewalk in Veronica's yard. There was yellow tape around the entire circumference of her house and her door was wide open. I froze, like somebody had suddenly turned off my nervous system. I ran out the door. If something had happened to Veronica I didn't want to hear it from my mother.

Paying careful attention not to look at the sheet on the ground, I attempted to cross under the tape outside her house, but was once again met with resistance by a tall thin black cop that a faint wind would take down.

"Sir, you can't go in there."

"My girlfriend lives in that house."

"No one is allowed in this area."

"What happened?" I asked grabbing my head.

"I can't discuss that with you."

"You can't fucking tell me if she's alright!" I yelled.

"No I cannot, sir."

The last thing I wanted to do was to go and ask my father to help me get in Veronica's house. My pride and fear were in a tug of war when he walked up and stood beside me with his hands in his pocket.

"How are you, Barry," he asked the scrawny officer.

"I'm holding my post, sir!"

"Good, good," my father praised him.

"That's not your business," he exclaimed as if I'd asked him a question.

"I don't remember asking you if it were."

"Gentlemen this is my son. He can go in for a minute," he firmly stated to the officers posted at the front door.

"Yes, sir," one of the officers at the door called back before disappearing in the house. I waited anxiously for him to return.

I wasn't moved by my father's sudden display of kindness, but I was grateful to know that Veronica wasn't the one on the ground under the sheet. The officer appeared back outside and waved me forward. I dipped under the tape and sprinted up the steps.

Her terrified eyes met mine when I crossed the threshold. She was seated between two female cops on the couch in her living room. Her body was trembling. Part of me was thankful to see her but at the same time petrified at the thought of what could have happened. Her clothes were torn and her eyes and lips were swollen. Dried blood was on her lip. A gash in her leg was bleeding lightly. She looked like she'd been in a horrible fight with someone. Pictures were shattered on the floor and furniture was overturned. Veronica's TV had been flipped over and a window shattered. I kneeled down in front of her and took her trembling hands. She hugged me tightly. The two officers got up to give us space.

"You okay?" I asked.

"No," she whispered.

"What happened baby, what's going on?' I asked, not letting go of her.

"I shot him, Myles, I shot him!" she said, crying hysterically.

"Who did you shoot, baby? Who is *he*?"

"He's been following me and…and…and threatening to kill me and Brooklyn. He came here in a rage," she managed to verbalize despite nearly hyperventilating. "I didn't know what else to do when he came at me. I fought him off and got to the gun. I ran out the house but he followed me," she cried.

"He knocked me down and I shot him! He's dead!"

I held her close to me trying to grasp what she'd said while she cried in my arms. I felt guilty that I hadn't been there for her like I promised.

"It's okay baby, it's okay. You did the right thing. It was either you or him. I know a good lawyer. She'll help you, don't worry," I tried to soothe her, still wondering who *he* was.

"Myles you have to do me a favor," she stated quickly as if momentarily checking back in from a daze. "You have to go in the kitchen and get my sister's phone number off the blue card on the refrigerator. It says Lisa Fairland," she said, pointing to the kitchen.

I looked up at one of the officers.

"You can't go in there sir," she hesitated. "I'll get it for you."

She left and came back with the card.

"Is this it, ma'am?"

Veronica nodded her head. She handed me the card and I sat next to Veronica and held onto her cold hands.

"Call her right away and tell her George found me. She'll know what to do," Veronica rattled off as if she'd been preparing for this day a million times in her head.

A voice on the other end of one of the police officer's walkie-talkie instructed them to bring her out.

"Ma'am you'll need to come with us." They both gently escorted her up from the couch.

"Where is she going?" I asked in shock.

"She has to go to the station for booking, sir," the officer said before placing a set of handcuffs around her wrists. Veronica broke down and began to cry harder. She tried to pull away and come back to me. I didn't know what to do.

"Ah come on, do you have to do that!" I pleaded. "Can't you just walk her out without those?"

"Procedure. I'm going to need you to step outside, sir."

I did.

"Myles, promise me you'll call Lisa right away."

"I will and don't worry, baby, I'll get you out as soon as I can," I tried to reassure her.

I kissed her on the lips and watched as each officer held onto an arm and walked her out of the house. I followed them out. The neighbors were out in droves whispering amongst themselves. Watching her walk to the cruiser in handcuffs with her head down was some painful shit. When she got in the car and they drove off past the questioning faces of the crowd, I wanted to tell them all to go to hell.

I glanced at the spot where the body lay and wondered who *he* was. Mother was standing on the porch when I passed the house.

"You alright, son?" she asked.

"No. I'll be right back. I need to go and move my car and make a call."

"Okay, baby."

It took me about fifteen minutes to call both Kymile and Veronica's sister and explain what I knew. Unfortunately, Kymile was in the Bahamas and wouldn't be back until the following Friday, but she promised to call one of her partners the moment we got off the phone to see what they could do and call me back.

The conversation with Lisa was bizarre. None of what I told her seemed a surprise. Cool and collected, she thanked me for the information and told me she would take it from there. I tried to tell her that I had contacted one of the best lawyers on the east coast for Veronica, but she assured me things were in place. I didn't insist. Lisa wasn't rude, just very matter of fact. I wondered if Veronica told her about me or if she just thought I was some stranger calling. Her sister was the only family she ever talked about. Just like the rest of her life, things were very secretive. I realized I didn't know much about her at all.

I found a place to park my car and solemnly walked back to my parents.

Mother was in the kitchen. "Would you like somethin to drink?" she asked as I dumped my body in a chair by the window.

"No, thank you."

"How is she?"

"As well as to be expected under the circumstances. By chance did you see what happened?"

"All's I saw was that strange lookin lil' man standin on her porch. I didn't think any more of it 'cause she let him in. I knows she don't let nobody in that house less she know'em. So I went on 'bout my business. Next thang I see, Veronica running out the house screaming at the top of her lungs and he on her tail. I called your father to come upstairs. Then I heard shots."

"I promised her I'd be there for her."

"Now don't you go blamin yourself."

"It's all so crazy. She said he'd been following her and making threats to kill her and Brooklyn, but she never said who he was, though. Why did you say he was strange looking?"

"Well he was a lil' tiny older man with dem tattoos all over his body and he had on bright, bright yellow shorts and yellow socks. Look to me like he coulda been her..."

I could not believe my ears!

Could it have been? No way! Big G and Veronica!

Suddenly things were adding up.

What were the chances Big G was the one she had been afraid of all this time?

There was no way in the world two people would be running around in bright yellow outfits. The tattoos. It was too much of a coincidence.

"It can't be," I blurted out loud, startling mother.

"Lawd have mercy boy, you 'bout to give me a heart attack! What's wrong?"

I rose to my feet. "I'm sorry, mother, I have to go. I'll call you later!"

"What's the matter, son?" she called after me.

I didn't have time to explain. Bursting through the front door, I ran down the street and got in my car. I felt nauseous and lightheaded. In my mind Veronica and Big G's world should have had no connection. The two of them together didn't compute. The thought made me want to earl. My head began to throb. First of all, he was much older than her, and secondly he was a raving lunatic! If it were true though, it would explain why she was so paranoid. The dude was a loose cannon.

Why would she be involved with a deranged psycho like him? I mean there had to be an explanation.

I dialed Kymile back.

"Hello?"

"Hey Kymile, sorry to bother you again, but I just wanted to give you a heads up that you can squash the phone call to your partner. Veronica's sister already has a lawyer."

"You positive? What happened?"

I really didn't want to go into detail because I had a more important phone call to make.

"Real quick, they booked her but her sister is on it. I'll fill you in when you get back. I gotta go."

I hung up from her and made a call to a connection I had down at the city morgue. Lucas and I had become acquaintances over the course of the last four years. I'd established a track record of identifying over ninety percent of the deceased patients who I'd seen at some point in their lives through dental records for the morgue. As a result, Lucas was impressed. We became cool to the point I had his personal cell phone number. This time I required his assistance. Although it was the weekend, Lucas favored spending more time with dead people than he did the living, so the probability of him being at work was high. I dialed his digits.

"Lucas here."

"Hey Lucas, Dr. Myles Rollins, how are you?"

"Hey Dr. Rollins, what a surprise! Our phone calls usually go the other way around. To what do I owe the honor?" he asked sincerely.

Lucas stood a little over five feet tall, weighed about a hundred pounds wet and had fire red hair that had no particular care about what it did on the top of his head. He wore a pair of glasses that were barely held together in the middle by dingy pieces of white tape. They sat loosely on his nose and he habitually kept shoving them back up on his face with his pointing finger. I wanted to go and buy him a pair of glasses, but I knew full well if I did he wouldn't wear them. He reminded me of the kid that had been an outcast in school who spent most of his time dissecting any animal that dared to cross his path.

"I need a personal favor, Lucas."

"Go on."

"You're going to have a body come in sometime tonight. Homicide over on Highland Drive in SE. He's a shooting victim about fifty or sixty years old. He's heavily tattooed and might be dressed in yellow shorts and yellow socks…I'm not making this up. When he comes in I need you to get as much information as you can on him as well as what happened and call me back."

"Oh you mean the stalker that caught one right 'tween the eyes?" Lucas laughed. "They already called him in. Probably won't be here 'til after midnight. He a patient of yours, Doc?" Lucas asked cautiously.

I wasn't sure whether I should tell the truth or not.

"No."

"You ain't rock-a-bye'em, did you?" he laughed uneasily.

"No."

"Okie dokie. I'll give you a call when he comes in."

"Thanks Lucas. I owe you."

More than anything, I needed a drink. Too much had happened too fast. I felt partly guilty for Big G's death because when he left the tennis courts he was an explosion ready to happen. To imagine that he was the source of Veronica's fear was mind blowing. The story that connected the two of them was one I couldn't wait to hear.

I didn't want to go back to my parent's house and didn't feel comfortable interfering with Veronica's sisters efforts to get her out, so I opted to have a few drinks at Treasures, a local sports bar in the neighborhood.

I don't remember much about the drive to the bar. My thoughts were a mixture of shit that didn't all go together: Mia, the kids, Q, Veronica, Big G, my father, my life.

I found a seat at the bar between two beautiful sistas and ordered a Grand Marnier straight. I spoke to them out of courtesy, but my body language made it clear that I wanted to be alone.

I swirled the liquid around in my glass before taking a swallow. Fate was an unpredictable visitor. Never in my wildest dreams could I have imagined that the man I was playing tennis with earlier in the day would be shot dead by the woman I was seeing. If Big G was stalking Veronica maybe he knew about us. I chugged the rest of my drink down to stifle my thoughts from running rampant. I'd checked my phone a hundred times to see if I had missed a call from Lisa with an update on Veronica, but she hadn't called. Hopefully, her sister would help her make bail as soon as possible. I had a few more drinks, paid my tab and headed home partly intoxicated.

Not long after I got home Lucas called.

"Hello."

"Doc, we are about to have the conversation we never had, Capiche? Capiche!"

"What convo?" I stated anxiously.

One thing was obvious about Lucas, he didn't need anybody else to entertain him, he did a good job all by himself.

"There were two bullet holes in his head. One dead center and the other in his temple. The female who put his lights out is a killer shot. Story is he'd been stalking her for quite a while. She moved around to keep him at bay 'cause he'd been threatening to kill her. I'm no expert, but what it looks like we have here is a classic case of self-defense." Lucas recounted for me.

"The coward could have used your services," he added. His choppers needed some work! This guy ain't seen a dentist in years! Oh, I almost forgot. She told one of the detectives he raped her and she got knocked up."

Told You So

Mia

THIS WAS THE third time Daphne had put me on hold. If she did it one more time I was gonna hang up on her ass. Bad enough I elected to drive and was stuck in gridlock rush hour traffic on the George Washington Bridge trying to get my ass home. I'd spent the longest day of my life with a client who was the wife of a very wealthy doctor. The heifer could shop anybody under the table. She'd already paid me fifty grand to design the color palate for two summer homes, one in the Hamptons and the other one in Key West. I had to follow her around pretending to be excited about the horrific suggestions she picked for color schemes when I could have done it by myself. I wanted to tell her that the money she was spending to furnish two houses that she'd probably live in for a month out of the year at the most could feed a small country, but who was I to judge. In essence she was feeding a small family which just happened to be mine.

"Mia, you still there baby girl? Where were we?" Daphne came back to the line out of breath. "I gotta get some exercise! I'm so outta shape it's ridiculous!"

"Where else I'm going in all this damn traffic! You got one more time to put me on hold and I'm hanging up," I threatened.

"Whatever, listen, like I was saying, whew, I don't like the looks of this right here. I'm glad you cut ties with your multi-millionaire lover boy. My PI's are the Crème de la crème; they don't miss shit. Your boy turned up clean as a whistle. They ain't find a spot, not a blemish on him, you hear me! No parking tickets, no warrants, unpaid bills, no passports, no child support. Really! How the hell you travel outta the country as frequently as he does and you ain't got a passport in your *supposed* name? That's some bullshit! I smell a fish! It's like he moving under another guise. He's got something to hide and he's paying somebody a few bills to keep it hidden. We know he got a passport. He's gotta have one. The question is whose name is it in?" Daphne concluded.

"Ty doesn't have any children so why would child support show up for him? That's so stereotypical. Secondly, when did this turn into an investigation about Ty? I thought you were trying to find out who was following me?" I asked half annoyed.

"If all the pistons were firing in your head and the cheese wasn't slipping halfway off the cracker you would see the correlation, baby girl. Might I remind you, the man vamoosed the night ya'll left the hotel, and didn't bother to explain why you couldn't reach him on either of his phones, one of which he uses for emergencies."

"And your point is? I still don't see what this has to do with my being followed, unless you're insinuating that Ty is the one following me, which if you are, would make you crazier than I thought you were."

"My God help her! Help her Lawd! Mia, what do you *really* know about this man other than how good he lays the pipe? Do you know any of his friends, have you met his relatives, anybody who knows him that you can talk to unbiased? If you recall, you were supposed to meet his friend that lives in Hawaii New Year's eve until he cancelled on 'yo ass at the last minute. I'd bet my last dollar you don't know if he has relatives because everybody around him either turns up dead or don't exist. I know the man should have a record of some kind because I know his *real* story. The one he didn't tell in Black Entrepreneur, honey. The average person wouldn't know that story because somebody has cleaned him up and made him look like he's always been an upstanding citizen. That's what people like me are paid top dollar to do. We polish them off, shine them up, clean up this, make that disappear, and miraculously, you've got a new athlete, politician, celebrity or what the fuck ever you want! Shit, here's that other call! This is paper baby. I'll call you later, love you!"

"Love you, too."

Daphne clicked over to the other line and I glanced out the window admiring the NY skyline from my standstill spot on the bridge. As much as I hated to admit it, some of what she said rang true. Most of what I knew about Ty came from the horse's mouth or magazine articles I'd read. When you put it all together it wasn't a lot.

To tell the truth, I had never checked into his story. I just took it at face value. Now Daphne had me wondering if I may have put too much trust in a man I didn't really know. Ty was a very powerful man and with power came enemies. The more I thought about his potential connection to my being followed I got angry and scared. Angry because my children were at risk, scared because I didn't have any idea what I might be in the middle of.

The thought had me second guessing my decision to allow Marcia to take the children on an overnight safari at the Bronx Zoo. Tiff and Brandon had befriended two other children in the neighborhood their age who had gone along for the excursion.

With them gone overnight, I'd have a few hours to catch up on some paperwork that had piled up over the past few weeks, and do a little bit of cleaning before Myles arrived tomorrow.

My ego hadn't quite healed from the night he rejected me. To add fuel to the fire, he didn't come visit last weekend. If I had any prior doubts that he was seeing someone else his no show confirmed it. One thing I never had to worry about was Myles turning down sex, especially when I had on anything tight or short. Tomorrow I planned to put all my cards on the table. I wanted my husband and family back and I intended to do whatever it required to make that happen.

Two hours after I'd left Manhattan I pulled up to my garage, thankful to be home, and hungry as a dog. After I ate something, the first thing on the agenda was a nice hot shower to rinse off the sweat and stickiness that had attached itself to me from being out in the heat.

I pressed the larger button on my garage door opener clipped to the visor and waited for it to come to a complete stop. For some reason the hairs on the back of my neck stood straight up as I was driving in. Instantly, I looked around but didn't see anything. I pressed the button again to lower the door back down, reached for my purse and opened the car door. Just as I did, I saw a figure coming at me. I tried to close the car door shut, but a hand snatched it and flung it open. In an instant, I was face to face with a dark mask, dragged out the car by my arm and over-powered in a split second. I fought to free myself from the tight hold but I was no match. The more I struggled the snugger the grip tightened. The chokehold covered my mouth. My hands were locked behind my back with the intruder's other hand. I was masterfully held hostage.

"I'm not interested in hurting you if you do what I say."

His mouth was so close to my ear I could feel his hot breath on my face. My heart was beating out of control. I felt lightheaded and dizzy from not being able to breathe. All the fear I'd amassed from being fol-lowed and hung up on was staring me in the face.

"Where are your keys?" he asked calmly.

I didn't realize until he'd asked that I had left them in the ignition. I tried to beckon my head toward the car but I couldn't move it because of his grip. I tried to move my eyes from side to side to see if he was alone. I wondered if he had a weapon, but it wouldn't have mattered if he did; his hands were weapons.

"Go get'em and if you ever want to move another muscle I suggest you not turn around or make any sudden moves."

He let me go and that's when I felt the gun in my side. Shaking, I did exactly as I was told. I was so nervous; I could barely get the key out the ignition.

"Here's what we're going to do. I want you to walk over to the door and put the key in slowly. We're going to walk over to your alarm and you're going to punch in the security code, not the emergency code. If you try to key in the emergency code and the cops come, they'll come in on a dead body. I don't have anything to lose. You on the other hand have everything to lose, it's your choice," he stated just as calmly as he had the first instruction.

I had no interest in dying so I followed his commands to the tee. I punched in the correct code, but had to do it two times because my hands were unsettled.

"Head over there and sit down. Keep your back to me." He shoved the gun deeper into my side.

I sat in one of my wingback chairs in my great room facing the window. My knees were knocking. The voice was beginning to sound familiar, but I couldn't place it.

"You got yourself involved in something way over your head, Mia. I'm only gonna say this once," he advised, sending a chill down my spine because I realized he had called me by my name.

"Who are you and what do you want from me?" I mumbled. In my mind, I had gone through every strategy I could think of to get out of this situation alive; however, I was at a disadvantage with my back to him.

"Turn the chair around."

He unhurriedly peeled the mask off his face with the same hand he held the gun with.

"Kwame?" I asked. "Have you been following me?" I stammered. His countenance said more than any words he could have uttered. The hatred, indifference and animosity he had for me emanated from his pores, heightening my fear beyond measure. I felt totally vulnerable but tried to give off an air of confidence. He'd lost a lot of weight and his locs were gone. He looked worn, tired and empty. There were heavy bags under his eyes, and it looked like he hadn't slept in days. His black pants, tennis shoes and jacket suggested Salvation Army or Goodwill. I wondered if his drinking were out of control.

"You ain't fooling nobody. I had your number the first time I seen you."

"I don't think you've been following me and my children around, putting us in jeopardy and trying to scare the hell out of us to tell me what you think about me," I said, trying to make a brave attempt at establishing some ground. The smirk on his face and the coldness in his eyes brought me back to reality. It was almost as if I was humoring him.

"You give yo'self too much credit. The only place I'd follow you is straight to hell to make sure you got a seat next to satan. You better be glad I got to you before you and your children end up dead, even though it don't make no difference to me one way or another," he said dryly.

His talking in riddles was heightening my angst. It petrified me to think he wasn't the only one following me.

"So why are you here? And why did you force yourself into my house if you don't give a shit?" I asked with cynicism, looking him dead in his eyes.

"Once again you got your blame fingers pointed in the wrong direction. I ain't the one putting your family in danger. You doing a good job of that all by yo'self."

What possessed me to fly up off the chair and stand toe to toe with him and his gun, I'll never know. I'd had my fill of insults, and he was right, there was gonna be a dead body in my house, his or mine. At this point I didn't care. My anger took over.

"Either you do whatever it was you came here to do or get the fuck out my house! Who the hell do you think you are? Does it make you feel important emphasizing other people's faults? You're not perfect."

Kwame didn't flinch or move. He grinned and broke out laughing right in my face. Part of me wanted to smack the shit out of him. The man was obviously not in his right mind. Nevertheless, if he wanted to hurt me he had plenty of opportunity, which led me to believe he had other intentions.

He walked past me and I turned on my heels to see where he was going, paying special attention to the gun. He sat down in the chair I'd been sitting in and crossed his legs. He looked around the room and then back at me with disdain.

"They say God takes care of babies and fools, and you're living proof that there must be some truth to that saying," he continued with his insults.

"Yeah well it takes one to know one," I retaliated.

"I'll never have grandbabies. Won't get the chance to 'cause some punk thought he'd send a message to the joker he had a beef with by taking out my baby girl," he began in a low tone while waving the gun around in the air. "She was a beautiful woman, just like her mother, long legs, big brown eyes and a smile to die for. Her mother did the right thing by putting me out when she was just a little girl 'cause I wasn't ready to give up the booze."

In the pit of my stomach, I had a nauseating feeling but didn't know why. Part of me had known all along that the deep hatred and loathing Kwame directed at me wasn't personal.

"In the beginning," he continued as if talking to himself, "I resented her mother for throwing my shit in the streets. I stayed away thinking I'd pay her back. When I sobered up sixteen years later, I found out that I was the one who had lost out in the end. Her mother's best friend was happy to tell me that before RosaLee passed away, she told my baby girl I was dead. In a way I was. Determined to find her, I spent years chasing dead ends. Then one day while I was watching television, there she was. I recognized her immediately. She was talking about her work at Monet's and then she mentioned her mother's name. She was even more beautiful than I remembered or had dreamed."

Kwame didn't have to say her name. I knew instantly that he was talking about Nina.

"I moved to NY from Florida the next day. A week later I got a job in the kitchen at Monet's. I had no intentions of undoing the past. As far as she knew her father was dead. Watching her from a distance was enough. I only got to spend two years with my baby before she was gone."

"Why do you feel the need to rehash your short comings with me? I'm not interested in hearing how you couldn't be a man and own up to your responsibilities. What the hell does that have to do with me?"

"I have come across a lotta people in my life but never anybody like you. You think ignorance is an excuse to shit on people," he said with apparent disgust. "I hope I get to see karma shove her foot up your ass one day."

I watched Kwame rise from the armchair and head to the front door. When he got there he turned to face me and stare me down one last time.

"I will tell you this much for your children. Ty killed my Nina. He may not have rigged her car, but the goons who killed her are the same ones on your trail. The rivalry between those thugs go back to the streets when they were gangbangers. I might get to them first thanks to the interest they've shown in you. Either way, you can't run from the fact that your choices might cost you a lot more than what you bargained for. I know. My Nina ain't stand a chance. She fell for the same smooth talking bullshit you did. But every dog got his day."

In that moment, standing there listening to him, the depth of my involvement with Ty hit me. My whole body trembled.

"The least I could do is warn you, but given your track record for caring about anybody other than yo'self, I probably coulda saved my breath."

I walked over to the front door and opened it. "Yeah, well why don't you just do that on the other side of this door."

Kwame gave me a once over look spiked with venom before walking out the front door. I didn't know what to do. I slammed the door shut and locked it. I stood in the same spot trying to grasp the full implication of what he had dropped on me. If what he said had any truth to it, he was Nina's father, a piece of information I couldn't help but wonder if Ty knew.

Damn, Mia, how could you have been so naïve! This must've been what Daphne was trying to tell me about Ty."

Now I regretted not listening to her.

The very first thing I could think of to do was to call Marcia on her cell phone to make sure they were fine, then I needed medicine. Carefully, I held onto the banister as I walked up the stairs. It felt like I couldn't make it to the medicine cabinet fast enough. By the time I got to the bathroom, my head hurt so badly, I had to take the painkillers sitting on the toilet seat. Luckily, I'd left a cordless phone in the bathroom.

"Hey Marcia." I attempted to disguise the fear in my voice.

"Hello Mrs. Rollins, is everything okay?" she asked.

"Of course! I just wanted to check on you guys and see if you're having fun?" I lied.

"We are! They are preparing for snacks and a movie!"

"Remind me again Marcia, what time are you all heading back in the morning?"

"Breakfast is at seven. I thought we'd leave after that. Is everything okay, Mrs. Rollins?" she asked again.

"Perfect. I miss the children that's all."

"Any more hang-ups?"

"No, but you don't need to be worrying about that Marcia. Enjoy yourselves!"

"Well don't you worry about us either. The children are having a blast!"

"See you guys when you get home. Kiss them for me."

"I will. Good bye Mrs. Rollins."

I felt a little better even though the painkillers seemed like they were losing the battle against my throbbing head. Daphne was going to love an opportunity to say I told you so, but at this point it didn't matter. I stumbled over to my bed and laid down on the floor in front of it to call her back.

"Hey honey, you still on the phone?"

"Yeah, hold on a sec."

Daphne spent more time on her cell phone than anybody I knew.

"Sorry 'bout that baby, what's up?"

"Kwame was waiting for me when I got home and forced me in the house."

"Say what!" She yelled in my ear.

"Yeah. Believe it or not he didn't come here to hurt me. He actually came to warn me."

"Warn you?" About what?"

"Well, I guess this is where you can say I told you so. He came to tell me that Nina was his daughter. Apparently, Nina's mother put him out when she was a toddler after he began hitting the bottle pretty hard. Long story short, he ended up finding her after she started dating Ty. He got the job at Monet's to be near her on the down low."

"Making sense," she interjected. "Go ahead."

"This is where it gets ugly. According to him, Ty and some 'goon' as he called him, have had a rivalry since they were teenagers. He said Ty was a gangbanger. Kwame seems to think that whoever killed Nina did it to send Ty a message. It looks like they might still be trying to send him the same message by following me. Kwame has been trying to find the people who killed Nina and I may have led him to them. That's why he's been tagging me."

"Bingo! I knew that motherfucker had some carcasses in his closet! He was too clean. What did I tell you! I knew it, I knew it, I knew it! So this explains the tail from the hotel and why he didn't call you back that night. No wonder you couldn't reach him. He ain't stupid. He knows you're being targeted, too. What was he going to say if he had answered…ahhh, yeah, Mia, I know somebody is probably following you. Don't worry about it though, they just might kill you? I hope you know you gotta cut him all the way off like a bad toenail! I hate to tell you this Mia, but dudes like that, when they got a score to settle they don't give a shit who gets caught in the crossfire."

"Thanks a lot, Daph."

"What you want fairy dust?" she asked coldheartedly.

"No, I just want to know that my family and I will be safe."

"Well you shoulda thought about that before you went picking up some stranger in a record store, bringing him home and fucking him," she reminded me.

"Did I miss something or did you think I called you for your sorry ass opinion?" I took the liberty of asking.

"You? Call me for my opinion? Never that! You don't never listen to nobody other than yourself. That's why it would be ludicrous to think that for a second! Did Kwame say what the beef was about?" she asked, shifting gears.

"He didn't say, but you know what he did have the audacity to say?"

"What?"

"That I was selfish and that I didn't care about anybody but myself. Can you imagine? How dare he think he knows anything about me? He even had the gall to imply that I would put my children in harm's way!"

"I can't! Baby girl how many times have I told you that you were selfish? I get it. He doesn't know you from a can of beans but he's telling the truth! Instead of licking your wounds, your focus should be on how you gonna shake this tail that might endanger your family more than what some 'ole drunk thinks about you. If I were you I'd be putting five universes between me and Ty. I swear somebody dropped you when you were a baby."

Despite the insult, Daphne was right. I was in way over my head. I'd potentially put people at risk that didn't have a clue.

My life.

"I'll work on that the minute I get off the phone with you."

"And stop sounding so fucking sad. It's time to put the big girl panties on. I know you ain't used to wearing those but its time. Think about the alternative. That's the severity of the shit you're dealing with. Bottom line. Do you understand?"

I did.

What you See Is What You Don't Get

Quincy

SEVEN-FIFTY. I WAS rollin up in Randolph's parking lot and the bitch was already crowded. I tossed the keys to valet instead of try'na find a park, hopped out and went inside. Casin the joint I saw Imani's sexy ass struttin ova to where I was.

"Hi Q," she said huggin me and pressin her titties up against me all hard. "You look handsome. We're over here."

I followed her.

"I made reservations so we got a good table," she told me climbing around the other side of the circle table.

I got in next to her.

"Thanks for agreeing to talk to me, Q. I know you were trying to get out of it," she said looking at me.

"What's up?"

"Okay!" she laughed. "Straight to the point I guess! Same 'ole Quincy."

A dude came over to wait on us.

"Can I start you off with something to drink?"

"I'll have a glass of red wine, please?" Imani told him.

"A Corona."

"Would you like to order an appetizer?"

"No," I told him.

"Yes. I'd like the crab cakes, please."

"Yes, ma'am. I'll put that order in for you and I'll be right back with the lady's glass of wine and for you sir, a Corona.

I stretched my arm on the back of the seat. She cleared her throat.

"I'm just going to say it. You know, I've kept this from you long enough Q, but my conscious won't let me do it any longer. I spent a lot of time working through you and me my first two years of college. It got so hard for me I had to talk to somebody," she said, looking down at the table.

"Seeing a therapist helped to keep me sane. The painful part about it all, was that I really did love you and I thought it was enough. I thought we could seriously work if you would have just let me in. I wasn't willing to let go of that thought even if it cost me my life, which of course it was costing me anyway."

I wanted her ass to get to the muthafuckin point.

"It hurt me that I never came to you and told you that I was carrying your child when I left."

Dude came back and put the drinks on the table. Imani swigged half her glass of wine down in one gulp.

"I ain't got shit to say 'bout that," I told her. I ain't mad at you for doin what you had to do."

She didn't say shit, just put her elbow on the table with her chin in it and looked straight ahead. I was checkin out a fine ass slim mommy that came in and sat at the bar.

"I didn't expect you to, Q. I just wanted to let you know."

The Irony of Fate – Part 1

Myles

I DECIDED TO FLY to Jersey instead of drive. Something about flying always helped me to sort through the shit in my head. Mia insisted on providing car service for me once I got to the airport so that I didn't have to drive to her house. That worked for me. Settling in my window seat on the plane, I got as comfortable as I could. The flight was full.

I thought heavily about the conversation mother and I had had a few weeks ago. It was part of the reason I didn't jump back into sleeping with Mia and slowed things down with Veronica. Until that conversation, I didn't realize how much time I'd spent ignoring what was happening in my life. Now, I was intentional about spending more quiet time to reflect on my choices, and I had to admit it wasn't as hard as I'd thought it would be.

At this stage of the game I was sure Mia and I were over. Too much to forgive. Mother was right. Our problems didn't start when Mia left. We were drifting apart long before then. Little did I know it had more to do with infidelity than a marriage that needed a tune-up.

The time I'd spent with Veronica helped me to realize that I didn't have to settle or be unhappy. Life was too short. I was grateful she'd been exonerated from the charges related to shooting Big G, and that although she was moving to avoid the memories of what had happened, she planned to stay in DC. I wanted to spend more time with her once I got my head together.

For the first time in my life I decided to heed my mother's advice and do me for a minute. My heart wasn't in a place to commit to another woman yet even though Mia and I had been separated for about a year. I still needed time to process everything that had happened. As well, the time had come for me to be honest with Mia. She had been laying it on thick every time I saw her and in pretty much every conversation we had. It was obvious what she wanted, but in my mind we had come to the end of the road. It was time to be honest with her so that she could go on with her life, too.

The plane began its taxi down the runway shifting my attention. I felt like my life was just beginning again.

The Irony of Fate - Part 2

Mia

IF ONE MORE *doctor told me that these goddamn headaches were all in my head I was going to go postal.*

Driving back home from the ER, I felt hopeless. The painkillers that were prescribed by my doctor for my excruciating headaches was no longer helping. I couldn't imagine having to deal with them for the rest of my life without any relief. He'd given me my last prescription after making some screwball remark about me getting hooked. I had managed to function with the mini explosions going off in my head the last few weeks by taking one pill a day, but I didn't know how much longer I'd be able to do that, especially given how bad they'd gotten. I was doing everything humanly possible to pinpoint triggers like the doctor advised, but other than breathing there were none. He suggested I lessen the stress in my life. I suggested he go to hell.

Merging onto Teaneck Road, I wondered why the phone calls and tails had come to a screeching halt after Kwame's intrusion. Although I didn't have a clue what stopped them, I was glad they had.

I didn't miss Ty like I thought I would even after I received a picture from his phone of him and India on a beach somewhere with a caption that read: you lose again bitch. It reminded me that I was grateful to be done with them both. Like I gave a fuck. She could have him. It had been a game for him all along and I had to admit brotha was good. My ignorance and trust in Ty made me feel like a complete fool. It was reminiscent of Dre all over again. Ty was a smooth operator. Brotha was good at his game, and I'm sure he had plenty of women like me to practice on. We made it easy.

Wine and dine a woman and she loses her head, back it up with being a multi-millionaire and she loses herself.

The children wanted to have a surprise party for Myles when he arrived. At the time I didn't have an excruciating headache so I agreed. I concocted an elaborate plan that included barbecuing chicken, turkey burgers, skewers and corn on the cob, making banana pudding, a fresh salad and homemade lemonade. Thanks to a throbbing headache, that eventually got scaled back to KFC and ordering a cake that would be ready a little later today from Cakes on my Mind. The children loved their cookies 'n cream ice cream cake.

I arrived home to find Tiffany, Brandon and Marcia, who had Saturdays off, already preparing dinner.

"Surprise!" they all echoed as I walked through the door. Ms. Marcia said we are gonna cook today for daddy!" exclaimed Brandon.

They had washed and seasoned the chicken, took out the turkey burgers, and put skewers on the corn on the cob. Tiff and Brandon were working on the fresh salad and Marcia was squeezing the lemons for the homemade lemonade.

"Marcia! You're supposed to have weekends off, remember! You can't let these two run things!" I scorned her.

She laughed. "They aren't running anything around here! We're a team!"

"Yeah, we're a team!" Tiffany and Brandon mimicked.

"Okay, okay! Have it your way! I'm going to go upstairs and change. I'll be right back to help."

"No mommy you can't help. We want to do it by ourselves."

Marcia winked her eye.

"Fine. I'll just go take a nice hot bath and relax then," I told them.

"Thank you, mommy!"

I could not have mastermind the opportunity to relax before Myles arrived any better. Somebody was looking out for me in a big way. Heading up the stairs and into the master bath to run my water, I remembered that last weekend marked the one-year anniversary I took the coward's route out by packing things up and leaving my family to move here. At the time it felt like my only option given all the lies and deceit I'd been carrying around. Feeling invisible day after day left me thinking I had no choice but to get out, get away, start over.

Peeling off my clothes and stepping into the hot water, I realized a bath was exactly what the doctor ordered. Life sprang back into my spirit after sitting there for a good while. When I got out the tub, I pampered my entire body with my favorite lotion and coconut oil, applied another coat of red toenail polish and slipped into one of my favorite sundresses, with no panties and bra of course. In the middle of brushing my hair I heard a car pull up. I tiptoed over to the window and peeked out. It was Myles. He looked like a King even though he was only dressed in a pair of jeans and a pull over shirt. I doubled checked myself in the mirror and went on downstairs to open the door. The kids and Marcia were in the backyard which allowed me a few moments to chit chat with him before they bombarded him.

"Hi Myles," I purred after opening the door. I reached up to hug him and he didn't resist like he had before. "How was your flight?" He smelled like dark chocolate.

He looked even better than he did the last time. He had an overnight bag on his shoulder, two gift bags in his hand, and I assumed they were for Tiff and Brandon.

"Hey Mia. It was good," he answered putting the overnight bag down. "How are you?"

He made no mention of the sundress. Even his hug lacked interest.

"I'm great now that you're here," I said, attempting to flirt.

He didn't bite.

"Where are my babies?" he inquired, awkwardly looking around the house.

Tiffany and Brandon came through the French doors that led to the backyard and ran to their father. "Daddy, daddy you're here!"

"There go my superstars!" he said kneeling down. Myles shoveled both of them up in his able arms. They hugged, kissed and loved on each other for a few minutes. It was clear why he was there.

"What's in the bag, daddy?" Brandon pried.

"Well, you're going to have to wait and see!" he teased. They walked over to the great room and sat down.

For the rest of the afternoon the three of them clung to each other like grapes on a vine. You could barely tell where one ended and the other began. Marcia and I were as useless as soap in a pigpen, but it didn't bother either of us one bit. When they had their fill of each other, Myles washed his hands, adorned an apron and cooked all the meat on the grill with Brandon's help. Tiffany, Marcia and I set the table and got all the necessities needed for us to eat out on the patio. I felt hopeful despite the obvious. I had my husband back even if it were just for a weekend, my children were happy, and this time so was I.

As we were cleaning up, Myles slipped up beside me and asked if he could speak to me alone. Because I couldn't get a feel for what it was about, I got jittery. I didn't think he'd take this moment to deliver bad news.

"Guys, will you excuse us for a minute?" I asked. I wiped my hands on my apron and followed him to the kitchen. I scooted up on the island and faced him.

"I hope you don't mind, but Tiffany and Brandon have been begging me for those Razor scooters. I had them hold two at the Toys R Us in… "Myles pulled out his cell phone. "Paramus off Route Four. Do you mind if I borrow your car to go and get them?"

I breathed a sigh of relief. "How sweet! Of course I don't mind! Do you want me to go with you? I know exactly where it is."

"I think if we both leave that'll raise their suspicion. I'll make the run and come right back. I have the address in my GPS."

"It's a straight shot. You can't miss it. Oh! That reminds me! You can stop by the bakery and get the cake on the way back! It's on the street right around the corner." I hopped off the island and got the address for the bakery from a magnet on the refrigerator.

The keys to my car were hanging in the key box by the garage door, so I pulled them down and gave them to him.

"Thanks, Mia. You can tell them I went to get the cake and whatever else you can think of to stall for time."

Tiff and Brandon were going to lose their minds when Myles came back with scooters and a cake. All the children in the neighborhood had those things.

I waved at him as he backed out the driveway. If Myles followed the GPS to the letter, I figured it would take him about forty-five minutes for both errands. He was efficient when it came to handling business. I went back out on the patio to play decoy for him.

I heard the sirens going up the street about fifteen minutes after he left, but didn't pay them any attention because we had a fire station in the neighborhood. I heard them going up and down the block all the time. Shortly after I heard the sirens I heard police cruisers go by. Something inside of my spirit made me uneasy. I picked up my phone to call Myles but he didn't answer. I began pacing the floor, calling him every five seconds, but the calls went into his voicemail. By now I was a nervous wreck.

An hour and a half into waiting, worrying and making up excuses to the kids as to why their father had not returned, I told Marcia to take them over to the playground across the street or around the corner to occupy them.

Moments after they left the doorbell and my cell phone rang at the same time. I checked it. It was my mother in law calling. She'd have to wait until I chewed Myles out for taking so long and not calling. I ran to the door and flung it open.

"Are you Mrs. Rollins?" a police officer asked me.

"Yes."

"May we come inside?"

I didn't move.

"Are you the Mrs. Rollins that is the owner of a two-thousand, four door blue Mercedes license plates, D_E_S_I_G_N N?"

"Yes."

"Is Mr. Myles Rollins your husband?"

"Yes."

"We're sorry to tell you there's been an accident and Mr. Rollins…"

Silence.

www.ingramcontent.com/pod-product-compliance
Lightning Source LLC
Chambersburg PA
CBHW070209260626
47160CB00002B/495